LAND

LAND

ALEX CAMPBELL

HOT
KEY
BOOKS

First published in Great Britain in 2014 by Hot Key Books
Northburgh House, 10 Northburgh Street, London EC1V 0AT

A CIP catalogue record for this book is available from the British Library.

ISBN: 978-1-4714-0225-8

1

This book is typeset in 10.5 Berling LT Std using Atomik ePublisher

Printed and bound by Clays Ltd, St Ives Plc

www.hotkeybooks.com

Hot Key Books is part of the Bonnier Publishing Group
www.bonnierpublishing.com

For Duncan, Laurie and Mae. My lifeboat.

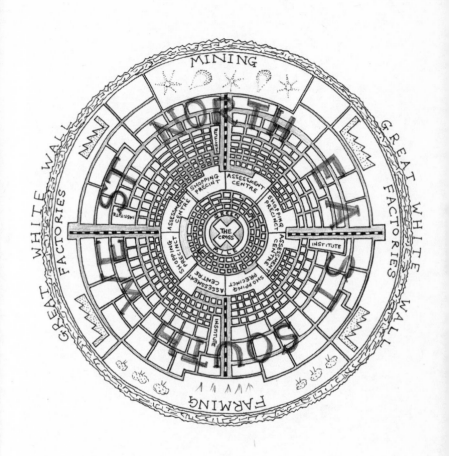

'To survive it is often necessary to fight and to fight you have to dirty yourself.'

George Orwell

Prologue

'Stories teach us about choices.' That was what my grandmother told me.

Seeing as Land forbade either, she made sure to pass on her own stories, of the Old World she had belonged to, of a time of leisure, pleasure, and imagination, when the past brought comfort and the future promised excitement.

I would curl up into the padded curve of her side and listen hard to every word. I invented pictures in my head; I relived her childhood emotions as keenly as if they were my own.

Over the years my grandmother's stories held me to her. Maybe that's why I never joined the dots; though why would I? Why ever would I have guessed they formed a signpost to my own destiny?

At the start of 2014 my grandmother was six years old. She lived in a sprawling house of toys and books and happiness. She loved the silvery pond in her garden, with its darting orange fish that teased the neighbour's cat. The school she attended had brightly coloured pictures on the walls and teachers who bent down to greet her, warm smiles as big as their faces. There she skipped round the playground arm in arm with other little girls who lived in houses just like hers.

But then the sea rose. At an unpredictable speed. With such little warning.

It swallowed up whole the house, and the garden, and the pond with the fish, and the school with the smiling teachers and the little girls just like her. It took away her toys and her books and the happiness that cocooned them. It would have taken her too, but her family was one of the lucky ones; they had a sanctuary – her father's sailing boat.

For the next three months this small floating space became their home. Taking with them her aunt's family, eight crammed into a boat that was tossed, and regularly threatened to turn with each swell of the temperamental mix of oceans. They lived by the cans of food they had stored and pills that purified the sea water. Weeks of aimless navigation brought extreme sea sickness, fever, then a gradual starvation that slowed their brains and evaporated their hope.

They buried my grandmother's younger brother first. Soon after, her aunt joined him in a grave beneath the waves. Then both cousins. Until the sea played coffin to her beloved father too.

Three of them remained. They shelved any hope of survival, and had almost surrendered life.

Until a miracle came at their last hour, a glistening light of browns and greens squeezed between the variant blues of sea and sky: land.

Abandoning the boat, my grandmother, her mother and her uncle walked across this high ground, foraging as they went. The weather at least was kind to them and after a time they stumbled upon their second miracle: a makeshift refugee camp, doing its best to survive on meagre rations and even less optimism.

More people drifted towards this camp daily. And every day more people died of disease and starvation.

Hysteria, panic and lawlessness reigned as scavenged food couldn't sustain the camp's growing numbers.

The survivors felt a renewed desperation to stay alive, to hope once again to know the fundamentals of their previous existence that they had so sorely taken for granted.

Above all things, people began to crave order. They decided they would give up anything – liberty, fraternity, equality – for order. They looked for leaders – the decisive, the strong, the visionaries – those they perceived capable of controlling the chaos.

Including amongst them my grandmother's uncle, those chosen swiftly did what was asked of them. They presented the edict for survival in a land stripped of civilisation, in a place where limited resources meant only the useful could prosper.

And so Land was born, on the last day of the last month of 2014.

Only those who could work, who would offer something towards Land's growth, were allowed to belong to this new State. The elderly, the sick – they were sent away; children only kept for their promise. Land was contained. Surrounded by newly made soldiers. Its citizens and resources protected.

So it was to be that my grandmother once more had a home, and food, and a school.

A life.

This story in particular was the one I recited over and again, dissecting each word, replaying every image, in a desperate search to make sense – to understand, to forgive . . . How could the person I loved beyond all others, do what she did – to the last survivors . . . of her own family?

Part One

The Pairing

Chapter One

Stay silent. Fix a smile. Keep on walking.

It was my mantra. Cultivated for survival over the past seventeen years.

Only, in the last few days, weeks, months, it had been failing me.

I pushed the remaining bread and cheese towards Cons.

January was nearly over. I had dreaded the arrival of this year for half my life. Now I was in it, and I couldn't press stop. Every bit of me seemed to be straining at the rules that had contained me through my childhood. I no longer wanted to remain silent. I wanted to scream: let me out!

I just didn't know who to start screaming at.

'Christy, no, you finish it. You need your strength today.' She moved the plate back my way. My grandmother would give me every bit of her breakfast if I allowed her.

'What for? Seeing Stella?'

'You know that's not what I mean.' The lines like brackets at Cons' mouth multiplied as she gave me a strained smile. 'But don't you go using the Pairing announcement to conveniently forget you're having dinner there tonight.'

'Can't I give it a miss . . . this once? Today's going to be bad enough.' Our Friday morning ritual – it always started with me trying to get out of my weekly obligation at Mum's.

'I gave your mother my word.' And ended with Cons insisting I had no choice.

Choices weren't commonplace in Land. It edged on fairy tale the very notion that Cons had been able to *choose* to raise me, aged two. Nothing here was left to fate. 'At least admit it for once, Grandma Constantine: Stella doesn't even want me there.'

That made Cons laugh. Such a rare sound; I liked it. She detested her full name of Constantine – 'too fancy'. And she had never wanted me to call her Grandma – 'makes me feel old'. It wasn't a welcome feeling in Land. There was no chance, let alone choice, of getting old here either.

'Whether that's true or not – it is simply something you must do.' Her kindly face was set.

Stay silent, fix a smile, keep on walking . . . the mantra might have been mine, but the sentiment was all Cons'. She had a list as long as her arm of things I *simply must do*.

I collected our plates up – thin, chipped state-regulation white china – and squeezed round the back of Cons' chair to the sink. Our small wooden table virtually filled the whole room. It was the only item of interest in an otherwise bare (state-regulation) white room. It used to be a desk; my father's when he was a child. Every mealtime I traced the name and number that was carved into the wood. *Hogan 425689.* It was the closest I got to him.

'I'm a woman who keeps my word, Christy,' Cons continued.

'I must stand by my promise to Stella.'

A sudden rush of fury flew up my chest. I slammed the dirty dishes into the basin. 'So then why can't she do something for you? Delay your Selection!'

Cons made a noise at the back of her throat.

She wouldn't tolerate erratic outbursts; she wouldn't discuss *It*. The black raincloud that had hovered above our heads since she turned sixty-six three weeks ago. Land controlled when you were born; it dictated when you died – and Cons was now living on borrowed time.

I stared down at my hands waiting until I could contain it – this growing anger inside. It felt like it would overpower me if I gave it a voice. Cons and I had never argued. I wouldn't start now.

'Christy – even Stella can't offer that kind of help. You know that.'

I sighed and turned on the hot tap, fixing my eyes out of the small square window above the sink while the pipes gurgled awake. Our flat was on the fourth floor of a typical Land six-storey tenement block. It gave us a view directly down onto the bowed heads beginning to flood the street, hurriedly making their way to their designated work . . . or to appointments at the Assessment Centre. Everybody rushed, nobody in my part of West Land ever strolled with ease. You got to where you had to get to. Or else.

'I know I keep saying this – but keeping in with Blues . . . it's vital for your survival, Christy. Don't overlook that.'

No, nor could I deny it. Over the years, Stella had stepped in – extra food, clothing; coal for the fire; intervening when Cons got arrested for assisting the labour of a woman unapproved for childbirth; when I had pneumonia aged nine and was borderline Selection.

But it still left me feeling pretty cold where filial love was concerned. She did those things for one reason alone: guilt.

The one good thing she'd done for me was give me to Cons. Because Cons loved me. That was a fact I brought out of my head regularly, examining it as if it were a piece of treasure I kept hidden. It was why I would always follow her rules.

'Fine. I'll go.'

'I know you'll go. You always go.' Cons leant over and patted me gently on the arm. 'You're my good girl.'

I thrust my hands into the lukewarm water, scrubbing at the plates like it was them annoying me. The description circled my head. *Good girl.* I was her granddaughter, she was biased. I no longer even knew what *good* was. When I was a child it meant eating everything on my plate (which in our area of West Land was never a lot); paying attention to tutors; obeying Cons.

What did being *good* mean now?

'. . . and you must promise to keep in with your mother, even after I . . . when . . .'

I glanced round. 'When . . .? Cons –?'

Cons caught the look in my eye; she smacked her lips together to make it clear any further discussion about her Selection wouldn't happen. 'You have to trust me, Christy. I know what is best.'

I rolled my eyes at the window. 'Okay . . . I vow to visit Stella until the day the Selection truck arrives for me.'

'No truck will ever come for you.' Cons clicked her tongue

13

as she rose from her seat, as if I had said something utterly ridiculous.

Cons had never lied to me. She didn't hide truths even if sometimes she avoided speaking them. So I didn't know how it was possible she could hope for something different for me than the fate that befell everyone in Land.

Unless she knew something – someone – I didn't.

I'd always blithely accepted Cons' reason for why she'd started leaving early on Fridays. A new rota at work, she'd said. Until Kara had spotted her.

'What's Cons up to? She was heads close with some man at the tram stop near the Institute. A Blue. I didn't recognise him – do you think . . .?'

No. No, I didn't think. Kara liked to suspect anyone she respected of secret mutiny against the State; she lived her life in constant hope of revolution. But with Cons I knew it was unlikely. Cons' life was spent keeping mine safe.

'I'm off now.' Cons leant round the bathroom door; she was ready to leave even earlier than usual. 'I'm sorry I can't walk with you to the Institute, today of all days.' She made anxious eyes at me in the bathroom mirror as I brushed my teeth. I stared back. Cons didn't look her age, not yet. Her skin was supple despite its map of fine lines. But I didn't like how her hair was starting to thin. Nor how its colour, the same as mine – chestnut red she liked to call it – and long still, like mine, was beginning to fade into shades of grey. Strands of which seemed to sink into the frayed outdoor coat she had on. Grey, for a midwife.

Colours defined who we were in Land. Cons' work was classified somewhere between Brown for the manual workers and Blue for the thinkers, the managers and politicians. Green was for children and students. Black for the State Troopers. It hid blood the best. The slave workers wore White; the State's joke – it insisted slaves keep their clothes spotlessly clean.

I rinsed out my mouth and moved towards Cons in the doorway. I would need to delay her to give me time to catch up. 'Don't worry. But can you help me find my tracer before you go?'

'Oh, Christy! Of all the things to lose today – don't they alert you on your tracer if you're chosen for the Pairing?'

'Yeah . . . must be subconscious –' I made a sound like a laugh – 'because I haven't a hope in hell of being picked.'

Cons' face tightened, deepening the crease between her eyes. 'I was accepted for Pairing when I was seventeen. And so will you be.'

'It was different back then.' Her ambition for me, to claim the life of a Blue, blinded her to our reality. 'The State didn't have your genes listed on any file. You were able to *choose* Grandpa.' I'd never known him, my grandfather. Land had done for him. Something else Cons preferred to avoid talking about. 'The State's not going to want to mix the DNA of an escaped rebel's daughter, Cons. They *are* creating their perfect master race after all. Besides . . .' I finished my sentence with a shrug that Cons read correctly.

'Christy, I won't even hear that you don't *want* to be Paired. Stronger as a two than a one, *remember*?'

'*We* are the only "two" I need.' That was my sole ambition.

For us to stay alive, stay together.

'Must I keep telling you!' Her hands began fumbling clumsily with the misshapen buttons on her coat. Cons saved up points for clothes for me, not her. 'To be Paired will be your ticket to live!'

By the time she'd found my tracer, already in my satchel where I'd packed it an hour ago, I was ready, but I hung back until I heard our front door slam shut. Then I followed, quietly, down the stairs into our bare-walled lobby. The only decoration: a poster with black, stark writing, pasted on to the glass of the entrance so you couldn't fail to read it every time you left the building.

Sixty years ago the sea rose, stripping countries bare, removing all life. It will rise again. Citizens of Land, strengthen our survival. We can't carry the weak: work hard, breed only on approval, die when your time comes. Only then can we survive the Second Coming.

Land lived under constant fear of another Armageddon, and those in charge never failed to use it to their advantage: they were taking no passengers.

Cons was already setting a fast pace on the crowded road ahead of me. I mimicked her as she crossed diagonally, keeping a certain distance, for what it was worth – because if she were to turn round she would instantly see me. There was nowhere to hide on the streets of Land. Roads were narrow, architecture was flat, pathways brightly lit, any foliage or tree trimmed to be no taller than a child.

I cursed under my breath as a large white perambulator blocked my path, transporting at least five babies with wide suspicious eyes to the state crèche. I careened around it. I couldn't risk losing her this time. Three Fridays now I'd tailed my grandmother. Three Fridays I'd lost sight of her.

I had to know who she was meeting.

If it *was* Dad.

I mean – I knew it wouldn't be. What a stupid thought. My dad – the only known fugitive in Land. As his mother, Cons must be under some form of surveillance. The risk would be too high, for both of them. For me.

But I was certain the meeting had to be connected to him. That somehow, some way . . . Dad was going to keep Cons from Selection. I had to help.

Cons back in plain sight, I took a moment to breathe in the return of sunshine – it was a welcome surprise after months of stormy grey. Cold, but bright; there was more sky on view than usual, large patterns of pale blue cut up by just a few clouds. I liked it that way, to see the sky in its entirety. Clouds had always struck me as being in conspiracy with Land, with its love of white. Above me, some of the flat, tenement rooftops still merged with the last of the snow that had covered the streets a month back. Beyond them, I could just make out the very tip of the Great White Wall in the far distance. Built against the ever-rising sea just outside Land's borders, it formed a twenty-metre-high protective circle around us; its last stone had been laid when Cons was just a young mother.

My eyes shot back to the street as I heard shouts, unusual in Land. A small crowd was forming ahead, blocking any view of Cons, a Black-clad State Trooper hollering, 'This is what Land's traitors look like; come see!' indicating the wall to his left as if he were calling an audience to a show.

Between a gap in the growing throng, I spied five scared-looking young men, stripped down to their underpants; winter's cold turning their skeletal frames blue; shivering, cowering like animals awaiting the slaughterhouse.

My eyes locked on one. I recognised him from Kara's block: soft brown hair and a pinched but gentle face. He wasn't more than twenty. My gut twisted in fear for him, but I couldn't stay and watch. I surged forwards, but more people got in my way, citizens assembling to prove themselves loyal. Combined voices began raining out like ammunition at the bowed heads of the boys:

'Land won't carry you!'

'Your kind will bring us all down!'

'Destroy all Resistance!'

My breathing hurried, I elbowed a path through Grey and Green and Brown-clothed bodies. *Stay silent. Fix a smile. Keep on walking.* I just hoped desperately the gory spectacle would have dispersed by the time Kara passed on her way to the Institute. Arrests like these, they were few and far between; mostly kept out of sight. To do it in public must have meant the Troopers wanted to send out a warning to would-be traitors. Which Kara was fast risking becoming. Lately, she was burning to retaliate, to risk trouble – to pay back the State for removing both her parents for Selection, her father when she was twelve, her mother two years later. My job: to stop her. Always.

I was nearly through when the crowd bunched and pushed me to one side.

'Get off him!' I watched a middle-aged woman in Brown with lank dark hair careering into the furthest State Trooper, her arms out. 'Leave my boy alone!'

I turned my head away – it was inevitable what was to come. I kept my focus on the road ahead as I heard the slam of a body onto hard concrete, a crunch of steel-clad heel on bone. I pushed on, creating distance as fast as I could from the woman's flailing shrieks; from the shouts of one of the boys, suddenly silenced by the pop of a gun.

I rubbed at my eyes. What difference could I have made?

Say nothing. Do nothing. It sat there as comfortably in my psyche as *wake up and eat.*

Survival, wasn't it? I clenched my fists tight, gritting my teeth. No – it was about protecting the ones I loved. Kara. And Cons.

I strode faster, beating out my emotion, until I caught up with her greying auburn hair bobbing ahead. Her long Grey coat had escaped its useless buttons and was flapping behind Cons like a pair of wings. I adjusted my pace to match hers, shading my eyes as the sun rose higher, its rays bouncing off the pure whiteness of Land's buildings. Some had been whitewashed recently so they glared particularly brightly. It wasn't so bad at this time of year, but when summer came, it could blind you. Kara always argued that was the State's intention.

We walked on in tandem for another forty minutes, turning to take a road that merged into West Land's main thoroughfare. Past the Institute, the entrance beginning to pool with Green students, the architecture started changing from identical flat-faced tenements into the comparable luxury of low-level apartment blocks. I wasn't far now from where Stella, and my stepfather, Syon, lived, amongst other Blues whose genes had proved their worth to Land. The kind who waited eagerly for their next move – into Central Land, to live in the houses that hugged the Cross, government's main office.

Finally I could see where Cons was going. Up ahead gleamed the wide glass doors of West Land's only entrance to its shopping precinct. Linking with West Land Assessment Centre next door, it was also the only way to access Central Land on foot – but you required approval for that. The tram stopped here; only Selection trucks and the small number of cars driven by elite Blues were allowed to use the underground road that ran beneath it.

Cons joined the line waiting to be checked into the precinct by a group of State Troopers. I hung back then did the same – only a few Blues and Greys between us. I watched Cons get through on just a nod. I should have known the Green of my coat would automatically make me stand out.

'Student – why aren't you at the Institute?'

I glanced up at the Trooper in front of me, trousers tapering into polished Black knee-boots; belted jacket; a reflected sheen on his round beetle-Black helmet. 'I have a little time before registration . . .' I took a breath, trying not to let him sense my nerves. 'I need a new pen,' I added quickly, evading his eyes. *Stay unnoticed*, Cons had ingrained in me since I was little.

'Number,' the Trooper snapped.

Silently, I pulled back my coat sleeve, revealing the blue-white of my wrist. The black tattoo of 823057 had been imprinted on me at the age of seven, when I was officially branded as a citizen – the 823,057th – of Land. A citizen you stayed until the day you failed an Assessment.

Or turned sixty-six.

The Trooper punched my number into his handheld computer. I chewed my bottom lip, watching impatiently as Cons' head grew smaller beyond the glass. I didn't dare meet his eyes – the familiar disappointment was palpable.

'Your files are inaccessible,' his voice grew more unyielding, 'What's so special about you?'

I licked my lips, hastily shaking my head, fear surging through me. 'Nothing.'

I knew it was irregular that my files were blocked. Kara was routinely stopped and humiliated over her history – that her father had concealed a neighbour from the Assessors; that Selection claimed her mother after she became bed-bound with depression. Cons' only explanation: Dad's escape was a state embarrassment.

Presently the Trooper muttered a terse, 'Go on then.'

I thanked him; it didn't do to show them ill manners. You could never tell the ones that were okay, maybe even half decent, from the ones whose uniform gave them licence for tyranny.

I rushed on into the covered expanse of concrete, glancing frantically inside each state-controlled shop within its warren of thin pathways. Most were plain, uninviting, shelves of unvarying goods. Cons would tell me how in the Old World she remembered her mother shopping like it was a job: 'We'd spend whole days browsing for things we didn't even need'. In Land, it was only about finding food and fuel that Cons' points could afford.

I couldn't see her anywhere. I was too late. Dammit. I'd lost her again. I stopped abruptly, frustration turning into a sudden spark of fury; why wouldn't Cons confide in me? I swung round to make my way back to the entrance, rummaging in my satchel for a pen I could pass off as newly bought if the same Trooper stopped me.

I felt his presence before I saw it: a flash of Blue coat moving away into the crowd, a face – with an expression of someone caught out.

I'd had my own shadow all this time.

A Blue. Following me.

Someone old enough to be my dad.

Chapter Two

Staring down into the auditorium was a lone black crow, perching on one of the windows in the Institute's high walls. I felt more of a kinship with that bird than with those around me: the girls creating the insect buzz of background chatter; the boys throwing soft punches and reaching out to slap hands.

Maybe it was because of Dad being a traitor, or because I hated how Mum conformed so beautifully, but I'd never felt qualified to be a paid-up member of any of the groups that naturally formed at the Institute: the clever ones, the sporty ones; the my-parents-are-Blues ones. You picked a pack – survival in numbers was the way it went – until you hoped to become a Pair.

Me, I was more suited to stand alongside that crow up there – observing, unobserved.

I'd said to Kara I'd wait near the doors at the back, but I was regretting it now as students kept flooding through, pummelling and pushing me into a sea of Green. All around me, different shades of the same colour. Only the State Troopers were assigned a uniform; everyone else made their own clothes, unless you were points-rich like my mother and paid others to make them for you. I was lucky that Cons was a good seamstress. The dark Green knee-length skirt I had on today fitted me just fine. The paler Green blouse my mother had given me; I hated to admit I quite liked it. My winter coat was an ugly, scratchy wool, but it was thick and Cons had sewn a softer piece of material round the collar.

I did better than most. But not as good as some – like my stepsister Astral, whose clothes went beyond required functionality. Finer fabrics with detailed finishes. It wasn't supposed to be about the way you dressed, but the likes of Astral would undoubtedly be picked for the Pairing today.

'Hey!' I muttered under my breath at a forceful shove from a broad-shouldered boy; it was lost to the air. I might as well have been invisible. Cons said to stay unnoticed; within the walls of the Institute, I'd clearly done too good a job: there were over five hundred students in my year alone, but only a tiny handful even knew my name.

What did it matter now? I thought back to the shopping precinct: could it have been Dad? My chest tightened. He used to be a Blue, I knew that much. And I'd long held an instinct he was looking over Cons and me. It was a child's fantasy maybe, like a god the Old World would pray to, but there were many times when I'd sense his presence. Like today, I would turn and be sure I spotted a body dash away, a wave of coat, a shadowy face staring up at our kitchen window.

Of course I had no idea what he looked like, other than Cons' description. The same dark red hair as us. My green eyes; Cons' strong, straight nose. I had tried and failed to draw the image she'd described, like the photograph Cons still had of her mother, taken in the Old World – the only keepsake of the past she had. History, sentimentality . . . that was all useless to survival now.

I glanced quickly back over my shoulder. I wished Kara would hurry. State Troopers were clustered in both back corners of the auditorium. Black-clad bodies, arranged lazily against walls – they were bored; it wouldn't take much for one of them to hassle a student purely for their own amusement. The Grey tutors wouldn't dare do anything to stop them.

'I'm not sure I can contain myself till we find out,' a pretty brunette screeched back at a gang of friends she was shepherding past me. They were collectively shaking with exhilaration. The Pairing – it was what most girls had been waiting for their whole life. One magical day of swapping Green for a white frothy dress; thereafter, *to be made stronger, as a two not a one*; your Pair's number tattooed for life beneath your own. No one wanted to stand alone in Land. It wasn't a good look.

'Believe me, if they couldn't track me on my tracer I'd never have shown up.'

I breathed out a real smile, pulling Kara closer to me. 'At last.'

Kara's mother had worked as a midwife with Cons. We'd grown up together in the state crèche near the hospital. I'd known Kara as long as I'd known my grandmother.

'There's a nasty stench of collusion in here. And I don't like it.' Kara drew her poorly made Green coat tighter. It was freezing in the auditorium; heating was a luxury in daytime unless you were in Blue work.

I prodded my elbow into her side. 'Oi, keep it down, you'll get us into trouble.'

25

She stabbed me back sharper with hers. 'Christy, don't be one of them. You can't be a wimp all your life.' I rolled my eyes at her, but gave up as she linked arms with mine. The physical touch was reassuring. I was more nervous about today than I'd realised. Less than half of the students in this room would be chosen for the Pairing, and Kara and I stood no chance of being in that fraction. I did all right in my classes and Kara excelled at science, but one of my parents was a fugitive and hers had been removed. It was inevitable: we were destined for second-class citizenship.

'We're better than this, remember,' Kara whispered into my ear, her breath a blast of warmth on my cold cheek. 'They can stuff their Pairing!'

I pulled my face back to take her in. The muscle in her cheek was contracting. She'd obviously made an attempt to look dishevelled today on purpose – her short hair looked like she'd backcombed it. Raven black, it paid homage to her father's side of the family, who had reached Land from India when the seas broke. Diluted with her mother's mix of Spanish-American, Kara's skin was a smooth caramel brown, her eyes an unexpected navy blue.

I had always envied her exotic heritage. My dark red hair, my pale skin that sunshine freckled in an instant, drew only from one obvious line of descent: British.

Not that either of us presented the new ideal.

When the Pairing first began, Cons told me how young people were joined, not on the colour of their skin or hair, but simply on their intelligence and well-being. It wasn't hard to spy a new trend emerging. You only had to look at any Blue, their fair hair and tanned, white skin. A different kind of superiority had taken over from IQs and health.

'I just want to get this pathetic freak show over with.'

Her tone made me nervous. 'Shush, Kara.'

'Just think: another five months and then we're free at last. A chance to make a difference the right way.'

I hissed back, 'With the work we'll be assigned . . .?'

'You know what I mean. The Resistance – that's where I'm bloody well heading once I'm out of here.'

I flashed a look at the Troopers closest to us. 'Stop it, Kara . . . not in here.' I placed a hand over hers, squeezing it hard. Any of the students bunched around us wouldn't hesitate to report her to the authorities, for cursing as much as treachery.

Kara shrugged at me then muttered, 'Finally,' as the Institute's principal took to the podium, drawing his diminutive frame up tall behind the lectern.

There was an immediate hush of quiet from the audience. Despite the fact I knew I wouldn't get picked, I felt my stomach contract; my breathing became shallow. I reminded myself of the pact Kara and I had made long ago: we didn't want to be Paired! We wouldn't live out our lives with some stranger, procreating at the State's command.

But I'd never admitted to Kara that sometimes the alternative scared me worse.

'Students, tutors and Troopers.' The principal was nodding his head brusquely at each grouping. His dark hair was greased back from a high forehead; glasses perched purposefully down his beaked nose so he could peer over them. His neatly tailored Blue suit underlined his status above the tutors in Grey behind him. 'Right now, and across all four institutes of Land, you are part of something crucial to Land's progress. At seventeen, you face the next stage of your life. If you are Paired, respect the great honour, 11024, our new leader, bestows upon you!'

I frowned. It was the first time I'd heard his number – it rang familiar somehow, but the recollection got lost as Kara let out a small puff of derision. Someone tutted behind us; I pressed Kara's hand tighter.

'If you are not Paired: accept the destiny Land places on you. For the greater good.' He drew out the last few words in a clipped, louder voice, then stepped aside, his arm swinging out behind him towards the auditorium's large white screen. As it flickered on, the window blinds dropped down, and the room darkened. Applause peppered the room as the obligatory citizenship film started.

'Wait for it: here come the happy people.' Kara sighed dramatically as the predictable moving shots of beaming, shiny, healthy citizens appeared on screen. It reminded me, unlike Kara, to try and resemble one. If you didn't smile and simper when it was expected of you then there was only one course of action. A little blue pill. Once a day. Sometimes for your whole life if the Assessors decreed it. Paid for with your own points.

Making people look happy. It was the only medication the State saw value in. Kara had been prescribed it twice since she was twelve. But for her last Assessment, at least, she had finally clocked on to Cons' doctrine that had seen me through: smile, open your eyes wide and agree, *yes*; save the sadness for yourself. But the way Kara was going now she wouldn't be off them for long.

The film began making its ubiquitous reminder of the promise we had made aged seven at our citizenship ceremony. Words that were as marked on my memory as my number was on my skin – *respect my body and keep healthy of mind . . . accept the State's vision of me . . . yield to the end of my time . . . all for the greater good.*

Then the Leader came on, a head and shoulders shot, his eyes directly facing the camera so he stared at you wherever you were standing. His grey hair was cut close to his head, like tiny metal shavings across his scalp. Only recently appointed, he began reciting Land's inception – the beginning of Cons' life here that her uncle had helped create. *'Borne out of a battle with nature, Land's early leaders recognised the only way to survive was to choose life for those who could honour it, and Selection for those who couldn't.'* The Leader didn't dwell on that history; the past was only useful for emphasising the policy of the present.

One half of his upper lip lifted as his mouth continued to move over artfully selected words. *'Now everyone has a distinct role to play. Land assesses each person's individual skills and merits from childhood, so it can be decreed how they will serve Land the best: whether they possess the natural qualities to be Paired and play parent to the next generation. By filtering out defective DNA we will master survival. This is the way we will defend ourselves against a second coming of the seas: by keeping gene-mixing high on the agenda, and the population as low as possible.'*

His eyes were at turns emblazoned then darkly serious – oh, he might be new, but he was already good at this. I could sense the auditorium swell and quiver with collective pride in the

State. As abruptly as the film had started, it was over; the lights went on, blinds up. I looked back up at the window; my sole black crow had flown away.

Under a cacophony of inhalation, students were reaching for their tracers, clutching them in palms that would undoubtedly be moist, despite the chill in the air. I nudged Kara; we unlocked arms and began fumbling in our satchels to retrieve our own. 'What's the point,' I heard Kara murmur.

I didn't really pay attention as the principal echoed parts of the Leader's sermon, interspersing oily beams of encouragement with thin smiles of warning. I hated that I was allowing myself to get this nervous. I looked down to where the tracer fitted snugly into my hand as if it had every right to be there. A shiny black casing that framed a tiny computer screen from which I routinely received state messages, universal reminders of the purpose and duty of life in Land, or notification of Assessment Centre appointments. More notably the tracers allowed the State to keep tracks on all its citizens, of where they were at any given moment. If your tracer remained static, or showed you in places you weren't supposed to be, then there was a problem. A big problem.

'Four, three, two . . .' The principal was counting down, as if it were some sick celebration. I could hear Kara's breath coming in derisive bursts beside me. I shut my eyes. *Kara and I, we don't want to be Paired anyway.*

There were shared gasps, some excitable screams, a scattering of moans – the last, markedly contained. The State of Land only wanted to hear appreciation, whatever you thought of your result. I opened my eyes, stared down, then blinked. I closed them again before I glanced across at Kara.

When she eventually met my stare she gave a slight twitch of her head. 'As expected.'

I tried to open my mouth to tell her. But I couldn't process its meaning myself. Why was it? How could it be?

That I had been chosen – for Pairing.

'Remember, we didn't want it, we don't care,' Kara was whispering, she was dipping down to look into my eyes, to reassure me, confusing my shock for disappointment.

I was about to speak, to find the words, when a long, loud moan rose from the crowd. Followed by a 'No! This isn't fair!'

The stiff Black uniforms from both corners stirred, beginning to force their way through the students to where the principal was pointing, a section in the middle, towards a girl's voice: 'I've done what you wanted!'

I couldn't see her from where I was standing, but there must have been a grapple as the crowd began to rock and sway about me.

By the time two Troopers pushed their way back towards the exit, the tear-streaked girl trapped between them was quiet. Lifted up, her feet weren't even touching the ground. The strain on her face highlighted her fear: *What was she to become . . . if she wasn't Paired?*

I watched her pass, my exterior impassive, even if my insides clawed with pity for her. She had created unrest; the blue pills were a certainty. But I doubted she would get off that lightly.

I looked back at Kara. Hoping she wasn't about to protest next. Her expression was caustic; her eyes narrowing as they stayed with the girl. I could sense her body trembling to move. I gripped on to her arm, before I felt my tracer vibrate again in my hand. Had it been a mistake? A second message to rectify an incorrect result? Kara and me, unPaired together.

I opened my palm and gazed down.

But that wasn't the message waiting for me.

The typed words – they didn't make any sense.

I could tell myself it had to be some piece of propaganda for the winners. Except for one thing. A personalised message always began with your number.

But this one…for the first time in my life, started with my name. My full name.

Christabel, now is your hour. Rise to it.

Chapter Three

'Christy!'

I inclined my head slightly.

'So lovely to see you!'

The same charade as every Friday. Standing there on the doorstep, Stella's mouth twitching over whether she dared kiss me or not. In the end, she chose to lightly grasp me, puckering her lips at the air beside both my cheeks, skin skimming mine in a puff of face powder and scent.

'Thanks, Stella.'

She stepped back from me.

I always enjoyed that it hurt, calling her by her name. Why would I ever give her the title of someone she had never been? I had decided long ago that 'Stella' fitted better, round about when Astral and Tom began calling her Mum.

I could have done worse; I could have called her by her number.

'Well, do come in.' She redressed her wounded expression. 'Dinner's about to be served.'

And served it was in this house. Like most Blues, their points bought them a slave who cooked, cared and cleaned for them.

I traipsed after her into their ground-floor apartment. The hallway alone could fit mine and Cons' whole flat. My stepfather Syon's status at West Land Council was rising and as your value to the State grew, so did your home. It was a simple equation.

I let Stella take my coat, enduring her weekly assessment of me – eyes feasting as if she were reminding herself who I was: her obligation; the daughter to feel guilty about.

In turn I stared sulkily back at her. I supposed she looked good, why wouldn't she? She worked alongside Syon at the Council. Their senior roles granted them rare leisure time, time to make themselves look attractive. Stella's hair – glossy as ever, golden blonde that fell with a well-tamed fullness to her shoulders – seemed lighter; I knew the kind of points it took to make hair dye.

'Seen enough?' I broke her hungry glare. There was nothing I hated more than being under Stella's microscope. What was she looking for? Did she hope one day my hair would lose the dark red that probably reminded her of Dad? Along with my green eyes, it was all that stood between me being a clone of her. A fact I didn't like. I'd have done anything not to have been born with the same features as hers, my face the same oval shape. I was as tall as her now too.

It helped to remind myself that inside we were different.

'You're growing more into a young woman with each week that passes.'

I shrugged and lowered my head. I hated it that when I looked back up I saw tears pooling in her eyes. Stella, basking in sentiment like a hot bath. She had no right to cry over me.

'Yes . . . not long now before I'm conscripted into Brown

factory work.'

Stella drew a finger under each eye, her smile glossing over my sarcasm. 'How did the Pairing go today?'

'As expected,' I mumbled ambiguously. We eyed one another awkwardly. I wasn't going to tell her something I hadn't yet confided to Cons or Kara.

Forcibly cheery, she replied, 'I remember my first Pairing as if it were yesterday.'

'Don't,' I fired out, then pressed my lips together. I had promised Cons that outside of our flat I would keep my thoughts to myself. A relatively easy promise to keep. Until my grandmother had turned sixty-six. 'I really don't want to hear about the day you were Paired with Dad. I think we both know that's unnecessary.'

Stella made a sharp intake of breath, her fingers shot to her neck, nervously nipping the skin there. I refused to feel bad for the comment.

'Naturally you will be Paired with someone equal to our family.' Syon's statement to Astral was finished with his usual sneer for my benefit. A sneer his sixteen-year-old son Tom was now duplicating perfectly.

Stella's glossy, manufactured family of four: sat perfectly spaced out around the polished wood of their dining-room table, which was decorated with freshly cut flowers (only the points-rich could afford to buy in nature). It made my seat, pushed in between Mum and Astral, all the more that of the unwanted guest.

'And what's next for you?' Astral asked tartly, tossing back her long blond hair as she speared food onto her fork. Like the rest of her family she'd automatically presumed I hadn't been picked.

I glimpsed Stella glancing anxiously at me.

'Whatever the State asks of me,' I replied pertly, affecting a smile none of them could argue with.

'Astral will have the life your mother and I enjoy. Maybe you might want to see your Pairing result as a failing on your behalf. If you want to stay alive in Land then take this opportunity to think about how you might better honour the State and all it's done for you.'

I glared over at Syon. When he talked he had a habit of closing his eyes, his lids flickering, as if his subject wasn't worthy of focus. His hair was thinning, but he wore it brushed up then back, as if it were still a full head. His broad features held the settled-in smugness of a man who imagined he would never face Selection. I would say that wasn't possible, except that lately there had been hints of rumours spreading – Blues appeared to be getting older; points were infiltrating Land policy.

Syon began deftly cutting up his meat; then chewed and swallowed before turning his head back to me, his eyelids closing as he picked up his lecture. 'Of course, you can't change your path. If you're not Paired now, it's very doubtful you will be in future years.'

Behind him, their slave leant over to refill his water glass. She was a new one. Dressed in a well-worn, bleached-White sweatshirt and skirt that contrasted with her dark skin, she couldn't have been much older than Astral and me. Syon liked them attractive, and this one was especially pretty, delicate eyes and curly hair almost as black as Kara's. She wouldn't have committed much of a crime to get here. Anything major, you faced Selection. No, a life of slavery came from petty theft – say a potato from one of the state-farmed fields, or three strikes of bad behaviour from a factory manager, or being caught roaming the streets after student curfew.

'We have an urgent duty as politicians to contain Land's population growth. It's more important than ever that only the very best are Paired and allowed to breed.' Syon dabbed at his lips with the napkin from his lap. 'The thing about you is –'

The loud clearing of my mother's throat interrupted his opinion of me. Syon slammed his hands on the table, shaking their superior china. He cast Stella a lingering look of resentment. She held it. It was an act of defiance I had never witnessed from my mother, the woman who licked the ground Syon walked upon.

But I wasn't about to thank her for it. I scraped my chair back. I'd eaten the main course – what did it matter if I missed pudding? I never got pudding at home. 'I need to go before curfew.'

Stella drew her eyes from Syon's and looked down at her tracer next to her plate. 'It's only seven o'clock . . . It's not curfew for another three hours.'

'I have to leave,' I said firmly and rose. Syon wouldn't bother to stop me. And Stella wouldn't want a fuss. Stella had never wanted a fuss. It was probably for that reason alone she had given me up aged two.

I had to hang around in the hallway. Stella insisted on getting a

37

parcel together like she did most weeks: food, soap, sometimes clothes. I would have routinely refused, but the extra food was all that stopped Cons giving me everything from her own plate. And soap and clothing, well, they supported my campaign for Kara and me to go unnoticed at the Institute.

I could hear laughter coming from the dining room. Syon's low growling holding court to his children. No doubt I was the joke. I might have felt sorry for them, that they had lost their mother in childbirth to Tom, if they had ever shown a speck of decency towards me. But to Astral and Tom, I was just bait. A reminder of how lucky they were.

'Here we are.' Stella rushed back into the hallway, a folded white paper bag stretched out towards me. She smiled easily as if she were at last doing something right. My insides stirred at the gesture. After last week I had told myself not to ask again, but I couldn't help myself. What if Dad *couldn't* help Cons? What if the rumours were correct – and Syon could?

I swallowed. 'I know what you said last Friday, but can you try . . .' *Don't beg. Don't cry. Contain yourself.* '. . . and do something for Cons?'

'Oh, Christy.' Stella's hands moved as if to cup my face, then paused midair. 'I wish you wouldn't keep asking. You don't understand. I wish . . . I wish I could, truly I do. It's impossible . . . it's more complicated than –' Her hands drew back to her own face. 'I can't,' she finished feebly.

We stared at one another. I blinked rapidly.

'I am *so*, so sorry, Christy.' She pushed the paper bag into my chest, pressing one of my hands against it.

I shook my head, refusing the kiss she was leaning in for, and turned towards the door, concentrating on just getting out of there before I exploded.

I was on the path when I heard her, a sing-song of a small voice as if she wanted it to travel despite its quietness. 'Now you've been Paired, you must be careful, Christy.' It took me a few minutes to digest, to turn to look at her. But when I did the door was already closing.

I fought the urge to return. To demand an answer: how could she have known so soon, when no one else did – that I had been Paired?

The roads were almost deserted now. Unless they had to venture outside for work, after dark most people stayed indoors. I walked slowly – I needed the air. My head was throbbing with a mix of confusion and frustration. I hated Stella for refusing to help Cons. How could she stand by and watch the one person who cared for me face Selection?

I pulled my arms across my chest as a cold wind whipped around me. And how did she know about the Pairing? She couldn't have been told! Syon plainly didn't know! And, *be careful*? What was that supposed to mean? That being Paired wasn't for the likes of me? She needn't worry: I agreed.

I dipped my eyes low as I heard the familiar marching thud of State Troopers' boots approaching from an adjacent road. I showed up clearly, courtesy of Land's florescent streetlights, attached along every wall. They spotlit the streets brighter than daytime, blocking out the stars in the sky.

I tensed as they came into view, as they stalked past me. 'Get home, pretty girl,' I heard one call, his tone mock-syrupy, pulling out of rank as the others carried on. Thumbs tucked in his belt, his eyes idly examined me from under the shadow of his helmet. I held my breath. Troopers weren't allowed Pairs or families; we'd all heard the stories of what this made them capable of.

'Stop!' We both turned at the shout from one of his colleagues. A trio of Browns were running out of a tenement entrance down the road. I quickened my pace as the Trooper darted after his pack.

It wasn't until I'd reached the last building before our own that I dared lift my eyes again.

Then I spotted it.

Standing out starkly against the floodlit white walls of our tenement.

I broke into a run. The boxed shape of the Selection trucks were a common sight at any time of the day but outside our flat, it meant something else. My heart began to rocket in my chest, pumping solidly into my ears as my legs drove faster still. All my other worries instantly evaporated. *Please no, please not Cons*.

I paused momentarily beside the truck's high-sided shiny black bodywork, right in front of the familiar red signage, **For the greater good**. There was no Trooper in the driver's seat. I dived into the lobby, tearing up the staircase.

'Cons!' I shouted the moment I opened the front door to our apartment. 'Cons?' I gasped, my breath coming in short rasps then, louder, 'Cons!'

'Christy!' In an instant she appeared in the doorway to our kitchen.

Relief bent me over double, my sides suddenly crippled with a stitch. I looked back up at her. 'A Selection truck . . . outside.'

'Oh, my dear. It's okay.' Cons' voice soothed as she put an arm round my waist, rubbing my back as I struggled to claim back my lungs. 'See – it's not for me . . .'

'For some other poor soul.'

I whipped my glance over Cons' shoulder, trying to locate a face to the low voice.

A man. A man in a waxy Blue coat that fell down to his ankles, was now standing in the kitchen doorway. 'Some other poor soul,' he repeated, not looking at either of us.

'Christy.' Cons pulled at my arm, to straighten me up. 'You're home early from your mother's. I wasn't expecting to have to do introductions, not tonight, but . . . well, you were due to meet him this weekend anyway, so no harm done . . .' She made a small smile for the man in the Blue coat.

I drew up closer to him. 'You,' I said.

We'd moved into Cons' bedroom. The only room in the flat with a small fireplace. It doubled up as our lounge, housing the scant furniture we could squeeze in around Cons' single, sagging bed: two chairs with grey cushions to make sitting on their hard wood bearable, a side table for Cons' sewing machine, and a squat, square trunk.

It was the same man that I had caught following me this morning. Of that I was pretty certain. 'This is my Christy,' Cons had said, introducing me before she left us alone – 'to make us all some tea'.

The room was warming up cosily. It added to my resentment

41

of this man, this man who clearly wasn't my dad after all, who'd chosen the chair closest to the fire, and was agitating the coals with the poker. I was on the bed behind him, hugging my knees to my chest. He hadn't removed his Blue coat. It covered almost all of his body but I could glimpse a high-necked jumper underneath, dark-Blue trousers with neatly ironed creases. I watched him as he leant forward and poked at the glowing coals. His brown hair was cut very short at the sides but seemed to sprout from his head on the top. It reminded me of the cress Cons grew in small pots on the kitchen windowsill.

'Who are you?' I eventually broke the silence; he didn't strike me as someone to initiate conversation.

'An old associate of your grandmother's.'

'It was you . . . I saw you, this morning. You were following me.'

He inclined his head towards the fire. 'Yes.'

'Why?'

He inclined his head again. He had a calmness, a quiet confidence that unnerved me. 'It's my job . . . to follow you.'

'*What?* Why?' I pressed the palms of my hands together and took a deep breath through the next silence. Cons wouldn't like it if she came back and I was at this man's throat. 'Cons has been meeting with someone . . . is it you?'

'Yes.'

My stomach tensed. 'Do you know my father?'

'You might say so.'

My heart sped up. 'Where is he?'

'I'm not in a position to answer that question.'

His words hit me like a slap. My body sunk lower on the

42

mattress. 'What do you want?'

'Like I said, it's my job to watch over you.' He said it as if he were telling me he was here to fix a leak, or paint a wall.

'I have Cons for that.'

'I wasn't implying that kind of care.'

I narrowed my eyes. 'Did you send me a message on my tracer?'

He twisted round in his seat, scanning me briefly. 'What did it say?'

I ignored his question, and met it with one of my own. 'What's your name?'

The stranger rose from his seat. He dropped the poker, stretched, then paced round the small room, picking up our few possessions and placing them down again as if he were in a shop. '454111.'

'I'm not calling you by your number.'

'Why not? It's what I am. What did this message say?'

'I need a name.'

He continued pacing, his eyes averted from me. 'You *want* a name – not need. It's the one thing the State got right. Give a dog a name and you attach feelings to it. I'm 454111. A number's just a number. There's no room here for attachments.'

'I'm not looking for any,' I bit back. This conversation was making me more nervous. How was I his job? Why had Cons invited this man into our home? I wished she'd come back with the tea. She was taking too long. I didn't like what it could mean. I pulled my arms tighter around my legs. 'And I'm not a dog.'

The stranger gave me a sideways look, his eyebrows – thick,

wiry – rose up and twisted into a lined forehead. Eventually he let out a sigh. 'If you must, shorten my number then. Someone a long time ago . . . used to call me One.'

'One?'

'If you must.'

I squeezed my eyes to dry them out, sniffed. 'It's less of a mouthful.'

His grunt of 'Indeed' held a hint of a smile to it.

'So?' Cons said, coming in with three mugs on a wooden board that improvised for a tray. 'Have you two got to know one another?'

'Why is this man –?'

'I thought you were going to call me One?'

I made a face at Cons as she placed the mugs down. 'Why is *One* here, saying his job is to watch over me?'

Cons drew her eyes across the man's face, this stranger in our tiny room whom she seemed to know so well. 'Is that all you've told her?'

He flicked a hand through the air and reclaimed his seat. 'The rest I'll leave to you,' he eventually replied gruffly.

'Cons, please?' The beseeching tone in my voice drew her quickly beside me, onto the thin bedspread that I knew wasn't enough to keep her warm at night.

She patted then stroked my lap as she asked eagerly, 'So, how did it go today? Are you to be Paired?'

'What has that got to do with –?'

'Just tell me, Christy . . . You've been picked?'

I nodded, and she joined in: she had already known the answer. I thought of Stella's warning. 'Has it been broadcast

44

or something?'

'No. You were destined to be Paired.' The expression on Cons' face looked satisfied at first, but then shifted into one of resignation.

'Destined? No – my destiny is to remain unPaired . . . to stay here, with you! The Pairing – it's not for me.'

Cons made a fierce shake of her head. 'I have looked after you, protected you. But my part in your life is done. It is your time now.'

'What if I won't do it?'

'Then my Selection will come sooner.'

I shook my head frantically. 'No! What do you mean? Why should it?'

'No one turns down the Pairing. If you do, they won't hesitate to Select me as punishment – yours and mine.'

I opened my mouth, fish-like, but only a moan came out. She was right. My shoulders slumped.

Cons came closer. 'Oh, my dear, my Christy . . . The Pairing – it is your calling, my sweet one. From the moment your father left, your fate has been fastened. The Pairing is just the first step.'

'My calling? Fastened to what? You're not making sense, Cons!'

Cons stayed tight-lipped. She was looking at her stranger. And he was staring into the fire. I took my hand and gently turned her face back to meet mine. 'Cons . . . okay; I won't risk them taking you. I will let them Pair me – but, please,' I dropped onto the floor so I was at her feet, 'let's finally talk about this: find a way for you to avoid Selection. You can't ever leave me!'

45

There was nothing I could do to stop the tears now.

Cons winced, moving her face close to mine until I could see every line and wrinkle, every fleck in her pale blue eyes. She watched me cry, before her hands reached out, gripping both my arms with a strength of someone half her age. 'Contain yourself, Christy. Swallow back your emotion. You need to be brave. It is time . . . You must stop surviving – start living.'

Chapter Four

I hadn't come to, not fully, yet. My body was stirring, but for one beautiful moment my mind remained stuck in another world.

Intuition told me it was preferable to remain there. A dreaming limbo.

Dad was with me. I couldn't see him clearly, but by sense alone I knew it was him. His mouth was moving, talking hurriedly yet kindly. His arms, solid as they looped around me; one hand smoothing my hair back away from my face, just like Cons might do. Then, all of a sudden, we were running, hand in hand, his palm thick and rough against mine. Our fingers tightly entwined; he wouldn't lose me again, *Not now I've found you*. There was a boat ahead, its triangular sail flapping in the wind, water spraying over its deck . . . a cabin door opening, an indistinct blur of a woman's face beckoning us both to hurry –

I awoke abruptly. My heart rate plummeting as my consciousness became familiar with my surroundings.

A comfortable smell of frying bacon was seeping into my room. Stella must have packed some into that paper bag; Cons' points never afforded us any meat besides offcuts of mutton or goat. The aroma wasn't temptation enough though. I dragged the sheet back over my head, closing my eyes again. I tried recalling the very last moment of my dream, urging it to take me back inside.

But already its detail was being erased, the last images slipping like water through my fingers. Till all that was left was a deep sense of longing.

Then I remembered: my *destiny* – to be Paired . . . That man – *One*. Cons had said nothing more; I'd heard him leave soon after she had ordered me to bed.

I swung myself up, legs out, the chill in the room hitting my skin like tiny knives. Pulling a jumper on over my thin nightdress, I joined Cons in the kitchen. Facing the stove, she was pushing the contents of our breakfast about a pan, blithely humming one of the tunes she said came from her early childhood.

'Morning,' I said softly, going over to her. I wanted to forget last night had ever happened. I wrapped my arms around her waist and pressed my cheek against the back of her neck, inhaling the warm scent that was Cons' alone. She was a close second to a dream about Dad.

'Sit yourself down; this will be ready in seconds.'

'Did that all come from Stella?' There were mushrooms either side of the bacon, some shredded onions and an oversized tomato cut in half.

'Like I'm always telling you,' Cons replied, a half smile appearing at the side of her face closest to me, 'stay in with Stella.'

'Right,' I replied drily, pulling away from her and picking out cutlery from the drawer.

I watched Cons scrape the contents out of the pan and onto

two plates. 'Here,' she said, passing me mine.

I took a fork, stabbed a piece of bacon and moved it onto hers. 'Take your fair share.'

For once she humoured me. We sat down opposite one another. Our usual places.

'Christy, we need to talk.'

The look on her face made me instantly nervous.

'The thing is, I didn't mean for you to meet 454111 like that.' Her head was tipped to one side as if she were trying to work out how she might have preferred me to meet him.

Neither of us had started eating yet. My right hand was now occupied, circling each of the six numbers that followed the scratched-out *Hogan* on my dad's old desk – our makeshift dining table.

'454111's a decent man . . . like your father.'

My eyes flashed upwards. 'I don't need another dad, Cons. That role is not vacant.'

Cons made a 'pah' noise and began shovelling up some mushrooms. 'Whoever said it was!'

Sighing, she dropped her loaded fork and leant towards me. The skin on her arms creased into small zigzag lines as she reached for my hands. Its age-worn looseness had begun to obscure and distort the two numbers tattooed on her wrist. Hers; and beneath it, my grandfather's. Damn them for marking her like that.

'Let me explain,' she said, opening and closing her mouth a number of times before she began in earnest, 'what I meant last night.'

I kept quiet, hoping I was still locked in a dream.

49

Cons looked behind her then got up and closed the kitchen door. Her voice more hushed now, she carried on. '454111 works in government – in security. Ostensibly, he is the State's mole in the Resistance . . . but really, he works for *them*.

'Christy, your father – he needs your help. You're seventeen now.' She spoke over the strangled sound my mouth made, her hand wafting furiously to indicate she wouldn't suffer any more dramatics. 'The Pairing is only the first step – there is a plan for you. Your father had clear ambitions for his daughter. He told me of them before he left. 454111 is here to help you fulfil them.'

All that moved in me was my heart, each beat quicker than the last. 'My father?' I eventually found the voice to utter. 'Ambitions for me?'

'He intended for you to rise up and do great things for the Resistance – for him – when you came of age. Which is now. Now, Christy.'

'Join the Resistance?'

'Yes! My dear, you come from a great rebel leader! His natural abilities run in your blood. You were born to continue his fight.'

'You want me to fight?'

'To spy, to inform . . . the Resistance need to get rid of certain people if they are to strengthen their offensive.'

My voice box strained, 'Get rid of people . . .?'

Cons' pale eyes turned sympathetic. She roofed her hands. 'The Resistance has to kill to stop others being killed.'

'You want me to kill people?' I asked, my lips trembling.

'It will be made easy for you,' Cons said, adding warmly, 'But let's not worry yet about what you might be asked to do.

Concentrate on what you are to become.'

I shook my head. 'This is what my dad wanted for me?'

'He always knew that you . . .' she paused and nodded her head at me as I shook mine some more. 'Yes, *you*, would be integral to changing things in Land . . . for the better – for everyone.'

'That's ridiculous! I mean . . . me? Me!' I looked down at the table. My fingers moved over to trace the carving of his name now, over and again, pressing harder each time until it hurt.

'There is more to this life than you and me alone. Don't you want to help shape Land into a place where people are free to choose their own destinies?'

'All I want is for you to stay safe,' I said, as Cons continued.

'The Resistance need someone on the inside – a young, innocent-looking girl like you, who would never arouse suspicion – Paired powerfully.'

I made a hacking noise. 'How will I get a *powerful* Pair?'

'454111 is certain of it. He can help – it was he who made sure you were picked.'

'He made that happen?' I blinked. What had I thought – that my genes alone had overridden my dad's traitorous history?

'Yes, and he will guide you into a government job when it's time to leave the Institute. To the outside, 454111 will simply be your mentor.'

'So this One must also know where Dad is?' Hope rose.

'Oh, my darling . . . As I've told you before, for *us* to know Hogan's whereabouts would be too dangerous.'

Then fell.

'But I do know this is what your dad hopes you will do for

him – what he's been waiting for, all this time, to ask of you.'

I lifted my hand away from the engraved *Hogan* and joined it with my other on my lap. I straightened up, lifting my chin. Then I said in a voice that I hoped matched Cons', in its quietness as well as its strength. 'I'll do anything to help Dad. You know that.'

I sat on my bed with the Pairing pamphlet I'd been handed at the Institute yesterday.

I felt nauseous. I wanted to see Kara.

I flicked listlessly through its pages, notes on a briefing to be held next weekend, then the big event – the Pairing Ceremony itself – a few weeks later. I needed a second pamphlet . . . something to tell me how to become a rebel. *Getting rid of people*. Suddenly that role felt much harder than being Paired off to some stranger.

I ran back over Cons' words from breakfast. 'The Resistance hope to see you Paired within the Blue elites who run government. It will put you in the best place to help . . .'

My stomach was pendulum-swinging between a tight ball of anxiety – I wasn't capable of working for the Resistance! – to another feeling: pride. Over the past fifteen years I had known what I felt for my dad. I was all too aware what a great man he was, what he had tried to do for Land's people. But I had nothing to tell me how he would look upon his daughter.

So yes, I felt proud – that my dad had pinned his dreams onto me. That he thought me – *me* – capable of fuelling the change Kara always talked about.

Except, I wasn't like Kara. I wouldn't help the Resistance

because I wanted a fight.

I just wanted my dad back.

We had joined a long line of sombre-looking workers waiting for the tram. Cons had suggested we take it to the shopping precinct because her legs were too tired to walk. She wanted to buy me material for a new outfit. 'You'll be mixing with the finely dressed soon. You must begin fluttering your feathers amongst the other peacocks.'

'We don't have the points,' I'd objected. 'Besides, Pairings are matched by some database somewhere – what difference can a new dress make?'

'Let's not be naive; times haven't changed that much from the Old World.' Cons closed her eyes temporarily as if she had transported herself back there. 'You must step up to who you're going to be.'

Browns and Greys mostly filled our queue. Saturday remained a day of work for most of them. (Cons was due at the hospital by lunchtime. Her shift would last until evening.) Only Blues were deemed deserving of the whole weekend off. Greens were given enough home-study to plug nearly every minute. As one of the State posters at the Institute reminded us, **Idleness is your downfall**. The message was a clear one. Stay busy, prosperous, useful . . . or face Selection.

So it was something of a novelty that being one of the chosen ones would grant me free time: the pamphlet said I no longer had to complete home-study until the Pairing was over.

'Here it comes,' Cons said. The tram was rattling down the thin metal track that was embedded in West Land's main thoroughfare; drawing a straight line from the outskirts to the shopping precinct. With its white, square face and lights that flashed red either side, West Land's only tram had given me nightmares as a child.

The queue surged forwards in anticipation as it stopped, its black wire crackling overhead. Last in line, we had to squeeze on. The State operated a tram schedule that ensured they were interminably packed. I was glad when a young man in Brown with a thin, drawn face gave up his seat for Cons.

When we came to the next stop, Cons glanced across at me, dragging my eyes with hers to the floor. Two Troopers were getting on. Their laughter, the easy manner of their bodies, a stark contrast to the slumped shoulders inside. Yet in an instant there would be a marked change in every passenger's demeanour; mine too. It was second nature. I pulled a small, forced smile onto my lips; my head up but my eyes dipped. Humility and happiness; the mastered look of a *contented, grateful Land citizen*. Dare to look miserable or nonchalant and they would report you to the Assessors – and their medicinal prescription for discontent.

Luckily these two seemed too absorbed in their own conversation as they forced their way through, pushing a middle-aged woman in Grey and the Green child next to her from their seats.

I could never ignore Troopers' presence, but now nor could I forget: I was being asked to be their enemy.

As we left the shopping precinct my mood had shifted a little, simply by spending time with Cons. She was a different grandmother to the one sat at the breakfast table plotting out my future in the Resistance. I was glad to have this version back. We'd searched through hundreds of rolls of fabrics in the large Green section of West Land's only material shop, finding amusement over the weirder types, 'dyed rat fur' the Brown assistant told us, and thumbing the more luxuriant.

Outside, the sun was shining again, taking the edge off the chilled air. It generally made things more bearable. Sunshine brought better health (over winter, many colds, innocently left unchecked, led to Selection); it brightened up the faces of the Greys and Browns scurrying past, as well as Cons'.

'When are you due at hospital?' I said, linking arms with her. She'd spoilt me, convincing me to let her use her points on a beautiful emerald-Green piece of material, a cotton so soft it felt velvety between my fingers. Indulged me with new tights as well, ready-made and glossy – so unlike the scratchy home-made woollen ones I wore to the Institute. Thankfully, tights, like socks and shoes, didn't have to be Green – these new ones were almost skin colour. Cons wouldn't let me see how much it all cost her as she jammed her points' card into the debit machine. But I was sure we wouldn't be eating much till she was paid next week's salary.

'Soon. But first I must take you somewhere. You need to . . . Well, you must meet him again.'

I didn't ask who. Dread began trickling through me. I pulled away from Cons, stopping as she walked on. I had been tricked. Cons had tricked me.

'Why didn't you say that's what we were coming out for?' I said.

She walked back to me, her face pinched.

'You could've told me.' I tried to keep my tone light for the benefit of those rushing by.

Cons pulled me in close to her, her eyes impeaching me with her first rule, *Don't get noticed*. 'Shush now, Christy. I'm sorry, I thought it might be better this way. I didn't want you making a fuss again.'

'A fuss?' Another fight with my emotions was stirring, fear mixed with anger. I was becoming breathless as my chest tightened. 'But I was going to call on Kara soon; I want to see Kara,' I repeated lamely.

'Kara? Christy, you've been a good friend to Kara, but Kara is no longer your priority.'

A flush rose up my neck. I wanted to stamp a foot like a toddler. 'Kara will always be my priority.'

Cons passed me a stiff smile then kissed me fleetingly on my temple. An action that promptly told me: *I love you, but pull yourself together*.

'When did you arrange this . . .?'

Cons' eyes looked cautiously around, then she hissed back, hardly moving her mouth, 'A message . . . on my tracer . . . this morning.'

'He has authorisation to send out messages?' I thought fleetingly of the one I had received at yesterday's Pairing announcement, **Christabel, now is your hour. Rise to it.** *Was* that him? He hadn't said so, but who else had the inclination – or authority – to send me messages?

Cons made a curt nod and we began walking again.

'Why not just meet him back at our flat?'

56

Cons sucked in her cheeks. I was testing her patience but then, if I was honest, I would say she was starting to test mine too. Sighing, she paused and leant her face against my ear, delivering words so scant and quiet I had to fill in the gaps. *I was to be seen with him – an elite, powerful Blue.* She put a cold palm to my cheek. I didn't want her to remove it; all of a sudden any touch of Cons' felt so precious. 'Please, do this for me.'

I drew my eyes over her tired, lined face. 'For you,' I mumbled.

Chapter Five

He was waiting for us outside one of the few cafés in West Land. I'd never been in one before – they were almost solely patronised by Troopers and Blues. I preferred my tea at home.

Standing with a rod-straight back, dressed in the same long Blue coat from last night, One's gaze was alert like Troopers', as if he were searching for trouble. I might never have assumed the boy standing near him, stamping his feet on the ground from the cold, was with him, had it not been for the way they jointly locked eyes with mine as we approached them.

I glanced round impatiently at Cons. 'Who's he?'

She flashed me a look that said *Be quiet*, stretching out an arm to One. He shook it formally, but with both hands, and then turned to me. His smile was one I recognised, the kind I forced on my Institute tutors. It didn't spread to his eyes, and it passed as quickly as it came.

So I gave him one just like it back.

'This is Salinger.' One signalled the boy to his side.

I merely tipped my head a little, trying to keep my eyes indifferent. He couldn't have been that much older than me. His nut-brown hair was curly, but cut short, as if he wanted to tame it. A direct stare shadowed by dark brows; a straight nose led to a curved mouth that seemed to twitch with puzzlement.

'Your son?' I asked plainly. Dressed in Grey, but smartly, in trousers and a jacket that said he may not be a Blue but clearly he had done okay since leaving the Institute. Unlike Kara's brother, Xavier. Xavier was clever, really bright in fact, but he'd been given Brown to wear, sent to work at a plastics factory.

Salinger made a short bark of a laugh. 'I'm no one's son,' he said, as One coolly added, 'He's my aide. Salinger, meet Christy. Christy likes names so it's a good thing you've got one.'

One and Salinger exchanged a look clearly meant to patronise me. I felt a dull thump of exclusion in the pit of my stomach. I shrugged to disguise it. 'Fine. Shall we get this over with?'

'Oh, I can see we're going to get on really well.' Salinger whistled on the air to his right.

I heard Cons utter an exasperated, 'Christy!' It made me feel like a child. She began pulling on her gloves. It looked like an act, so she didn't have to meet my eyes. 'I have to leave – get to work.' Cons put her lips together decisively, then she tapped my cheek, peeling off my fingers as they clasped hers. 'You need to spend time with 454111 and Salinger now . . .'

Silence. It was a joke. Silence.

A protracted silence that amplified every other sound – slurp of tea, chink of cup, groan from my hungry belly.

I opened my mouth to say something, anything; then closed it again. Was Cons' whispered admission, that the meeting was for us to be seen in public together, simply that: to be *seen*? Not heard? I shifted uncomfortably in my seat. Maybe I'd failed some test already. Maybe they were working out how to tell me I wasn't who they thought I might be. Well, I could have told them that.

I stared round at the café. White wooden tables and chairs were laid out close to one another, illuminated brightly under blocks of strip lighting. We'd already been served a cup of milky tea each by a perky-looking waitress in Brown with badly dyed yellow hair (probably lemons from the café larder) and clearly on the highest dose of blue pills the State administered.

One, directly opposite me, suddenly cleared his throat.

I looked back at him expectantly. But no words followed. It was as if silence was the way he conducted every meeting. I'd decided he was probably in his early forties . . . about the same age my dad would be now. A scar, shaped like a smile, was drawn on the underside of his chin. His nose was bent a little to one side; his grey eyes – the way they drooped at the edges – gave him a doleful appearance that seemed at odds with the way he held himself: upright, chin raised. In control.

In contrast, Salinger, beside me, appeared restless. He kept flicking his black tracer over in one hand and moving the cutlery around his place setting with the other.

I exhaled loudly and finally gave in. 'So, One, is there anything in particular you wanted to talk about?' My words affected saccharine sweet.

Next to me Salinger's voice cracked. 'One? She's going to call you One? No one's called you One since –'

One's expression halted him.

I looked between them. 'Since?'

One's mouth fidgeted as if he might answer but instead

he adjusted his coat and said, 'No – nothing particularly,' his gravelly voice deadpan. 'It's simply good to meet you.' As if last night had never happened. 'We feel we already know so much about you.'

I narrowed my eyes. 'I wish I could say the same.' I wasn't going to let him reclaim his tortuous silence, so I continued. 'I understand you're going to steer me through my Pairing?'

'You can steer yourself through that. We're here as your mentors, to guide you in your career,' he answered bluntly.

I shrunk a little until I caught those doleful eyes; they were sliding sideways. I followed their trajectory, towards the swathes of Black and Blue, talking loudly, being seen being great. He was ordering me to censor my conversation.

I brought my cup to my lips, taking a small sip to stop me making a fool of myself again. But curiosity got the better of me. I frowned. 'Won't my career be decided upon by the Assessors?'

'That's right . . . they spotted your potential a long time ago.'

I swallowed his lie; let it settle. Then it struck me; the class schedule I had been given since I joined the Institute, aged eleven: political theory, debating class, land policy and development. Just how long had One been *guiding* me in my career? Had this all been thought through, from the very beginning? 'When *did* they spot it . . .?' The clipped edge left my voice. Layers of my past were being stripped away.

'Your talents are finally being honoured. Only a few students are chosen for a future in senior-level government. Which is why you are to be mentored for such a career by us,' One answered, every word fit for public consumption.

I nodded vaguely. I was trying so hard to read between his lines my mind was beginning to blur.

'Though first you've got to prove to us you're worthy,' Salinger butted in, then added, 'of what the State asks of you . . .' as if he were editing his first statement.

It wasn't hard to guess it was meant personally. I twisted in my seat to face him. His eyes directly on me, wide, dark brown, they seemed to penetrate mine as if he were trying to take every piece of me out and examine it all over, like the Troopers did sometimes when they wanted to intimidate you. For some reason it took every bit of strength in me to pull my own eyes away.

'I *thought* it was you.' An oily voice came by our table.

One coolly looked round and made the same smile he'd given me outside. At least he wasn't selective, I thought. I followed his gaze upwards, nervously mimicking One's mouth.

'You're picking them off already are you?' he continued to One.

I'd never been this close to the principal of my Institute. I only ever saw him at a sensible distance, usually when he was behind a lectern, like yesterday. Up close his skin was marked with small acne scars. His greased dark hair shimmered under the strobe lighting, as if he'd pressed it close to his scalp with beeswax.

I held my breath, waiting to hear how One would answer. Taciturn as ever, he took his time responding. He made a miniscule adjustment to the cup in his saucer, then another of those smiles again, before, 'One of yours. 823057 has been personally selected for a future in our new Leader's government.

Only the best will do, isn't that right?'

Behind his glasses, the principal drew straining eyes over me. He clearly didn't have a clue who I was.

'Good, good. I always thought you'd go far, 823057.'

I coughed back a laugh and thanked him.

'I'm glad West Institute keeps meeting our quota,' he added to One.

One raised his cup. 'Keep passing them to us.'

The principal was dismissed, that was clear now by the way One sharply averted his eyes. Enjoying the experience of watching the scene unfold, at first I didn't catch his retreating remark. Then it caught up with me, as if the principal's words had simply taken time to blow my way. 'Your uncle – I mean, the Leader – is doing such a tremendous job . . . Do give him my highest regards.'

I turned, wide-eyed, to One. I wanted answers, even if he had to give them coded. 'Your uncle?'

The stare One returned was blank.

'The Leader is your uncle? How did you –?' I lowered my voice, trying to keep my tone dull for the benefit of neighbouring tables, as if I was debating eggs, scrambled or fried.

My questions were met with a nonchalant shrug.

'My family . . .?' I danced my eyes so One could be in no doubt this time of the meaning behind my question. How could One have convinced *the Leader* to promote someone like me for a career in his government? I mean, the fact I was Dad's daughter had to be on some file, somewhere!

I held his gaze. I did what Salinger had done to me and tried to read into it. Maybe it worked, somehow, because One

63

stretched out his fingers then furled them into fists, before he said, 'One of the reasons you were chosen is because your files are impeccable . . . not a stain upon you. Believe me, that's rare.'

It was the most number of words One had used since I had met him. But they spoke volumes.

No one knew who I was.

He had created a whole new version of 823057.

Chapter Six

Was I imagining it? Or was there a new attitude towards me at the Institute come Monday? I mean, the way Tutor 567341 gave me back my report from last week – 'You're showing great logic in this' – wasn't normal. Through the whole year he'd never even noticed the girl on the back row with her eyes down.

Now, sat in my debating group (which claimed a new meaning for the verb 'to debate', seeing as each side was forced to back Land's policies), Tutor 446728 kept picking on me to speak up, spoiling my six-year run of silence. Suddenly she actually seemed interested in my anodyne views: *Yes, I believe the edict to tightly control birth rates is an invested one*.

Was it just because I'd been chosen for the Pairing? Or had the Principal talked to his staff about the student now associated with the new leader's nephew?

The Leader's nephew. Cons hadn't denied it. Not that she'd affirmed it either. She'd returned, shattered, from her shift on the maternity ward on Saturday night.

'He is?' was all she'd said when I'd told her. But it didn't come with any accompaniment of surprise. More a tone of *Why's that relevant?*

'You never told me how you know One.'

Cons had rubbed a hand across her eyes and let out a tired sigh. I felt mean, for pressing her yet again. 'I've known him since he was born, more or less . . . though there were gaps when I didn't see him at all.'

'So, a family friend?'

'You might call it that.'

'But how? I mean, he's not just high up – he's *really* high up.'

'As our family was once.' Cons looked offended. 'Don't forget – my uncle was one of those who formed Land!' Then she let out a snort of a laugh that sounded jaded. 'How the mighty can fall – clearly I chose the wrong man to partner with.'

'You chose for love,' I replied solemnly. It was a fact of our family history I cherished. 'But One is happy –' I lowered my voice to a whisper – 'to betray his own uncle?'

Cons chopped a hand through the air. 'This new leader rose from being Head of the State Troopers, that's why he still wears Black. He abandoned his family long ago. One, as you call him, might work alongside him, but he's not close in any other way.'

'You're sure we can trust One?'

'Don't look for *doubts*, Christy,' she cut into me. 'Be patient. Keep things simple.'

Simple. Her voice, like burnt treacle, made it sound as if it was.

Trust Cons. Trust Dad. Now: trust One.

What choice did I have but to trust them all?

The tutor's droning voice brought me back to the present. I tried to focus on the policy test being handed out, but the print swam. The answers were all predetermined anyway – I just had to keep saying *yes*.

When the bell finally trilled for end of class, I was one of the first to jump out of my seat. I had to hurry and catch Kara. I never had got to hers over the weekend. I couldn't put it off any longer: I had to tell her – I was to be Paired.

'How've you been?' I didn't mean to sound so forced; it came from trying too hard to appear like nothing had changed. 'Did you do much at the weekend?'

We were crammed into the last cubicle of the girls' toilets where we always met, down near the Institute's slaves' living quarters – the White workers who endlessly cleaned and prepared for students. We'd already checked we were alone, and left one of our tracers in the cubicle next door, so if anyone tracked our whereabouts we'd been in separate toilets.

'Do anything? Fat chance – I had five bloody essays to finish. How about you, you get lots?'

It was a natural cue. *No. And here's the reason why.* Except that the words refused to come easily. 'I . . . the thing is . . .' My voice split. How did I break it to her? When I wasn't allowed to tell her the rest?

'Christy! What is it? Is it Cons? They've not taken her?'

'It's not that.' Thankfully, it *wasn't* that. 'It's . . .' I looked her straight in the eye. 'The Pairing. I've been chosen.'

Kara's face bolted like I'd just punched her. 'Why didn't you say on Friday?'

I shook my head. 'I was in shock . . . I'm sorry.'

'You're going to refuse, right? Show them you won't be one

of them!' Kara grabbed my shoulders. 'I'll be there alongside you – we're in it together, remember?'

My forehead twisted. 'If I say no – they'll make me a slave; they'll automatically approve Cons for Selection . . . I don't have a choice.'

Kara's expression was turning fierce, desperate. 'But, Christy, if we don't take a stand – how else will things change?' The same expression that had got her put on the blue pills twice.

I took a breath. Couldn't I give Kara something to hope for?

'They chose you, but not me.' Kara lowered her eyes; her long black fringe falling down across her face. She made a short laugh. 'It figures, right? Despite your dad, you still tick their boxes: you don't argue back, you're pretty, you're clever . . .'

'Hey – you know it isn't that! You're smarter than most students here!' I shook her sleeve. 'You don't conform: the way you look, cut your hair . . . you tell them you're different, you're special. And they don't like that. So they will never choose you, because they don't want people who think for themselves. Haven't you always said that?'

Kara began picking at the collar of her shirt. It was fraying badly. I would need to pass some new clothes her way before she got reprimanded for it. She breathed out heavily through her nose. 'I would just have liked to be picked, so I could tell them to stuff it. To show them what I think of their bloody stupid Pairing.'

I put my hand under Kara's chin to lift it up. I feared for her when she talked like this. I realised at this point that I had no choice. 'Listen, if I tell you something, you must swear, swear on Xavier's life, not to tell anyone.'

Kara made a face, then, slowly, a nod of understanding.

I unlocked the toilet door and looked out, scanning the row of sinks. Above them hung a line of black and white propaganda posters. So you could remind yourself of what Land asked of you each time you washed your hands.

'Wait here.' I stepped out, checking the other cubicles were still empty.

Rejoining Kara, I pulled her down onto the floor with me, as if somehow that would contain the noise of our voices better.

I bit down on my lip. Was I being stupid? It was so dangerous to tell someone, anyone. My eyes glanced over words faintly carved into the wall behind Kara. *They have taken everything.* Probably scratched out by a slave, desperate for a voice. Who was I kidding – of course it was stupid! But I had to – I had to keep Kara surviving.

I took my voice to its lowest tone. 'Haven't I always wondered why my files were always blocked to Troopers? Someone's been controlling my files.' I rolled my eyes upwards as if government were just upstairs. 'A man, with links to Dad. A double agent.' I had to keep words to a minimum. The rapid beating of my heart reminded me that every word uttered came with risk. 'Kara, I've been given a job to do. To help Dad. Okay?'

I kept looking at her until I saw in her eyes that she had caught up.

'I can't say any more.'

'No,' Kara whispered hurriedly, 'no, you can't. You shouldn't even have said this.'

Slowly, I watched a smile as it began a journey across her wide mouth. A genuine smile – such a rare thing for Kara. But

I always loved it when it happened. It completely changed her, brightening her face in a way that made her beautiful.

'Amazing; bloody brilliant! The rebellion's really starting!' Kara mouthed silently.

I smiled with her. I knew what it meant to her. I had spent all these years fantasising about Dad coming back, but Kara had dreamt of something far bigger – a revolution.

I just wished I wasn't one of the people tasked with delivering it.

Hordes of Greens were making their way out of the Institute grounds now the final bell of the day had rung; that's what made his Grey stand out, nothing to do with his presence otherwise.

I paused, staring at him from a distance. Who else would he be waiting for but me? I used to get jealous of Kara on the few occasions Xavier would come to meet her at the Institute's tall metal gates. I would have liked an older brother. But I didn't want Salinger.

'You okay?' Kara had stopped alongside me.

'I know him,' I mumbled, nodding my head in Salinger's direction.

The collar of his short, metal-Grey coat was up against the cold. His hands were casually dug into his trouser pockets; his feet stamping the ground like yesterday.

'I have to meet him alone,' I said to her, grimacing when a group of girls in front of us smiled and giggled as they passed by him. Why? It wasn't like Salinger was a Blue or anything.

'I don't suppose this is a happy coincidence,' I said drily

when we were finally face to face.

Salinger clicked his tongue. 'There's no such thing. I'm here to walk you home.'

I jumped as Kara drew up against me. 'I'm Kara. A good friend of Christy's.'

I strained my eyes at her: why hadn't she left? After what I'd confessed to her, after what she knew of me and boys (in that, I didn't know any), I thought she'd guess who Salinger was to me. Then it twigged. All Kara had talked about the last couple of years was joining the Resistance. Finally: here was her chance. Angry with myself for not thinking it through, I took it out on Salinger. 'I don't want you walking me anywhere!'

Salinger simply shrugged and grinned at Kara. 'Salinger. Pleased to meet you.' He used a different tone. 'You had a good day, Kara?' Nice. That was the word. He was being *nice* to her. They started talking about her last class, chemistry, Kara's favourite subject. Kara was telling him how her dad had been something of a genius in chemicals before his Selection.

'So clearly you're not at the Institute yourself?'

And what was that, the change in Kara's demeanour? The way she was holding her body, pushing forward a hip; one finger rubbing against her lower lip? Kara wasn't wary of boys like I was. She knew ways to handle them. But this was Salinger.

'No, I'm eighteen.' Salinger flicked the Grey collar of his coat. 'Work in government now.'

Idiot. He was lapping it up. I wanted to drag one of them away. I just wasn't sure which one.

'I'm keen to get working.'

'Yeah? It's not all it's cracked up to be.'

71

I almost shoved him. Couldn't he just shut up? Didn't he see how Kara was hinting for him to get her in with the Resistance? Couldn't he see her fraying collar, her badly cut hair? I didn't want them taking advantage of her. She was safer out of it.

'Do you live round here?' Kara was now asking. My insides cringed for her. She was trying too hard.

Salinger shook his head. 'South Land.'

'You do?' I interrupted, surprised. It was the best region to live. I hadn't thought about Salinger – or One for that matter – living in homes, with other people, cooking dinner . . . Now I tried to picture it I found I wanted to know a bit more, despite my indifference to him. I had an unexpected urge to know . . .

'Are you Paired?' Kara asked the question for me.

Salinger made a half smile as he shook back the sleeve of his jacket, showing his wrist, his own, sole, number tattooed there.

It made Kara's dark blue eyes grow brighter. 'Me neither.'

'Who wants to be?' Salinger laughed, before he made a gesture with his head for us to leave.

I ignored his last remark, clearly aimed at me, and passed a hand out to stroke the side of Kara's threadbare coat. 'Don't you have to go to the shopping precinct?' With Xavier working in the industrial outskirts of West Land, Kara had to get all their food.

'I'd rather walk home with you two.'

My stomach dropped, but I had to say it. 'No Kara, that's not a good idea. I'll see you tomorrow.'

Looking back as Salinger and I sloped away, I saw she was still in the same spot, a forlorn, distinct figure, despite the constant rush of Green around her. I felt a hot rush of anger. I had been mean to my best friend, all because some guy I didn't even like thought I needed to be met from the Institute. Suddenly I was the one being walked home by an older brother.

Until I reminded myself it was Salinger, not a member of my family. 'You could've warned me you'd be turning up.'

'And how do you propose we do that?'

'One sent my grandmother a message on her tracer.'

'454111 has those privileges. It might have escaped your notice but I'm a Grey, not a Blue.'

'No. It hadn't escaped my notice,' I cut in, my voice neat.

Salinger glanced sideways at me. His face showed no sign of hurt. Just bemusement. This only annoyed me more.

'454111 will meet us back at your flat.'

'And I can't be trusted to make my own way there? What are you, some kind of stalker?' I regretted my words the moment they came out.

'No, but you're some kind of *girl*, so you would probably go chatting to other girls and never find your way home. Our time is precious, you know.'

I took back my regret.

But I kept my mouth shut for the rest of the way home.

One and Cons were installed at the kitchen table. I bristled immediately to see One in my seat, his arm resting over Dad's name and number.

We only had room for two chairs in the kitchen; Salinger went and leant against the sink. I stood behind Cons.

It didn't feel like my home any more.

73

'This won't take long,' Cons turned round and said to me. Then she nodded at One as if she were granting him permission to speak.

He cleared his throat and eyed me briefly before returning to Cons. 'The plan is for Salinger to come by every Monday, Wednesday and Friday evening until the Pairing. Any more visits might attract suspicion. Ostensibly, he is here to tutor Christy on my behalf for her future in government.'

I looked at the back of Cons' head, but she didn't flinch. So then, one good thing to come out of this: at last I'd be officially relieved from Stella's Friday dinners. I waited for One to expound on the true purpose of these visits.

'And what is it he's *really* coming for?' I asked testily when, typically, he didn't.

'Is that not obvious?' One drew a hand back through his spiked short hair. 'Salinger is a skilled Resistance member, been doing it since before you could read, practically. He'll teach you all you need to know to execute the activities we'll ask of you. There won't be as much chance for that kind of intensive training once you're Paired.'

I looked across at Salinger. He was already watching me, his dark eyes doing that trick, their visual interrogation.

'Will he be teaching me how to kill?'

Cons' face shot round at me like I'd said a dirty word.

'Well, will he?' I looked at each of them.

One shifted his body in his seat. 'We'll keep death simple. Most of our assignments won't involve weapons – just a pill.'

'A pill?' I spat out.

'A pill,' One repeated calmly, his voice a faint murmur, 'that kills; no skill necessary.' He made a small smile. I returned it with a scowl. 'Swift, undetected. Formulated for us by a Resistance member working in the science labs. So far we have made two assassinations this way, by dropping into the victim's drink a pill that causes immediate heart failure, or gives them some fatal bug that looks like food poisoning.'

'Surely the State will get suspicious?'

'Not at first. We use a different concoction each time. And remember, this is Land. Autopsies, collecting evidence – they're timely. The State only ever makes such effort when there's a definitive sign of murder. And there won't be. Land's approach to human life will protect us: once you're dead, you're dead.'

'Ultimately, yeah, they'll begin to put two and two together,' Salinger began saying. 'But by then it'll have served our purpose – it will have weakened government. The Resistance can start their attack.'

'But first: you get Paired,' One said, tapping the table in front of him.

I swallowed back the growing lump in my throat. My heart was thumping heavily. 'Do you know to whom?' Was the accompanying spasm in my stomach from fear? It felt too pleasant. Excitement? No – what on earth was there to be excited about? It didn't matter who I was Paired with. Did it?

'That's not in my control.' One held his hands up.

'Then whose control is it in?'

'Christy!' Cons swung round fast in her seat. 'Patience.' Her current keyword. *Stop asking questions. Stop seeking answers.*

I glared back over at Salinger – Resistance's boy genius – to see if he was enjoying the way I was being treated, but he was no longer looking at me. He'd picked up a knife from the side of the sink and was examining it as if it were some new invention.

'You must prepare for life as a Pair,' One continued, 'None of us can train you in that.'

I drew my neck back. I didn't even want to ask him what he meant. But for once One decided to expand. 'It's doubtful you will be approved to reproduce soon . . . not when you're yet to finish at the Institute. But there might be a chance that –'

He stopped talking as my mouth made a croak of a sound. I meant to say 'Stop'. I flashed Cons a fierce look of *stop* instead, as she twisted round.

'It has to be raised, Christy,' was all she said.

I shook my head, mortified. Angry at them all. How dare they discuss something so personal!

'Needless to say, you need to be on your guard,' One went on. 'Manage your relationship wisely. People aren't Paired for love, remember; you're there to breed.'

Nausea was climbing up my oesophagus.

I'd nearly asked Kara today, what it was like with a boy. I knew Xavier brought home his unPaired workmates. Recently, she'd told me about a first kiss with one of them.

I cut a hand through the air. 'I'm not going to be reproducing,' I said vehemently. I wouldn't stand for my fertility being debated like they were farmers discussing which livestock to mate.

'If you're approved, you won't have a say in the decision.' My eyes shot across to Salinger. What did it have to do with him? Eighteen, he'd said he was. Yet here he stood, relaxing against my sink, acting as if he were already my middle-aged tutor or something.

'Don't you tell *me* about *my* choices.' I stabbed my finger in his direction for extra emphasis.

'Christy!' said One and Cons at the same time, though One's was more of a question; Cons' of admonishment.

Salinger made his usual show of bemusement, brown eyes creased, mouth twitching.

My face grew hot despite the cold of the room.

When no one spoke again, I threw my hands in the air. 'Fine. I'll reproduce . . . I won't reproduce . . . whatever it is you want of me.'

A suggestion of a smile passed over One's lips. It duplicated the smile of the scar under his chin. 'I'm just saying it's unlikely you'll be approved yet – but practise avoidance. Keep your Pair happy, but when he wants anything more –' One made a puff of exhalation – 'then you point him in the direction of the State Troopers.'

I couldn't cover my ears; I knew better than to do that with Cons sitting stiffly in front of me. But I lowered my head and wished I were anywhere but there.

No one had much control over their life in Land. But all of a sudden the State seemed tame in comparison to the three people sat before me plotting my future.

It wasn't till later when I was curled up in my bed after receiving my first basic training from Salinger that the same nausea struck again from One's earlier humiliation. I hugged my body. I had no experience of managing boys. Full stop.

Direct them to the State Troopers, One'd said. At least I knew what he meant by that. Relationships were only condoned through the Pairing; children only by approval – so any additional needs men had, State Troopers especially, were taken care of by Land. By the state-run brothels in the outskirts, filled with slave workers. The girls and women sentenced there, usually for an unapproved pregnancy, were stamped with a red cross below their number: a lifetime of servicing men.

None of us would ever dare do anything with a boy that would risk a future there. Their presence was the best contraception the State had going.

But for One to suggest I tell my Pair to use one rather than bother me . . . I curled up more tightly into myself. I was out of my depth – at every level. Even though I could hear the soft snores of Cons coming from her room across the landing, I had never felt more alone.

Chapter Seven

Salinger was there for my third night of Resistance training that week. It was going just as badly as the previous two. After yet another lecture on why I was failing to unpick the front door's lock, he kept up haranguing me as we went back into the kitchen. 'You must practise on the nights I'm not here. We're running out of time.'

'Maybe I should have been told about my job months – years – earlier then!' I snapped back. I was tired, and annoyed with myself.

'How were we to know you'd become so important?'

'Important?' My lip curled. 'What are you on about?'

Salinger's expression shifted uneasily, as if he'd said something he shouldn't have.

'What is it?' I almost screamed at him. *Did* they know who I was to be Paired with – was that it?

'Nothing. It's nothing.' He shrugged. 'We just didn't envisage you'd be such an asset till we started working with you.'

I fixed my hands to my hips. 'Is that your attempt at sarcasm?' I wouldn't have known whether to be flattered or horrified if it wasn't.

Salinger screwed up his mouth and flipped a hand in front of his face. 'Take it how you like. You usually do. I'm done.' He stood up, collecting his things to go.

I made a huffing sound in reply. If it wasn't for Dad's hopes for me, and for protecting Cons, I'd kick One and Salinger's training to the kerb right now. I clearly wasn't right for this; I was failing every test Salinger set for me: information recall – memorising Salinger's hand-drawn maps of Land and the Cross, as well as a list of government positions, names and numbers; teaching me to talk like a true Land follower; reciting their prepared backstory of who I was and why I had been picked for fast-track into government. Then: picking locks; physical defence moves; scouting a room to assess the people in it, exits, manoeuvres . . . it all spun round my head, making me breathless – too much to take in too soon. I was so strung out I couldn't learn any of it properly.

Cons arrived back from work just as Salinger was leaving. She clocked his expression as they exchanged goodbyes; promptly picking up on the mood left stewing in the kitchen.

'You need to show Salinger more respect, Christy,' she said, her voice laced with disappointment in me.

'I can't help it. He puts my back up . . . thinks he knows it all.'

'Well, he probably does.' She made a long sigh. 'Remember, he and 454111 are not here to make friends.'

'I know that,' I mumbled, watching her collect some meagre vegetables from a cupboard and begin cutting them for our supper.

'There has to be distance. The relationship you will have with them isn't like you and me. They won't care for you like that.' Her voice was sharp, mimicking the sound of the knife as she diced.

'Like I want them to!' I returned fast, my jaw stiffening. I was reminded of the people who *did* care 'like that'. Besides Cons, there was Kara.

Two. It was so few.

'But your dad cares for you,' Cons offered, as if she'd just reached the same sum. 'And that's why you're doing this, right – for him, and for me?'

I felt my jaw slacken. Of course. She was right. Get Paired into an important Blue family, and I might delay Cons' Selection myself. Honour my father, and maybe – one day soon – I would meet him again.

I was sitting on my bed, glowering at the dress spread out next to me, as if everything was its fault.

Cons had worked hard at it. Every moment she wasn't working this week, she'd be head bowed over our ageing sewing machine, pins stuck in her mouth, her fingers raw from threading. I'd told her it didn't have to be so fine. *It's not like I'll be wearing it for the Pairing* – the State provided a dress for that. But she was determined. The result: the finest dress I'd ever owned, in an emerald-Green that almost matched my eyes.

I rubbed at my neck, took a breath, trying to stem the nerves racing round my veins, quickening my heartbeat. The briefing for the Pairing – it started in two hours. Everything was moving too fast.

I roughly picked up the dress, squeezing it as if it were a person I could hurt. Then I gave in. I stood up, lifting it over

81

my head. I didn't want to admit it: wearing the dress was like sliding into another skin, soft and gentle. I pushed my arms through the short sleeves, let the hem drop to my knees. It smelt of Cons. It had her hard work and skill etched into every cut of cloth, each stitch. I rolled the thin tights slowly over my legs, careful not to snag them – they gave my perpetually pale skin an unnatural glow at odds with the rest of me.

I just had to do something with my hair now.

Peering into the small tarnished mirror that rested against the wall on my chest of drawers, I played with piling it up above my neck. It gave me an uneasy resemblance to my mother. I let it hang back down like usual. It seemed too young: the hairstyle of a schoolchild.

Why did they all believe I could pull this off?

'What's wrong?' Cons said, appearing at my door. She must have heard the slam of my hairbrush.

'I don't look right. I won't fit in.'

'You are beautiful.'

'I won't look like the others.'

'Why ever not?'

I pulled a face. Where did she want me to start?

'Here,' she said, her hardened fingers deftly playing with my hair until it became a loose knot at the nape of my neck. She pulled out thin metal grips from her own and stabbed my hair with them. When she pulled soft tendrils back down around my ears I looked less like Mum. More a grown-up version of myself.

Cons' eyes stayed with my reflection. 'Seventeen,' she said suddenly, her voice whimsical, as if she'd drifted off somewhere else. 'Back in the Old World, hardly anyone got partnered for life at seventeen.' Cons made a little twitch of a smile. 'Well, unless they were . . .'

'Were what?'

One of her rare laughs trickled out before Cons pressed a hand onto my shoulder. 'Things were different then . . . never mind.' Her features tightened; she was back in the room again. 'Let's go; are you ready?'

I placed my hand over hers on my shoulder, to keep her there. 'I'm scared,' I said, a little startled by my own admission.

'There's nothing to be worried about – not today. Remember: keep things simple.'

I weaved my fingers into hers. I wished I could magically rub away the pale brown age spots, tighten the loose skin there . . . shave years off her age.

'This is what Dad wants?'

Cons inhaled deeply; her hand seemed to press down harder on my shoulder. 'It is.'

Her use of the present tense was all I needed to hear.

I smoothed down the skirt of my dress. 'Then I'm ready.'

Even Cons stretched her neck back, her voice becoming wondrous. 'It's been so long since I was last inside the Cross, I'd almost forgotten how beautiful it is.'

'I thought all Land buildings were constructed to be purely functional,' I whispered drily.

'Right . . . until you come to the place where you need to believe in a greater power. Or the place where the people in power need to think themselves great.'

I nudged her back; it was so unlike Cons to speak so disrespectfully in public, but she seemed spellbound.

My own eyes had been out on stalks since we'd exited the other side of West Land shopping precinct. I'd never had a reason to seek approval to step into the circle of Central Land. Circling the Cross, tenement and apartment blocks were swapped for white-painted houses of different shapes and sizes. There was so much space – so much green that wasn't part of my wardrobe. Evergreens allowed to grow tall and shadow streets; lofty deciduous trees dotted with round buds ready to shoot come spring; lawns like thick carpets in front of homes with borders of flowers in the pastel colours of a sunset sky. Where the houses ended began a wide strip of grass – the Green Mile, that circumnavigated the white outline of the Cross, where nearly everyone who lived centrally worked.

I'd purposely taken my time crossing the grass; there was so little of it in West Land. I'd halted Cons like a little girl when I'd spotted a bird tugging a worm out of the earth. 'A wagtail,' Cons commented; she always did like to fill in the gaps the Institute didn't see necessary to teach us.

Now, inside the Cross lobby, we stood poised on a floor of shimmering white marble, our necks strained, gazing up at a domed ceiling. Its peak was filled with coloured glass – it let light through in rainbow shards of colour; purples, yellows, pinks, turquoise.

'We'd better move on.' Cons lowered her eyes, collecting herself. Behind us, clustered family groups were pouring through the entrance, Blues with their Green son or daughter nestling between them.

We copied them, handing in our coats at a cloakroom. As soon as I was without mine I wanted to snatch it back. I stroked my hands down my new dress to make sure it hadn't hitched up, patting the knot at the back of my hair, checking my tights for pulls from the tram journey – then caught Cons smiling quietly across at me. She had tied her hair into a plait and wound it round her head like she did for work. 'Don't worry; you look lovely,' she said.

I made an awkward face back, but let her take my hand, and we followed on behind the others to registration.

I knew I should be working already – trying to place myself within the map of the Cross that Salinger had forced me to memorise, but I soon lost sense of the many corridors as we trailed others into another high-ceilinged room, this time pierced by slim white columns.

Registration was at a semicircle of white-covered tables behind which Grey staff faced boxed computer screens, their fingers furiously tip-tapping over keyboards.

'Number?' ours said tartly when we were gestured forward, her eyes fixed on her screen. Like the room around her she was extravagantly decorated: pink wax on her lips, a brown line under both eyes. A Grey scarf floated around her neck, so thin it had to be for decoration rather than practical warmth.

I pushed my wrist out.

The woman glanced up, her forehead creasing, like I was showing her something distasteful. 'Number?' she repeated acidly.

Cons gently lowered my arm, reeling off my number on my behalf. As the woman tapped it into her keyboard, Cons

85

gave me a quiet look I understood. I should have guessed by the setting alone: things were done differently here. 'There are six rooms hosting lunch. You will be in group "First".' The woman's face had markedly brightened.

'*First!*' Clearly even Cons was surprised at the work One had done on my files.

'Your dad and Stella were in Third,' Cons added as an aside, then caught her breath, her body stiffening. She never mentioned the 'D' word outside the flat.

It was so unlike Cons, my nerves almost turned to laughter.

The next room we got shepherded into was the largest, most elaborate yet. This one I remembered from Salinger's crudely drawn map – right in the centre of the Cross. In two weeks' time, this would be where the Pairing would take place. But for now, the perfect circle of the Great Hall was lined with stalls. Crowds of smartly dressed bodies milled amongst them, heads poised, eyes searching confidently for those they knew, assessing those they didn't. More people stared down from a large, curved public viewing gallery above.

I edged closer to Cons. 'What do we do?'

'We act like the others,' Cons sighed, as if she were exhausted that she still had to explain it to me.

I gazed around, trying to find a quiet place where I could go and do just that. There were no windows in the room, just three large screens on the walls. It took me a while to realise the film they were showing was real time, of here, right now. I dipped my head straight away; I didn't want to risk catching myself because then I would see: I looked nothing like anyone here.

We stood, waiting to go into the anteroom hosting group First. In the end, Cons had forced me through to each of the stalls, urging me to take everything that was being given away – goods of such colour and texture and sparkle, the like I'd only seen at Stella's – made by the artisan Grey workers who catered solely for points-rich Blues. I picked up a pot of pink lip wax, a similar shade to the woman at registration. Having put it on, I kept licking at my lips; they tasted of sweet fruit. My hair had more grips added to it, but with sparkling silver gems; I imagined them like tiny iridescent stars in my hair. The white paper bag I was gripping bulged with jewellery, more make-up, a small white clutch bag; tights like the ones I had on. Still vaguely distracted by the novelty of taking anything I wanted, I hardly noticed Cons suck in her breath. 'Just what we need.'

I followed her eyes; my puff of annoyance matching hers. 'Let's go.' I tugged Cons away; too late.

'Constantine.'

'Stella.'

Their greetings were mutually curt. It had to have been at least eight years since they'd been in the same room together: I had been nine the last time Cons felt it necessary to escort me to my mum's house.

'You look stunning, Christy.'

'Doesn't she,' Cons interjected when I said nothing.

I wouldn't compliment her back. Stella's many points paid for her to look this good: a pastel-Blue tailored dress and silky cardigan.

I glanced back at Cons. Her simple Grey trousers and faded

Grey shirt looked dreary in comparison. And yet Cons did a far more useful job, outside the home as well as in. It wasn't fair.

'I'm so glad I found you, Christy. We missed you on Friday . . .' Stella paused, her expression straining. Clearly she was still trying to work out how this miracle could occur: her unPairable daughter, to be Paired. 'I can't tell you how pleased I am for you. Such an exciting day . . .'

She didn't look excited.

'You seem well?' Stella turned back to Cons.

I watched as my mother and grandmother held a brief look. Stella's demeanour was usually a pathetic one, from ever trying to please Syon and his spoilt offspring – but I noticed a shadow of something hardening her dainty features. How dare she harbour anything but gratitude for Cons.

'They've opened the doors for group First – we should go.' I placed an arm around Cons' shoulders. I wanted to show that my solidarity unequivocally lay with my grandmother.

'First?' Stella said; I couldn't tell if her expression was pleased or punched. Surely the latter. 'Astral's Fourth . . .' She halted, stiffening visibly. I followed where her gaze had gone. Two thirds of Stella's family were approaching.

'Tell me this isn't true.' Syon said, as he and Astral joined us.

My mother stepped aside, regrettably closer to me, and replied, 'Isn't this a surprise: Christy has been chosen after all,' her voice unnaturally high.

I exhaled at Stella's lame act, casting my eyes quickly over my stepsister, standing the other side of Syon. Her shoulder-length blond hair was swept up into a style that mimicked Stella's. The red wax painted over her lips gave them an extra pout. I licked mine again. So we were both getting Paired: finally we had something in common. Since we were little girls, Astral had made it distinctly clear she wouldn't share my own mother with me. I'd tugged her hair only when she'd pulled mine, but it was still me who had got whacked by Syon for making her cry.

'There are a couple of boys in here I suppose they need to Pair with *someone*,' Astral was saying, her eyes adding an extra sting to her words as they flicked critically over my dress. She was still metaphorically pulling my hair. I just wouldn't retaliate any more. Stay silent, *stay silent*. But I wouldn't, couldn't, fix a smile.

'I wouldn't think the State ever capable of making mistakes.' Syon's mouth grew into a wide grin as his eyes fluttered to shut me out. His thinning, bouffant hair added at least another couple of centimetres to his height. 'But there you go.' He snapped his eyes open. 'Let's carry on,' he uttered coolly to Astral.

My eyes flew back to Stella. *Go with them*, I wanted her to read in them. But hers were fixed on her feet, her hands squeezing together. 'Well, I just want to say again . . . how it's such wonderful news . . . about . . .' Her eyes slowly rose up to meet mine; they made one of their Friday dinner sweeps around my face. 'The Pairing. *Isn't it?*'

Why was she asking me? Like she wasn't sure of the answer for herself?

If only she knew what I was being Paired for. I was so angry, I could almost have told her. Instead, Cons interjected again. 'It's all perfect, Stella.'

* * *

89

I did the mathematics: if there were six rooms, then in here there must be about a hundred and twenty students. So, sixty boys. One in sixty – my Pair – in this room.

The sheer thought nearly had me turning on my heel. Except Cons had a tight grip on my arm. She steered me on, through an atmosphere of Blues' easy confidence. Cons was the only adult in Grey, besides staff. Students and their parents slanted their gazes at us as we passed. It wasn't hard to read their eyes; they hoped I wasn't to be their Pair. Even Cons must have felt the chill as gradually she circled us to a place where I was always more comfortable: a back corner of the room. I pulled some seats across for us. She wouldn't admit it, but the sigh Cons made when she sat down showed her legs must have been aching from standing for so long.

I stroked her shoulder. 'Are you okay?'

She tried to brighten her face. 'Of course. Here it is; where it all begins, Christy.'

I glanced across the entire room. 'Which one do you think he might be?'

Cons' face displayed her prescribed answer.

'You're right, it doesn't matter,' I agreed, but I continued checking every boy in the room. '. . . It's just . . . what if . . .' I began to picture the fear that stalked my dreams lately: a faceless stranger; rough hands forcing their way onto my skin; wet lips trying to lever mine open, 'I don't like him?'

Cons blinked several times but kept her eyes fixed beyond me. I could tell she didn't like the question any more than I feared the answer. Her face changed expression then finally flashed with gentleness. 'I keep telling you, focus on the present;

90

don't fret over the future. Keep things simple . . . wait and see who he is first. Now why not go and get us some lunch.'

Simple. Focus. I swallowed back my fear – I wasn't here to meet a boy; I was here to protect my grandmother.

I filled two plates from a table displaying food like some fantasy meal – woven dough baskets with bread rolls; sandwiches cut into the shape of their contents; fresh vegetables trimmed into objects – tiny boats and lofty crowns. Food made to look attractive: the idea seemed preposterous when Land's resources were so carefully managed.

As we ate, three girls rushed over, claiming seats near ours, their heads bent close in confidence. A brunette, two blondes. Apart from Cons, I was the only red-haired person in the room. I looked sideways at them as they suddenly laughed conspiratorially. 'I'd give Tobin a ten; Marcus a six – that *nose*, I'd better not get him,' one of them said.

I tried to concentrate on the fish-shaped sandwich in my hand, like I was working out the origin of its pink, sinewy content.

'I like the look of *him*,' another giggled. 'There, the one with the brown curls.'

I swung my eyes in the direction of their shared gaze, my stomach squeezing until I saw who they meant. I cursed myself silently. Why on earth would Salinger be here! Like he had a monopoly on brown curls! I put the sandwich down; I'd abruptly lost my appetite. Like Cons said: I needed to focus. I made a fierce swipe at my mouth with the back of my hand, removing its sticky smear of pink.

* * *

The actual briefing was short. Led by a woman in a stiff Blue dress suit with mushroomed blond hair that didn't seem to move with the rest of her; a tiny smile that pulled up only the edges of her thin mouth. She took us through the Pairing ceremony, what would be expected of us – mainly to stay quiet and recite what we were told. Then we were subjected to the obligatory citizenship film, the Leader reminding us that, '*Pairing individuals to be stronger as couples, and controlling breeding, secures Land's future survival!*'

The end of the film was our cue to leave. Even Cons seemed to realise we had no part in the self-congratulatory socialising going on. I couldn't act that well yet.

The moment we exited back into the Great Hall, she darted out as if she'd been hovering in wait for us all this time. Cons, in front of me, didn't see her.

'Don't forget me, will you?' Stella said, so quietly it was clearly only meant for my ears.

I both shook and nodded my head, uncertain of how to answer. Finally, I gave a plain, confused, 'Bye.'

She didn't move as I continued to walk away. I passed one last glance back at her as I caught up with Cons, her glossy leather shoes rooted to the spot.

It was Stella's features that caught me. They were pinched, as if she were in pain.

For the first time I felt a little sorry for her. I gave her the briefest of smiles.

It had the opposite effect to what I expected. She made short continual shakes of her head; her painted lips mouthing an emphatic, anxious, '*I'm sorry.*'

Chapter Eight

'I get it,' I said, exhausted.

'Then why did you just do it all wrong?'

I glared up at Salinger from where I was sprawled, ungainly, on the kitchen floor. 'I get it, all right? I'm just tired.' In the small space of the kitchen, table pushed back, he'd moved on from teaching me defence to attack moves.

'It's our last time to practise for a while, probably. Come on. You have to swing your leg round faster, sharper in with your elbow.'

I shook my head. 'I've had enough.' And I had, too. Three weeks of training now, and I was still failing at jamming a metal hair grip into a keyhole to unlock it; was hopeless at learning protocol for tailing someone. I had no natural skill for espionage; certainly none for attacking. My head was in a perpetual mess. Cons was continuing to sneak disappointed glances at me. I couldn't forget Stella's ardent apology at the briefing. I'd hardly seen One lately to quiz him more on his plans for me.

Then there was Salinger – annoyed, patronising me.

I needed a break, from it all. From everyone. Except there wasn't time.

'You're tense because it's the Pairing on Sunday.'

I pulled myself up onto the nearest chair. 'Don't presume to know how I'm feeling!' I didn't take the trouble to disguise my outrage. Salinger got to me so much I never bothered to contain my feelings, to censor my words with him. Which was practically a first.

Though I wasn't going to go as far as to admit to him that he was right. Of course I was tense about the Pairing! I wasn't sleeping. I couldn't eat properly. My chest was riddled with so much anxiety I could hardly breathe straight. In just two days' time, I would be Paired and partnered, punctured with someone else's number on my skin, for life. From then on – a spy! Putting my life on the line and removing others'.

Cons kept saying *Keep it simple* – a new mantra to supersede *Stay silent. Fix a smile. Keep on walking.* Yet nothing of how I felt seemed simple.

When I wasn't dreading who I might be asked to kill, I was imagining a faceless boy. I would be sitting in class and I would find my mind floating off into *Who will my Pair be?* I'd forget myself and get this small squirt of excitement pop in my stomach when I imagined a hand holding mine, fingers stroking my face . . . arms bringing me close. Imaginings that I'd never dared entertain before.

Other times I'd wake up in bed, my skin dripping with sweat from a nightmare about a thick-set brute, who would force himself on me every evening in the name of being my other half.

'If you must know, I am excited, not *tense*, about the Pairing.' The half-lie felt comfortable on my tongue, so I continued.

'Because at least it means afterwards I spend less time doing this.'

'Good. Fine. Glad we're agreed on that.'

Salinger took the chair across from me and began picking moodily at the bits of food Cons had left out for us. Some bread, cold mutton and beans. She was out at her night shift. Cons usually found a reason to get out of the way when Salinger was here.

'Well no one forced you to come and train me.'

Salinger eyed me, before throwing his head back and chucking beans into his mouth as if it were some kind of sport.

His silence only added to my heightening irritation. 'I said, no one forced you.'

Salinger brought his head back level. He seemed to temporarily lose his cool as he spat out starkly, 'No? No one forced me? What do you know?'

'Nothing!' I spat back. 'No one tells me anything!'

Salinger's brows pulled heavier. What was that behind his eyes? Remorse? If it was, it passed quickly.

'Yeah well, no one told me much at the beginning either. Learn fast, follow orders and don't ask questions.' His eyebrows straightened out, as if he regretted his statement. 'Unless you want to die, take your training seriously.'

I pushed my chin forward. 'I do take it seriously.' I blinked furiously so the tears couldn't pool at the bottom of my eyes. This boy knew nothing of what I took seriously. Cons' life. Dad's life. Kara's. 'Sometimes I would just like more information on what's going to be asked of me! The jobs I'll be given. *Who* I'm going to have to get rid of!' I felt bile rise in my throat, like it did whenever I let my mind drift to that detail of my 'destiny'.

'You've heard One – your first assignment won't come until you're in a good position, until you're ready. Right now, you just need to listen, and learn. Okay. Let's do another study of the Cross and Land maps, looking specifically at where key officials live and work. Then we'll go over the workings of a gun again.'

I sighed heavily. I hated the way he talked to me. Teacher to student. 'No need – the maps are burnt to memory now. And I really don't see the point of learning to fire a gun in-mind only. Virtual government, virtual gun. You'll be teaching me virtual Pairing next. You play boy, I'll play girl.'

Salinger reddened. I hadn't been expecting that.

When he cleared his voice to speak it was monotone. 'You know I can't bring a gun. It's too dangerous, in case I'm checked. We have to work with what we've got – our heads, our instinct.' He enlarged his eyes as I squinted mine. 'If you have either?'

I screwed up my face, resisting the urge to scream at him.

'This is futile.' He threw the beans back into the bowl. 'You've not even got the right attitude. You don't care for change, just your own situation.'

'I *do* care,' I answered, my mouth clenched. I thought of Salinger's observation getting back to Dad. The idea hurt.

'Your heart's not in it – and that's dangerous for us all.' Salinger folded his arms against his Grey woollen jumper.

His first statement was correct; but his last terrified me. Almost daily I was having vivid visions of them all being tussled into a black Selection truck – Cons, Dad, One, Salinger. All because I couldn't pick a lock or load a gun.

'What do you know of heart? You don't even have any family to fight for!'

It was unfair of me. But I was too exhausted to take it back.

Salinger's mouth contracted. His brown eyes didn't scrutinise mine for once – instead, he seemed determined to look anywhere but at me. He pushed a hand back through his short curls. 'It's stupid,' he said to the kitchen table. 'You're not right for this. You don't even understand what they're asking of you.'

'I am! And I do!' I lifted my head up high; then felt stupid when I spotted Salinger's satisfied half-smile.

'There – passion at last,' he said.

I stared back down at the carved *Hogan* on the table. Why couldn't I just tell him the truth? That I was scared I wouldn't be able to do what they were asking me?

'It's not your fault,' Salinger continued, as if he were reading my thoughts. 'You have no experience in any of this stuff. You're a child still.'

My eyes shot up. 'You're only a year older than me!'

'Yeah – and d'you want to know what I've done and where I've been in my eighteen years that qualifies me for this job?'

'Yes I do!'

I hadn't realised we'd both half risen out of our seats until Salinger sat back down again. My answer had stumped him.

'Well I can't tell you.' He was rubbing his chin stiffly with his hand like he was sanding wood. Perennially bemused Salinger – had I finally got to him?

'You know everything about me. I know nothing about you.

Why did One choose *you*?'

'He didn't. I went to fight for the Resistance when I was a boy.' He sighed heavily. 'I wanted payback. 454111 brought me into line, guided me into how to fight with my head.'

'Payback for what?' I asked hurriedly, forgetting to hang on to my customary hostility.

Salinger made a jerk of his head. 'You should ask him.'

'By him, I take it you mean One?'

'Yeah, *One*.' Salinger still bristled at my calling him that, even though I'd noticed he'd slipped it in a few times himself recently.

'Well, thanks for disclosing so much; I feel like I know you so much better now,' I replied, my mouth faking a smile. If he wouldn't talk to me, he might as well just go.

'My experience isn't under scrutiny here.' Salinger pushed his neck forward. 'Yours is. You need to *want* to help the Resistance – like that friend of yours you asked 454111 to enlist? Kara? Shame she can't trade places with you.'

That was the final straw. It stung.

I sifted through words that could hurt him back. My eyes even scanned the table for what I could throw at him.

He had no right to bring Kara into it. She was another part of the sum of what was making me tense right now. Yeah, I'd asked One to recruit her. Because she hadn't stopped begging me to get her into the Resistance – Kara didn't understand why I wanted to protect her from it. But One's answer a week ago had been unequivocal: 'No chance'. I'd only relayed it back to her the other day – and I hadn't seen her at the Institute since.

'You don't know anything about Kara,' I snarled across at him.

Salinger massaged his neck with both hands, then stood up. 'I'd say good luck for whoever you get at the Pairing, but I'm pretty sure you're going to end up with who you deserve.' He reopened his mouth, was starting to say, 'I didn't mean, I –' when I cut through him.

'Just as long as he's nothing like you.'

Salinger shook his head as he reached for his jacket. 'For your information I never wanted to do this. This wasn't my idea. All right? You haven't a clue what you're getting into.' His mouth had pulled taut, his words whistling through his teeth as he said, 'You really haven't.'

I clenched my fist, trying hard to resist the urge to scream a profanity for 'Get out'.

'I am trying to help you the best I can,' he continued, striding across the short length of the kitchen. 'So the least you could have done at any point during this tedious time together would have been to say thank you.'

He didn't slam the front door; we both knew to keep our anger quiet from neighbours outside. But he might as well have; the force of the fury surrounding his exit stayed with me long after he'd left.

My hands rubbing the tops of my arms, I went into the hallway, facing the closed door. I half hoped he might come back for some reason. I suddenly wanted to say sorry.

I wanted to try and explain why I was acting the way I was.

I wanted to tell him, tell someone, that I couldn't cope. That yeah, okay, he was right, I didn't really know what I was getting into. But nor did I know how to admit that.

When it was clear he wasn't returning, I turned the handle and opened the door.

I stepped onto the landing; and heard a quiet 'Thank you' pass from my lips into the air.

Chapter Nine

By the time I stirred on Saturday morning, the argument with Salinger had added another layer of anxiety to the hard rock permanently lodged in my chest.

Maybe that was why I jumped out of bed at the sound of Cons opening the front door to a male voice. Though I didn't know why it had me searching for my best Green blouse, or brushing my hair out in a way I didn't have to for a Saturday morning stuck at home.

Nor why my heart sank so heavily when I saw it wasn't even Salinger.

It was One.

'Hello,' I said sullenly, not daring to look at him; Salinger had probably already filled him in on last night. He had come to lecture me for it. Or to tell me Salinger had thrown in the towel. Tension pulled at my insides. Why should I care if he had?

But One didn't even mention it. 'I will formally visit you at your new home on Monday,' he had begun to say, sitting at my spot at the kitchen table, his hands hugging a steaming mug of black tea. The fact that he didn't take milk fitted him perfectly, '. . . establishing my relationship with you to your new Pair and his family.'

Cons pressed my fingers round a mug too. 'Drink, it'll warm you up.'

'I have to move in there straight away?' I spoke to Cons, not One. 'In the Pairing pamphlet it says you're allowed a month to decide whose family to live with . . . So there's no rush.'

One was staring over at me as if I were out of my mind. His thick, wiry eyebrows nudged into one another, forming a bridge above his bent nose. 'But the whole *point* is that you move in there – and *fast* – so you can be at the centre of things, pass on information. You do understand, don't you?' he asked, as if he were checking we still spoke the same language. 'We need you planted as soon as possible.'

My eyes drew back to Cons. Plants needed soil, and sun. 'Then will you come and live with me?' And watering. I shifted in my seat, warming to the idea more. 'I mean, you can, can't you? Why shouldn't you come and live with me and my . . . ' I couldn't say the words out loud – *new family*.

'Oh, that's really not possible, Christy.' Cons smiled indulgently back at me like she used to when I was a child, fantasising about the future job I would like.

'Okay, then he can come and live here.'

'Oh, Christy. Where would he sleep?'

I tried to imagine it – my Pair, sharing my single bed. I had taken it for granted I would have my own room, like Syon and Stella did. I didn't want some stranger watching me sleep. But if it meant I stayed with Cons . . . 'In my room, I don't care.'

Cons' mouth twitched; she looked over to One, as if she were waiting for his say-so before she answered. I could never get to grips with which one of them was in charge – at times it could have been either. But right now, it was clear: One was running the show.

'You have to move into Central Land: alone. Otherwise this won't work,' One said, a gruff sound to his voice as if he were getting a cold. 'Clearly you are still thinking with your emotions – you must stop that. There's a good reason why State Troopers aren't allowed to Pair, to breed – so they avoid any form of empathy. The same applies whichever side you fight for in war; you have to cut out feeling.'

'You mean become cold, like you and Salinger?'

'Christy!' Cons fixed indignant eyes on me.

One's joined hers. 'You *live* in society; you don't need to have a love affair with it.'

I couldn't listen to any more. I made my excuses and fled the kitchen before I fell out with One too. I was merely a cog in the wheels of his rebellion. A trained animal learning tricks, for when I was required to perform.

Needing something physical to occupy me, I went into Cons' room to sort out the ash in the fireplace. I wanted a fire suddenly. I wanted to curl up near its warmth and imagine that tomorrow was never coming.

I bent down in front of the black slate hearth – then I heard it; the click of the kitchen door closing.

Curiosity quickly overruling anger, I stepped back quietly into the hall, placing my ear gently against our flimsy kitchen door.

'Why not? Why shouldn't I get something that pleases me out of this arrangement?' One was saying. It was hard to imagine his stoic face behind making any appeal for pleasure. Nor could I picture what would please him. My Pairing?

Cons murmured something so quietly I couldn't catch any of it except for the words '. . . what's best for Christy, not you.'

But One's low growl of a voice continued to carry through the door. 'This *is* best for Christy. I am looking out for her.'

My mouth made a small involuntary smile. I'd never heard One use my name before. *Looking out for me.* I liked the way that sounded.

'It will be a good Pairing. Isn't that all that matters?'

Then he did know? Had One hand-picked my Pair?

'You can't get distracted by sentiment,' Cons said.

I heard movement; I imagined One straightening that stilted frame of a body before he answered. 'I never am – not since she died . . . You of all people should know that . . .' I could only make out snatches of his conversation. 'It makes sense all round . . . good for Christy; good for her.'

I drew in my breath through the silence that followed. Since who died? And: *her*? Was there another girl One was *looking out* for? My stomach churned with uneasy jealousy. Another Resistance member? What did she have to do with me?

There were more murmurs from Cons before I caught her saying: 'The relationship will be your downfall if you don't stay cut off. No attachments, remember?' The cruel edge to her voice sounded nothing like my Cons. I prickled. What was she saying? One couldn't care . . . for me?

'You are doing this for Hogan. If only . . .' Cons' voice dropped to a hum; I pressed my ear harder against the door but couldn't catch her last words.

It went quiet before the sound of a chair being scraped back. I retreated quickly into Cons' room.

'It is not a good idea.'

I made a face, tugging on my coat. 'I'll be fine.' I was going to win this fight. Cons wasn't going to stop me going out. More so after what I'd heard her say to One this morning. I needed to see Kara; I had to check she was okay. 'Besides, you're on shift tonight – you won't even be here.'

'But the Pairing – you should be resting, ready for tomorrow. Kara can't be your problem.'

'I just told you – I didn't see Kara at the Institute these last few days. I have to check she's not ill. Make sure she's back Monday – you understand that, don't you, Cons?' You got to five days absent and the tutors reported you to the Assessment Centre. Kara *was* my problem.

Cons tutted, then sighed. 'You must keep things simple: detach from Kara.'

I stared at her, open-mouthed; her words were reminiscent of the way she'd spoken to One this morning – *no attachments*.

'I'm telling you, Christy: don't go.'

Usually I would do anything Cons asked of me. But everything was going to change after tomorrow. Including Kara and me. The State might make me change institutes. The pamphlet said that could happen.

'I'll be back before curfew.'

It was about four miles between our tenements. The view changed the further I went. It was the main reason Cons fought – and usually won – for me not to walk to Kara's after it got dark. There was little crime in Land – there were too many deterrents against bad behaviour. No, Cons worried more about the law-keepers than the law-breakers. Selection trucks were more plentiful in Kara's part of West Land, so there were more State Troopers there too. Yes, it was a risk, so close to the Pairing, to attract any Trooper's attention, but I had no other choice. Besides Xavier, I was all Kara had.

Spotlit under the streetlights, I kept my eyes dipped to the ground, head level, my face wearing its concrete smile each time I caught the dull thud of marching Troopers. So far, there hadn't been too many. A cold snap had appeared this week, patterns of transparent ice still shone across the road; it probably accounted for the notable reduction in trucks too.

After an hour's fast stride, I arrived outside Kara's block. Near the outskirts, close to the plastic and metal factories spewing out their foul-smelling smoke, the white paint of their building had a grey tinge to it. On most days, a mushroom of fog hung above the tenement blocks here, blocking out the sun, extinguishing hope's light.

I charged up the communal staircase, two steps at a time; their small flat was on the very top floor.

'Christy.' Xavier, Kara's older brother, opened the door; his head bowed, his arms wrapped around his thin body as if he were trying not to take up too much space. 'Am I glad to see you.' His voice was faint, meek, as if it were at a distance from him. He hadn't always been like this. The old Xavier used to brim with gentle confidence; had worn his good looks with ease: brown skin, uncommonly smooth; eyes, coal black; thick, dark eyelashes fluttering like butterfly wings above them. Two years of factory work had dried and cracked his skin; dulled his eyes until they'd seemed to detach from whatever it was that used to operate behind them.

'I haven't seen Kara at the Institute. I was getting worried.'

'She's been off. She's just been in bed – thinking time, she says.' Xavier made a tiny, desperate shake of his head.

'Really?' I should have come sooner. Lying in bed all day – it was what their mum had done. Xavier and Kara would take her tracer out with them routinely each morning and evening, just to make it look like she was moving around still. Cons had done her best to cover for her at work, taking some of her shifts.

But their concealment could only last so long. No one was cleverer than the State of Land.

'Let me see her.' I walked past him into Kara's room. It was even smaller than mine. I could only just fit into the space left around the thin mattress on the floor.

Kara was lying fully dressed on her bed. The lights were off; Xavier's meagre salary couldn't always afford the electric meter. But from the outside light coming in through the one small window, I could see she was staring up blankly at the ceiling, as if she were being forced to watch some citizenship film up there.

'Hey, Kara; what's wrong?'

She glanced round, rubbing aggressively at her eyes as if she wanted to erase what she had just seen there. 'What are you doing here?'

'I was worried.' I reached over, feeling for her forehead, wishing hard for it not to be hot. I knew the points it would take even for the most basic of medicine, never mind what would happen if you were diagnosed with something the State refused to cure.

But her head was as cool as the air in the room.

'Talk to me. What can I do?'

'Nothing. I've just been really tired, that's all. I needed some time to myself,' Kara added, as my forehead crumpled with concern.

'Pairing tomorrow, then?' she said, moving to sit up, her black fringe falling across her eyes. 'Your big day.'

I couldn't decipher her tone. Indifferent, mostly.

'I'll still be around for you. We won't change, will we?'

Kara made a despondent smile.

I knelt down by her legs. 'You've just got to hang in there.' I licked my lips. 'However you feel about things, promise me you'll be back at the Institute Monday. Promise me, Kara.'

Kara gazed over at the wall. She was only a wearing a T-shirt and skirt; she had to be frozen. 'If you promise me you'll get me enlisted into the Resistance . . .'

I tilted my head, appealing to her.

'It's just,' Kara bit down hard on her bottom lip, 'I need it, Christy . . . I need life to change sooner.'

'I know you do . . .' I breathed out through my nose. Keep Kara surviving, hopeful; towing the line – that was my job too. 'Listen, leave it with me; I'll get you recruited somehow.' I felt my face flush with the fib.

Kara's face brightened; she shook her fringe back. Instantly, I felt worse.

'You mean it? You'll try again? I have to help, Christy.'

I did my best to keep the truth from my eyes. 'Sure.'

'All right: I swear I'll return Monday.'

'Thanks.' I breathed out, smiling at the 'good girl' expression she pulled. 'I know it's difficult; but we can't risk our lives, Kara.' I sounded like Cons and One: empty words, glossing over the detail. *Keep things simple*: get Kara back to her classes.

'So what have you been lying here thinking about?' I gently stroked her bare knee. Goosebumps were littered across it.

And that was when she said it. Four stark words I never expected her to throw at me.

Four words I would never have thought possible.

Four words an unPaired girl should never utter.

'I missed my period.'

Chapter Ten

I was trying to keep it together for Cons' sake. Walking across the Green Mile towards the Cross – *déjà vu* of the briefing two weeks ago. Except this time I was filled with double the dread.

It had rained heavily through the night, so the grass was sodden. Our feet sank as we tramped over it, but it smelt good, a wet freshness like air packaged up. I clutched my Institute satchel tighter to me as the main entrance to the Cross came into view. It was all I carried. I'd not brought much with me, just overnight things, the white clutch bag and lip wax I'd got free from the briefing. The rest of my stuff was packed in bin liners in my bedroom, ready for One to deliver tomorrow. His formal introduction into my new home.

We didn't stop in the lobby this time, but after registration we were directed back there, towards a door to the dressing room for group First girls.

'I have to leave you here,' Cons said as we stopped and faced each other amidst the crowds of people still spilling in.

I took her hands, my eyes pleading, *I don't want to do this*, as my mouth betrayed them and made a smile. 'I guess the next time I see you I'll be a two, no longer a one.'

Cons made a funny movement with her face then she pulled a hand from mine and stroked my cheek, dropping it flat against my collarbone. 'You're going to do fine, Christy. Just fine.'

It sounded more like she was talking to herself than to me. Her face started quivering – was she trying not to cry? I'd never seen Cons shed a single tear.

'That's right. I'll be just fine,' I reassured her. I was starting a life built on lies – so I lied some more. 'I'm looking forward to it, in a funny way, this next part of my life.' I stretched my lips as far as they would go before they risked collapsing under the truth. 'You watch: I'll make you proud. I'll make Dad proud.'

Cons leant into me. Her arms, both frail and strong at the same time, swung round my neck, pulling my head against hers.

I breathed her in. *Don't make me do this*, I silently told her. *Take me back to my childhood*.

She drew back and looked at me quizzically as if she'd heard my thoughts. Her hand lifted and gently tapped under my chin as if she were trying to lift it. 'Remember these two things,' she said, her lips batting against one another as if she were considering some new taste.

'The first: I love you.' Her voice nearly broke on the last word, and I began pulling her towards me again. But she resisted. She hadn't finished. 'And the second: this isn't about us, it never has been. It's about . . . it's about the greater good.'

She had stepped back, her fingers trailing my neck, my shoulder, my hand, until she stopped touching me altogether. 'I'll be watching you,' she said softly.

Then she turned and blended into the crowd. She didn't once look back. I stared across the lobby, up at the coloured glass dome. Its rainbow shower wasn't as bright today – the sun was obscured by grey clouds – but it still emitted a spectrum of faded yellows and purples.

What I was going to do – getting Paired, helping the Resistance – it was going to liberate colour.

'Didn't you read your pamphlet? You choose a dress,' said the young woman with a neat face and starched Grey lace collar, when I asked her what it was I should be doing.

When I still didn't move from the doorway, she relaxed a little. 'Go try a few on, see which fits the best. Then find a dressing table and get yourself ready. Okay? They will call you when it's time for the ceremony.'

I walked further into the room, eyeing the rails of billowing white gowns that occupied most of the space in front of me. I started flicking half-heartedly through them. The sizes were mostly standard. There wasn't much scope for getting fat in Land. Too thin and you'd be flagged for not doing well. That was why you never saw people close to starvation, like Kara said her grandpa had in the Old World. He'd told her that some children where he came from showed ribs bowing under transparent skin, faces the shape of skulls. Kara's grandpa thought Land was all right.

Maybe he'd never realised that you wouldn't find starvation here, because those close to it were annihilated before it could ever manifest itself.

It was a sobering thought to hold in my mind as I tried to find a style I could vaguely bear wearing. Most were overly fussy in thick, shiny materials, with fat jewels added around necklines; wide silky ribbons replacing buttons. Some had white fur trimmings, others cascades of tiny fabric rosebuds or scores of pearls. Like everything about the Pairing process, their excess seemed at odds with what Land projected. But then wasn't that the idea? Excitement and indulgence. To launch you into your state-controlled, prosperous future! Land did so love happy people.

I found it, finally. The only plain style on the racks. I hated myself for actually taking a moment to admire it once I'd put it on. It had a satiny feel to it, clinging to my body from a short-sleeved bodice and dropping down beyond my ankles into a scooped train at the back. Its only nod to fussiness was a braid of minute embroidery around its neckline. I grabbed some flat satin pumps from a shelf; I wasn't even going to contemplate heels.

Folding my emerald-Green dress into my satchel I lifted up the bottom of my train to find a vacant dressing table. Most were already occupied; a hum of excitement rising from the girls sat at them. Sheer thrill glowing in their made-up faces, in the little bubbles of squeals they shared at one another's dress choices: this was their special day, collectively. The one they'd dreamed of as little girls – a day to meet their happy-ever-after. When one became two.

I found a spare table, sat down heavily and pulled out my clutch bag and lip wax, then stared glumly at my reflection.

Cons had already put my hair up for me, using the jewelled hair grips I'd been given free at the briefing. There wasn't much else to do besides add a bit of the lip wax. It had been Cons who had convinced me to use it. 'Put some colour on your face and already you're playing at being someone else.'

I started to apply it with my finger, highlighting my mouth from my pale skin, no longer me, Christy; I was being the undercover Resistance member.

Behind my reflection, other girls continued bobbing companionably, excitedly, from one another's tables. I watched them, then refocused on my own face, and thought of her . . . my one and only friend.

Kara had to have got her period by today. She had to.

I tried to picture her, on the toilet, seeing red, the relief that would rapidly flood through her. I fixed my eyes on my unnaturally pink pout. I had asked Kara why she let it happen. Why she let a boy get that intimate with her. Her answer was still haunting me: *I wanted so badly to feel something . . . I just wanted to be . . . alive.*

'Stand quietly, not a rustle of dress, please. The Leader will soon be addressing the audience in the Great Hall.' We'd been ushered, via a back door, into the same anteroom as the briefing. The same woman in Blue, with the rigid hairstyle, was speaking. The boys from our group had joined us, dressed in white suits and shirts. I stayed at the back so I didn't have to look at any of them.

Stiff-haired Blue continued: 'Remember – you will be Paired first, and then the Leader will conduct the official ceremony, when you will make your promise.'

I fiddled nervously with my clutch bag. All the way here on the tram, it had helped me to picture Dad somewhere close – the version of him I had permanently drawn in my head, with friendly green eyes, thick auburn hair. Watching us.

'We will get our call to enter in just a short while. Please prepare yourself.'

Now I tried to imagine him standing right beside me, his hand tucked into mine, my fingers curled into his palm.

'We have just two hours to get through nearly four hundred Pairings. So when your number is announced, you must step up quickly to receive the Leader's blessing. Staying in your groups means your Pair won't be far from you. This is a solemn event, remember,' she added, fixing stern eyes on two girls at the front whose shoulders were shaking with suppressed giggles.

I took a slow breath, trying to calm down the drumbeat thud of my heart.

The woman smacked her lips. 'At the end of the ceremony, you will seal your promise with your Pair's number. After that, you return to this room to meet with your new families.' She stopped talking as muffled sounds of cheering seeped into the room from the Great Hall beyond. There followed the sound of a low, harsh voice. The Leader's? More cheering, then quiet. Next: clattering footfall accompanied by a backdrop of slow applause.

Our eyes were all fixed on the door into the Great Hall when it swung open.

I hung back on purpose. I would have been the very last to leave if it weren't for one blond boy with a heart-shaped face, insisting with his arm that I go before him. I picked up the trail of my dress and followed closely behind the end of the long white gown in front of me, trying not to stand on it.

Beyond, the circular room had been transformed. White

115

glossy material hung down in elaborate drapes from the public gallery that sliced across the far wall. Filled with families of those to be Paired, they were all moving their hands in a rhythmic clap as our group followed our woman in Blue in a parade around the room.

I tried desperately to hunt out Cons from the faces – there were so many of them. Where was she?

My eyes flew back to the floor as I stepped on someone's foot. The criss-cross of white carpet paths we were being led round was edged with shoes and clusters of gown hems. Pots of miniature evergreen trees were dotted along the way, decorated with tiny white fairy lights that twinkled and reflected off the dense mass of shiny white dresses. Squint your eyes and you could believe the stars had fallen amongst a thick layer of snow.

The music was clearly supposed to be rousing, in tune with our footsteps, but its incessant beat was starting to resonate in my head like a hammer. I was becoming breathless.

Finally we were taken to the only area of the hall left empty, up near the front, in the middle, herded like sheep into quarters cut up by a cross of white paths. The music halted. I looked up. The new Leader was standing on a small white-covered stage. He loomed larger in real life: tall, broad-shouldered. Grey hair cut close to his head, a smart Black suit. His hands were held in the air, palms down, as if he were waiting for quiet. But there was already silence.

I inhaled, exhaled, lifted my eyes again to the public gallery. I just wanted a glimpse of Cons.

Instead I caught sight of myself – my pale face a round dot amidst the blanket of white dresses and suits, pictured live on all three screens above. I bit down hard on my lip, willing the cameras to move on. Would it be obvious? Would they see they had a traitor in their midst?

'How wonderful it is to welcome the new pioneers of Land's future . . .'

I tuned out as the Leader expounded on Land's greatness, focusing instead on his hands; he used them to mimic his speech, raising, clenching, shaking them; stretching them out. His eyes were doing the same; squinting, then enlarging, as he made each point.

I didn't know his real age. I doubted he would broadcast that fact. Because he looked at least Cons' age if not older. *Exemptions, exceptions* . . . the rules bent for the power-makers.

'Pride' and 'obligation', I heard him holler. I reminded myself of Cons and Dad and Kara – my three reasons for doing this.

'Sacrifice,' next. I thought of the day the Selection truck came for Kara's mum. How Kara had clung to her mother's waist until the arresting Trooper had picked her up by her long, thick hair and hurled her against the doorway.

Kara had cut nearly all of her hair off that night.

'Only the strong can survive.'

I turned my eyes to the floor. I was starting to get dizzy. The dress felt tight across my chest, trapping breath in my throat.

I had to hum in my head or else recite one of Cons' stories – anything to shut out that stout, pompous voice. In the end I chose the words of a tune Cons had taught me once, from when she was a girl. *London's burning, London's burning, fire, fire; fire, fire, pour on water, pour on water* . . . repeating the rhyme, over and over.

London had well and truly burnt to the ground when I looked up to see the Leader raise both arms over his head and drop them down like he was starting a race. Then he jumped down to the floor from the stage with the agility of a far younger man. A thin woman in a tight Blue trouser suit announced herself as director of the Pairing and took over the stage. And in an instant I heard it: the first of the numbers.

It was starting.

The Leader and his trail of assistants were getting closer to my group. So many couples had been called now, hurriedly stepping forward onto the white path. I'd been anxiously watching their expressions up on the screen closest to me – students facing their Pair for the very first time. I saw elation on many, though was that only due to the presence of the Leader? I was sure I spotted concealed disappointment too, a twitchy hand brushing against a brow, or eyes that narrowed while mouths stayed wide.

My legs were starting to ache from standing so long, and I needed the toilet now. I was glad at least for my flat shoes; many girls around me were step-hopping in their heels.

823145 was called out over the microphone. It took me a moment to realise why it was familiar. Astral's number. I stared up at the screen as the camera zoomed in close on her face. Her fixed smile took over her entire, overly made-up face; it was hard to trace her true reaction. I tried to see the thick-set boy who stepped forward to meet her, but he was soon lost behind a blur of white dresses and suits.

Stella. It was the first time I had thought about my mother

being here, watching her precious stepdaughter in her big moment. I scanned the gallery again, until finally I saw her. She was standing at the far end, but at the front – she must have arrived early to get that position, for Astral. Except, the thing was, her eyes – they seemed fixed on me. I glanced away, trying to work it out, then looked up again. She was turned away now, talking to Syon beside her. I felt a dull punch in my stomach. I wouldn't seek her out again.

Behind me, the Leader was getting closer.

My heart ran away as I heard it. '823104 and 823057.'

I shuffled forward, blinking in the artificially bright light. I imagined Cons' kind eyes on me, from somewhere up there, holding me in her heart.

I stepped out onto the path, my heart thumping in my chest, my mouth dry. The Leader's thick body came close to mine. I didn't look as his fingers lifted and tugged mine across until they felt new skin. Soft skin that squeezed my own, as the Leader's thick hand pressed down on both, sanctioning our union: '*Be you ever Paired for the greater good.*'

The next numbers were already being called out.

I could sense the closeness of the stranger who held my hand in our stack of palms, but I couldn't look. My eyes were fixed on the lapel of the Leader's Black jacket. Why wasn't he moving on? The next two numbers were called out again. Still, the Leader remained rooted; I could sense him staring at me. But I didn't dare lift my eyes to meet his.

Had I done something wrong? Were they onto me already? What if One had betrayed us? I would face the Assessors in a flowing white dress. I would have lost Dad's fight before I'd even got started.

I tried to keep breathing, stay focused. I held my body taut, waiting for one of the Leader's assistants to pounce on me, shout out an instruction – or arrest me.

Instead I heard it; one strongly put, but faint, word, before the Leader's heavy palm lifted itself up and away. His Black suit was striding on, around the side of me, on towards the next couple.

It reverberated in my head as my body relaxed.

A simple, stark: 'Christabel.'

Chapter Eleven

Christabel. Had he really said my name? The question left me reeling, so that for a moment I forgot I was attached to somebody else's hand. Why would the Leader even want to use it? The State preferred numbers to names.

And then I noticed it. Moist, warm skin, sticky against mine; fingers that were flexing intermittently as if they were trying to communicate.

Slowly, I gazed up.

The boy with the heart-shaped face, the boy who had politely stood back to let me leave the room before him. That was my first thought.

My second was his smile. A comfortable, welcoming smile. A smile that was rare in Land: it stretched to and shone in his eyes; eyes that were a mix of blue and grey. The colour of twilight.

We weren't allowed to speak to one another yet; I had recalled that instruction at least from the pamphlet. But with his gaze alone this boy seemed to be trying to say whole sentences.

I didn't know what words to form back with mine. What was there to say besides *hello? I'm sorry? Sorry you went and got me?* His thumb was circling my palm; despite everything I found I was curious about this new sensation. I looked down. His fingers started weaving with mine. I lifted our hands slightly, finding a strange sort of pleasure from how they moved together, as if temporarily I was anchored somewhere.

The Leader climbed back onto the stage and led a round of applause from the public gallery which he then halted abruptly. It was our cue. This stranger and I, our hot hands still clasped together, faced the front like everyone else in the room, starting a recital of the promise we had been instructed to learn by heart. I tried to listen to the sound of my stranger's voice, but it was hard to catch it above the drone of words around me: *Together we will uphold Land's laws, abide by Land's diktats, sacrifice the individual . . . for the greater good.*

The Leader drew his arms up and proclaimed, 'Do you promise to remain committed to your Pair as long as the State of Land decrees it?'

My breath quickened; I joined in with the cacophony of 'I do'.

I steeled myself for the Leader's final words. 'Then I pronounce you Paired, what was once one, is now two. Go forth and fulfil Land's destiny. For the greater good.'

For the greater good echoed once more round the audience. I silently mouthed the words, gulping in pockets of air. This boy, this stranger in front of me, was now part of my life. It was no longer me, just Cons and me. I had a new life. For as long as the State of Land decreed it? No – for as long as my father needed it.

The crowds above were encouraged again in their slow, rhythmic clapping as we paraded in our Pairs now along the snow-white carpeted path, between the small twinkling trees.

We were led towards the back of the room. I'd not noticed them as we came in – the line of small white tables hugging the back wall. Men and women in Grey with white masks over their mouths, white plastic gloves covering their hands, awaiting their first customers.

I'd been here before of course. Aged seven, waiting in line with Kara at West Land Assessment Centre. It had been Kara then squeezing my fingers, tugging me forward, reassuring me it wouldn't hurt for long. This time it was a strange boy with smiling eyes and a hot hand whose fingers tightened around mine.

I separated my hand from his as we reached the front of the queue, sitting down at spitting distance from neighbouring tables. The attendant at mine silently pressed the back of my wrist down onto the white paper cloth on the table. I didn't look as the buzzing needle hit my skin, making the first of its tiny punctures. I gritted my teeth, swallowing back the burning pain as the ink began to mark the pale skin beneath my own number, with his. *823104*. Thanks to Salinger's lessons in recall I could already remember it in an instant. Not that I'd ever be able to forget it. This stranger's number was a part of me now, whether the Resistance won or not.

He turned, a wide beam cutting across his face, once we'd left the Great Hall and entered the same anteroom as before. 'Ouch, that hurt.' He held up his wrist to show my number, scored under pinpricks of drying blood.

I gently dabbed at my own wrist. 'It's sore.' I didn't know what else to say.

'But finally, we can get introduced the normal way!'

I nodded. I had to start: act in a way that wasn't me. Like talking; like looking confident. *Start.*

'You know, I saw you. When we were here in this room back at the briefing. I said to my friend –' he laughed – 'Ha, you don't want to hear this, do you . . .?'

I blinked. His confidence made me shrink. *Say something.*

'I saw you, that's all . . . I noticed you.'

He noticed me?

'And I thought . . . yeah, you know . . .' He took my hand again, holding it loosely in his own. 'We've not even done names – what's yours?'

I cleared my throat. At last, something I could provide an answer to. 'Christy.'

'I'm Tobin. Great to meet you, Christy.' He clasped and shook the hand he still held in his. When he'd finished, I claimed it back. Damp with moisture, I wiped it on my dress; it wouldn't be mine much longer.

'Nice to meet you,' I said cautiously. The concrete nest of anxiety in my chest was unravelling a little. At least one piece of the unknown was over – I now knew the face of my Pair. And I had to admit – however irrelevant it was – I liked that face. There was a boyishness about Tobin's features: round mouth and eyes – except for his cheekbones, sculpted and high, his smile pushing them up even further. His blond hair swept over his forehead in a thick fringe; it was a little longer than most boys wore theirs. I instantly liked that about him.

'Weird how the Leader lingered, don't you think? I thought we were going to have a threesome. Imagine that. In fact, no, don't.'

I licked my lips. 'You didn't hear him say my name?'

'I don't think so. Why, did you?'

'Tobin!' We both glanced up. A glamorous older woman was coming towards us.

I heard Tobin moan under his breath; his arms stayed stiff as she embraced him heartily; a muffled 'Congratulations! I love you, my darling boy.'

It instantly made me glance around for Cons.

'Tobin! Is this her?' Those glamorous arms came at me now. I glimpsed Tobin rolling his eyes as I was tugged just as eagerly against this woman's breast, her pale Blue blouse silkily soft against my skin. 'My name's Bea.'

I managed to introduce myself before I was pushed backwards, a pincer movement on each of my arms as Bea examined me. Her eyes appeared moist. 'Lovely. A picture! We've done so well!' Everything she said seemed to end with a breath of exclamation. Her wet eyes blinked from me to Tobin and back again. She was well-presented, like Stella. A little older maybe, mid-forties or so; she had more lines framing her features than Stella. Or maybe she just smiled more – right now her smile imitated her son's, pointing directly up to her eyes.

Rigidly, I held my own mouth in check, waiting for the inevitable enquiry about my background, my family, their status. I was ready with my story, the not-strictly-untrue one Salinger had pressed on me: I was the great-great niece of one of Land's founders; no father – the stepdaughter of a prominent West Land Council member; a student chosen for fast-track into government. But she didn't ask for it. Her hand was beckoning excitedly over her shoulder. 'Meet the others!'

'Audley,' said the broad-faced man who joined us, with

grey-streaked hair and kind eyes. He was more subdued than his wife but appeared similarly pleased to meet me. 'And this is Ella,' he said, pushing forward a girl with a bush of light brown hair and a tiny, mouse-like face. She looked younger than her 'nearly fourteen years old'.

'Your new family!' Bea held her arms aloft. And for just a second there, I could have almost believed it.

Tobin and his parents were circulating, offering and receiving congratulations around the room. I should have been moving with them – getting to know who they knew. But I still couldn't find the faked version of me, at least not until Cons showed. I wanted her here, I wanted her to come and enjoy all this free food – even more lavish than last time – see the cloth napkins shaped into swans, inhale the honeyed scent from the many vases of fresh flowers across the room.

'A bit much, don't you think?' Tobin's sister Ella, sitting beside me, was nodding her head at the food table's centrepiece – an ice sculpture of a Paired couple that was now starting to slowly melt.

I smiled companionably with her. Ella didn't seem to share the exuberance of the rest of her family. It might have been nice to claim her as an ally. If I wasn't here to deceive them all.

'Do you think we should join in?' I looked over at Tobin's parents, who were holding court in the centre of a large group. Tobin was next to them, but he didn't look like he wanted to be.

'Nah. I never do very well in situations like that . . . usually end up putting my foot in it, annoying Mum with some comment.'

I watched as Bea flew her arms around, her beam widening as she talked.

Ella was still chatting to me. '. . . Unfortunately I didn't get their ultra-sociable genes – what with being adopted and all.'

I drew my neck back. 'You were adopted?'

'Yeah.' Ella scrunched up her small features. 'As a baby, though. Mum couldn't carry any more children after Tobin but she'd been approved for another . . . and so along came me. They love me just the same as Tobin,' she added with a cautious smile. And I didn't doubt it. Bea appeared to adore her whole family with a passion as forceful as her smile.

Cons still hadn't shown. Lunch had been cleared away. I had already been back twice into the Great Hall. Slave workers, blending into the dressed setting in their Whites, were already hard at work, beginning to roll up the carpet and cart away the miniature trees. Storing them, ready for next year.

The public gallery had emptied completely, the screens had all been turned off. I hurried back towards the lobby; guests were already starting to put on their coats. Most people had a Pairing party to go to.

'Not found her yet?' Tobin asked when I returned. His parents, I could tell, were itching to leave. They had friends and family arriving at their house soon to congratulate us, the happy Pair.

'I don't want to go without her.' Cons had been invited of course. 'She won't know where to come.' Which was when it crossed my mind. Cons wasn't coming. This was her way of saying *Over to you now*. Was that what she was thinking, that look on her face, out in the lobby? Was she telling me I was on my own?

I couldn't decide whether to buckle under the self-revelation or straighten up taller. In the end I did neither. It was Tobin who said, 'Why don't we go home for a bit, then you can pop back to yours to see if she's there – bring her over. The party will go on well into the evening.'

I had a job to do.

I followed through with that reminder after each person sauntered over to congratulate me and enquire after my health, and my family, and my progress at the Institute. Generally, my prospects for survival.

I had a job to do.

Tobin and I were standing side by side in his family's sprawling lounge. One half of it was squared off with white leather sofas around a large, open fire. The half we were in was empty apart from a round shiny wooden table holding empty wine glasses and bowls of snacking food.

I was busy practising what Salinger had taught me to do, logging names and numbers and government positions in the new file I had ready and open in my head.

I was improving with my conversation each time I shook the next hand thrust in front of me, every time I batted back a question, be it merely polite or coolly interrogative.

Yes, the large glass goblet of Audley's home-made wine that I was gripping might have helped somewhat too. My first ever taste of alcohol. A taste I'd been enjoying far too much since it had been placed in my hand, mainly because of the warm, hazy sensation, like sunshine, spreading through me. It bought me some of the confidence Tobin took for granted; it loosened my tongue. If I'd known it helped so much I would have started drinking a month ago. Clearly I would make a better Resistance member drunk.

I was still trussed up in my long white dress, though I had discreetly let out the side zip just a little under my arm as we made the short walk back to Tobin's family house. A short walk – their home was in Central Land – to a white, angular house on the southern side of the Cross. It was enough to tell me: this Pairing was a great one. This family: the elite of the elite. One, Cons: they would be pleased. Maybe the wine helped, but that thought alone did something strange to me. It emblazoned me. Like I'd passed my first challenge.

I *could* do this.

I *would* do it.

'Do you still want us to go and find your grandmother?' Tobin's eyes were on me. We were experiencing a rare moment without one of their many guests in front of us. His cheeks were a little flushed; the roaring fire was making the room unbearably hot.

My bravado of the last minute left me: I did want to see Cons. 'I can make my own way there. I won't take long.'

'No – I'll drive you in Dad's car.'

I swallowed back my surprise. The *new* me should be used to knowing people rich enough to own cars. The *real* me knew no one. I had a sudden hazy vision of driving theirs. The freedom of having wheels to get you places, rather than walking or taking the tram. I could drive round the whole of Land till I found where Dad was hiding.

'Do you want to see your room first though? Mum and Ella have spent weeks – no, months – on it. It used to be Dad's study. He's grumpy we've moved him into that far corner of the lounge instead.'

I stared over at an elaborate wooden desk in an alcove across the room. 'I'm sorry.'

'Don't be. Mum says at least she gets to see him that way.' Tobin raised his eyes to the ceiling, as if that sentence meant he was annoyed by one of his parents.

We headed out through smiling guests. Their hall was a room in its own right, with a white marbled floor like the one in the Cross lobby. The stairs swept up to another floor. A two-floored house. I had only ever dreamt of their existence.

'I like your staircase,' I heard come from my mouth; that wine was doing the talking for me again.

'Good, this is your home now . . . till we get our own.' Without warning he reached out and grabbed my hand, bending his lips down and kissing my knuckles. He smiled as he looked up again. I hoped it was his own intake of alcohol giving him that look to his face. 'Come on; let me show you your bedroom.'

We climbed the curved stairs and went into the first room off the landing. 'Here.' Tobin cast his arm around the room.

It was so big it took a while for my eyes to take it in. And then I had to start again, to take note of all the detail. It looked fit for a girl. Just not me. It was painted white, but with a trail of silver stars along the upper wall. The cushions on the bed were plumped full, silver and purple; there was a bedspread, a silky Blue. Artisan furnishings that you never saw in the shopping precinct. And a double bed. I wasn't sure what that might mean. But Tobin had said this was my room, not 'ours'. So briefly I let myself imagine the luxury of spreading out in it.

On the drive over he chatted nonstop, like he could speak more freely now. 'Mum and Dad do my head in. I'm just so relieved to be Paired. We can start planning, find our own place. Get away from them.'

I blithely nodded. I couldn't really deal with what he was saying. The closer we got, the more I just wanted to see Cons.

'I mean, I don't see why we should wait five months until we finish the Institute. I have points. I could get us somewhere, even if it's not in Central Land.'

I stayed silent. Like One would let me leave that house, that position, that family. Besides, why did Tobin even want to? He clearly didn't know how good he had it. 'It's just over there,' I interrupted him, pointing out the sharp edge of our thick tenement block.

Tobin pulled the car over, looking up and around as if he didn't trust where I'd brought him. 'I've only ever been out of Central Land to go to South Land Institute,' he said by way of explanation for his alarmed expression. 'This looks different.'

I shrugged. 'Thanks for driving me – Cons and I can make our own way back.'

Tobin pulled a face and drew his hands wide above the steering wheel. 'You're not going to invite me in?'

I tugged my mouth into what I hoped was a friendly smile. 'I'll see you back at the house,' I said, pushing the foreign brightness of his mother into my tone as I grabbed for my satchel. I'd need to change back into my Green dress before walking anywhere.

'But . . . why . . . I mean, how about I just come in for a bit? I don't want to go home yet.' He twisted his mouth comically.

'You've got to save me from my overbearing mother.'

In another life, another version of me, maybe I would have fallen for his endearing entreaty. But I wanted to see Cons alone. I doubted she would come to the party. 'I won't be long, a couple of hours at most.'

Tobin made a dramatic, resigned sigh then leant over and kissed me; a soft brush of a peck on my cheek that made my skin instantly blush. I turned to get out before he could see it. He was probably the kind of boy who would have been pleased whoever he'd got – just keen to get away from Mummy and Daddy. I had to remember – the wine had put me off my tracks – that this was a sham of a Pairing.

I could hear Cons in the kitchen the moment I came through into our flat. My heart lifted. Okay, so she would probably be cross I'd come chasing her. I simply wanted to take our usual seats at the table, tell her I was doing okay.

'Cons.' I was breathing her name out the moment I pushed open the kitchen door, ready to accept one of her hugs. Ready to tell her that Tobin seemed nice; that his family were up there, way up there.

I halted in the doorway. My heart seemed to jump, then stop. 'Where is she?'

Somehow, it was already present, the answer, filling the room around One like a cloying black smoke, stifling my lungs, blurring my vision.

I already knew.

Part Two

The Assassin

Chapter Twelve

'It was what Cons wanted,' were the first words One had uttered. 'She offered herself up for Selection.'

'No! It's not true!' Violently, I pushed at him, over and again; showering my fists against his chest; clutching and twisting handfuls of his coat. 'You tell me where she is!'

None of it displaced him from his rigid, seated position; nothing altered the impermeable expression on his stiffly held face.

It was only when I began to raise my voice, ordering him: 'Leave! Get out!' – that he finally moved, rising slowly, adjusting his coat. 'I will talk to you when you've calmed down,' he said blandly, crossing the hall and closing the door behind him on Cons' room.

I stood there, clenching my fists tighter, an eruption bubbling, readying to blast out of me.

He was lying!

Cons would never give herself up freely for Selection! Cons wouldn't leave me without saying goodbye. One had to tell me where Cons had gone! I stepped forward to follow him but my legs gave way; my body buckling beneath me. It wasn't true.

Was it? I fell onto the floor, an abrupt blackness flooding my eyes, as if a blind had been drawn.

I shifted upwards, my body stiff, my head hurting. I was covered by a sheet, still dressed in my white Pairing gown. It took me a moment to realise I was in my own bed.

Another moment more to remember what had happened. My blood chilled.

I clasped a hand across my stomach as it clenched in agony. Cons?

I drew my knees up into my chest, clutching at my face with my fingers. What was I fighting for, if Cons had left me? Why would she do this to me? I pulled at my hair. I wanted pain; I wanted physical pain to overtake this agony. Every breath felt impossible. I wanted Cons! She had never given me the chance to save her! I screwed my hands into fists to beat myself as strangled sobs began lurching their way out.

I didn't remember much of the days that followed. And they must have been days, because I recalled the light ever changing in my room, from yellow daylight to artificial white-grey from the streetlights.

I had no intention of getting up.

Now and again I woke to creaking footfalls around the flat: One. Twice a day he would come into my room. Brusquely force my head up and push a thick, tasteless soup down my throat, followed by water. I was too dazed to stop him. The loss of Cons consumed me.

I knew what would soon happen. If I remained in bed.

Five days was all it took. Five days until the Institute would report me, and the Assessors would come. Selection: it had to be my only escape from this interminable ache of missing Cons.

Maybe that was why One chose the fourth day to say what he did.

'Christy.' He roughly shook my shoulder. I turned, expecting his soup and water routine. He was crouching by my bed as usual, but he had no food with him. I turned back to face the wall. Squeezing my eyes shut, I willed sleep to take me. I hated the waking hours.

'You knew Cons was due to be taken some time this year. What difference does it make that she chose the day?'

I covered my ears to block out his voice.

'Christy . . . You have to listen to me. There is something Cons tasked me with telling you.'

He caught me at the last sentence. But I still gave no sign I was paying attention.

'*My leaving is Christy's beginning.* They were Cons' words.'

He let out a long breath through his nose. 'Her death was part of a grander plan – hers, your father's – for your future. For everyone in Land who wants a future.'

My eyes sprung open at the mention of him. Dad. I stared steadily at the white wall in front of me. In all of this, I had forgotten him. Or maybe he had forgotten me. Together, we were supposed to have protected Cons.

Slowly I craned my neck until I could see him. 'Why,' my voice broke; I swallowed, '. . . did Cons leaving me have to be part of any plan?'

One sighed, he drew his hands wide; his drooping eyes

seemed to drag further down his face. When his words came they were heavily enunciated, as if he were reading from a prepared script: 'Because it was part of a deal, in exchange for bringing you up . . . she had promised to bow out once your time came, when you were Paired into your future.'

'A deal . . . with *whom?*'

One shook his head, rubbing a hand across his thick chin. 'Your grandfather.'

I sat bolt upright, roughly pushing the tangles of hair from my face. 'Both my grandfathers are dead!'

'No . . . Hogan's father, Jacob, is very much alive.'

'No – Cons said Land did for him. Those were always her words!'

One made a shrug. 'I suppose it did. Our last Leader convinced Jacob to give up his family in exchange for becoming Head of State Troopers. The State took away anything of the man he once was.'

It was like a flash of lightning in my head. A sudden crackle of a memory, of a number spoken publicly – the distorted digits that had marked the crepe skin of Cons' wrist underneath her own.

'11024 . . . the Leader's number. It is my grandfather's number . . .' My head felt as if it were about to explode. 'The Leader? He is my grandfather?'

The connection brought another: his using my name at the Pairing! Then another: the message on my tracer when I was picked? *Christabel, now is your hour. Rise to it.*

'He knows who I am?'

One bent over, clasping his hands in front of me as if he were about to beg me for something. 'Your grandfather – he

139

has his own plan for you. As his only grandchild, he was always keen you should follow him into government.'

He inhaled through his nose. 'Just like Cons has always marked you out for helping the Resistance.

'When your grandfather became the new Leader last year, suddenly we saw how we might best use you. We are hijacking your grandfather's ambitions for you.'

I watched One, this wooden man, whose words were now darting like frenzied fish at feeding time around my head. All the blood seemed to have drained out of my body. In the space of a few days I had lost one grandparent – and gained another.

'Why did Cons never tell me about him?' I said, my voice surfing on small gasps of air.

'Part of the deal was to keep your relationship to him secret. The Leader is cut off from family. He wants you to work alongside him . . . but he doesn't want you to know who he is. Cons had to abide by this request – so he would trust her.'

One rubbed at his forehead. 'Cons' part of the deal was to groom you for future leadership . . . Your grandfather wants great things for the last link to his DNA. He tasked me with watching over you, to oversee Cons was raising you as a proud Land citizen.'

'But instead you let her raise me to become a rebel,' I uttered blandly. Nausea was spreading up my throat. Had Cons only taken me in to groom me?

'You will make the perfect infiltrator; the ideal weapon for the Resistance. The Leader is surrounded by guards all the time; he shares and conceals secure information with guile. No one knows the whole picture of his policy. If he starts to care for you, trust in you – we can make him vulnerable.'

I glanced wildly round. 'Make him care for me?' I pressed the heel of my hand against my forehead. 'Cons should have stayed alive!'

'I told you – she made a deal with the Leader. He didn't want you to remain close to your grandmother once you were Paired as he wished.'

'She should have fought against him!'

One licked his lips brusquely. 'Cons was convinced that, with her gone, you might find it easier . . . to detach from your old life, and accept your fate.'

'Detach from my old life?' I repeated the words slowly, each syllable crumbling the foundations I'd been raised on. 'My fate – working for the Resistance?'

'Your fate . . . as your grandfather's assassin.'

I pulled my head into my neck. The words hung in the air between us. 'What did you say?'

'To overthrow the Leader's power, we need to eradicate the Leader. Soon – we hope – you will be in the best position to do it for us. If you get his trust, you will have the best access. Our plan is to make it seem as if he brought about his own death . . . the implosion of power.'

I drew both hands down my face. I couldn't believe what I was hearing. 'I have lost my grandmother, but I still have a grandfather . . .?' I made a short gasp. 'And now you are telling me I have to lose him too?'

'Assassinate.' One pronounced the word as if he were spelling it out for me.

'You want me to kill my own grandfather?'

'We told you your role might require you to remove certain

people.'

'You talk about it so coldly.'

'The State has taken lives. Your *grandfather* has taken lives. Countless times.' His eyes stayed on me; his hard face softened, just a little. 'You are crucial to us, Christy. You are at the centre of the war for change . . . the centre of a long-fought-for plan – your grandmother's, your father's.'

'And yours?'

He nodded solemnly. 'And mine.'

I shook my head. 'I was doing this for Cons.'

'Then still: do it for Cons.' He leant over me and placed his wide hand on my shoulder. It was the first instance he'd ever touched me in all the time I'd known him. Maybe that was what jogged my mind, stirred me to join up the dots. '*You're* the Leader's nephew . . . which means . . .'

'I'm your father's cousin. Yes.'

My mouth gaped open; I checked his stiff face for expression – did our relation mean anything to him?

'How else do you think I got involved in this? We were family. Hogan and I were like brothers. I had no mother; Cons virtually brought me up along with him.'

'You and Cons,' I breathed out. Suddenly it was like I had always known. Their silent familiarity; the way they both had of regarding the other. 'So then you do know where Dad is?'

One made no answer. Did he still not trust me?

'I have always loved my father,' I stated hotly, as if I had a sudden urge to compete with One for Dad's affection.

'Yes – that is why Cons knew you would want to avenge his betrayal. You see it was Hogan's own father – the then Head

142

of State Troopers – who called for his arrest.'

'I raised my chin. 'I need to see Dad.'

'Right now it's not possible.'

I let out a choked groan, turning away from him. My past was tripping through my head, images of what I thought had been a contented childhood with Cons. All those stories of the freedoms of the Old World, contrasting with Land's cruelties. *Contain yourself, Christy. Don't cry, Christy. Fix a smile, Christy.* She had packaged me up.

Cons had played a game with me.

I was only ever collateral – from the very beginning.

I finally got up later that day, swapping my stale white dress for a cool shower. Maybe I abandoned my death wish because of what One had told me. Or maybe it was simply built in: the desire to live.

One was still there when I walked into the kitchen. From the look of the room, white dishes piled high in the sink, remnants of tin cans and glass bottles cluttering the counter, he must have been living here these past days. Clearly I was too precious a commodity to the Resistance to risk losing.

'Don't,' I said as, unusually for him, he began talking the moment he clocked me. 'I'm up. I'll be at the Institute tomorrow. You don't have to watch over me any longer.' I rubbed at the throb in my head.

'This is my job,' One answered gruffly.

'How could I forget?' I blinked at him. 'That's where I sit.'

One looked down at the chair, tilted his head then rose and moved to the seat opposite.

'Do you never take off your coat when you're inside?'

His shoulders lifted and dropped, but he removed his coat, hanging it up neatly behind his chair. The Blue suit jacket he had on underneath was ironed with creases down the arms.

I reclaimed my chair, instinctively scooping my hands over the table to create a wall around the scored number and signature of Hogan, as if I were protecting it from One.

'By tomorrow you must go back to your Pair's house.'

'I've not said I'll fit in with your plan yet! I can't kill my own grandfather!' I spat out, my eyes holding his fiercely. Anger was fast overtaking grief.

One circled his neck then stood up and poured out tea from the metal pot on the hob. He banged a mug down in front of me, spraying black liquid over the table. 'No milk left,' he mumbled. It was a sour reminder – without Cons' salary, I had no points to even buy any.

I drew a finger over my wrist; the inflammation had gone down around my new tattooed number. They had me cornered – I had to return to Tobin's family, if I wanted to survive in Land.

'What does your grandfather mean to you, Christy? Nothing! You don't know the man. He abandoned your grandmother, betrayed your father!'

'Cons still should have told me about him!'

'I've already said: keeping it secret was part of their deal. Maybe Cons also feared you might seek him out. She knew that what you wanted beyond all things was to save her from Selection.'

'The irony,' I muttered under my breath.

'Are you tempted by him – now you know who he is?' One was eyeing me strangely.

'Tempted?'

One stretched his palms wide. 'By the privileged life you might own. *Sit at the right hand of your grandfather.* Reap all the benefits power brings . . . Automatic survival based on who your family are.' There was a bitter tone to his voice.

'No! I am not tempted. Are you?'

One sighed heavily; he didn't answer.

'How long have you fought for the Resistance?'

'How long?' One briefly sucked in his cheeks. 'Put it this way – I kept my head down in government . . . until you were seven years old. When I chose Cons' side.'

I narrowed my eyes. 'You weren't always loyal to Hogan?'

'No. I wasn't,' he said matter of factly. 'I couldn't be loyal to my cousin; because I had somebody else I had to remain faithful to, to protect. To do that I had to stay out of trouble. That same person became my motive to fight . . .'

I leant forward; I wanted to hear more. But One made an abrupt toss of his head. 'It's all immaterial now. I switched, backed Cons' cause . . . watched you grow to be useful to the Resistance instead of the Leader . . .'

I shook my head. 'I can't kill him. I'm not capable of killing anyone!'

'I wouldn't even be here if I didn't think you were. Cons raised you to survive; Cons raised you to think. I have been near, watching over you since you came to live here, as a small child. I have followed you for all these years, trailed you, shadowed you . . .'

'*You?* It was *you* . . . I sensed watching me?'

One made a slight inclination of his head. 'Always.'

Chapter Thirteen

One said he wanted a decision from me by the end of the
next day. Today.

I didn't see how I could make it. Kill my own grandfather?
How did you decide on something like that?

I hardly functioned through Friday morning classes. The
facts of my new existence wouldn't stop flooding and fogging
my mind, keeping me breathless, my body numb.

But they weren't the only pieces to my nightmare. I'd almost
completely forgotten the other – until I spied her across the
lunch hall.

Kara's face echoed mine, intensifying with concern, as we weaved
our way past the Green backs of students tightly packed around
the white bench tables in the Institute canteen. When we reached
one another we shared cautious smiles, our exchanged look
mutual: we'd save our words for when we were alone.

'Have you got your period?'

We were squashed into our usual cubicle in the toilet block
near the Institute's slave quarters.

Kara's fierce blue eyes ignored the question. She placed her hands on both my arms. 'I was getting worried. I thought you'd been sent to another Institute; I went to your flat, to ask Cons. I could hear her inside, but she didn't answer the door.'

'It wasn't Cons . . . it was someone else. I didn't hear you knock,' I said plainly. 'But first, tell me, did your –?'

'What do you mean? Who was it if not Cons? Have you been there all this time? What happened at the Pairing?' She pulled up the bottle-Green sleeve of my jumper, her eyes narrowing at the newly marked black ink beneath mine. '823104. Has he done something to you? If he has I'll –'

I made a curt shake of my head, dwelling briefly on Tobin, on his comfortable home and his smiling twilight eyes. One had said he'd explained my prolonged absence to him and his family by my grief for Cons. I was due to collect my things from the flat; then One would take me back there tonight – whether I decided to become my grandfather's assassin or not.

Tension clawed at my insides as I found the voice to tell her everything.

Kara drew in her breath when I finished. Her eyes had darkened over Cons' leaving. But lit up when I whispered what I was now being asked to do. 'They plan to get rid of the Leader?'

I frowned. 'Kara . . . I can't do it.'

'I'll do it. Christy – tell them. I'll kill anyone.' The muscle along Kara's jawline twitched in eagerness. I could almost smell the retribution for her parents oozing from her pores.

'It's not that simple.' I sniffed. 'How could Cons do this to me, Kara?'

Her eyes darted around mine, growing brighter still. 'Christy – Cons left a legacy behind: for things to get better.'

I pulled back, leaning my head back against the wall of the cubicle. Didn't even Kara get it? My grandmother had made my childhood a training ground. Then abandoned me to a war I never chose!

'Get them to enlist me. Then I can be at your side always. Christy – it makes sense, we have to kill. With death comes birth.'

I gazed down. Her hands had left mine; they were making tiny, comforting circles across her flat stomach.

I held my breath, my body tensing, staring up into her eyes. 'No . . . Kara, no. Tell me you're not.'

Her voice came back, tight, hushed. 'I am.'

I heard the front door go soon after I'd got back to the flat. I didn't wait for him to enter the room; propped up at the kitchen table I uttered a loud, clear, 'I'll do it.'

'Do what, cook me dinner?'

My face tightened, as Salinger rounded the door. All those nights in training . . . he'd been in on the secret – what I was really being trained for. For some reason Salinger's part in it stung more than One's.

'Where's One?' I put out the question brusquely, avoiding his eyes until I had no choice but to look at him.

'Charming as ever,' he replied, that languorous body of his heading straight for the sink. He helped himself to a glass of water, as if it were his own flat. When he turned, he tapped the now-empty glass against the end of his nose. 'I wanted to say I'm sorry, if you'll hear it . . . about your grandma. I know how much she meant to you.'

'I've told you before – don't presume to know how I feel,' I replied acidly. I wasn't going to accept any olive branch. Right now, it was easier to be angry at Salinger than to make him my ally. 'Why are you even here?'

'It's my job to be here.'

'A job. That's right – all I am to everyone is a job.'

Did my words bruise him somehow? Was that why he turned back round to face the sink? I tried to spy his reflection in the window beyond, but his head was cast downwards. 'You've got to remember that none of us get to choose our jobs in Land.'

I pulled at my bottom lip.. 'Right: I don't matter to you.' Why did I say that? To push him to say I did?

Salinger lifted his eyes to gaze out of the window. Now I could see his reflection I saw he looked tired, resigned somehow. 'One's asking a lot of you, and yet you should know –' His voice was lost to another click of the front door.

One entered soon after; he cast an abrupt hello to us both then directed his eyes at me. 'Want me to sit there, and take my coat off?' One of those faint smiles of his was playing on his lips as he promptly did both then leant towards me. 'Decision?'

'And this is your answer?'

I made a curt nod. 'You help her, I'll help you.'

'She'll need to help herself. You can take a horse to water.'

I should have been used to One's abrasive manner by now, but his attitude still hurt. Did the man not feel for anyone? 'I just need you to arrange the necessities for Kara. Set up an appointment with . . . someone who can stop her pregnancy. Leave the rest to me.'

I didn't add that my part was going to be the hardest. Kara was refusing to even contemplate 'removing' it.

'I won't, I can't . . .' she'd said with venom this afternoon, raising both hands as if she were going to slap me for even suggesting it. Kara had found her fight at last.

'It's a deal then,' One said. 'Good. So, to business – we'll inform you when there's a directive you'll be suited to. The quicker you step up to the day job, harden yourself, the sooner you'll become ready to do what really matters. Agreed?'

Fight. Kill. Make change happen. And bring it about soon.

It was all I had in my power to save Kara; besides Dad, the only person left I cared for.

It was a strange group we formed as we made our way to Tobin's – in a car I'd never even known One owned. I hadn't been in a car my whole life. And suddenly in the space of a week I'd been in two. Strange, when Cons had talked of beginnings.

We'd spent the last few hours recapping my basic training. With a different edge. Suddenly it seemed even more important, to learn how to attack or defend myself. Though I still flunked at it: Salinger had me pinned to the kitchen floor seven times in a row; my elbow kept missing his chest, my fists going wide.

'Hopefully you'll never need to physically attack anyone,' One had said in an elongated sigh as he helped me up.

'So you want me to kill people but you're hoping I might not need to defend myself?' My face had flushed with instant anger. Contained yet angry – was that the perfect temperament for a murderer? If so, Cons had done her job well.

'As you know – for now, we're keeping death simple. We won't ask for much skill from you at first,' One had replied levelly. 'In the meantime I'll arrange for you to have some more time with Salinger at my house. We'll build up your strength, your reactions. We'll make an excellent assassin out of you yet.'

I couldn't match his grim-faced smile.

My heart was pounding harder now I was standing by One's car. It looked like every other car in Land, spray-painted black like the Selection trucks. They were in such small demand they were manufactured to the same specification – like cars from her own grandparents' days, Cons used to say; stocky and square, with tyres that seemed too big for the car's body.

I got inside next to Salinger, pressing my hands, damp with nerves, onto the blue leather of the back seat. My Institute satchel was on my lap. The few bin liners with my clothes and toiletries were in the rounded boot. I'd taken nothing sentimental from Cons' room. Not even the old picture of her as a baby with her mother. One had said the flat probably wouldn't get taken up by another tenant for a while: 'You can always go back for more.' I wasn't sure I wanted to. There was only one part of myself I didn't have the courage to leave behind: Dad's desk.

It now claimed one half of the front bench seat. Salinger had helped me unscrew the legs, stealing great pleasure from it. 'Fine impression you're going to make, rocking up to their grand house with some old kitchen table.'

As One started the car, Salinger edged closer. 'I need to give you this.' He opened his hand. The little blue pill they had talked about sitting there comfortably between the tracks of lines on his palm; sealed in plastic and looking smugly innocuous. A mirror image of the ones the Assessors prescribed, the happy pills Kara used to take. Except this little pill wouldn't be making anyone happy.

I caught One's eyes on me in his rear-view mirror. Checking for my reaction.

Salinger cleared his throat, then said, 'Right now, the priority for us is to get rid of – in short succession – the key figures in government. We will be asking you to help with that.

'We will weaken the power base . . . portray the Leader as losing control of the State –'

'And then, finally, eliminate the Leader, I know,' I cut in.

'Right,' Salinger said, his tone uncommonly soft. 'Remember, the poison is indirect, so it's not really like it's you ending their lives – you're just the messenger.' He made a small, encouraging smile.

'If it's me who drops a pill of death into their drink, it's me who murdered them.' I sat back. 'I don't need you to sugar-coat this. I've already told you I will do it.'

'I'm just saying. It's no easy task we're asking of you . . . the trick is not to think about what it is you're doing – until you're there. In the room with them. Block it out by fixing your mind on the end result instead. A new Land.'

I turned my head towards him. 'How many have *you* killed?' I genuinely wanted to know. I hadn't meant to let the scoff seep into my voice. It came too naturally now.

Salinger ignored the question. He slanted back away from

me, pushing his hand out for me to take the pill. 'This one's for you. Keep it with you at all times.' The hint of warmth had left his voice. 'You can't afford to be tortured for information. If you ever get caught – to protect the cause, you use it.'

I stared at the dot of blue nestled in his palm. Then I took it; securing it in the pocket of my satchel. 'I'll put it somewhere safe when we get there.'

Salinger nodded. One's eyes returned to the road.

I slunk down in my seat. None of us were ever going to be friends. Wasn't that what Cons had said?

'I have killed plenty.'

I glanced back over at him. Closer to the window now, Salinger's face was half lit by the bright glow of streetlights, half in shade from the darkness of the car. He looked as if he too had lost someone important.

I noticed One's eyes had moved back towards us in the rear-view mirror. But this time they weren't assessing me. They were watching Salinger.

We crunched down the well-maintained white pebble path. I'd last walked to my Pair's front door in a floor-trailing white dress. Only five days ago; already it seemed a lifetime.

Rapping hard on the black-painted front door, I gave a curt, 'You can go now,' to One and Salinger either side of me. They were making me feel like some kid being escorted home after breaking curfew.

One made a noise like a cough. 'We'll see you inside,' he said.

'Need to sneak that kitchen table of yours up to your room before they send it packing . . .'

I glanced at Salinger, holding my dad's desk, then back to One. It wasn't about tables, or seeing me into my new home. It was obvious: they wanted to make sure I wasn't about to run away, or tell all the moment the door opened. It was their job to see I did mine.

My job. *Keeping death simple.*

'Oh, my darling. You poor thing.' Bea's eager arms pulled me into her silky chest the moment she flung the door open. 'Selection, even when it's your time to go, is always such a sad moment. We all feel for you.'

I inhaled Bea's sweet perfume. Her grandiose sympathy, for some reason, I could take. It felt like something close to a normal reaction, if I knew what normal was. To Bea I was simply mourning a grandmother.

She stood back to let us in, and that was when I glimpsed the rest of them, a welcoming committee. My charade of a new family, standing as if they'd all assembled moments ago. Clearly they had been expecting our arrival. One must have kept us to a schedule I hadn't even been aware of.

'Hey there, Christy.' I found I was glad for the big smile Tobin gave me as he took my bags from me. His 'I hope you're okay' seemed sincere, concerned. If I had any tears left, they might have sprung to my eyes at such genuine sympathy.

One had strode with his usual aloof confidence into the centre of the large hallway. He was pumping flesh with Audley; he'd mentioned they knew one another from government. In my absence he'd already established himself and Salinger as my 'mentors'.

The scene was set. There was no turning back now.

One had moved on to Ella. I could hear him asking her about the subjects she was doing at the Institute. His voice held an uncommon warmth to it. I felt a prick of envy; he never spoke to me like that.

Salinger, beside him, was replying to some comment from Audley, 'I agree . . . 823057 is privileged to be handpicked for government fasttrack. Her great-great-uncle, of course, was one of Land's founders. Exemplary genes, like her Institute record.'

Using my number – it was proof enough that I wasn't an individual to either of them. I turned round; Tobin smiled at me. It still reached his eyes.

Clearing my throat, I spoke loudly. 'Thanks for bringing me. You must need to get off now.' I wanted them both out of here.

Everyone stopped talking. One, his eyes still on Ella, made a short nod.

'I'll just get this up to your room then,' Salinger said.

'It's going to be my desk,' I explained to Bea. She was staring disconcertedly at the rough, marked wood making its way up the stairs. I followed it.

'You've landed on your feet,' Salinger muttered as he navigated the table through the bedroom door.

Even with my shoes on, I sank into the soft carpet of my new bedroom. Carpet – our floors at the flat were a mixture of wood and stone, whatever the builders had to hand when the tenements were quickly constructed decades ago.

'Resting your head on a silken pillow, how about that,' Salinger murmured as he propped the table up against the one piece of wall free of matching white furniture. He began twisting the legs back on.

He was mocking me. I reached out, snatching the table leg from his hands. 'I'm entirely capable of putting it together myself.'

'Is there a problem here?' Tobin had appeared in the doorway, his eyes glaring at Salinger. 'I'll help Christy with it later. After all, that's what Pairs do.'

Salinger stared back at him. His hand was still fixed to the table leg we were now both holding; it flinched. For a moment I thought he was going to do something other than screw it into the table.

I looked between them. 'That's very kind of you, Tobin; I'd appreciate it,' I said, giving him the sort of forced, sweet smile Salinger had never seen on my lips. I might fight on the Resistance's side, but it didn't mean I had to play on Salinger's.

Tobin put his hand forward, taking the table leg from us both, his voice barbed. 'I think we need to see you out, Salinger.'

I lay in my new oversized bed, having just soaked in the huge tub of an en-suite bathroom that belonged to me alone. My first bath after a lifetime of showers. I'd been fed a meal that would have lasted me a week in my old life: roast chicken, fried potatoes and all kinds of vegetables. Cooked pears for pudding. When I'd said I was tired Bea had insisted on coming with me to my room. She had wanted to show me all the clothes she had bought that filled a large wardrobe and three chests. 'I guessed your size when I saw you. I got all kinds of styles and shades of Green; some jewellery too. I hope you like it all.' I had affected a gracious smile to match hers. A month back the sight of so many lovely clothes might have overwhelmed me. Now they simply seemed ridiculous compared with what I was here to do.

There was nothing of the old me left.

I didn't even bother unpacking my old Green clothes. I would carry them to the State bins in the morning.

I pulled the covers up tighter, even though the room was overwarm, curling up into myself. A feeling had clung to me since One and Salinger had gone. No matter how much I wanted them to leave, I couldn't chase it off.

It was the same feeling that would scrape down my insides when Cons would take me over to Stella and Syon's, leaving me there for Friday night, in the days when I was too young to walk back alone. I would do as she had told me to – I wouldn't cry, I wouldn't make a fuss. But in my head, through my guts, a rage battled within me.

People were always leaving me.

Chapter Fourteen

'They are?' I said back to Bea, helping myself to a glass bottle of juice from their giant fridge. Bea kept reminding me: *'This is your home now.'*

'They are.' Bea beamed across their meticulous, spacious kitchen. She was home early from work. Tobin was still at his classes at South Land Institute, extra lessons that Bea and Audley paid for. They weren't taking any chances; why rely solely on good genes when points could assure them the best future job for their son? 'Isn't that great?'

Great? It was the worst news to be greeted with. I really didn't need this at the end of my first full week living with them. A week that had been spent either waiting, with shredded nerves, for my first assignment, or failing to convince Kara to let One's contact visit her and do what had to be done: get rid of that baby. Before it got rid of her.

So I didn't need Bea's enthusiasm for life right now. And I certainly didn't need this.

'Are you not pleased?' Bea's generous smile was starting to wane. In her mind: *What girl wouldn't cheer at the prospect of her mother and stepfather coming for dinner tonight?*

I caught myself in time, widened my mouth. 'Of course; it's really kind of you . . . to arrange it.'

Bea's perky smile replanted itself. 'Oh and your stepbrother Tom is coming too, and Astral is bringing her new Pair!'

My stomach slumped in on itself. 'Fantastic,' I forced out.

Their slave girl stepped in from the back door, dressed in a spotless White blouse and trousers., her hair pulled back fiercely into a ponytail; I empathised with the way she skulked round the edge of the room, trying to remain invisible. Even to me. I'd tried my best to catch her eye since I'd moved in; I'd asked her name, but she only answered with a monotone repetition of her number.

Bea twisted round, catching sight of her. She told her 'wait' then swung back to me, her face turning serious. 'You know, Christy, you're looking tired . . . you're working too hard. We have a rule in this house: no studying after dinner, that's family time. And you've been breaking it every evening, missy.'

Leisure time, family time – I was now moving in a set of people who thought time their privilege. 'We Blues work hard so we can get to play hard too,' I'd heard Audley say to Tobin recently. As if the Blues were the only ones who grafted. I thought of Xavier at his factory job, his mind wasted, arm muscles permanently strained; of Cons at her midwifery, working long shifts into her sixties.

But I nodded as if I agreed with Bea; what other answer could I give? I was one of them now. Thankfully Bea became preoccupied directing the slave girl on the food to prepare for tonight's menu. I took the chance to escape, retreating like I did every day, shutting myself into my new bedroom.

It had become my sanctuary. I could breathe in here. I threw my juice bottle on the bed and lay down next to it, flat on my back, stretching my arms up over the silky bedspread the slave girl made each morning – even if I remembered to do it myself.

I pressed my eyes shut; waiting was all I could do. For my first assignment . . . my last. Waiting for One to arrange the 'accidental' introduction to my grandfather. For Kara's belly to grow bigger.

Waiting to be reunited with Dad.

Waiting to get found out.

'You in?' A sharp knock on my door.

Or waiting for Tobin to make another move. That problem might have been pretty tame in comparison, but I felt just as inexperienced about my role as a Pair as I did about all the other things closing in on me.

I lifted myself up from the bed, uttering a reluctant, 'Yeah,' that I tried to make sound more encouraging. I wished he would stop doing this, seeking me out all the time.

He opened the door, standing there in my doorway, my golden, blue-eyed Pair.

'She's doing my head in.' She. Bea. It had become a recurring complaint from Tobin every day this week.

He came over and collapsed next to me on the bed, sending my bottle rolling with a thud onto the floor. 'I'm just this minute back and already she's started in on me. *Do this Tobin; think that* . . . We've got to start searching for our own place, Christy.' It was all Tobin talked about; it was all he had on his mind – our future together. And how he wanted it to look.

'We get our jobs in four months' time . . . we've got to leave then.'

'We' this, 'we' that – Tobin was born for being a Pair.

'She only wants the best for you.' I tried to make my voice cheerful. 'You're her son.' I was running out of excuses for why I was in no hurry to live alone together . . . even *be* alone together.

'She wants what's best for *her*. What fits her idea of what I should be.'

I made a face of sympathy. When really I wanted to shake him. Yeah, Bea fussed and worried, but she cared about him – it was plain to see, she really cared. He had nothing real to be concerned about; his world was wrapped up in cotton wool.

Except, of course, for the fact that he was Paired to an assassin.

'Wouldn't you prefer it to be just you and me?' His eyes blazed with a suggestion of what he wanted that time alone to entail. I fidgeted and glanced away.

I kept resisting even a simple kiss or hug. Telling him *not yet* over and again all this week, telling him that I wasn't ready. I was tired.

Which lie next from my pack? Because, the truth – what was that?

The truth was: maybe I liked him. I mean, there was a lot that was easy to like about Tobin. For starters, his heart-shaped face; his smiling eyes. I liked his hair, the way his fringe bounced when he talked as if it had the same boyish eagerness for life as he did. I liked the way he backed up Ella when his parents reproved her for speaking her mind, and he always held the door open for the slave girl.

Tobin lifted a hand, drawing a line down the curve of my jaw. I held my face still. It wasn't that I didn't want something. When I wasn't having nightmares over Kara and killing, I slept in dreams of arms around me that weren't my own. Sometimes, even in my waking hours, I imagined what that closeness with Tobin might feel like; whispered romantic words into my ear, hot breath on my skin. A large part of me had begun to ache for the touch he kept trying to give.

It was mine for the taking: life, here, with him – cocooned, taken care of, blind to the real picture of Land's atrocities. I could tell One: no more, and just . . . live . . . as Tobin's Pair. Such a tangible option – I could almost reach out and stroke it.

Until I remembered – Dad, Kara.

I pulled my head back. His hand dropped back down onto the bedspread.

I couldn't ever forget the reason I was here. For all I knew, the Resistance might be planning to remove Audley or Bea. Their existence protected my identity, but they were both instrumental to the success of the State. Audley headed up the Department of Industry. Bea was a prolific communications specialist. She was behind the posters that had recently appeared above the sinks in the Institute toilets: **Frailty will sink us**. Land would be weakened without both of them. That thought had begun to trouble me a lot when I let it.

I got off the bed, away from Tobin. I had to *stay focused. Keep things simple. Keep death simple.* It didn't matter who died, if I didn't care for them.

'I really need to get some work done before dinner,' I said, watching how in an instant hurt showed in his eyes. Tobin had never learnt to form a mask. Why would he have to?

'That's okay, you do the work; I'll just sit here and watch you.' He lay back on the bed.

'No, I need to be alone,' I said plainly.

Tobin lifted his head up, watching me at a slant. 'All right, I get the message.' There was a grumpy tinge to his voice. 'I'm going.' He got off the bed. At the door he turned, a frown forming, casting a shadow above his eyes. 'Is it me you're not happy with . . .?'

I chewed at the inside of my mouth. All the training Salinger had put me through, all the pep talks One had made me endure – they'd never prepared me for this. Girl meets boy.

I straightened my back, bringing my best, practised smile to my face. 'Of course I am,' I lied. 'I just need time . . . you know, to get used to things.'

Tobin tapped his fingers against the door. 'So you keep saying,' he said. 'This isn't how I imagined it. Us.'

'I know.' I tried to smile encouragingly. But he must have noticed by now. How my smile never reached my eyes.

'I always worked too hard at my home-study.' It was a classic Stella-ism. Another one of her feeble attempts to make a connection with me.

'But I wish Christy would have more time for us . . .' Bea made her point again. 'Get to know us better, right?'

I glanced at Stella as she nodded rigidly. The three of us were grouped round the lounge fire. Stella's powdered cheeks had turned pink from the heat. A good few centimetres smaller, she stood in Bea's shadow; prettier maybe, but not as effervescent as Bea. I had to wonder if Stella thought it: *Here's another capable woman to take my daughter off my hands.* I kept catching her surveying the length of the room. Larger and finer than hers; I was certain this new family of mine had come as a shock. Stella wouldn't have envisaged me Pairing so well. Yet, after her emphatic, 'I'm sorry,' at the briefing, wouldn't it be natural to assume that now I'd done okay she might look pleased? There I was – her daughter – no longer an embarrassment for her and Syon; no longer living in a hovel in an unappetising area. No more a one but, hey, a two!

Yet instead she looked close to miserable. I could see the corners of her mouth fighting to tug her fake smile downwards.

I couldn't work the woman out. And I didn't have the time, or inclination to do so.

Her daughter was a soon-to-be killer.

You must be so proud.

Dinner announced, I waited till everyone was seated around the formally set table and my empty glass refilled with wine before casting my eye over the rest of Stella's family. Besides stiffly exchanged greetings I'd purposely avoided them back in the lounge. Astral's Pair was now sat opposite me, partially blocked by a glass vase of freshly cut white roses. He didn't have a lot to recommend himself: broad-shouldered, heavy built, with a bullish, squashed face. Maybe that accounted for the distasteful look on Astral's face next to him, like her Pair's breath was bad or something. Until I noticed it – still visible, despite a thick layer of make-up – shades of purple and yellow

164

below her right eye.

Syon on her other side looked oblivious to the fact Astral was practically moving onto his lap to get away from her Pair. No, Syon was too absorbed in ingratiating himself with Audley. Tom, too. Their expressions grew more slippery as Audley rose at the head of the table, lifting his glass.

'A toast – to our new Pairs here tonight!' Audley's kind eyes embraced us all. 'They walk taller as a two than a one. As a couple they will strengthen the backbone that makes Land prosperous! For the greater good!'

Tobin, next to me, brought his arm around my waist as we all stood up and raised our glasses.

'Another toast.' Syon's eyelids closed as he interjected. My lips twitched with silent derision at his smug tone. 'To the State Troopers – who today rounded up forty Resistance members responsible for the power station explosion; a few of their key players included.' He opened his eyes, lifted his glass. 'To eradicating all who betray Land!'

Everyone repeated his last sentence. I merely opened and closed my mouth. My breath was quickening as we retook our seats. I ignored Tobin as he whispered in my ear, 'Have I told you you look lovely tonight?' I wanted to swat him away like a fly; what did I care how I looked? This was awful news. I'd heard about yesterday's bomb at the East Land power station. That the Head of State Troopers had been shot dead when he'd arrived to survey the damage. Despite the loss of life on both sides, I'd been relieved the Resistance were finally making a big gesture. But now to hear so many of them had been caught? Forty must severely deplete their numbers! And what if 'key players' meant Dad? My stomach shrivelled. I pushed away the soup that the slave girl had just placed before me and glugged back more wine. Trying to keep the strain from my voice, I turned to Audley. 'Who were the key players?'

'Nobodies . . .' he said. 'Mostly young men and women who don't understand what we're trying to do here.'

'Who don't deserve to be in Land. Selection is too good for them.'

I whipped my glare back to Syon at the sound of his voice. He was now slurping at his soup with satisfaction.

'Ignore them.' Tobin's whisper was back in my ear. 'They don't know how to have fun.' He refilled my glass.

Again, I knocked it back. But not to chase the kind of fun he probably had in mind. To stem the rising panic threatening to disarm me. Instead, all I got was the beginnings of a headache. I leant forward and grabbed a bread roll, biting into it to mop up the pool of alcohol in my empty stomach.

Syon was commenting silkily to Audley, 'Youth. Why is it always the youth who need to fight back?'

'Present company excepted, of course.' Bea, at the opposite end to Audley, made one of her wide beams round the table.

Audley gave a weary sigh. 'I suppose the old realise what life is really about: to live is to survive, not to dream.'

'Hear, hear,' Syon said, eyelids shut, his fingers fluffing up the fine hair that was starting to flag above his forehead.

'But what is so wrong with dreaming?'

Everyone looked over at Ella, sitting quietly between Audley and me. Over this week I'd often heard her ask the defiant questions I couldn't, in her soft, yet solid little voice. She reminded me a little of Kara at the same age, when the fire was starting to catch.

Audley panned out his hands at his daughter. 'Dreams belong to the Old World, Ella, my dear. We now conduct our lives in a war with nature, our enemy. The sea is waiting at our boundaries, a constant threat to our existence – Land is no place for dreamers. We have to live by nature's rules: only the fittest can survive.'

Or the richest, I thought, narrowing my eyes at Syon. The effect of the wine was making me forget any vague act of respectful stepdaughter. I caught Stella make a small gesture; a shake of her head, a warning not to mess with her pair. I defied her; and glared at him a little longer.

'At least the civilians who got killed in the bombing were all from East Land.' It was Tom speaking, in a tone that imitated his father. His anaemic brown hair had recently been cut incredibly short. It made his thin face look more severe. He laughed. 'In the survival of the fittest, what do the citizens of *East* Land matter?'

'My father is proposing we get more brutal with students. That's where the problem starts after all.' I looked round sharply at Astral's Pair. His top lip was screwing up over his words. I didn't know his name. He had arrogantly introduced himself as 792569. It was thanks to Salinger, forcing me to memorise numbers, that I could still recall it.

He continued, leaning enthusiastically towards Audley, 'You've probably heard – as Director of Security at the Education Department, my father's trialling the installation of Youth Troopers across the institutes next week.'

Maybe it was the way I was staring at him that made his eyes meet mine.

'You're a student being mentored for a senior state position?' His voice was haughty, hanging off a sneer. 'What do you think? The best students chosen to catch the worst – flush out the *ringleaders* before they have the chance to emerge?'

I pictured Kara targeted, surrounded by a hungry band of his Youth Troopers. 'Serious intentions beget serious punishment,' I said, without a thread of emotion, while inside a new inner voice I didn't entirely recognise raged, *I will kill your father before your kind gets to touch my friend.*

It was over. I only had to get through this charade of goodbyes and I could take the curve of a staircase back to my bedroom, away from them all. Solitude.

'I was just saying to your mother how pleased she must be with you – to have 454111 guiding your career into government. Such opportunities happen to a very small minority,' Audley said, steering Stella over to me as he helped her on with her coat. I sometimes wondered if Audley was trying to work out what had singled me out. He was just too polite to ask.

'One, I call him. And yes, he is very attentive . . . like a father to me,' I replied archly for Stella's benefit, watching her face to see if the lie did anything.

'You know, the Leader himself had a mentor: the previous Leader. Made him give up his family so he could become Head of State Troopers.'

'So I heard,' I said and glanced at Stella. Because she *knew* – she had always known. The Leader – her ex-Pair's father. 'Leadership is nothing if not full of personal sacrifice for the greater good.'

'Spoken like a true potential leader yourself,' Audley stated rousingly and stepped away from us both.

Stella started buttoning up her coat. She gave me a strange, slanted look as she uttered a quiet, 'Well, goodbye then,' and bent in to air-kiss around my cheeks.

I noticed her eyes straining, as if she were trying hard to focus on me. I thought it might be the wine on her part too, until they widened unnecessarily, as if she wanted to say something she couldn't. Then it struck me. A spasm of fear shot through my veins. All these odd glances, the words she used: were they warnings?

. . . What if Stella had been aware right back then, when she abandoned her two-year-old daughter? The plan that Cons was weaving for me?

Was she watching for it now? Checking to see what I was up to? What if she informed Syon?

I licked my lips then parted them, looking for the words that would best convey my suspicion. 'When you left me with Cons . . .' I said quietly, letting it hang there, as if in those six words were buried all I needed to ask of her. I wasn't expecting her reaction. Her eyes flashed back at me, with a fury I'd never witnessed from Stella before.

It was only when she gave her answer that I realised. It wasn't me she was angry with.

'You mean – when Cons *stole* you.'

Chapter Fifteen

My tracer bleeped me awake – there was no chance to nurse my hangover from last night's wine. One had sent me a message: he wanted me in his office, *now*.

I got dressed quickly – in what, I didn't care; I'd already syphoned off half of my new clothes to Kara. The look of privilege – she needed it more than me.

Cons stole you. Stella's words wouldn't stop following me as I brushed my teeth, as I grabbed an early breakfast in the dining room, alone but for the quiet shadow of the slave. I didn't want to but I would have to go and see her, demand an explanation – what she meant; what she knew. Why she would say that?

My post-wine headache was worsening, echoing my dread as I dragged myself across the Green Mile. One summoning me into the Cross so early on a Saturday could only mean one of two things. I was to meet my grandfather, or they had an assignment for me. I wasn't sure which was worse.

My clothes, the way I was starting to hold myself (no one in Central Land felt the need to lower their eyes or mark their expressions with humility), meant the cluster of State

Troopers at the Cross main entrance let me through with only a cursory check.

I'd not been invited to One's office before, but I knew exactly where it was. The maps Salinger had since destroyed were branded in my memory.

Salinger was there, at a desk by the door. I knew he worked from One's office; as a Grey he'd have to work Saturdays even if One didn't. But it still took me off guard. I sucked in my breath, replying a purposefully clipped 'Hello' to his.

'Come, Christy.' One beckoned me over to him. I felt Salinger's eyes on me as I crossed the room. It was a large office but sparsely decorated; typical of One – blank, white-painted walls; his desk, sprawling blue metal, uncluttered except for a boxed computer screen, his tracer, a pad of paper and a sharpened pencil – lined up, as if awaiting his inspection. As I reached him he nodded, picked up the pencil and flipped it between his fingers. Then he bent over the pad and scribbled on it.

Time to meet Grandpa was written in small, tight script. My chest tightened, despite having half-anticipated it. One watched me, waiting for my answer. I gave it with a curt head tick.

Another scribble on the pad. This time: *Keep calm – follow instinct. Make him care.*

One's sad eyes flexed; I nodded stiffly.

Opening a drawer in his desk, he took out a box of matches and promptly lit one. Tearing off the piece of paper, he lit it at the corner, tossing it into a blue metal bin as its edges curled black. My insides seemed to burn with it.

I had to make little skips in my stride to keep up with One as

171

we approached the broad staircase at the far end of a corridor. Here, suddenly the floor became covered in white carpet as soft and springy as animal fur. I tried to stay at One's heels as we climbed up to the next floor, a pair of black painted double doors at its far end.

A thin Blue woman with pale, choppily cut hair, was sitting behind a desk outside. '454111, is the Leader expecting you?' she asked in a raspy voice, then drew suspicious eyes up and down me. 'And who is this . . .?'

'The Leader will understand,' One replied and stalked to the door, rapping his fist loudly before the secretary could stop him.

On a growl of 'Yes?' we entered.

The room beyond was four times the size of One's – and immaculately dressed: on its white walls neatly hung state posters from over the decades, black-and-white printed messages reminding citizens how to conduct themselves, live their lives, accept their fate.

He was standing behind a black, leather-topped desk, staring out of a large semicircular window behind. It overlooked the Green Mile, and beyond: I could see the spread of South Land tenement blocks past the flat roof of its Assessment Centre. A view enclosed by a sky so pale blue, it seemed to bleed into the edges of the fat, feathered clouds sailing through it.

Gradually he turned. He saw me. And stalled. Two animals assessing one another.

The man I'd watched on citizenship films; the man whose hand had sealed my Pairing to Tobin. He wasn't expecting me.

The Leader of Land.

My grandfather.

'Leave us.' I heard his voice crackle through the space between us. He directed his stare at two State Troopers I hadn't even noticed, standing behind us, guarding either side of the door.

Once it had shut on them he stared frostily at One. 'What is this?'

'She knows.'

Those penetrating eyes of his narrowed.

One kept his own wide as he lied. 'I didn't tell her . . . she guessed for herself. I thought you'd want to be informed immediately.'

My grandfather's gaze switched to me. I answered as One had primed me to, 'Your number was on my grandmother's wrist.'

The Leader twisted his mouth, enlarging his eyes in a look of arrogant despair. 'She promised me she would remove it.'

'She didn't.'

I watched him. Waiting. For what? What was I searching for? A link? A spark of connection? Love? Hate? Something? Anything? An undercurrent of feeling that might be hiding within the sharp packaging of his fitted Black suit; lodged in the fissures of lines scoring his lightly tanned skin: I was directly related to this man.

He drew his head up, the light from the window glinting off the short grey hair that covered his scalp like metal to a magnet. His tongue dug around in his back teeth; hostile ruminations seemed evident in his eyes. Finally he rolled his shoulders back. 'Christabel,' he said simply, starkly.

Christabel. I thought of that message on my tracer, his comment at the Pairing. He liked to use my name.

Did I mean something to him already?

The Leader's fingers plucked at his lips as he brought himself around his desk, slow strides across the thick white carpet, until he was standing close to me. His gaze travelled from the hair on my scalp down to the heels of my shoes. His eyes – the piercing green that were mine, eyes that Cons had said had been my dad's – scrutinising every detail of me as if he were considering an important purchase.

I wanted to speak as he began circling me; I wanted to shout, to ask a million questions that were tumbling into my mind, spreading like wildfire. Yet I stayed mute. I wasn't here to demand truths. I was here to make my grandfather let me in. To make the Leader trust me.

His eyes returned to my face. I swallowed. Was it part of my act – the reflex that made me lift a hand, to reach out to touch him, the sleeve of his coal-Black jacket, his chest, his cheek, any bit of him? To know this was real. This was my grandfather.

He stepped back before the tips of my fingers found him. His voice came out more distinct, devoid of any tinge of emotion. 'Know this – I have no intention of declaring our relationship to anyone. It is irrelevant. I won't risk any public connections with your father. I left my family behind a long time ago, and it has served me well.'

'I understand.' My voice came out at a distance.

'Do you? I cleansed you of your history, alongside mine. The last Leader permitted me to delete Hogan from both our files. You see what I have done for you? You have always simply been an old woman's granddaughter; a descendant of one of Land's founders. Your father never even breathed.'

I drew my own breath in sharply, fists furling. Out of the corner of my eye I glimpsed One's gaze straining, silently reminding me: *Contain yourself*. A thin line of sweat was coursing down his temple.

But I had to let something out. I kept my voice light, the tightness lodging firmly beneath my throat. 'Your son.'

The Leader made a short bark of a laugh, pushing his head back so I could see the black of his gaping mouth. Then he drew it back level. 'What does that even mean? Hogan started hating me and what I stood for from twelve years old; well before I was made Head of State Troopers. I was no loss to him as a father, he made that clear. I have no family. I stand alone.'

He retreated back to his side of the desk, the window behind framing his head and shoulders, before he added, 'Now you have guessed our connection, maybe you will also have deduced the reason for your sudden, stellar rise in the ranks. Naturally, I have engineered it.'

I held myself straight, uttered a simple, 'I see; I am grateful.' *Make him care*. 'You have made the right decision . . . Grandfather.'

The Leader gave a grunt of contempt at the last word, then slanted his head. 'Let's not confuse what I've done with grandfatherly affection. It's because I can trust only my own DNA to continue the work I am doing, to further what I have achieved.' He scoffed through his nose. 'After all, it's the first rule of survival to leave behind your gene pool when you go.'

'And yet you are using my name, not my number,' I replied in a heartbeat.

I held my head steady. Did my quarter of his DNA mean

that much to him? Was he forgetting that half of his genes went rogue?

His returning smile seemed to have some warmth to it. The possibilities pricked at my skin. I needed to remind myself: I was playing a part. This was an act, getting this impervious man to acknowledge me as his kin – wasn't it?

'I use your name because I want to. There may be no room for attachments here; we have work to do, but you still have my blood – good blood – running through your veins.' His head slanted in the opposite direction as if he were gauging different impressions of me. 'I have been very pleased to hear of your progress from 454111. Your grandmother kept that promise at least . . .'

'She brought me up to be loyal to Land . . . till the day she met her Selection.'

Did I imagine it, or did some deeper emotion cross his face? A softness? 'Yes, I was glad she kept her side of the bargain.

'So – you know who I am. Fine.' The Leader tapped a finger against dry lips. 'I must ask you then: are you ready, Christabel?' He pushed his head forward over the wide desk, staring into my eyes as if he wanted to see through them. 'Are you up to the task? To work for me, to shadow me, learn from me? To prove yourself worthy, able, of sitting at my right hand?'

'I am,' I answered steadily; pushing away a recurring thought: I'm *to kill this man*.

'Are you ambitious to take up the reins of leadership of Land one day?'

'I am.'

One fidgeted next to me. Clearly he hadn't expected this

176

measure of success so soon. 'She has been brought up for this moment,' he said, recovering himself.

'Hmm.' The Leader's eyes flickered out of the window, then back at me. 'Well, seeing as you have found out the truth about us, I think there's no point waiting until you graduate from the Institute. You might as well start straight away. It's safer that way. For all concerned. To keep you close.'

His tanned, creased face pulled into a rigid smile, but his head slanted again, as if he was still working out if I fitted the bill. 'But I can't stress it enough: no one must know of our relationship, only that I have hand-picked you based on your natural abilities, your academic achievement, for future leadership.'

I straightened taller, stiffening my features. I nodded.

'You will honour me.'

The last sentence was an order, delivered with a ferocity that said: I have no choice.

'And when I tell you the time is right – you and your Pair will have a child. Our line, our inherited brilliance, will continue.'

My mouth opened and closed; I had no words to meet that.

'Now I have work to do. And you need to start to prepare yourself for yours.'

'I will see to it,' One interjected. His hand reached out and clenched my arm in a tight grip. Clearly he was anxious I might ruin it at the last moment; he steered me quickly across the white carpet, back towards the black double doors.

I caught a grunt of assent behind us before the Leader's voice carried over the expanse of the room. 'I expect great things from you, Christabel.'

I let out a sigh, only audible to myself. Didn't everyone?

Chapter Sixteen

'It went well. She's been made a Blue already. We can start,' One said under his breath to Salinger as we re-entered his office.

I followed One back to his desk. 'Wait, you hoped he'd make me a Blue?'

'Hoped . . . anticipated – nothing's ever certain,' he said. 'You can start here next week; I'll get you your own office beneath his.' He tore off another piece of paper from his pad; writing quickly, he pushed it to me.

The Leader must confide in you. We want knowledge. When I nodded, he bent and scribbled again. *Now, you can do more – remove a key target.* My blood went cold. I didn't move. An assignment to kill? It seemed a poor prize for winning my grandfather over.

I watched him crumple up the paper into a tight ball, setting it on fire and throwing it into the metal bin like before; the flames licking high as if they were hungry for more.

'Right now: you go with Salinger for instruction; don't let us down.' One jerked his head at Salinger. 'Go – the both of you. Get to work.'

I turned, blithely following Salinger towards the door. I

was a Blue. I was to work with my grandfather. I was about to undertake my first assassination. It was too much, too soon. It was as if the fog already enveloping me was becoming denser . . . I only had One and Salinger to light the way – two people who cared little for me. They were double agents – for all I knew they could turn triple . . . I spun on the spot, strode back to One's side and whispered close to the side of his face, 'I saw my mother for dinner last night.'

One pulled his chin down, inclined his head, but said nothing.

'She made an accusation. She said Cons stole me.' I paused to steady my voice. 'What did she mean?'

He drew his hands wide across the empty desk. 'When Hogan . . . was disgraced, your grandfather deemed your mother unfit to raise you. He didn't trust her.' He let his voice trail off, made a small twist of his stiff neck.

He didn't like emotion from me, his mechanical soldier. I pushed my face in front of his. 'Stella never gave me up?'

One looked at me, his eyes impeaching, *What does it matter?* 'As well you now know, mothers tend to be reluctant to give up their children,' he offered tersely.

I pulled back from him. The allusion to Kara stunned me. One knew that Kara was still refusing to take the appointment he'd arranged for her. How could he draw a parallel with Stella? 'But my mother let Cons take me?'

Suddenly his eyes flashed with a hint of rare feeling. 'Don't you understand the choices we have to make? That Stella had to make? It was between dying fighting for you or living to see you. Which would you choose?'

I felt like a fist had rocketed into my stomach. Stella had

179

never let me go?

I had despised my mother – all these years – for something she wasn't guilty of?

'Salinger, will you take Christy now?'

I twisted round and gave Salinger daggers, as if everything was his fault. If I could kill with my eyes alone, I would already have a death on my hands.

We remained silent as we walked across the Green Mile. Salinger kept shooting glances my way, but I wouldn't meet them. The sun was taking the edge off the cold, but I had my arms wrapped round my body as if it were frozen. I needed to find a way to manage the battle inside me.

I didn't want my heart to melt towards Stella; that wouldn't help. And Cons? She stole a child from its mother? Then the Leader. What were my feelings about *him*? To kill the grandfather I'd thought already dead? I had to work harder to rid myself of emotion altogether. Encase my heart in concrete.

'Just over there,' Salinger said, pointing ahead at a house – whitewashed walls and a grey slate roof. He was taking me to One's. A few roads along from Audley and Bea's, his house appeared modest in comparison – single level and squat – but it was still in the coveted southern area of Central Land. A black-painted garage was attached to one side. Salinger led me into it, via a back door that he locked behind us.

'To anyone else, I'm giving you driving lessons.' He indicated One's black stocky car on the concrete floor as if it were part of our secret meeting. 'You can take it for a spin once we're done, to look legit. One thinks you should learn to drive anyway.'

I nodded eagerly, losing myself for a moment in the idea of being able to get behind the wheel.

'But first let's get on with the practical stuff, recap defence moves. Then we'll talk over your first assignment, okay?'

We sat, both of us breathless, in the front bench seat of One's car. Still stationary, the windows were steaming up from our body heat. Across the garage floor, we'd spent an hour going over every conceivable defence and attack tactic that might help me. I'd concentrated like I'd never done before. I had to; I knew now what was coming. Every move Salinger reminded me of – a neck lock, a sharp knee to the groin, a stab of fingers into eye sockets – it might make the difference between my life and someone else's death.

I'd fallen over so many times I could feel bruises staining my skin already. My stomach, winded repeatedly, ached now as if I were hungry. Yet I found myself emitting a faint glow of pleasure when Salinger, his arms draped forward over the steering wheel, turned to me and said, 'You did well.'

I shifted uncomfortably, unused to praise from him. 'I've no choice but to do well – if I want to stay alive.'

'You're going to be doing a great thing. Land will thank you.'

I bit the inside of my mouth and nodded.

'Just remember, certain people need to die, if life is to get better for –'

'Who is it?' I interrupted him. 'I mean, thanks and all that, but I don't need the pep talk. Stop pussyfooting around – tell me who it is you want me to kill, and when.'

Salinger looked into my eyes. 'Okay.' He arched his eyebrows. 'They're appointing a new Head of State Troopers. The last

181

one died, if you recall: shot by a "rebel" when he was called out to the East Land power station bombing . . .'

I glanced at him; his face was still. 'I remember.' I caught the look in Salinger's eyes. 'Was that you?'

Salinger didn't answer; a twitch of his head did it for him. He leant across me and flipped open the car's glove box, taking out a small wallet; inside, one blue pill. 'You'll be using one of these. One's glad you've been made Blue, because it will mean he can get you invited to this new guy's inauguration, Wednesday evening.'

Four nights' time. I had only four nights to prepare. 'Too soon – I'm not ready,' I said aloud before I could stop myself. But it was the truth – I wasn't ready: I'd not yet found the killer inside me.

Salinger drew a long breath through his nose. 'The first time is the hardest. It will get easier. Think of it as hardening up for the big one: the Leader. It's not going to be easy, I know.'

I blew out my cheeks. 'You can leave it at information only, okay?'

Salinger started tapping his thumb against the steering wheel. 'I'm just saying . . . I know One's asking a lot of you – to take out your own flesh and blood.'

'And how would you know?' I replied, beginning to blithely examine my nails to show him they were more interesting than his opinion.

'I don't, I can only imagine.'

'Do you even do that? Imagine? You and One, you're just Resistance machines. You've even both managed to escape Pairing.' I bristled at myself for my childish, petulant tone of voice; it was always too easy to take out my tension on Salinger.

'I've never been Paired because I'm a Grey, with a shady past that, unlike you, 454111 couldn't erase. And 454111? His father made him become a State Trooper when he turned seventeen. He only got out when he was charged by your grandfather to take on Resistance surveillance work instead.'

'One . . . was a Trooper?'

'Don't knock him,' Salinger growled back. 'It wasn't his fault. What could he do? What can any of us do when choices are made for us? *His* father – your grandfather's brother – when he was alive . . . he was a brute. Makes the Leader look like a cuddly animal in comparison. You know the real reason 454111 never mentions his name?'

'One chooses numbers over names.'

'It's not a choice if he hasn't got a name. His father wasn't into them. His father wasn't much into sons either.'

I made a face, starting to feel a little foolish for my outburst. I tried to see One as a nameless child: it was hard; there was so little in One's demeanour to suggest a childhood. Except for those sloping, sad eyes.

Salinger lifted his shoulders matter of factly. 'My mother used to call him One.'

'What?' I prickled, despite the intriguing revelation. For some reason I felt cross with myself.

'Yeah. My mother and One . . . were –'

'They were together?'

Salinger chewed his lip. 'They met when I was two. Began an unapproved affair. Back when he was a Trooper.' He rested

183

his chin on top of his hands on the steering wheel, gazing out the car window at the back of the garage door as if there was a landscape there.

'Why did it end?'

'She died.'

'Selection?'

Salinger chose not to answer. Instead he said, 'My mum chose the name for him, One. Besides you, she was the only person to call him it.'

I swallowed. I didn't want to feel sorry for One; I didn't want to feel sorry for Salinger. I didn't want to feel bad about using One as a name. I moved awkwardly in my seat. 'I didn't realise,' I said, trying to keep the sting out of my voice. It seeped through anyway. 'I won't call him that any more, if you don't like it.'

Salinger let out a pithy, dry laugh. 'Funnily enough, I have started to like it. Mum would have wanted people to name him. That's why she did. He was much more than a number to her.'

I coughed, trying to clear the bite from my tongue. This version of their shared background . . . I was finding it hard to digest. *Because it didn't include me?* 'So that's how you know each other?'

Salinger splayed his hands across the steering wheel; his forehead all screwed up as if some memory he was replaying wasn't a pleasant one. 'I was six when she died; One promised her he'd take care of me . . . he got me a place in a state orphanage – made sure I graduated from South Land Institute, even though I'd got tied up in the Resistance . . . He secured me a job in government, to protect me from arrest.'

184

Already, I'd swapped the picture of One as a child for Salinger. It was easier to draw – dark-eyed, unruly curly brown hair, holding on tightly to the hand of the larger, sturdier One.

'He made sure I survived. He's a good man.'

I raised my eyebrows.

'Really, he is. He's hard work – well, you know that – but . . . He has a strong sense of duty. He felt he had a responsibility for me.'

Salinger glanced at me, a fleeting, tight grimace pasted across his mouth that reminded me of Cons. When she wanted me to know a conversation was now closed.

'You need to be ready for Wednesday. We're counting on you.' He changed the subject. His mouth was set in lecturing mode again, but the eyes that grazed over mine seemed to have an apology attached to them.

'Wednesday,' I repeated. Suddenly even the sound of the day had changed.

'If nothing else, just make sure you stay alive,' Salinger said.

Stay alive. What if I didn't? My blood went cold. I took in a breath. 'Can I ask you a favour?'

'You sure you've got the right person?'

I made a face back at him. 'Believe me, if I could ask anyone else, I would.'

'Nice; go on.'

'Our deal – if anything happens to me on Wednesday, will you still look out for my friend Kara – and her baby?'

'One's given you the name of his contact. There's nothing more we can do.'

'Yes, but, if I get caught . . . will you help her?'

185

'Sure, I'll give her my advice: hot baths; falling down stairs; knitting needles . . . '

I drew away from him, my face flashing with outrage.

'Well, how do you propose I help her?' Salinger gripped the steering wheel. 'She needs to get rid of it; if she won't, you have to distance yourself from her. If you're not to jeopardise your work with us.'

I couldn't translate his tone, whether he really meant what he said or not. He'd spoken without feeling, as far as I could tell. I was stupid to have thought this insight into his and One's past meant they owned any proper emotions.

I had to grit my teeth to keep my voice low. 'I am doing *your* work to protect *my* friend. She's more important to me . . . than any of this.'

Salinger watched me, examining me, his mouth twitching familiarly between bemusement and annoyance. 'Nothing is more important than the work we are doing. Our lives don't matter – haven't you cottoned on to that yet?'

My eventual quiet reply of 'Yes,' seemed to subdue him.

He breathed out, lifting his palms from the wheel. 'No one can help Kara if she won't help herself.' His impenetrable eyes did a search of mine, but frantically this time. 'If she goes ahead with the birth, the baby will be stripped away from her. Kara will be branded with the mark of the brothels – until she's too old . . . or no longer serviceable, whichever comes first. Then it's Selection – you know that, Christy. There is no other way of looking at it. Get your friend's head out of West Land's smog. Tell her to wake up and smell the shit. Abortion – it's the only choice she has.' He had removed his hands from the steering wheel and was twisting them together as if he were trying to fend off the cold. I had never seen him so agitated. 'Kara does not want to end up in the brothels, believe me. There is no finer hell than one of those places.'

I stared at him, momentarily forgetting my anger. 'How do you know what the brothels are like?'

He glanced at my expression and then hurriedly added, 'No, not like that. My mother was . . . my mum was sent there. Visiting her brothel, it was the only way I got to see her, before –'

'You were an unapproved baby?'

A grey shadow moved over Salinger's face, as if every light had just gone out. 'No. I wasn't the unapproved one of her children.'

He watched me again, but it wasn't with a smile this time. His lips stretched out thinly, his eyes focusing ahead. End of conversation.

Chapter Seventeen

I was a Blue. Just like that. Bea had busied herself on Sunday buying outfits for me.

I'd been at work since yesterday.

And tomorrow – tomorrow I'd be a murderer.

I lay in bed and repeated my latest mantra. *Kill one to save thousands.* Land took those we loved. I was to take back. This wasn't murder. I was setting wrongs right.

I only had to work on believing it now.

I forced myself up, showered. Dressed in one of the many Blue dresses Bea had forced upon me, and went down into the dining room, hoping to grab breakfast then make a quick exit. Instead I walked headlong into an argument between Bea and Tobin.

'Because it's not what I want to do!'

'Want? It's about what you *have* to do.' Bea's voice was quiet compared to Tobin's. His mouth uncommonly twisted, it loosened a little when he saw me; his eyes rolling upwards. He wanted me onside.

Clearly so did Bea. 'Christy, work some sense into my boy will you? He's saying he won't take a job in government!'

'Mum,' Ella let out a quiet entreaty. 'Tobin doesn't see things like you do.'

Bea flashed a glare at her daughter. 'Stay out of it, young lady. Your opinions are already causing you enough trouble with your tutors.'

Ella made a sigh of exasperation. She was doing a lot of those lately.

'Tell him, Christy!' Bea pulled a face at me.

I chose the furthest chair from any of them. 'But Tobin won't know his job for another few months?' I said, purposely evasive, filling my mug from the teapot on the table before the slave girl did it for me.

'Oh, we know what Tobin's job will be – after all the legwork we've put in,' Bea replied.

'I thought it was based on your genes, and academic achievement?' I stated blithely. Like I didn't know by now that was only half the story.

'Right; but there's also a column entitled Loyalty. Tobin comes from respectable, hard-working stock. Like you do.'

I almost choked on the hot tea. Bea wasn't mean. But she was ignorant. I half listened as Tobin returned to the main thrust of his argument, a plea I'd heard before. 'I don't want to work in government, Mum! Listen to me! I want a job in farming. I won't be trapped behind some desk all day like you and Dad.'

I poured some cereal into my bowl and ate hurriedly. However endearing Tobin's lack of political ambition might be, I had no time for his trifling problems; nor the head space to care.

* * *

'Walk with you?' Tobin caught up with me at the front door, shoving things into his Institute satchel.

'But you go the opposite direction to the Cross.' I tried to disguise my reluctance.

'I don't mind,' he shrugged. 'I have some time before registration.'

I swung the strap of my own satchel across my body and began to walk. I could have started using any one of the work bags Bea had supplied me with; but for some reason it felt strange getting rid of my satchel. I'd been a student for over thirteen years. I still felt like one, beneath this surface Blue.

We both began shrugging off our coats the moment we got outside; I lifted my face to the sun, favouring its warmth over conversation.

The Cross was in sight by the time Tobin started one. 'Now you're going to be earning, we should definitely find our own place, Christy, okay?'

I didn't answer, keeping my eyes fixed ahead.

'Listen, I know things have been tough for you, losing your grandmother, moving in with us . . . I think a fresh start might help us.'

I sniffed and made a face in answer that could have meant anything.

'At least humour me with discussing it!' he said, almost as hotly as he had spoken to Bea before. 'You've got to start giving me something, Christy. We're a Pair! Don't keep me at arm's length. Stop this ice-queen act!'

I halted abruptly, rounding on him. A spoilt boy's tantrum. I had no time for his dream world. Tonight I had to kill a man!

'*You* stop with this ridiculous idea of moving out. You don't know how easy you've got it!'

He raised his hands in the air. 'Whoa there; she speaks.'

I pushed my neck forward. 'Don't you realise you are one of the lucky ones? Even your sister Ella gets that! You've no idea what's going on outside your idyllic bubble!' I didn't wait for his answer. I'd said too much; he'd forced me to make cracks in my mask. If anyone had heard me . . . I glanced around – there was no one close. I took my eyes back to his. His response to my outburst shone there. Nothing about Tobin was closed off.

I made a sound of despair and started to stalk away; I wasn't going to feel bad. Maybe he needed to get hurt. At least he wasn't still trotting alongside me, so I had accomplished something. I moved faster to chase off all feeling . . . I couldn't be responsible for giving Tobin a happy-ever-after. People were dying every day through Selection for no other reason than the wrong opinions or poor health. I rushed on into the Cross lobby, flashing my eyes at the Troopers, daring them to stop me. They wouldn't now I was a Blue. One of the elite. The untouchables.

'Come with me.'

He'd been standing in my doorway for a good few seconds. I had purposely not raised my eyes from the policy document on my desk to meet his. It was One who had instructed me to keep my door open always. The office One had found for me was at the bottom of the staircase the Leader used to access his own suite of rooms. He got a view of me each time.

I glanced up as he spoke, affecting surprise that he was there.

'Where to?' I smiled.

He scowled. 'Bring pencil and paper. You will need to take notes.'

I grabbed both and followed him down the corridor. It was what One had anticipated – that I would be invited to shadow the Leader.

But I wasn't prepared for the meetings I was forced to observe. A series of interviews for a new post my grandfather had secretly created – the Head of Population Control. A role to lead his soon to be announced policy: the Culling.

After I'd been released, I clock-watched until it was a respectable time to leave. I should have made immediate arrangements to update One, away from the Cross. But I was more concerned for Kara. The Leader was initiating severe plans to get rid of *'undesirables'*. Kara wouldn't survive any new cull of the unfit; soon her secret would be worn like a beacon on her protruding belly. I had to try one last time to make her get rid of it – in case, after tomorrow night, I never had another chance.

I hadn't seen Kara since Sunday morning – and then only briefly, when I'd taken the tram to hers to tell her I'd be leaving the Institute, becoming a Blue. Kara had been distracted. She'd not even pressed me for her own part in the Resistance for once; as that baby grew, her mind had a new preoccupation.

'Hey, stop! Come here! You – stop.'

The collective shouts flew out on the air before I'd even reached the Institute's tall metal gates. The bell had just rung when I saw them: Youth Troopers. They must have been instated just yesterday. Already, West Land Institute had started its witch-hunt.

Their Black trousers and jackets mimicked the State Troopers – minus the helmet, the gun. Thin Black neckerchiefs were tied under their chins; a red fabric star on arms inscribed with their slogan: *Damn or be Damned.*

I watched them hassling particular students as they left, their prey apparent – those with tatty clothes, with badly cut hair, the ones whose eyes darted nervously. Four thick-set brutes nearest to me had collared two young boys, teasing them on their shabby Green appearance.

'Say it again!' one Youth Trooper with shorn fair hair growled, knocking off the smaller boy's glasses. 'I heard you whisper it. You disrespected Land; I heard you!'

Another echoed him. 'You say it again!'

The two boys' faces swung round in frightened denial as the Youth Troopers closed the circle around them; their thick bodies obscuring the boys from my view as if they were swallowing them whole.

My body twitched to move. Why? What could I do? Nothing!

I felt the twist in my stomach loosen when I finally spotted Kara. At last, she was finally following the code I'd always nagged her to: eyes down but her head held level. A smile fixed. Though she had to be hot in that thick coat of Tobin's. I'd stolen it from him last week; it was roomy enough to keep her changing figure concealed.

'Christy!' Her mouth broke into a quiet smile as she reached me, though her eyes struggled to match it. The Youth Trooper shouts were growing around us. Greens were rushing to get out unnoticed.

'I'm going to come home with you,' I said, trying to make

my face appear nonchalant, so she wouldn't guess my reason why. Kara nodded, her gaze fidgeting. I tried to keep her eyes on me. I could tell she was itching to intervene; stop the Youth Troopers from their worst. 'Let's go.' I pulled her away.

I insisted we go get provisions first, using the points card Bea kept regularly topped up for me. The old Kara wouldn't have been keen on handouts from Blue elites but her attitude had changed; she was trying to protect that thing growing inside of her. For the same reason, she let me treat her to a tram ride all the way back to hers.

We spent time cooking together in Kara's thin galley kitchen – it almost felt like the old days. I was glad I'd restocked her cupboards; all they'd had left were a few carrots, some grain and a palm-sized piece of cured goat. I had to keep a better check on her, before she starved.

Taking our bowls of stew into her bedroom, we sat down to eat on her low mattress.

I started to fill Kara in on the last two days, my food lodging in my throat as I whispered to her about the party I was attending tomorrow night; my eyes finishing my sentence, 'I have a mission.'

'Once I'm me again –' her hand circled her bloated stomach – 'remind them I'm ready to fight with you.'

I couldn't eat the rest of my food. I placed my bowl on the floor. Her comment was my cue. I licked my lips, preparing a lie, my last resort. 'Well, actually, you could join the fight now. I've got the go-ahead for you. They want you in.'

I watched my friend's face brighten at my last remark; regret stabbed at me, but I couldn't lose faith now. I might be dead by tomorrow – I had to hold on to the end goal: to keep Kara safe, alive. 'You're needed, Kara . . .'

'Yes, yes, tell them yes, Christy! But delay it, I mean.' She made a little shrug. 'I can't right now, what with this inside, encumbering me . . . but once the baby's born . . .'

'No, Kara, we can't wait. The war needs to be fought right this moment. Think about it. If you weren't pregnant . . . If you give this baby up . . . then we can fight together. We can –'

Kara's shoulders rolled back; she glared at me, her head tipped sideways, as she placed her bowl down beside mine. 'Don't! Christy, don't! I told you last time – I won't hear it again!'

I swallowed, working out my next move. 'It's not too late . . . You're only a few months gone –'

'I said, no!' Kara stood up suddenly, her hands tapping agitatedly against her legs.

I stared up at the underside of her swelling stomach, then got up too.

'But how are you going to hide the pregnancy from Troopers and tutors? How will you hide the baby when it comes?' I kept my voice to a low hum when really I wanted to shout. Why couldn't she get it? Why wouldn't she see? 'Kara, no one – *no one* in Land can hide an unapproved baby! Even the Blues face punishment if they don't obey childbirth policy.'

'I will find a way . . . I have to find a way. It is my baby.'

I raked fingers through my hair, twisting it nervously round my neck. This thing in her: it was the enemy. 'Kara, you have no other choice. I don't want to frighten you . . . but there's going to be a new policy – a culling of . . . undesirables. When that kicks off, if anyone even faintly suspects you of being pregnant, you can forget about facing a lifetime in a brothel – it will mean automatic Selection. Destroy the baby before it destroys you!'

Kara's head lurched at my last words, her mouth gagging as if she were about to be sick.

I hated this baby; it was killing her already. I had to protect my friend from it. I had to find more words to fire like ammunition. 'It's not even a human being yet. It doesn't think, or love . . . it won't feel any pain . . . It's just a blob of DNA. It's nothing!'

A low moan fell from between Kara's dry lips. 'What's happened to you?' She raised her palms flat in the air, as if she were creating a wall between us.

I ignored the gesture, shifting even closer to her. 'You've got to listen to me. That baby will weaken you and it will kill you. It is a parasite – stopping you from living.'

The slap hit me like a cold wind against my cheek; the sound of a door slamming; so fast that for a moment I hadn't realised it had come from Kara's own hand. My fists rose, tightening; what all my training had taught me, a guttural reaction to any attack: to hit back.

'You're going to thump me? Beat me, pummel me, into doing what you want? This time I won't do it.' Kara's lips curled, revealing her top teeth. 'For years, since Mum and Dad died, I've gone along with your version of how I should act. What *you* want! How *you* want me to behave! And I've done it so you wouldn't worry; so I stayed safe – for *you*! That's what it's always been about! Christy's way of doing things! Preventing me from helping those in need! From making a difference! All those times you've held me back from getting involved in a fight. You would never let me risk my life. Well you won't stop me this time!'

I lowered my fists, moving my hand to cover the sting on my face. 'Kara, no; listen!' I had done this all wrong.

'I want you to go now. I need you to leave.'

'I just want to protect you.'

'No! No, Christy, that isn't it. You want to protect some idea of what I am to you! I can't be your dad and Cons and your best friend all rolled up. I am me! Kara! With two dead parents and little to live for . . . until now! This is *my* life; this is *my* choice. The risk I take is mine. I want you to go. I don't want to see you here again. You're no longer part of my life. I don't know you any more.'

Her face was wild; the same look she wore when she witnessed the atrocities of the State. She was seeing me like one of them.

'I said, go, Christy! We fight in different ways! . . . I never want to see you again!'

Chapter Eighteen

Wednesday. I was hovering near the drinks table under the guise of listening to some group of Blue women extolling the benefits of gender-specific jobs. The most verbose was now expounding her views on slave workers. 'We have to accept men have attributes different to women. Household slaves must be female. It annoys me when –'

I tuned out of what annoyed her. Like I'd finally tuned out the echo of Kara's hateful words. I couldn't think about losing my best friend. I had to focus. I had to get through this party.

We were assembled in the room in the Cross cut by slim white columns. Guests wore their finest Blues – all here to celebrate the start of the new Head of State Troopers' career.

Only I was here to end it.

My target had already made the requisite rousing speech from a white-dressed stage: 'I will increase the numbers of Troopers on the streets; continue zero tolerance against any students who break their curfew, against any factory workers observed congregating. I will champion the roll-out of more Youth Troopers. We will fight student conspiracy with our own; hit the next generation of the Resistance before they have the chance to hold a firearm.'

His manifesto was enough to galvanise me. My fight tonight – this was personal. Kara might hate me – but I still had to protect her.

Like Salinger had taught me, I'd carefully assessed the situation the moment I'd walked in, between Audley and Bea. Tobin hadn't been invited; tonight's party was for Blues only. I estimated two hundred to two hundred and fifty of them; Central Land elite only. State Troopers lined the walls, having saluted their new head; a long table at the back of the room stood as a makeshift bar where slaves made drinks to serve.

Audley and Bea were at the opposite end of the room. One was a guest; but aside from a briefly exchanged glance of acknowledgement, mentor to protégée, we'd kept our distance. The Leader had shown up briefly at the beginning but had since left. The only person I needed to keep my eyes trained on was *him*. The man with the broad shoulders and large nose, dark hair cut razor-short. The man I was going to kill. His second drink was the same choice as last time: coppery-brown liquid, with ice, in a short glass. So far I hadn't been quick enough to interfere with either.

I just had to hold tight, smile when it was expected of me at this loquacious group of women; wait patiently for his next drink order. I could see he was coming close to finishing his current glassful; it was going down faster now that the formalities were over with.

I already had it planned what I was going to do. As the slave worker began to make his next drink I would innocently go enquire about the bottles lined up behind. The pill was nestled into the white clutch bag I'd used for the Pairing. As the slave turned to look I would drop it in.

I would have to fix my body just so, so nobody behind could see anything. That was the crucial bit. One trusted me to become invisible, to go unnoticed. He had watched me all these years to know it was the one thing I was good at. The only aspect not helping was the dress I had on. Bea had given it to me this evening and I hadn't known how to decline. Long and satiny, it lengthened my body and exposed my skin in ways that made me self-conscious; it drew too many looks from men around me.

As another woman in my group picked up the rant on the uselessness of slave workers – 'I need to nag mine about dusting the top shelves –' I saw it; his hand rising, beckoning, passing over his emptied glass.

I made sure no one noticed me slide away. I headed towards the table, parallel with the slave worker holding his empty glass, my face fixed with the look of a girl who simply liked the taste of wine, and needed another.

'I wanted to say hello!'

I recognised him instantly. John, 568992, Agriculture Department; he'd been at Bea and Audley's post-Pairing party.

'You've been made a Blue prematurely; I've just heard from Bea! You're one to watch, then!' He was swaying like he'd had too much to drink.

'Yes. Nice to see you again. I'm just going to the bar.'

'Get the slaves to do that for you! Come on, let's find one.' He placed a hand overfamiliarly on my back; his smile reached his eyes in a way I didn't like.

'No, I want to see what's at the bar,' I replied – a little too harshly, but I didn't have much time.

'You don't have to be all aloof now you're a Blue you know, girly.' His head snapped back. I had to keep my cool. 'We can be friends!' He bore his teeth, his hand gliding lower down my back. If I could have got away with using one of Salinger's defence moves – I would.

'Later, maybe. I need my drink.' I wafted my empty glass in the air and barged on past him.

I was too late. The same slave worker was already passing back, drink held aloft. Dammit. What if that was his last? I watched as she passed it to the new Head of State Troopers, my stomach sinking as he made a quick sip. Then he started to walk away. I imagined One's eyes on me from somewhere in this room, summoning me to act, to think. The Head was moving towards a door at the far end of the room.

I had no choice. I had to follow him.

I slipped out, pushing through the same heavy door as it swung back. I could just see his head disappearing beyond another set of doors, heading down a long stretch of corridor. There was a staircase at the end. I knew from the map in my head that the Head of State Troopers' office was on the floor above.

The ladies' toilets were right beside me. I rushed in; two women were chatting at the sinks. I feigned going to the loo, rustling toilet paper as I took my tracer out of my bag and secured it behind the cistern, out of sight.

I flushed, smiling insipidly at the women as I washed my hands. Returning to the corridor, I carried on down it, towards the stairs. I wasn't sure what my plan was. But I had to go through with this: like One said – follow my instinct.

The corridor above wasn't lit. The only light came dimly through the square glass of the office doors, from the strip lighting across the Green Mile outside.

Only one door was wide open. I paused, readying myself with an excuse. I could feign too many glasses of wine . . . I was looking for my mentor's office . . . slur my congratulations on the new job. Get closer, a hand on his arm; act as obsequious as Stella did with Syon. Flatter him. Maybe I could thank Bea for this dress after all. Drop the pill in while he watched my face not my fingers.

I moved round into the light of the doorway, my opener ready on my lips. My mouth in an easy smile, belying the ferocious rhythm my heart beat against my chest, preternaturally warning me: stop, go back.

He wasn't there. The sprawling office was empty. But he had been here: on the wide mahogany desk by the window, sat a tumbler of ice in copper-coloured liquid.

I stood, motionless, my frantic heartbeat still talking: *Do it and get out, quick. He'll probably be back any minute.*

I moved over to the desk, slipping the pill from my clutch bag.

My blood froze. Dammit! How could I be so stupid! I'd meant to get it out of its plastic casing earlier! I started fumbling with its sealed edge, digging a nail in to burst it. Finally the tiny blue pill was out. I held it between thumb and forefinger over the top of the glass. *Do it*, a voice was screaming in my head, *you're running out of time*. The tips of my fingers felt numb, like they were jarred and wouldn't open. This was it: *this will make you a killer.*

I had to do it. I couldn't think of him as human – as the boy he once was, the older man he would have been. Head of State Troopers – he won't have any family to miss and mourn him.

There was a click of a door behind me.

Chapter Nineteen

I spun round, the pill still fixed between thumb and forefinger.

The new Head of State Troopers was standing, his back pressed against the closed office door. 'I might ask what you are doing, but it seems pretty clear.' A sneer pulled at his thin mouth; brightened the dots of eyes in his large, angular face. 'You were about to put something in my drink.'

Blood pounded into my ears. I had failed.

'The Leader's protégée no less! Hand it over, you silly little cow.' He began making strides towards me across the expanse of office, his palm out.

Cons, One, Salinger. They had been wrong to think me capable.

'Who's managing you then?' His lip curled as he assessed me. 'You give me their names – all of their names – and you never know, maybe you will face a lifetime in a brothel, rather than Selection. Shame to waste your pretty face.' He stank of something sour. There was a drink stain down the front of his smartly laundered Black jacket.

'Tut, tut. What will the Leader say?'

He was enjoying this. He had nothing to fear from me. Some

silly girl, invisible in Land.

Maybe that was what made me act, and act quickly.

I used the move Salinger had pressed on me over and again. I charged forward. My knee thrust up into his groin. A swift turn, my elbow striking him in the face. I didn't have the strength to overpower this broad, stocky man. I just needed to stun him, to give me another chance. He let out a thunderous groan of pain; I twisted round, his hands were holding a bloodied nose; his body bent over.

I had only a moment. I shoved the pill violently into his mouth, pushing my fingers down his throat, forcing that pill in until I felt it slide down his oesophagus. He had started retching. I had to get my fingers out before he vomited it up. He bit down as I retrieved them. My body seized with pain; he twisted me round, holding me tight against his chest.

I watched him reach out, scrambling with one hand for the black tracer on his desk. I struggled wildly to try to stop him, kicking at his shins, but he held me firmly. I knew what that red button at the bottom of his tracer did the moment he depressed it. Audley had the same button on his. *Just for those in power*, he'd explained. *A direct alarm to State Troopers*. They would track him here within minutes.

It was lost. For me. All I could hope was that the pill was making its way into his stomach, spreading its poison through his veins. At least if it was to end now, I could have achieved something.

Then in a heartbeat his hold loosened. A rattling gurgle behind me. I turned; his hand was pressed against his chest, clutching at it . . . He was having a seizure.

'Get help. Help me,' he was moaning now, his mouth foaming up, his eyes popping in agony as he fell to the floor.

I employed the hardened part of my heart to peel my own eyes away. I had to get out of here. Now. I scanned the room for any evidence, grabbing up pieces of torn plastic from the pill's casing on the floor and shoving them in my bag.

Salinger had been certain that, as long as they believed it was a heart attack, they wouldn't check for anything else. Regardless, I had no time to remove my fingerprints: they were all over him, right down his throat, even.

I moved to the door, scanning the greyly lit corridor outside. No one, yet. I started to rush along it, but already I could hear the sound of heavy footsteps on the staircase beyond. I turned back in the opposite direction. I wouldn't get to the other end of the corridor before they saw me. I tried the first door to my left. Locked. Another, opposite. Locked too.

The footfall was getting closer.

Another door, this time with no glass window. It opened. I rushed in, closing it gently behind me as I caught the pound of boots outside. I crouched down. It was pitch black. I could smell bleach; next to me I could feel the wooden handle of a brush. I was in the cleaning cupboard.

More feet thundered past; calls for a medic.

I made my appeal over and over: *Please let him be dead*.

I lifted my head, my pulse charging, when I heard the shout: 'He's still breathing.'

My own breath stopped.

I had to get out of here. I had to run. But where? And dressed like this? I wouldn't even be able to collect my coat without being seen. I was trapped.

I thought of Tobin back at the house – would he hide me? He wanted an 'us' badly; enough to take this on? Maybe he would, but how could I possibly ask him? It wouldn't be fair.

No, I was alone in this. I had always been alone in this. Cons had seen to that.

I squeezed my eyes shut, and maybe it was because I started thinking about Dad – where he was, whether he was close, waiting to hear how I'd done – that a miracle happened.

'He's gone . . . his pulse, it's stopped. Cancel the medic, no point now.'

I waited, and I waited. I waited until I caught the heaving sounds of a body being lifted. I waited until I heard the door to an office being pulled shut. I waited until there was nothing but utter silence outside.

I had no idea of time. But I was more or less certain the event taking place below would have been cut short. Celebration fast replaced by commiseration.

I picked up my tracer from the toilet downstairs then returned to the party room. I tried to look like I'd simply had too much to drink, swaying and smiling like a naive girl who couldn't take her wine.

Only a few guests still lingered. I moved faster as I spotted John, 568992, talking closely with a tall woman in one corner. I kept up the drunken facade as I went to collect my coat, exiting out the main entrance.

Breathe in, breathe out; my throat was dry, my head thumping. I had to keep going, keep moving; wipe my mind of what had just happened, of what I'd just done. A Selection truck pulled up behind me as I started to cross the Green Mile – incongruous in this area, its red signage, **For the greater good**, illuminated under a bright wall light. It must be for *him*. The same trucks were employed to take away the dead, as well as the living.

I quickened my pace. Winter was still evident in March, now it was night-time; the temperature had dropped to freezing. But even the cruel chill in the air wasn't enough to account for the way my body was trembling.

It had taken me a while to realise I wasn't walking in the direction of Tobin's house, but on through the empty shopping precinct into West Land. My Blue meant I passed Troopers unchecked; curfew no longer applied to me. It took me a little longer to realise where I was instinctively heading.

I inhaled as I slid the grip from my hair into the lock. I wasn't going to knock and wake them all up. I only wanted to see her. The silvery light from a full moon competed with the luminous streetlighting; I was floodlit by both. My fingers manoeuvred nervously, trying to make it seem to any passing Troopers or curtain twitchers that I was simply jostling with a key. I breathed out when the lock clicked and the door pushed open.

I edged forwards, eyes alert. It was quiet; good, everyone had to be in bed already.

Closing the door gently behind me, I slipped off my party shoes so they wouldn't make a noise on the polished hardwood floor. The streetlight shone a torch through the hall window onto a stack of white boxes in front of me. Someone was moving in, or out.

I tiptoed towards the door that led to their corridor of bedrooms. Stella's was next to Syon's at the end.

The curtains were closed. I had to make my way in the dark to the lighter outline of her bed, my free hand out in front of me, feeling for any obstacles as my eyes slowly adjusted. Once there, I sat down near the curled shape of her body under silky covers. Her mouth was open, emitting pants of warm breath. A sudden urge took me – to get in beside her hot, sleeping body; curl up around her. I'd never slept with my mother, at least not that I could remember.

'Stella . . .' I gently rocked her. 'Mum?' I uttered quietly. I couldn't risk waking the others.

She stirred, blinking open her eyes. 'Christy?' she said, rubbing at her face, pushing herself up.

She squinted, staring at me. Devoid of make-up, her hair hanging messily unbrushed about her oval face, she looked younger than her forty years – a mere girl, snapped out of sleep.

'My goodness, what are you doing here? Is everything okay? What's wrong, Christy?' Her panicked voice came out in short, light stabs of breath, like beats of a butterfly's wings.

I licked my lips. 'You said Cons stole me. Why did you let Cons take me?' I swallowed back the tears that immediately pricked at my eyes. I wouldn't cry. I just wanted answers. I wanted to understand – why? Why me? Why this life? Why had they all colluded to make me a killer? I wrung my hands. I still couldn't get his face out of my head; the popping eyes of the Head of State Troopers; the sound from his throat as he was robbed of oxygen.

'Oh, Christy, you don't know how long I've been waiting for you to ask that.'

'You've known – haven't you – all along, what they had planned for me – that I would be picked for the Pairing . . . what they would ask me to do?'

'What have they asked you to do? You don't have to do anything you don't want to!'

'Don't I? What choice do I have?'

Stella sat up straighter, dressed in a wispy, pale nightdress; her eyes shot all around my face, as always – searching. Her mouth forming a small, sad smile, as her hand reached out. She tucked a loose piece of hair back behind my ear. 'The same dark red as your dad's; like fire.'

Instinctively, I jerked from her touch; her hand stayed poised midair. It had been so long. I'd never even let her hold my hand when I was a child. I'd been set to pull away from her ever since I could remember.

She dropped her arm limply onto the bed. 'Fire – was your father's problem . . . The same fire in his head as he had on it . . .' Her words came out on breath still jolted and jumpy, as her eyes held mine.

'Why did you want this for me?' My voice broke.

'Oh, my dear. I would never . . . I never wanted . . .' She took a gulp of breath. 'From the moment you were born . . . Hogan was filled with hopes for you . . . dreamt that when you were grown you would fight alongside him – lead the next generation into revolution, should he fail.

'Even as a baby you had such a bond with him – daddy's little girl . . . Cons was so angry over Hogan's fate, she was eager to pick up the mantle . . . She was determined to realise her son's vision for Land.'

'And you let her groom me for that,' I said flatly.

Stella shook her head furiously. 'No! What mother would want that future for her child? All I hoped for you was that you got Paired to a nice boy! Grandchildren . . . Security. That's all I wanted for you!'

I saw it with her – a picture that had been slowly forming at the back of my head. Tobin and me, enjoying a contented life like Bea and Audley; children playing at our feet. It could have all been so simple. 'Then why did you let Cons steal me?'

Stella made an O with her mouth. 'There was nothing I could do. Without Hogan . . . I had such little strength . . . he threatened me – your grandfather . . .' Her eyes strained at me.

'I know . . . who he is.' I answered her gaze.

Stella nodded. 'He threatened me with Selection if I didn't give you up to his guardianship. He would have put you in another family – had you adopted. When Cons stepped into the fight for you – I had to back her. I had to choose sides, or else I wouldn't ever see you again.

'Cons promised me access to you. As long as I swore to tell you nothing of your past – of your family, of the Resistance plans I suspected her of . . .'

'You should have told me the truth!'

'You were so young. As the years passed, I became petrified . . . I told myself not to interfere in Cons' raising of you, in case I jeopardised your view on life and made you hate me!' She shrugged. 'You hated me anyway.'

'And after Cons died? Why didn't you come to me then?'

'Would you have listened?' Stella pressed her lips together and picked at the sheet covering her legs. 'You have always been so full of animosity towards me.'

I let out a loud sigh, bringing my hands up to cover my face. Stella reached for them. 'I would have told you all I knew, if you'd come to me . . . You never came. You're seventeen; I thought it was too late. You'd been brainwashed into one of them.' Her eyes, still skipping over my face, were misty. 'Oh, Christy . . .' Her fingertips followed the line of my jaw. 'I've failed you, I know – I'm sorry . . . I should have fought back against your grandfather, your grandmother – even Hogan. I just didn't know how to do that, *and* stay alive for you. But then what use have I been alive?'

Bile rose through my throat. Part of me wanted to sting her – *Yes, you should have! Yes, you should have fought harder!* But looking at her face, I saw nothing but pain . . . and love. My mother had loved me all this time.

I took a small breath. 'I'm sorry . . . I'm sorry that Cons stole me.' On many levels, I was truly sorry about that.

Stella's sad smile seemed to dissipate into a brighter grin. 'We can talk now . . . I can help you . . . I can tell you about Hogan.'

'Do you know where he is?'

'I do.' Stella inhaled deeply, fixing melancholic eyes on mine. My heart paused as she opened her mouth. 'He –'

'I thought Astral moving back home today, renouncing her Pair, was bad enough. But this?'

Both of us whipped our eyes to the door. Syon was standing in the doorway. The room lit up in a golden glow as he turned on the light.

212

'Let me just check I heard correctly?' His voice was silky smooth as he stepped closer. 'Cons groomed you to take up Hogan's mantle? Hogan – the rebel leader?' His eyelids closed, twitching in speech.

I bolted up from the bed, my breathing shallow. My eyes tracked his as they opened again. 'You heard wrong,' I said softly as his mouth snaked into a gleeful smile.

Stella was kneeling up on the bed. 'This has nothing to do with you.'

Syon's eyelids flicked shut again. 'Christy, I underestimated you. Hugely.' He pressed his lips together effeminately. 'They warned us at West Land Council that this was happening – infiltration – and to be on our guard. But I never expected you. I won't allow treachery to dirty my family!'

Stella got out of bed, moving towards him. 'Christy is *part* of our family. Any slander you spread about her will bring us all down too.'

Syon's cheek twitched; he looked from Stella to me. It was clear her words had drawn some effect. He pulled his gaze back to Stella, raised his hand – slapping her so hard she fell flying back onto the bed.

I was next to him in a second – swinging out my foot, jabbing him hard behind the knees, forcing him to kneel. I locked his neck against me with my arm. 'How dare you touch her,' I hissed into his sallow cheek.

'Quite the little fighter, aren't you?' His face twisted in my grasp, his breath smelt stale. 'I knew it was impossible you'd been made a Blue under your own merit.'

I tightened my grip till he let out a high-pitched moan. Could I twist his neck till it broke? I was a killer now. Why not? My mind spun with the times he would hit me for the lies his children told about me. He had never disguised his hatred of my presence in his house. Now, he would have me arrested. Why let him?

I felt the light touch of Stella's hand on my shoulder. 'Let him go, Christy. Leave Syon to me.' I'd never heard her sound so strong, steady. I turned to see her; her expression was uncommonly steely. 'Please,' she added when I didn't move.

Syon darted away from me as I released my grip. 'I am sending this little bitch to Selection for this. And neither you nor her can stop me.' He stabbed a finger at both of us, his other hand massaging the pink ring round his neck.

'No, Syon,' Stella answered calmly, a new strength to her voice. 'You need to think about how it will look. Astral has left her Pair and run home to us –'

'Astral will go back.'

'Astral's Pair beats her black and blue – she will not. You need to manage yourself, or else you will never get promoted.'

Her last words silenced him. 'Come with me – and I will tell you a big secret.' Stella flicked a glance at me. 'About Christy. But not in here. Let's go to your room. I will tell you something that will put an entirely different spin on this.'

She was going to tell him about the Leader being my grandfather. I began to shake my head at her; that wouldn't help. Surely it would only make things worse. But what choice did she have – either of us? We were gripping onto a cliff-face. About to fall. As Stella followed Syon out of the bedroom door she turned to me, her mouth forming pained shapes of silence: *Go. Go now. Get out!*

'How did you know I would be here?' I said, slowly glancing over to the door as it creaked open.

I was curled up in the corner of Cons' room, tucked in between the wall and the end of her bed. I'd hardly noticed I'd kept the key to the flat with me at all times.

In my hand I clutched another small, wrapped blue pill, the spare one I carried around with me, tucked up in my lip-wax pot . . . in case.

Salinger sat down on the floor in front of me, hugging his knees and placing his chin on top.

'One,' he shrugged. 'He tracked you . . . He told me to come rescue you.'

'I can't be rescued,' I managed to say. My mouth felt thick, as if I'd been punched there.

'The Head of State Troopers – he died. You did it. Sudden heart attack in his office. One was on the scene soon after, saw it for himself.'

I shook my head. I didn't have the voice to explain how badly it had gone.

Salinger was trying to meet my eyes. 'Christy – you did good.'

'It's over. Syon knows about me. They'll be coming for me soon. I went to Stella's. I don't know why . . . I wanted to ask . . . Syon heard us talking . . . He knows, and Stella won't be able to stop him exposing me. It's over.' I opened my palm, staring at the pill there. 'So I do as you ordered – I kill myself; I protect you and One.'

Salinger rubbed his chin – I knew he would have to come to the same conclusion. Instead he made a grimace. 'I will alert

One straight away. One will fix it. Syon's a nothing – he's not even in Central Land – it'll be his word against yours. Stay strong, and we will send him to Selection for his lies instead.'

'You don't know Syon,' I replied.

'I know One,' Salinger said. 'He will take care of this.' He leant forward and closed my hand round the pill, extending his other to help me up. 'Let's get you home.'

'I am home.'

'You know what I mean,' he said softly.

'I'm no good at it. I nearly got caught by the man I assassinated. And now I might have landed you both in it. I can't do this. This shows I'm not what you need.'

'You need to get some sleep.'

'Are you not listening to me? I'm not right for this job. Even if I survive Syon – I can't kill again. You picked the wrong person for the job.'

'That's your choice,' Salinger replied. I looked up at him, waiting to see the bemused smile, or the taut way his forehead creased when he was annoyed. But there was neither. He meant it.

'There are no choices.'

'There are – if you look for them.'

The tone of his understanding broke me. My voice cracked. 'I want to see my dad.'

'Then you should demand that until they tell you where he is.'

I stared back at him; he continued. 'You have to take more control. Don't let everyone else dictate what you do. None of us really know what's going to happen.'

'We're going to bring about change! Aren't we? Even if I go to Selection tomorrow, what I did tonight . . . it's going to mean something?' It had to. Death for life. I couldn't have stopped another human heart for nothing.

'I hope so,' Salinger said, nodding his head slowly.

Hope. I wasn't sure I knew what it looked like any more. But I'd never seen a face express so little of it.

Chapter Twenty

All was lost. I knew it – in the spread of despair shrouding me as I woke. I had killed; now I was to die.

I had killed. I tried to check how it made me feel . . . to have taken another human life. Yet all inside me was numb. My heart beat sluggish and slow; my mind fast erasing all memory. I was becoming the machine Cons had dreamt of.

The machine that might be switched off in the next few hours if One couldn't contain Syon.

I got up, washed and dressed quickly; I had to get to work, face my fate.

I made sure my blue pill was safely secured in my trouser pocket.

Descending the stairs, I caught Bea joining Audley in the dining room for breakfast. I shot past the open door before they noticed me. I could overhear Audley announcing solemnly that the new Head of State Troopers had died last night.

'Who will replace him?' Bea asked agitatedly. She wouldn't waste time mourning or remembering the man. No one was of consequence, of any use, once they were a corpse. Only the living mattered. 'Keep your head down, Audley,' Bea continued.

'You don't want to be chosen . . .'

One was sitting in my office before I could take myself to his. He stood up, beckoning me with his head as I started taking off my coat. 'Put that back on, we're going out,' he said, his face set in concrete.

I didn't ask him why or for what as I trailed him out of the Cross. He must have lost the fight with Syon. Was I even going now, for Selection? I put my hand in my pocket, feeling for my blue pill. It could all be over soon.

As we stepped onto the Green Mile, One finally inclined his head to me, the edges of his eyes drooping even lower. 'Your mother's been taken for Selection.'

I halted, my slow-beating heart suddenly accelerating, as if it were hurrying my blood away. 'What? Why?'

'For the murder of her Pair.'

My insides pinched with dread. 'She killed Syon?'

'Salinger alerted me to your problem late last night. I went to Stella's flat first thing this morning. She'd already been arrested, taken away. Her stepson, Tom, found her standing over his dead body, with Syon's gun. Come on.' He picked up his stride across the grass.

I reached out, pulling him back by his jacket sleeve. 'You can stop it, can't you, One? I mean – it would have been self-defence!'

One flicked me a curt look, but his sad grey eyes held me with . . . pity? 'It wasn't. No doubt she did it for you.'

I swung my head, darting in front of him, to stop him moving on. '*Stop* it!'

'I can't halt Selection. Stella's confessed to murder. There is nothing anyone can do now.'

'Then the Leader . . . the Leader can prevent it!'

This time One grabbed at my arm, bringing me close to him to hiss in my ear. 'No! Stella has killed a member of West Land Council! And she's your mother! Hogan's ex-Pair! The Leader's not going to touch it – even asking will ruin the progress you've made with him!' He drew breath, loosening his grip on me. 'Christy – I am taking you to see her. That's all I can do. Okay? That's all we can do.'

'She can't die for me, One.'

'She stayed alive for you . . . It's not that different.'

I waited in the reception area of West Land Assessment Centre, amidst a crowd of agitated Browns and Greys trying hard to fix smiles before their appointments. I bit down hard on my nails. I'd not been called for a routine Assessment since being picked for the Pairing. I glanced at the strained faces around me; they looked as wretched as I felt.

One was talking to the centre director, pulling strings.

He returned, pushing me hurriedly down a series of thin corridors to a white metal door at the end.

She was already in there, sitting at a table in a room like the one I'd been in for my last Assessment.

One stayed back, near the door.

'This is happening too quickly,' I hurried out as I fell clumsily into the seat opposite her. 'You can't do this. Invent a story – tell them it wasn't you!'

She looked the same as last night – hair messily tousled, her

220

face bare of its usual make-up. Her Blue coat open over her girlish nightgown. 'There were witnesses.'

'You should never have done this for me!'

Stella's head tipped both ways; her face filled with warmth. 'Why not? I am a mother. That's always been who I am.'

I squeezed my eyes. I couldn't handle this. Something deep inside of me was about to burst out. And yet, looking across at her, she suddenly appeared as peaceful as I'd ever seen her. I tightened my hands into fists on the table. 'There has to be a way I can save you,' I said, my voice strangled.

Stella reached across, placing her hands over mine, pink fingers against my pale white skin. Their touch was unfamiliar. 'Even if there was – and there isn't – I don't want to be saved. Made a slave . . . or sent to a brothel. I'd rather die. And die knowing at last I've done something meaningful for my daughter.'

We both heard One clear his throat in the background. I read his command instantly, his warning against careless talk; so did Stella. She lifted her face to him. 'I want to tell her . . . Can't I . . .?' she asked, impeaching him.

One must have shaken his head behind me, as her expression fell a little before she struggled to reset it brightly.

'Tell me what?' I asked as she squeezed my hands.

'That . . . I did love him, you know.' Stella made a conciliatory smile. 'Hogan. I loved him.'

I gripped her hands tighter. 'You really did?'

She squeezed her forehead, as if she couldn't get a measure on her answer. 'Hogan was passionate and so energetic. Full of love for everyone he cared for – you, me, his mother.' She tipped her head to her shoulder. 'But Hogan's greatest love was for his own dreams. It preoccupied him to the point he forgot about us. Saw his baby as his future.' She sniffed. 'The expectations parents put on their children . . . I just wanted you to be safe . . . happy. Isn't that all you should want for your child?'

I thought back to the farce of my childhood with Cons. 'Yes,' I agreed.

'Mum, don't let them do this.' I leant into the table, my heart racing faster. 'You can't die for me; I should be the one dying,' I whispered, out of One's earshot.

'Don't you dare feel guilt over any of this.' She let out a small smile. 'I hated Syon. He was a bad Pair, a nasty father – he only loved his children as long as they provided a reflection of himself. He had no qualms about abandoning Astral to a violent Pair. No.' Stella smacked pale lips together. 'I have done everyone a favour. And it was easy – I'd often dreamt of it before,' she continued, her pretty eyes distancing as if she'd begun talking to herself. 'I knew he kept a gun – in the top drawer by his bed – he was so paranoid. I took him into his room so I could reach it. So I could use it. My only regret is Tom coming in at the gunshot, Astral soon after – seeing their father like that. Though maybe losing him will save them too . . . in a funny way.' She cocked her head, serene eyes trailing mine. 'If – when – things get better, maybe you could look in on them both . . .'

I nodded my head. Though I doubted either would want me doing that.

'I don't want you to go,' my voice strained out. I clenched

my lips together as they started trembling.

'It's fine, really. You're old enough, bold enough – I've never been much use to you.' She lowered her voice to barely audible. 'I can't say I like what they're doing to you . . . but I admire your conscience. You deserve to live a free life.'

'I'm not doing this for me.' I shook my head, my mouth twisting in anguish. 'It's just my job.' My breath was coming hard and fast. My feelings were struggling to catch up with what was happening. I'd never allowed myself to care for Stella – but now I could sense the beginning of a love that might rapidly grow if she could only . . . 'Stay with me.'

Stella gave me a pained look. 'I can't.' She flicked her head at One. 'Just promise me that you will act for yourself; do what you think you should do – what's right . . . for you.'

'We haven't got long,' One murmured from his corner. 'They said five minutes only.' He was anxious about what she might say; I could hear it in his tone.

I gazed frantically at Stella. There was too little time to make up for all these years.

Stella took her hands from mine, lifting her slim arms up until her fingers clasped round my face. 'I have always loved you. I just wish I'd done more to protect you.'

'You've done more than enough,' I said and smiled back at her; a smile I made sure reached my eyes. Stella had killed – was to die today. It was as grand a sacrifice as anyone had ever made for me.

Chapter Twenty-one

I convinced One I would be okay. I did my best to show him I'd contained all the emotions whipping furiously round my chest – just so I could get away. I had to be alone; I had to walk and keep on walking – something, anything, to chase away the violent ache around my heart.

My nerves were ragged. I could hardly breathe. This was happening. This was really happening. First Cons, now my mother, facing Selection because of me.

It was all I could do to keep out the image of Stella being led away to face her end. If I pictured that, I'd lose it; I'd collapse right now onto the road and wait until a Selection truck scooped me up. And I couldn't do that. Stella was going to die to save my life – so I had to stay alive. I had no choice. Salinger was wrong: there were no choices.

Soon, my grandfather's new policy, the Culling, would start. Thousands more would join Stella – like Kara. I had to focus. *Stay silent. Fix a smile. Keep on walking.*

A mixture of distress and anger hurried me down and around every street of West Land, then into North. Treading mile after mile as I held my grief for Stella in a tightly spun ball in my stomach. I had to escape this pain; this loneliness.

I must have walked aimlessly for hours, circling North, then back through West; gradually the azure blue sky turned navy, workers and students began making their way home, retreating inside their flats. To escape the crowds, I took a left into a quiet street near the outskirts; the zigzag roofs of the factories behind me.

I didn't know if I could go home tonight. I didn't know what home was. *What has happened to you?* Kara's words from yesterday were starting to drill a hole inside my head. What was I without Cons? Without Kara? Without my mother?

I caught the sound of footsteps tapping behind me; I made a sharp turn down another, smaller road; I wanted to be completely alone. Like Dad, I wanted to find the impossible: somewhere to hide in Land.

This road was deserted; on either side were squat, rundown tenement blocks, spotlit dirty white by the bright streetlamps. But I still wasn't alone. The footsteps echoed behind me. I moved faster, to dodge company; the possible interrogation of a Trooper.

And then: 'Christy!' It travelled, ghost-like, across the space behind me, a gentle, male voice. A soft entreaty. From someone who knew me.

I twisted on my heel, glaring frantically around the decrepit street scene behind. The footsteps had ceased. There was no one there.

I breathed slower, stilling everything; my ears pricked. But there was only the faint clatter of pans from adjacent streets; the occasional whir from the tram on the main road. I turned back; I had to be hearing things.

As I came closer to the end of the street I heard it again – footsteps – before, 'Christy!', louder this time. Definitely a man's voice – urgent, desperate. Someone was calling to me.

I didn't think; I felt. There was only one person who would be calling me from a hiding place. Only one person I had been sure all this time *was* watching me, following me. At last, he was here; he had taken the opportunity of a quiet spot to seek me out. When I needed him most.

He knew I had no one left – except him. Dad.

My stomach began to throb with desperation to see him. I raced back to the spot from where the voice had travelled.

My father's daughter – *that* was who I was.

'Christy!' Now it was coming out of a thin alley between two tenement blocks. I squeezed through, walking sideways to make my way into the gap.

I had to get to him before any random noise, like a Trooper passing on the street, startled him away. He was putting his life at risk, meeting me like this. I could just make out the edges of a jacket, hovering around the corner at the far end.

I moved faster, the sound of my feet bouncing off the walls that closed in on me. Now I could glimpse an arm in Brown, a shoe jutting out; the rest was out of view, but I imagined the head of dark red hair, the strong, lean shoulders, the wide smile, from the picture in my head.

I still had Dad. He would help me see; explain to me why he and Cons had had no choice but to do this to me. How it didn't mean they didn't love me. He would hold me and protect me from the pain of losing Stella before I'd ever known her.

I used my hands against the walls to move me faster. I was nearly there now. I was almost beside him.

I rounded the corner, a grin cutting my face in two.

A covered head, eyes widening through the holes of a dark mask. Hands rising and clutching at my arms.

I forced out a fist, jolting the body back; moving, running spider-like back down the same gap in the walls, scraping my face and arms against the rough brick. Thick hands clasped at me again, before another body trapped me from the opposite side. My arms were being forced down by my side; my face shoved violently against the wall in front of me, smashing my nose. Pain shot through my face; I tried to twist my head round to see who they were, but I was pinned against the wall; I couldn't move, could not even speak; my lips were pressed, splayed, brick dust filling my mouth. I struggled, trying to get some leverage – if I could free one arm I could jab out with my elbow one side, push a kick at the other. I had to get away!

A mouth came close to my ear, the same male voice who had shouted out my name, but harsher now, hissing, spitting on my cheek. 'Make a noise and we will beat you to within an inch of your life.'

The hands twisting my arms behind me loosened just a little. I took my chance and jerked back with both elbows, full force into the chests at either side.

Something slammed onto the side of my head. My sight blurred with dots of light, a sharp shock of pain rattled through me. Everything went black.

Chapter Twenty-two

I came round slowly, my mind not yet tuned to my body. When all of me finally synced, I became painfully aware of an intense, rhythmic banging in my head, as if something wanted to break out of my skull.

I lifted my head gingerly. Then panicked. I'd opened my eyes to pitch blackness. Why couldn't I see? I went to rub at my eyes, but my hands were tied; my ankles too, bound behind the hard chair I was sitting on. A gag was pinning my lips back against my face. They felt inflamed. I squeezed my eyes shut, blinked rapidly – my lashes brushing against something. A blindfold?

Had I been arrested . . .? How long had I been here? Where was I? Back at West Land Assessment Centre?

Yet the masked man – he had been in Brown, not Trooper Black?

I struggled to free my hands, my wrists burning as my skin chafed against the rope. The throb in my head intensified. I could sense swelling on my forehead where they'd knocked me out. My nose felt stuffed with dried blood. I fought the binds again. I had to do something. If I couldn't escape, I had to at least reach the blue pill in my trouser pocket. Land had controlled my life; it would not control my death.

Keep death simple. My low moan came out muffled through the gag. I wouldn't be here if I hadn't let emotion take over; hadn't dropped my focus . . . I'd made my own death simple.

The door creaked open. My head turned sharply, light sparking through the blackness. I breathed hard as feet strode towards me. My aching mouth bit into the gag, vainly trying to tear it away so I could at least speak to them.

'Well, looky here! Who's woken up then?' To my right; a young woman's voice.

My muffled voice made noise back; I wasn't even sure what I wanted to say. If they were Land's disciples, then what was there to say?

'Ready to get down to business?'

'Shall we tell you who we think the double agent is, and you can just nod?'

I swung my head from the female to the familiar male voice the other side.

I thought of One, Salinger. I had to do what I did best: stay silent. I must protect them. Fleetingly, my mind jumped to Tobin. Would they arrest him? For being Paired to an assassin? Picturing it made my head bang faster; I regretted my last argument with him. No; *Stop it, clear your mind*. No more emotion! *Be clever* . . . remember Cons' safety belt of rules: simple; focus.

Maybe there was still a way I could get out of this. I played my trump card. 'You have no idea who I am; you ask the Leader!' I snarled, but all that came out was indistinguishable noise, a mouth filled with cotton wool.

'Shut your Blue face.' A hard push against my shoulder; my

chair wobbled. I twitched my body to stay upright. 'We do the talking. You just nod!'

I tilted my head – why insult my being a Blue? Unless –

'We know you're under the mentorship of 454111. Now, you tell us: is it him who is betraying us? Is he true to the Resistance . . . or to the State?'

These weren't government workers.

'Was it 454111 who spread rumours about our unit? Got us thrown out of the Resistance? Did he give away our hiding place to Troopers?' It was the male voice this time.

I wriggled violently. They had to remove the gag: I needed to talk! I had to make them see – I was on their side. One was on their side! They'd caught the wrong person!

Another punch, this time at the side of my face; my teeth caught my tongue, the taste of metal as blood filled my mouth.

'Stay still!' the woman shrilled. 'Just nod if it's true! Someone set us up! And we're going to find out who! You tell us! Is 454111 the enemy? Answer!'

She sounded like she was losing it. Slowly, I shook my head.

'Do you know who it is? Who's betraying us?' The male voice, beginning to sound equally agitated.

Again, I slowly shook my head.

'She's lying,' came the female. 'There's no point to this; I told you. She's a Blue – let's do her and get out of here.'

I sucked in my breath; the fabric round my mouth strangling my voice as I tried in vain to shout, 'I'm one of you. I'm with you!'

'Kill her,' the woman said again. I braced myself.

Feet scuffled forward, then two dull popping noises rang

through the room.

Their sound forced my body into an arch. I'd been shot. I searched for a new pain around my body, but it was overpowered by the aches of those already there. Was it fatal? Was I dying? I summoned up my last image of Cons; my imagined pictures of Dad. Joining them, Kara, Stella, One, Salinger . . . Tobin. What had it all been for?

I could hear feet striding towards me again. I braced myself. I felt woozy. Was I fading?

My gag was being pulled down from my mouth, my blindfold gently tugged upwards. My eyes met two dark brown ones I knew well.

I don't know what made me do it. My lips were bruised and sore, my head was banging. I was in a state of utter panic and confusion. I wasn't dying?

But the moment I saw those eyes, it was all I wanted to do. The relief at still being alive. At still being here.

I pushed my head forwards and kissed the soft lips beneath the eyes.

I held my mouth there, taking in the warmth, the life that seemed to pulse within his. They felt like Salinger's should feel.

I pulled back.

Salinger's mouth remained slightly open. His eyes bore into mine. He seemed to be struggling with his next breath.

Then he straightened up and turned towards the voice as rough as sandpaper behind him.

One, crouched by two bodies lying splayed on the ground, a black gun aloft in his hand. 'Salinger, untie her. Hurry – can't you see she's in pain?'

Chapter Twenty-three

I stood, massaging the raised pink welts around both my wrists. Salinger's eyes were still on me as I stared down at the two corpses lying on the ground. My would-be killers. Their faces were as pale white as Land's buildings, almost completely drained of blood, except for a black-red circle, central on both their foreheads as if it had been drawn with ink.

They were younger than I'd imagined – a boy and a girl, both in Brown, but they probably wore Green not so long ago. The girl's light hair splayed, fan-like, above her head; the boy's corkscrew black. How could I have thought he was Dad? The irises of their unblinking eyes had rolled backwards; only the whites stared out at me, until One bent over and gently closed the girl's eyelids. He stepped over her body and did the same to the boy's.

'Did you know them?'

'Members of the Resistance.' One shrugged.

'Yes,' I replied, then I stared directly at him till he lifted his eyes to meet mine. 'How did you find me?'

'After what you went through this morning, I've kept a close track on your movements today.' He made a resigned face when I frowned. 'Which were pretty erratic. Your tracer –' he indicated my satchel lying against the wall – 'if they knew what they were doing it would have been the first thing to take off you . . . amateurs, dangerous amateurs. The Resistance is full of them . . . the young who dream.'

He sounded like Audley. 'They wanted me to confirm that you were a traitor. They believed you were on Government's side.'

'Shush,' One silenced me, stabbing his finger up at the ceiling then down at the floor. Yet I was sure there was no need. The room we were in was bereft of furniture; silence sounded in and outside the flat; it was surely a derelict building. 'What the hell were you doing walking round here at this time of night anyway? Have we not taught you any sense, taught you how to act now you are who you are?'

I swallowed. *Who was I?* Lowering my voice I said, 'Why would they think you had betrayed them?'

'I have to work both sides, remember; pretend I work for the State.'

I stayed staring at him. Something didn't add up.

He went on. 'Look: everyone is on edge. Everyone believes they're being betrayed. It's what this kind of politics does to you. What these two believed of me is irrelevant.' One sucked in his breath and crouched back down beside the girl, mumbling to Salinger, 'I'll do her, you check through the boy's jacket.' Without looking up, he added, 'They must have been following you for a while. No one knows you're on our side. Stupid fools.' He cursed under his breath. 'Probably thought they'd struck gold finding you out here. They'd never dare launch an attack like this nearer Central Land.'

'They picked me off because of my closeness to you.'

One shook his head as if he didn't agree. 'They will have heard about you. Your number's being bandied about in certain circles. There's a buzz around your future.'

'Yes, it's a buzz you are falsifying about me, remember?' I hissed back. 'Shouldn't the Resistance know whose side I'm on?' I dropped my voice to an almost mute whisper. 'Can't Dad trust his own group to keep me secret?'

One glanced sharply up at me, a look on his face as if he'd just remembered again that I was there. 'It hurts?' he said, indicating my head. I raised a hand and gingerly touched it. There was an egg forming just above my forehead. When I pulled my hand back blood stained the tips of my fingers.

'Here.' One pulled a handkerchief from his trouser pocket and thrust it towards me. 'Hold that against it; stem the bleeding till you can get yourself cleaned up.'

I took it, wincing as I pressed it hard against my head.

'Unarmed,' I heard Salinger murmur. He swung his eyes up at both of us.

'So you didn't need to shoot them?' I interjected. What was One playing at!

'They might have talked.'

'You killed your own side!'

'I don't have a side!'

My face freeze-framed with disbelief.

I caught Salinger glaring intently at One. 'You need to explain it to her. Tell her. She's lost her grandmother, now her mum . . . Christy could've died tonight; she deserves to know what she's fighting for.'

One halted his check of the girl's trouser pockets. His mouth made a chewing motion as if he were eating something. He straightened up. 'Why? Christy doesn't care what she's fighting for as long as she saves her friend. Isn't that right?'

My eyes stayed with his stiff features; fearful doubt was spreading, mould-like, through me. My voice strained with disdain. 'Who have I killed for? *What did Stella die for?*'

'These *kids* –' One spat out the last word – 'there are many more of them, but the Resistance is shattered. Doesn't know its arse from its elbow. It's a mess. They care only for taking power from the Blues – as if that alone will be a victory! Will bring peace! They will swap one type of war for another.'

'What are you talking about? It can't be a mess. *We* are the Resistance! We're making real progress – your words!'

One put a finger to his lips to shush me again. Then he raised and dropped his shoulders as if they hung heavy above his torso. 'Wherever you get human beings, you get chaos. We can only concentrate on what we have to do.'

I went closer to him, so he could hear the emphasis in my next whisper. 'What . . . are . . . "we"?'

'A few Resistance members, some officials in government . . . me, Salinger . . . you.'

'What? So few? And why government workers? I don't understand.' I stared back down at the two bodies at our feet. 'Did you betray them to the Troopers?'

'I did.' One raised his chin as if I were about to attack him. 'I betray everyone. That's my job. I'm playing a difficult game, manoeuvring, manipulating . . . murdering . . . passing weapons to the Resistance and then informing on them to government . . . Starting a war that hopefully neither side will win . . . so, with those I trust, we can stage a coup.'

I heard Salinger cough; his eyes motioned to One: *Continue.*

One held his hands out like weighing scales. 'We are striving for a balanced, peaceful state. The Resistance want anarchy. If they gain power they intend to eradicate all Blues – mass elimination of all those living in privilege. Equality for all others – but in a system that squashes life out of the living. Sound familiar?'

I swallowed; my mouth was dry. Everything hurt. My mind was swimming away from me. 'I've *never* been fighting for the Resistance?'

One released a long sigh. 'You hardly wanted to belong to anything – so how could I tell you things weren't as simple as Cons believed them to be?'

'Cons didn't know?'

One shook his head.

'You deceived Cons?'

'It wasn't my original intention.' He pinched his nose. 'I switched my allegiance to Cons when I was angry. Raging. Someone I cared a great deal for . . . had died.' One halted as his voice broke, jerking his neck as if he were dislodging something from his throat. I glanced at Salinger, remembering what he'd told me – *his mother*. His eyes were staring right into me; filling with anxious concern.

'How did she die?' I asked stonily.

One wafted his thick hand through the air above his head, but Salinger cut in. 'Tell her. She should know all of your story – *our* story. She has a right to know. It's her story too.'

One almost sneered at Salinger as he said, 'You want her to know, you tell her.'

Salinger took a breath. 'One got my mum pregnant . . . She kept it secret; like your friend's trying to. But at the birth, she was found out . . . she ended up in a brothel.

'The baby – a girl . . . luckily, was put forward for adoption. We don't know where she went.'

I gazed back at One, trying to work him out. He avoided my eyes.

'Mum wouldn't let One take any blame; even allow him to try and break her out. She made him promise just to take care of me. He could only visit her as a paying client. Took me sometimes. She died eighteen months after going in there . . . a client – a Trooper – got her sent to Selection for refusing him.'

'I'm sorry,' I said, my eyes alternating between him and One. 'For all of you.'

One scrunched up his mouth, pushing a hand through his spiky hair. 'There – so now you know our sob story. It was anger over her that drew me to the Resistance and Cons . . .'

'But then . . .?'

One swung his head. 'Anger fades. I became disillusioned with the Resistance's beliefs, their vision. Yes, I wanted change – I wanted more freedom for people – but not their way, not either way. I began to channel out my own cause . . . for a better Land.'

'A better Land?' I repeated his last words faintly. I couldn't grasp what 'better' was any longer.

'I'm no idealist – all power is corruptible. But absolute

power is destructible. We must remove absolute power from Land – achieve a balance, between survival and compassion, that Land's people deserve.'

I moved away from them – my right leg forcing me to limp – and crossed the room. Stopping at its one small window, I looked out onto the broken-down building opposite, bathed in outdoor light. What I could see of the sky was painted an inky purple-black.

I could hear rustling behind me as One and Salinger resumed their check of every hem and turn-up of the victims. 'Tell me it will be worth it.'

'It will be worth it.'

It was Salinger, answering me again. His stare, as always, fixed on me, penetrating mine. I had to look away. But not because I wanted to.

'And what about my dad? If I agree to your cause I will be betraying my father.' I coughed back the lump in my throat, but my voice still came out throttled. 'I thought that boy was him tonight – the reason I got caught was because I thought at last he'd come for me.'

'Shit, Christy.' One stood up abruptly. His stiffly held face, illuminated moon-like in the dimly lit room, looked almost as drained of colour as the corpses. He rubbed both thick hands across his cheeks. 'Have you not realised by now? Have you not woken up and looked around you?'

Salinger straightened up too. He stared across at One. I couldn't tell whether his expression was urging One to keep talking, or to be silent.

One chose the latter.

I swung my eyes between them. 'Looked around me? What do you mean?'

Salinger came towards me, close, his arms lifting from his sides, like the gesture Cons would make when she wanted me to embrace her. His mouth moved; for a second there I thought he was going to kiss me again. And, for a fleeting moment, it felt as if that was all I wanted. To feel his lips against mine, to taste their warmth.

And then he spoke. Plain words that shot through me, shredding my insides. 'There is no Dad. Not any more.'

'My *dad*,' I repeated, as if we weren't talking about the same man.

One let out a noise like some kind of growl, his eyes straying to the floor as if another dead body lay there by his feet. Salinger shoved his hands into his jacket pockets. 'Your dad died . . . sent for Selection the moment he was caught out in Resistance activity. Fifteen years ago.'

'This is some kind of joke, right?' I looked from One back to Salinger.

'It's not a joke.' Salinger shook his head sadly. 'They should have told you from the very beginning. You should have been allowed to make up your own mind what, who, you're doing this for.'

I twisted away from him; my whole body was trembling, rocking, as if it were pulsating against some inaudible beat. 'My dad . . . has never been alive?'

A stroke of silence, then – 'No,' One said bluntly.

'I don't believe you. You're saying this so I'll join your cause, not his.'

'Everything else is true.' It was Salinger again. 'What your father asked of you. How he wanted Cons to raise you, to continue the mission he had started. I suppose he *has* been alive, in that sense.'

My mouth made a strange sound.

'No one ever actually said he was alive,' One's gruff voice sounded behind me. 'You had already decided that for yourself, when you were a small child. A fairy tale you believed in. Children from the Old World had Father Christmas or Jesus . . . you had your dad. Cons encouraged it, said, "Why not let her believe, if it makes her happy?"'

'Makes me happy?' I spat out, turning round. 'I have spent nearly my entire life searching, waiting, for a man who never existed to save me? I have killed to follow a man who was never there?'

The pain rocketing around my body had suddenly abated. Now a new pain tortured me. A kind that wasn't physical. Worse than when Cons died, or when I said goodbye to Stella this morning.

What I wanted to believe? No; what Cons had led me to believe! 'Stories help you make choices.' That was what she had said. Her stories had been my life's compass. And here was her most powerful one yet – to guide me towards the only choice I must make: my father, alive and watching over me. The father who would one day come and save me.

This story of hers – it finally stripped all my childhood bare. Everything . . . was meaningless. All that remained: the instinct to stay alive. That was her only legacy to me.

Suddenly I could see what Stella had been straining to tell

me. She should have been stronger! Stella should have *interfered*! Someone should have told me the truth!

'I'm very sorry,' One answered, his voice tired, as if he'd given up. 'Cons convinced me it would give you a reason . . . to fight. Who was I to take that away? We needed you.' He exhaled quietly. 'Maybe I was wrong . . . but all I can ask now is that you switch your loyalty from your dad to me. We can still bring about change – not that dissimilar to the one Hogan dreamt of in the beginning.'

I followed One's gaze – down to the girl's lifeless face on the floor between us. I didn't want these two rebels' blood on my hands too. They should have lived, not me. I meant nothing to anyone.

'What choice do I have . . .' It was a quiet statement to myself, not a question. I was already a killer. All I had left was to make death mean something. 'A better Land . . . You'd bloody well deliver it.'

'I will do my best.'

I faced the window again, trying to stem my body's shakes. Someone had been and scooped out every fibre, every tissue and sinew of my insides. Made me hollow. A girl without a father. A thing; a weapon; a nothing.

When I eventually turned back round, One was crouched down again. He'd be staring at the face of the girl in front of him, except his eyes were squeezed tight shut.

But Salinger's, that mud-brown gaze, was still on me. His mouth slowly moving.

I knew what he was asking for. He wanted to offer his sympathy too. He had known. Along with those other lies,

Salinger had known this one. And he knew what my dad had meant to me.

So he would know too why I peeled my eyes away from his.

Why I couldn't even bear to look at him. Never again. Not like that.

Chapter Twenty-four

One dropped me off in his car; it was late, the house lights were out – good. I just wanted to reach my room. Get out of this dress stained with my own blood, take a bath and wash my wounds.

I stopped in the doorway; Tobin was sitting in the shadows, on my bed.

He started talking the moment he saw me. 'I can't do this any more; I can't be in this Pairing with you, the way you treat me. I don't know what's worse: my parents forever breathing down my neck or the fact you hardly even acknowledge my existence.'

Not now. I couldn't deal with this now. 'I've been working; I need a bath. Then I want to go to bed.' The curtains were closed. He couldn't see the state I was in. I tried to walk without my limp as I made my way over to the bathroom.

'I want more than this,' he continued. 'I'm going to have more than this – with or without you . . . I'd just prefer with.'

I entered the bathroom, locking the door behind me.

I must have spent an hour in the bathtub. I cleaned up my bloodied nose, then the gash on my head, placing a cold flannel against the lump there, moving it onto my lip, the burns on my wrists. Before I lay back in the warm water and allowed him back in. For one last time. Dad.

He'd *never* been here. Watching over me.

Now he had to go.

A rough hand inside my head seemed to start scrubbing away at his image, at the red hair and broad shoulders, at the fingers that would clasp mine and the arms that would keep me from falling. Until it was all gone. Nothing remained.

I put my head under the water and stayed there until my lungs gasped for breath. The child in me had been swallowed up whole.

When I came out of the bathroom, hobbling towards my bed in a clean nightshirt, I spotted it: the undulating shape of Tobin, lying on his side under the covers emitting soft, tuneful snores.

I didn't have the energy to wake him. So I just climbed in. It was cosy, snug, curled up next to Tobin's sleeping body. I'd only ever slept next to Cons, as a child. I found myself moving in nearer until his back shaped into my stomach and chest – suddenly I needed human warmth like never before. His closeness diverted me from the various aches around my body; from the black abyss growing inside as Dad vacated my head and heart. I shifted even closer; it made him stir. He turned round, murmuring sleepily, his hands snaking round my side, holding me tight to him by my waist.

I winced as his hands pressed against my bruises, and then sighed. They seemed to fit, our bodies; slotting in against one another as if they were built to connect.

Our faces close, our mouths were breathing hot air onto the other.

'I've no one to talk to.'

Tobin drew a hand down my face. 'Talk to me,' he said sleepily.

'I can't.'

He answered with his mouth, a kiss, full on my lips. I didn't mind the ensuing pain from my injuries. I wanted this, I wanted to know closeness. I began dotting small kisses across both his cheeks, his nose, his chin, to show him it was okay. I liked it. Then his lips returned, showering kisses in reply across my face, in my hair, on my neck, as if I'd unlocked some invisible gate.

Finally he pulled my head down onto the curve between his neck and shoulder.

I had thought I would never sleep again after tonight. But lying there, warmed by Tobin's body, comforted by the loop of Tobin's arms and the soft sound of his breathing in my ears, the dreams started to come.

Dreams of seas, both hostile and kind. Of boats that beckoned me to hurry; of families and babies coming together, breaking up.

Dreams that betrayed the hardening heart of my waking hours. Of the mother I had hated. Of the dad I had loved.

Of a life spent living . . . not surviving.

Of an orphaned boy with deep brown eyes.

Part Three

The Rising

Chapter Twenty-five

When I was little I used to wonder: if I kept watching my reflection, could I catch time out, see my face age? In the two weeks since the attack, it was as if I had. I had grown older each day. Not visibly, like Cons had – hair greying, new lines carved into her skin – but in ways only I could detect.

Looking at myself now in the white oval mirror attached to my dressing table, my green eyes stared back with the kind of hardened experience I recognised in the women and men in Brown, returning from the factories. Even my sulky mouth seemed to sit in a different fashion against my face, pulled back into a straighter line . . . of resignation.

I was no longer a child.

I finished tying and tucking my hair up from my neck, pushing grips into it until it all stayed in place. Grudgingly I went over to the full-length mirror on the back of the wardrobe door. Not to admire myself; I just had to check: did I look the part? The silky, sky-Blue dress began at a halter neck, skimming my skin till it dropped down to my ankles. Would I blend in well tonight; one of them? Superior, points-rich, powerful, no longer invisible – but noticeable.

Thanks to One I'd become something of a minor celebrity in Central Land. I'd heard my story circulating through the Cross corridors: the Leader's protégée who had fought off insurgents who'd kidnapped her to some forgotten street in the bowels of West Land. One's version of events. Guarding me further, he said, from suspicion, while at the same time, the story threatened both sides. He was playing his game so well.

I pinched my cheeks to bring some colour to my pale skin. I had become my own story. I was almost starting to think of myself in the third person. There was little left of the old me. And there would be no new me. Just the empty shell of an assassin.

'Ten minutes till we leave, okay, Red?' Tobin's blond head peered round my door. He had taken to calling me that this past fortnight, like we'd known each other for years. 'Your hair is what made me first notice you,' he'd said.

'You're looking good.' He sloped over to me; his embrace came naturally. I no longer stiffened at his touch.

'Smell good too,' he said, kissing my neck. 'Guess what? I put in our application for a flat on my way home from the Institute today. We're on our way, Red.'

I made a thin smile at him in the mirror.

'Not getting cold feet are you?' Tobin pulled away; a suggestion of a scowl appearing between his brows. 'You agreed: we need to get out of here?'

'No, *you* agreed *you* need to get out of here,' I corrected him, then made my smile warmer. 'Course not.' I shook my head. 'I'm still in.'

I was in – why not? After that first night sharing a bed

together, things had wholly changed between us. It wasn't real – but it was a pretence I'd started to enjoy. So why not get somewhere private to retreat to? I had enough salary and privileges of my own now, I no longer needed Bea and Audley for theirs. I was on my own, so why not spend solitude wrapped up in Tobin's arms?

I reached up, fingering the bottle-Green collar of his shirt, the same tone as his jacket. I was getting skilled at being a Pair; when to touch, what to say. 'You're looking good yourself.' He did, too: smartly handsome, his hair brushed neatly and tucked behind his ears; it was even longer these days – an open act of defiance against Bea who was constantly on his back to get it cut.

'A rare compliment, Red. If only I had time to act on it . . . but Mum and Dad are waiting downstairs.' He made his customary roll of his eyes. 'They're insisting we all arrive at the party together.'

'I don't mind that. Tell them I won't be a moment, all right?' We shared a conspiratorial smile: his for our planned life together; for a shared bedtime later. Mine: it dropped the instant he left the room.

I stayed put in front of the mirror, turning my head one way to see if I could spy it still; the purple bruising that had bled into my hairline had almost completely gone now. The accompanying lump had disappeared. All healed, like the attack had never happened. On the outside.

Only inside my head did the scars shine red and raw.

I'd gone to the Institute gates a couple of times over the last two weeks. Both times, Kara had forcibly blanked me.

Approaching four months' pregnant – how much longer could she keep disguising her bulging belly? After she reached five, six months, she was bound to balloon. But what could I do? If she wouldn't even speak to me? She was on her own too.

I had no one left to fight for. No magic pot at the end of the rainbow to charge towards.

I didn't know if I wholly believed in One's slanted version of change . . . for the greater good. But I knew one thing – finally, I could fight, kill. It was all I had left to offer.

I sucked in my breath. A fight. I went over to my bed and picked up my white clutch bag. Nestled inside was the pot of pink lip wax; inside that, two tiny blue pills: one – mine, still in its wrapping; the other – out, ready, waiting to be used.

Tonight would only be my second assassination. But I was facing it as if it were my twentieth. What was one more life now? There would be no glitches, no mistakes, not this time. I was going to execute it like my grandmother had groomed me to. I was a weapon. *That was all, remember?* Not a daughter; not a granddaughter; not a friend; not really a Pair. A weapon. That was all.

I clocked my target the moment we entered her home, greeting her guests; styled hair and broad smile plastered to her head. The new Head of Population Control. I'd first met her at her interview with the Leader two weeks ago – the day I said goodbye to Stella. Clearly she'd got the job – now she was throwing a party for her colleagues in honour of it. It was what Blues did. Get promoted, get celebrated; survival's great.

It was a good thing she was so admired – it meant the whole

of the ground floor was overcrowded; elite Blues and their Green offspring rubbing up close to one other, voices rising in a cacophony of self-satisfaction. It would make the task easier.

One had known I was to be invited. '*Perfect opportunity,*' he'd told me just yesterday, via the usual scrawled note on his desk. Salinger had been sitting rigidly behind us. The memory of it brought his bemused face sauntering, unwelcomed, into my head. I breathed out: *Stay focused.* I'd hardly spoken to Salinger since the attack. That kiss we shared when he pulled off my gag – I'd made sure Tobin had swallowed it up whole a hundred times over since. I had no feelings of that nature to spare for anyone. But certainly not Salinger. Our relationship was business only. I wasn't going to be forgetting that again.

Tobin's hand squeezed my waist as we forced our way deeper into the room. 'I need a drink first, Red, if I have to talk to any of these people,' he whispered into my neck. 'Promise me that when we get our own place, we won't have to go to so many of these phoney parties.'

I made a face of affected solidarity, as if my life held the same simple frustrations as Tobin's; underneath, I calmly assessed the room: *where is she? What is she drinking? How to position myself?* 'Let's head to the bar then,' I said.

I offered to drive us all back home. Last week I'd got Tobin to finish off the lessons Salinger had started. I got into the car at any opportunity. I liked to control the engine's small measure of freedom. And right now, I needed its distraction – an excuse not to join in their post-party banter.

Tobin sat up front with me, his hand planted protectively

on my lap. Audley and Bea were in the back; they were already discussing the premature absence of their host, last seen climbing the stairs, clutching her stomach.

I acted interested; slanting my head in concern. If the pill I had slipped into her drink was effective, the Head of Population Control would be dead from suspected food poisoning by morning. I had kept it simple, I had stayed focused. I had asked for the same drink, in the same glass, with the same amount of ice, as the one I saw her drinking. I had dropped the pill into mine. I had circled Tobin unwittingly round her table. I had placed my glass down next to hers, talking animatedly with Tobin; I could tell he'd enjoyed my unusual burst of verbosity. I had picked up her drink. We had walked on. I fixed a smile.

I wouldn't dwell on the life I had snuffed out; on her grieving Pair of twenty years, on the ten-year-old son she would leave motherless. I had to stay focused on the reason she had been promoted. The new initiative for dramatically reducing the population that was gaining noise through the white corridors of the Cross, featuring in fragments of conversations in its canteen: the Culling.

'You should never leave your own party,' Bea was saying, tutting under her breath.

I murmured agreement along with them, like one of their family. They had no idea I was there, an interloper, driving their car, taking them back to their home, blood on my hands, diminishing their happy lives; wrenching open the crevice in their secure existence.

Land has too many citizens. Too many to protect when the sea rises. And it will rise. We are counting on YOU to condemn traitors to Land and its vision. Damn or be damned.

I stared down at the printed words. The poster had been distributed round the long polished table, in the high-ceilinged state meeting room that led directly from the Leader's office.

'This has gone out all over Land today – into the Institutes, shop windows, communal tenement areas.' It was the Head of Communications speaking, Bea's boss: a dark-haired man with a handsome, tanned face, which dramatically shifted expression with every word. He was good. I could learn from him. 'This will underpin the *Damn or be Damned* campaign – a precursor to the next stage of sifting out all undesirables.'

Blue-suited shoulders round the table jostled, voices murmured in unison to be seen championing the Leader's new policy. I glanced over at Audley, there in his position as Head of Industry. His grey hair was ruffled, his face looked tired, a strain pinching at its skin. I could tell it wasn't suiting him; the straight path to elimination of 'undesirables' the State was taking.

I sat up more erect, like my grandfather at the top of the table. I was to his right hand as usual, but back a little – I wasn't a head of department. But I had the Leader's ear.

These past weeks, I'd worked hard; wrapping up my grief for Stella and burying Dad under a determination to eke out every piece of knowledge from my grandfather. And I was making quick progress. The Leader witnessed my apparent 'coldness' over my mother's death; it bought me favour. He was starting to trust in me, become accustomed to my presence – like I was an extension of himself. After all, wasn't that what family was? What Cons wanted from me, and what Bea wanted from Tobin, was what they wanted for themselves.

I was learning every detail of every policy my grandfather was discreetly juggling and filtering them back to One for his double-sided manoeuvres.

Then every night I'd go home and curl myself into a ball around Tobin. His arms my only relief.

'*Undesirables* – that takes us to 437191: update me on yesterday's bomb in North Land,' the Leader growled. The Head of Communications sat down with a carefully planted, obsequious smile – opposite him, the latest Head of State Troopers rose. A wizened man with grey skin and a bald head that shined darkly as if he'd polished it along with his Black helmet. If I did my job well he would be dead at his desk by this time tomorrow.

'Leader, we are currently looking at nearly one hundred casualties; twenty dead. The wounded will be assessed for Selection, once we've run checks to see if any were the culprits.'

'I don't want to know casualty rates, man; I want to know your plans for arrests! For retaliation. How you intend to flush out those responsible?'

The bald head sprang back then bowed with contrition. 'I am sorry, sir. I misunderstood . . . My Troopers raided all the homes of those on the current list of rebel suspects – we are filling cells at the Assessment Centres. We will work quickly; loosen their tongues.'

The Leader flicked a thick hand through the air as if he were swatting flies. 'Do it. Then dispose of them – all of them. Anyone on any list should face automatic Selection from now on. It is too late for second chances.'

I clenched my teeth, then my fists. I couldn't allow myself to feel for the plight of others.

The Leader raised his chin. 'And the other matter? The untimely demise of our Head of Population Control last night?'

My insides tightened. I hid my guilt, mimicking my grandfather and lifting my chin a little higher, fixing urgent, demanding eyes on the speaker's shiny bald head. 'We have checked through the guests attending the party at the Head of Population Control's house last night. As yet we have no reason to suspect foul play. But we will remain alert. We are watching, searching for moles, Leader, as you have instructed; forming an internal list.'

The Blue shoulders now rustled as if a sudden wind had blown in; *no one wanted to be on any list*. I turned my face more aloof.

'I will appoint a new Head of Population Control immediately, to initiate the Culling.'

I kept my posture straight; my expression warm with collusion, as my blood grew cold.

'We must not wait any longer; Land needs to be cleansed,' the Leader snarled. He stood abruptly, kicking back his chair, and began walking the length of the table behind the stiff backs of his heads of state. Like them, I stared respectfully, wondrously, at him: hail Land's saviour, who will guide us through future floods, protecting us from overpopulation and threats to our security.

'Only a specified number can fit on to the ark that is Land.' His voice was so strong it seemed to leave an echo. 'With the seas forever rising, our perilous future can only accommodate so many. And yet!' He raised a finger and then patted it against his lips as if the words weren't old, well rehearsed. 'In parallel we must look ahead: keep growing a master race of intelligence and skill that will invent and innovate ways to fight back against nature.

'The Culling: to make room for the next generation of chosen ones, we must erase those who hold no worth to Land. The Culling: to achieve elimination quicker – bypassing Assessments. The last leadership was effective but lax. Too many unapproved babies slipped through the net; too many undesirables passed by the Assessors. Our apathy has allowed this rebel force to flourish. We need to seek out the rats threatening to rock the boat. We must stamp them all out. Now.'

His voice halted; the table recognised the silence as an opportunity for applause: loud clapping resounded. I stared around at the faces as my hands joined in; everyone wore the same open-mouthed unctuous smile, myself included. It was hard to tell who truly backed the Leader's plans; who, like Audley, I suspected, were merely going along with the status quo. It was my job to fill the Leader with doubts about some of them. Confuse him. I would start with the Head of Communications.

'Do you have them?' The Leader had stopped at the seat of the Head of State Troopers who directly lifted up a box. The Leader dug his hands inside, pulling out handfuls of what looked to be yellow badges. He scattered them across the table like autumn leaves. One flew down onto the floor by my feet. I picked it up. It was cut to resemble an eye; the black outline of an iris at its centre.

The Leader continued, 'As of today, these are being distributed by State and Youth Troopers – to anyone on any Assessment or rebel list, to anyone they deem even slightly traitorous to Land's core values. We will encourage the culture of informing – from tutors, managers, neighbours; we all know who needs to be wearing one of these.'

He took a breath, pressing his lips together, then added, 'The yellow eye . . . it will make the Culling simpler.' He walked back towards me, his squinted green eyes focussing heavily on mine, as if he were saying, 'Do you see? Are you learning how this is done?'

My grandfather trusted me. Then a faint smile pulled at the edges of his lips.

My grandfather was starting to care for me.

Chapter Twenty-six

I awoke wrapped up in Tobin's arms, like I did most mornings now. Our mixed-up limbs were enveloped in a sticky heat, despite the cool breeze coming in from the open window near my bed. Within the last few days, Land's weather had promptly exchanged winter's cold for sunshine. Its climate, like its politics, tended towards the extreme; April's premature heat heralded an early summer.

I lay for a moment, listening to the untroubled rhythm of Tobin's sleeping heart, watching his lips moving faintly as if he were talking in a dream.

He was becoming a bad habit; every night now we shared a bed together, even if we were always modest in our nightclothes. It had sent Bea fretting – she'd recently given us both *The Talk*: 'No sex, not under my roof. Not until you're approved for children!' It was one rule I wholeheartedly agreed with; no matter how much my body might tingle for more as Tobin's hands roamed my skin in the dark. Even if we did get approved, there was no way I was bringing life into this world; no way was I going to risk ending up like Kara. A baby wouldn't bring back love . . . family. That bubble had irreversibly popped with my fairy tale of a father.

I took in a final breath of Tobin, his calming scent of sleep, before beginning to disentangle myself, careful not to wake him; I couldn't face talking this morning. My mind had to stay fixed on what I had to do. *Breathe in. Breathe out. In, out – don't think, don't feel.*

But as I pulled my arm from under him, Tobin made a grunt, stretching his body out. Half opening his eyes, he leant over sleepily and caught me in a tight hug.

'Let go; I have to get to work . . . I'll be late.'

'I don't like having a Pair who's out of the Institute before me.' His mouth pressed down against mine. He kissed me like I was his. 'A few more minutes, cosying up together, Red . . . you know you want to.' He laughed unselfconsciously, his hands tracing the contour of my waist. Then complained, 'You take things too seriously,' as I grabbed both his hands and forced them from me.

Like spring's heat, security was intensifying all around the Green Mile. Central Land was becoming paranoid as the Resistance offensive stepped up. Over the past few days alone, Land had seen constant blasts of insurgence. A group of Troopers had been set on fire; another four had been locked into the back of a Selection truck, the engine switched on with the exhaust plugged up. Two days ago a bomb blew up and destroyed a North Land café, and everyone inside; another exploded in South Land Assessment Centre yesterday.

Unrest was catching on. Fear was spreading round the pillared rooms and high white walls of the Cross. How rebels were getting armed; making explosives: the Resistance must have recruited members – on the inside.

One seemed pleased with progress, in his rigid, restrained way.

I dropped my bag in my office. I'd never bothered to personalise the room. It mimicked One's in its austerity: just the necessities – a desk; my boxed computer screen; pencils, sharpened. I adjusted the scalloped collar of my navy-Blue shift dress, straightening the hem at my knees. The clothes I wore were purposeful: a dutiful follower keen to one day lead . . . a girl they would never conceive a traitor.

I pulled out my lip wax, opening it and tucking the loose pill inside into my fist.

I made straight for the communal kitchen a few corridors down. It was where the secretaries on my floor made drinks for their bosses. I didn't have an assistant yet. I made my own tea. That was why I was able to watch her routine all this week.

I knew she'd be there, exactly at this time. The secretary to the Head of State Troopers. Stirring milk into the fat white cup I knew now to be his. I had planned for her verbosity to assist me – and as predicted she was chatting non-stop to a colleague about some disloyal Brown passenger on the tram that she had proudly turned in to the Troopers. Neither of them noticed me lean across to open a cupboard door; my hand hovering briefly over the steaming, dark liquid behind her.

It was done. Another heart-attack victim in the making. The job of Head of State Troopers: clearly it was too stressful.

Calmly, I continued to make my own drink then strolled back down the corridor with it. He was just a number, I told myself. Just another number.

'I've been waiting for you to arrive.'

I caught myself before I jumped; my grandfather, standing rigidly behind my desk, his Black suit starched and creased. 'Good morning, Leader,' I said, shedding all evidence of my traitorous act from my expression.

He surveyed me as he was wont to do these days; his green eyes displaying a confusion with what I was to him. I helped him out. 'I greatly admired your speech yesterday at the heads of state meeting.'

He raised his chin, breathing in loudly through his nose. 'I want to hear you making speeches similar to mine soon.'

'I do too,' I clipped back, echoing the tone in his voice. He had to think that we were one and the same.

'Good. Now come with me. I've just appointed our new Head of Population Control.'

'If it needs to be done, I'll do it.'

We were sitting, the three of us, in One's car in the garage – One and me on the front seat, Salinger in the back, as if were playing some child's imaginary game of a fun day out. To give us an excuse to get away from the office and talk, we'd just returned from a real trip – to see the damage left by yesterday's bomb in South Land. A woman had sacrificed herself to take out an Assessor at her appointment, as well as the walls of the room they were in. The Resistance were closing in on Central Land.

'I said, if it needs to be done, I'll do it,' Salinger repeated in earnest to One.

I gritted my teeth. I had purposely not turned to acknowledge him the whole time we'd been in the car. If I could, I avoided him altogether these days. I never liked to be reminded of that stupid kiss. 'I'm doing it,' I asserted. 'He's my Pair's father'.

One cleared his throat. 'Tell us again what happened.'

I cast my mind back. I'd thought it was some joke at first when I'd followed the Leader into his state meeting room. Audley sat, shoulders back, halfway down the long table; his hands clasped stiffly in front of him.

'Meet the next Head of Population Control. Of course you two know one another well already.'

Audley pulled at the edges of his mouth. It was plain he didn't want the job. Not one bit.

'Population control currently takes precedence over industry – so 488724 has been transferred.' The Leader looked at me. He was starting to value my opinion. He wanted to know if I thought it a good appointment.

'I told him afterwards I thought Audley weak, unimaginative,' I now told One. 'Clearly, I played it wrong; the Leader didn't seem to think either attribute a problem for the job.'

One danced his head at me. 'But you're right. It's a role we must target, if we want to delay the Culling.'

'Agreed. I have to get rid of him.'

One moved his mouth as if he were systematically repeating my words. The weather had forced him to abandon his ever-present long, waxy coat. Somehow he looked more vulnerable without it. 'Plan the best way. Do it soon.'

I heard Salinger shift restlessly in the seat behind me. 'Hang on. You live with Audley!' I sensed him lean over the front seat. 'Christy! Let me do it.'

'No – it's mine,' I answered plainly, blinking away the picture of Bea and her happy family.

'This isn't a competition, Christy!' There was a critical edge to his tone I didn't like. 'First you insist on being the one to take out the new Head of State Troopers when that was supposed to be my job – now this! You're not supposed to *want* to kill!' His face was bent close to mine now. But I didn't turn to see it.

'No? Then what the hell am I supposed to want? This is war!'

'Will you stop it?' One butted in, sighing as if we were both trying his patience. 'Stop squabbling like children. I told you, Salinger – Christy was confident she could take out the Head of State Troopers easily, swiftly. It was a job for either of you – this morning Christy got there first.'

He planted his thick hands over the creases on his trousers. 'Christy is best placed for taking out Audley.'

I heard Salinger sit back, grunting something that sounded like 'taste for death'. I ignored him. What did he care who I killed?

'However – we've got to stop using the pills. Time now to use a real weapon – one that makes government start to panic,' One continued. 'We need both sides to step up quicker with their reactions – before our final act.'

'A real weapon??'

'A gun. You'll be needing it soon anyway.' He opened the car door. 'I have one for you – it's in the house.'

'I've only been trained to use a gun on paper.' I coughed, correcting my voice as it broke. 'I've never even held one.' I'd thought I would be slipping a pill into the glass of water Audley

264

routinely took with him to bed. Could I put a gun to his head?

'I'll teach you the basics now.' One shut the car door behind him.

'Are you really going to do this?' Salinger spoke quietly.

'I'm instructed to kill my grandfather – what's the difference?' I adjusted myself, agitated. 'Audley's just the starter before the main course, isn't he?'

'Can you even hear yourself? You're like a . . . a . . .'

I stared fixedly at the garage door and finished his sentence for him. 'A monster?' I inhaled deeply. 'Wasn't that always the idea?'

'You don't have to kill Audley. I don't know him; I can do it. Or better still – no one kills him. Let's not fool ourselves the Culling won't still go ahead even without its new head.'

Was he right? Was it futile to kill Audley? Why *was* I insisting I do it? Tobin's father. The boy I slept wrapped up with. Bea's Pair. I'd be turning her from a two back into a one.

I dug my nails into my palms. I couldn't let myself care.

'You're on a killing spree.' The same edge lined Salinger's voice. It made me swing round at last. We locked eyes. Salinger's looked weary, spent.

'Audley lives in the same house,' I said, my tone strained. 'I have access.'

'I'll tell you now – hate won't salve the pain. I've been there – it just makes it worse.'

'You no longer have the right to give me lectures!'

'And you were never very friendly – but when did you become so damned mean?'

I twisted back to face the front, scratching at the blue leather seat. 'I'm just doing my job, aren't I? The one you trained me for.'

One climbed back in. 'We need to hurry; we've been in here too long already. Here.' He handed me the gun. 'Go in and out through a window – make it look like a rebel breaking in. We'll quickly carry out some aim practise now.' He tapped the metal handle weighing down my palm. 'You need to become familiar with it. We're not far from our end goal. When heads of state are sufficiently depleted it will be time to . . .' He let his voice trail off.

'Remove my grandfather,' I stated blankly.

One's reply was a low, silent hiss, like the sound of a pipe letting off steam. 'Remain controlled, Christy. Keep it in your head: a few men need to die . . . or thousands of others will.'

Chapter Twenty-seven

I stayed awake into the night, until I could be sure everyone else in the house was sound asleep. I couldn't face the thought of unwrapping Tobin's arms from around me to go directly to shoot his father dead. So, instead, I retrieved the gun from where I'd hidden it – carefully wrapped up within my toilet cistern – and left with it. I intended to drive aimlessly for an hour before I returned to fake my break-in.

I circled South Land, then drove across into West, fighting an urge to continue past Kara's. I spotted the poster I'd seen passed around the heads of state meeting stuck to countless walls, and pasted on windows. The stark black-and-white message repeated multiple times becoming part of ordinary language: *Damn or be Damned.*

On my route back, down the main thoroughfare, a blast of noise and colour suddenly appeared on the road in front: fire was raging through buildings near to West Land shopping precinct. A rebel bomb. Troopers were filling the scene, their thick Black boots pounding concrete as they raced round, hollering random orders at Brown fireworkers.

I drove slowly past bright orange flames dancing in and out

of windows, as if *they* were playing at rebels, taunting the water hoses trying to catch them. White stone had been charred black. Pieces of peeled-off burnt paint swirled through the air like a swarm of black moths. I'd occasionally heard an explosive shake the ground; I'd listened to the numbers injured, killed. But aside from this morning's comparatively tame visit – I'd not yet witnessed their fallout.

They were largely Blue-occupied flats in this area; their residents were now flooding out of doorways, filling the gaps between the Troopers and fireworkers on the floodlit street; their faces presenting fear and confusion: chaos was replacing order's grip.

I swerved round the debris cluttering the ordinarily bare street, shards of glass mixed in amongst torn pieces of curtain, smashed white crockery. A leg; my guts contracted – a body was no longer attached to it, shorn at the knee. I swung my eyes away, only to spot another mangled limb wrapped up in rubble; then more: misshapen dust-covered bodies, blown from their apartments while they slept.

Maybe it was what I'd just seen; maybe it was knowing it was One supplying the explosive material to the rebels, but I'd had enough of death for one night. As soon as I pulled the car back into the garage, I bottled it – I couldn't end Audley's life, not tonight. Suddenly, all I wanted was to be back in bed, with Tobin's warm arms around me. Before I could no longer sleep next to him again.

Not that I slept through the last few hours left of the night. I lay my head lightly on Tobin's chest, trying to let the rise and fall of his ribs rock me into a stupor, but my mind whirred too fast with my heart. If my eyes closed, the backs of my lids showed images of Audley, slain, mixing with those torn bloody pieces of Blues.

By the time I arrived at my office next morning, exhaustion hung off me like a second skin. My spent body was a stark contrast to the frenetic buzz of tension and shock running down the Cross corridors. Last night's bomb attack in West Land had caused the most Blue fatalities yet. The State couldn't allow the attacks to reach the power hub itself. I knew they would move soon on the Culling: I had to remove Audley tonight. I had to – I couldn't be weak again.

'823057, you're wanted downstairs in the lobby.' My nerves already jagged, I jolted as a Trooper filled my doorway. 'A Brown. Says he has an appointment.'

I nodded at the stiff face beneath the polished helmet, quickly closing the data report I'd been finishing for One on my screen – my own list of the Cross officials I had observed, who he might be able to trust when it came to it.

I blithely followed the Trooper down to the lobby, not even thinking about who it might be – until I saw him. He was standing nervously near the entrance, two Troopers either side, their eyes hanging heavy on him. I could tell who it was even with his head inappropriately bent down, just from his hair, raven-black like his sister's. The sight of it made me yearn suddenly for my old friend.

'Thank you; he's right. I have an appointment with him,' I said abruptly to the Trooper who had come to fetch me. They wouldn't dare question me. My voice had become something, inside these walls of power.

'Xavier?' I uttered quietly, tonelessly. 'Everything okay?' As if I were asking him about the weather or something. I steered him away, to stand beneath the glass dome and its rainbow shards of colour. 'What is it?' He looked so out of place here, his clothes drab and ill-fitting – mud-Brown trousers and a faded Brown shirt that was creased and wearing thin at the elbows.

'Is it Kara?' I asked under my breath, sensing the fear begin to spread through me just from saying her name.

His dark, sunken eyes stayed pointing downwards. He made a short shake of his head. He wouldn't dare speak. Not here.

'Does she want to see me?' Is that what I wanted? I wasn't sure; part of me needed to keep Kara shut out. It felt better that way. Save for the nest of Tobin's embrace, I was alone now.

Xavier scratched at his cheek, finally looking up at me. His black eyes gave his reply.

'She's been found out?' The hushed words surfed my breath, my stomach tightening against the answer. I flicked a glance at the Troopers; they were talking lazily amongst themselves.

Xavier shook his head; his eyes continuing to make an appeal for me to understand.

'It's coming?'

This time, a curt nod.

Another trail of terror began worming its way through my body. Frantically I started to assemble thoughts against actions, as if I were facing another assassination. 'But it's too early.'

Xavier spoke finally, an agitated whisper. 'It's happening now. I had a hard time getting here.'

Part of my mind sparked with sudden optimism. The baby was premature by months – I knew the facts from Cons' midwifery – so chances were it would die naturally. Kara's pregnancy would be over without further fight.

I reached out to place a hand on Xavier's arm. 'Let's go.' And then I noticed it. No wonder he'd had a hard time getting here. Badly sewn onto his worn shirt sleeve: a yellow badge – the black outline of an eye.

We were back at Tobin's house to get the car; I didn't speak again until we reached the garage, wheeling round on him once we were safely inside. 'It's okay to talk now. Are you certain she's in labour? I mean, it's really early . . . it must be a miscarriage?'

Xavier pushed a trembling hand through his hair. 'She lied to you. She wasn't sure at first whose it was. She's over seven months pregnant.'

My mouth gaped open, then closed; opened again. She lied to me about when . . . whose it was? She'd let me think he was her first. 'How many boys has Kara slept with?'

Xavier lifted his hands, they were shaking. 'I should have stopped her . . . There were a few of my friends who she . . . I just liked seeing her having fun.'

'Why would she lie to me?'

Xavier's eyes turned sheepish. 'I think she worried you'd disapprove of her . . . nag her harder to get rid of it.'

I felt my stomach shrink. Had Kara feared me?

'She's in pain, lots of pain,' Xavier said quietly. 'And really scared . . . I didn't know what to do . . . I thought, what with Cons being a midwife – I didn't know who else to turn to.'

I placed a hand on his shoulder to try and calm him down.

271

'It's okay; you did right. And Kara wants me there? She wants me to come?'

Xavier stared at anything but me.

'She asked you not to get me?'

A nod. I didn't know what to feel. That Kara would be in her hour of greatest need and not want my help? How had we got to this point?

'Okay, well let's get over there. I'll go collect some supplies from the house.' At the garage door, I turned back to Xavier. 'Do you agree – we need to act – do whatever has to be done to save her, to keep Kara alive?'

'She won't let you get rid of it,' Xavier interjected, already reading my mind.

I exhaled heavily. 'Well then, let's just hope it's dead on arrival,' I said, not making an attempt to disguise my real feelings with him. 'It would be the best solution for everyone.'

I grabbed the car keys from the table in the hallway, then raced into the kitchen. The slave girl was there, mopping down the tiles. She passed back a brisk 'Hello' to mine without even looking up at me. I didn't bother to explain myself; it wasn't as if she'd dare tell on me to Bea. She spoke to no one unless spoken to. I grabbed a heavy-duty white paper bag and threw in a sharp knife; any food I could grab from the fridge and the antiseptic cream Bea used for Ella's dry skin. My hand hovered briefly over Audley's home-made wine – I didn't like the reminder of him and my promise to kill him tonight, but what other pain relief did we have? I grabbed two bottles.

Heat was rising up from the roads, making the air above them shimmer and shake. It was sweltering inside the car but we kept all the windows up. We didn't want to be heard.

Last night's rebel activity remained in evidence; remnants from West Land's bombing still littering the streets. Troopers seemed to be everywhere. At least one in five people we passed already had the yellow eye attached to their arm, like Xavier. They were walking targets: stones or stale bread being thrown at their heads, jeers being tossed out by other civilians. I noticed a bunch of Troopers surround one middle-aged woman in Brown, flicking aggressively at her badge. I stared back at them in my rear-view mirror as they pinned her against a wall. When they backed away she was lying splayed, completely still on the floor. A Selection truck veered up alongside her.

I'd been too long in my Central Land bubble. 'When did it start getting this bad?'

Xavier sunk lower into his seat, hiding his Brown shoulders completely from the window. 'Since the rebel bombs started. Then loads of us got given these yellow eyes over the past few days. I had to use your number just to get past the Troopers on my way down. I hope you don't mind.'

I shook my head. 'It was brave of you to come all the way to the Cross. Did Kara get a badge?'

'Not yet. She's been keeping her eyes down, mouth shut, for once.'

I thought of Kara struggling to conceal a bump that was in fact approaching full term, fixing a smile, staying silent. I hit the steering wheel with the heel of my hand. 'Kara should have told me, let me help her.'

Xavier shrugged gently. 'We're the lucky ones; many I know

have failed Assessments recently, been shipped off in Selection trucks.'

I gripped the wheel tighter. 'I should have done more.' I should have killed more; I should have helped stop this sooner.

'I've brought Christy,' Xavier said, as we followed the drone of low moaning to Kara's bedroom. The small room was dark, airless; the curtains shut out most of the daylight, keeping all the heat in. I switched on the ceiling light; it flickered then shone a pale yellow onto Kara's body, heaped under a threadbare off-white sheet.

'I'm here, Kara,' I repeated softly, my heart thumping; I half expected to see the baby there, already out. What would I do with it then?

There was a low rumble of a groan and Kara's bundled body began to unfold. She stared around at me. 'Get out, I don't need your help.' Her caramel skin looked closer to grey; her blue eyes were shot through, blood-red.

'Please, Kara.' I moved closer to her. 'It doesn't matter now. I'm sorry for the things I said.'

'You never came back,' she spat out at me.

'I tried! You walked right past me twice at the Institute.'

'You didn't try hard enough! I was angry, I wasn't going to –' She stopped, her face convulsing, a throttled whimper seeping out between gritted teeth. Her body arched; she clamped a hand over her mouth, a high-pitched moan escaping.

'I'm here now,' I said in a rush, moving to her. 'So you're more gone than you told me,' I stated matter of factly; I wasn't going to argue with her now.

274

Kara slumped back down to the mattress, her face loosened as the pain faded. 'Eight months. This pain . . . it's agony . . . comes in surges . . . then goes again.'

'We can get through this.' I reached out, stroking her short black hair; it was sodden with sweat. 'Will you let me help?' I took her silence for consent. 'Can I see what's happening?' I indicated her swollen belly with my eyes. Even near full term, it was still just a small ball of a bump stuck onto her thin frame.

Kara stared back at me; her eyes distrustful, but gradually she nodded.

I took a breath. I had to get this right. I'd done everything to banish Cons from my head, but now I had to allow her back in. Memories of watching her, listening to her work as a midwife. I'd heard plenty of her talk about the women who gave birth just fine only to die days later from infection; the State had little interest in helping women who couldn't survive births. No one would dare touch Kara if we had to take her into hospital.

I shot a look at Xavier. 'I need your help; get me boiled water and clean towels . . . Take these.' I handed him the knife from the white paper bag. 'Sterilise it in boiling water.'

Gently I pulled the sheet off Kara and pushed up her nightshirt. I stretched her legs apart, scanning between them.

'Is everything okay?' Kara breathed out.

I didn't answer; besides a baby, I didn't know what I was looking for. Kara's whole groin area looked a mess – swollen pink and bloodied. Observing Cons hadn't stretched this far. I pulled her nightshirt back over her knees. The mattress beneath her legs felt sodden.

'Your waters, when did they break?'

'My waters? Was that what it was . . .? I thought I'd wet myself.' Her voice was squeezed. 'About an hour or so ago.'

'And do you feel the need to push?'

'When it hurts, yes, I think so.'

'Okay, then we need to start.' I could feel my own insides contracting. 'I'll be a minute. I'm going to help Xavier. In the meantime –' I went to the paper bag, taking out and twisting the cork from one of the bottles of wine I'd brought – 'drink this. It'll help the pain.'

Kara took it eagerly, taking large gulps back. I could easily have joined her, if I hadn't needed a clear head.

I followed Xavier into the kitchen. 'She's going to start pushing. But listen – it's crucial, we need to agree –' I circled him until he looked at me – 'what to do with it . . .' I watched his face darken. 'You know she can't keep it, Xavier.'

'We can't kill it.'

'It will die anyway; you see what they're doing out there. There won't even be the sniff of a chance of adoption: straight to Selection for both of them. They're not offering any second chances any longer. You don't know what they're doing.' I forced my hands back through my hair, stretching the skin taut on my forehead. I had to keep it together. Focus. 'They want to cull people where they can. Soon, they're going to start killing thousands of people without any Assessment process.'

Xavier's eyes searched mine. '. . . They're going to just kill us all?'

'I'll try to protect you. I promise. But first we need to save Kara . . . This is the way to save Kara.' I fixed my eyes on his as he started to turn away. 'With any luck it might not even come to it . . . it might die naturally as it comes into the world, if we don't help it breathe.' I paused. I didn't recognise my voice any more. 'But if it lives . . . your neighbours will hear it. Damn or be damned, remember? They won't –'

'Most of our neighbours are okay,' Xavier's soft voice cut through me.

'Xavier – most people are *okay*, until they fear for their lives!' My lip curled involuntarily. 'It's called self-preservation – most humans practise it . . . at the expense of others.'

'Kara won't let you.'

'Kara won't know. We tell her it died naturally.' I was certain now: I had to see this through. Killing life that got in the way of survival – it was the only answer.

Maybe I was more like my grandfather than I cared to admit.

Xavier swallowed hard, nodded, then shook his head. He hadn't said to do it, but he hadn't said not, either. It was answer enough. He wanted his sister saved, didn't he?

We took the towels and water back in, the knife I kept wrapped up in another towel, to keep sterile. I knelt back down at the end of the bed, lifting Kara's nightshirt again. 'Kara, okay, listen to me: when the next pain comes, you push; push what's inside of you out,' I said, with all the authority I could muster.

Then we waited, in silence, all three of us, in the hot room, until again Kara's breath started to quicken, inhaling rapidly as if she couldn't get enough air.

'Push,' I urged her.

Kara's face scrunched up, her eyes tightening shut. Her lips quivered, then a loud scream rattled out.

'Kara!' I exclaimed, panic shooting through me. Their neighbours right now might be stepping out of their front doors, checking what the noise was about; State Troopers staring up from the street directly below. 'Remember you have to be quiet! Xavier, give her something to bite down on – you have to help her stay silent!'

'I can't any more . . . I can't . . . it hurts too much. It's a pain like death.' Kara reached for the bottle of wine and drank ravenously, a calf to a teat. 'I just want this all to stop.'

'Kara, Kara, look at me, please – shush,' I exclaimed quietly. 'Remember, we can't let anyone know. We're all dead if anyone hears us. Troopers are everywhere outside, they're just waiting for an excuse to knock down any door . . .'

'I want my mum. I want her, Xavier.' Kara stared breathlessly at her brother. 'I wish she were here . . . My mum. I want my mum.' Kara repeated the last few words over; she was starting to sound delirious. I looked at the wine bottle in her hand; it was nearly empty. Stiffening, she moaned loudly again; Xavier shoved a piece of clothing into her mouth and Kara's eyes widened as if they were continuing the scream for her.

'Push, push, Kara,' I hissed. Her face twisting in agony; another arch of her back and then she slumped back onto the bed. I crouched lower, gazing into the bloody gap between her legs; and there it was. Just the top part of a head, crowned between Kara's legs; a small mound of thick black hair, matted with a cap of blood and mucus. I inhaled sharply. The damned baby, this thing who had taken over my friend, taken her away from me.

'Push again,' I said, my voice shaky, 'at the next contraction.'

I could feel beads of hot sweat running down my back; I had to be ready. I couldn't allow it to live. I could do this. I killed life. I didn't create it.

The whole head barged through on the next push. Its shrivelled skin the colour of milky tea, smeared in a creamy mucus; its eyes squeezed tight shut, as if it didn't dare look at where it had landed.

I breathed in, out; I ordered myself: *now*. I forced a hand forward. Kara's shallow panting was becoming more laboured; Xavier's eyes were on her. I closed my palm down, such a tiny nose, a miniature mouth; it wouldn't take much. It had made no cry yet, it hadn't worked out how to breathe; it was ill-equipped to live without support; *so do it now before it discovers its lungs. Before it has any idea it ever lived!*

Kara's body convulsed; her back curved again as a long, muffled shriek trailed out from her mouth. The rest of the tiny body slipped out on an oil slick of reds and pinks onto the limp mattress. My hand was still hovering over its face as its eyes blinked open. Black, black eyes, like pieces of coal. Eyes that seemed to fix on mine.

There was silence, a shroud of serene silence, hanging over the room. The only sounds came from the street below; the odd door slamming from the other flats in the tenement as people arrived back from work; the echo of Troopers' boots as they marched the road below; the whir of a passing Selection truck. But inside, we were so quiet the neighbours wouldn't even know anyone was in the flat.

Xavier was in the kitchen, making some broth with the food

I'd brought, for Kara when she woke again.

I should have left by now, but I couldn't. I wanted to stay near him. Kara's baby.

Kara had been weak from blood-loss, but she'd let me put him to her breast, hold him there as his small mouth worked out for himself what he was expected to do; she'd winced with pain but then began humming contentedly to him as she stroked the top of his thick black sticky hair. She was still in pain; said her stomach burned. She'd finished off the rest of the wine – it had sent her to sleep since.

I just hoped rest and nourishment, and Bea's antiseptic cream, would be enough to heal the damage she'd sustained.

And so now I sat, her baby boy snuggled up in the crook of my elbow, as if it was what my arm was built for. He was born surviving; grasping at life.

And in a matter of seconds, a different version of me had risen, from the one poised to extinguish life from this tiny body. How could I have even been that person? I would die – I would kill – to protect this baby. This amazing, tiny miracle.

Love. That was what it was. A reminder of what it felt to love: Cons, Kara . . . a dream of my dad; what I might have felt for Stella. It was filling me up, every corner and crevice inside, stuffing itself in tighter as if there was no end to it. Yes; love.

I was already addicted to watching him; I couldn't stop. Examining every minute fingernail and eyelash. How his tiny hands curled up into fists under his chin, as if he were resting his head upon them to ponder life. Those dark, owl-like eyes that roved back and forth, as if he were wisely assessing his situation.

I bent my head low to breathe him in, nutmeg and vanilla, a sweet aroma of comfort. I kissed the top of his black hair, fluffy now after I had spent time washing and drying him; he released a little murmur, a tiny, tuneful sigh of satisfaction.

His name was to be Sunil. Kara had murmured it, her lips pressed against his head, while she held him for the first time. 'Sunil. Like Dad.'

'Why?' Xavier had asked softly. 'Grandpa named Dad Sunil because of the dark blue of the ocean that had carried them to Land; do you really want to honour that same sea that traps us here?'

'I'm not naming him for the ocean,' Kara had said back to Xavier, her voice faint and woozy, 'I'm naming him for the colour of the clothes I hope he will wear.'

'You want him to be a Blue when he's older,' I stated resignedly.

Kara lifted her chin shakily. 'I want him to fit into this world. Not like me.'

I caught the look on her face. All Kara fiercely stood for meant nothing. She just wanted her baby to survive. If that meant wearing Blue, so be it. She would sacrifice her own beliefs for that.

She was a mother.

Chapter Twenty-eight

It was past midnight by the time I drove the car back into the garage. I was beyond tired, my eyes could hardly focus, and yet at the same time a new energy ran through my veins. I'd thought Kara foolish to believe hope and love would come packaged up in a baby. But both were now back in my life, pumping round my body, as if I'd been born again myself.

I couldn't, wouldn't take Audley's life from him now. I wasn't sure I'd ever be able to kill again. Sunil had ruined me.

I would have stayed there all night with them, but I had to plan – I had to protect my new family, think ahead. A germ of an idea had begun to form as I sat there cuddling Sunil's weightless body. The Leader – he was the only one with the authority to manipulate the database for Pairings . . . for childbirth. If I could find a way to convince him, some story about why I couldn't have children of my own, I might just pull it off. I had to pull it off. We were in an impossible situation; we had days, maybe only a matter of hours, till someone heard Sunil cry and reported him; Kara had to get back to the Institute by the end of the week.

It was our only way out – but I couldn't do this by myself any more.

What's more – suddenly, I didn't want to.

'Red!' My bedside light switched on. 'You're home at last – I was worried.' Tobin rubbed at his eyes as he sat up in my bed, his hair crumpled against one side of his head. 'What they got you working at that keeps making you so late?

I mumbled a 'Sorry,' lunging towards the bathroom. I'd imagined we'd have this conversation tomorrow morning, when I was lucid again.

'We've had a nightmare time of it here tonight,' Tobin continued, stretching arms out to me, then dropping them. 'What's that?'

I followed his eyes down. Dark red stains, like splattered paint, covered my blouse; I hadn't even noticed.

'Is it blood?'

'Not mine,' I breathed out as his forehead became lined with concern. 'Let me get washed first, get out of these clothes; then we'll talk. I'll tell you where I've been.'

He jumped out of bed, would have come into the bathroom with me if I hadn't closed and locked the door on him. 'What is it, Red?' His voice stayed close to the other side as I ran the tap, peeling off my stained clothes. 'What's wrong?'

He exhaled loudly, the other side of the door, when I replied, 'Just wait.'

'We've had our own troubles here tonight . . . Mum's lost the plot big time.'

I splashed my face with warm water, ran wet fingers through the tight tangles perspiration had formed in my hair. 'What are you talking about?' I called back, pulling my nightshirt over my head.

'It's Ella. She was given that yellow badge to wear today.'

I opened the door. 'Ella got the yellow eye?'

Tobin nodded his head solemnly then pulled me into a hug, his arms tightening round me as if he wanted to stop me from leaving. I pulled my head back. 'How on earth did Ella get the yellow eye?'

'You know Ella – she's always asking her quiet questions about the State. The tutors never report her because of who Mum and Dad are . . .

'But this morning – was something different. My timid little sister – she was caught tearing down posters in the girls' toilets – some with the slogans Mum came up with.' He made an ironic grimace.

I shook my head, picturing Ella, with her mouse-like features and slender limbs, the yellow eye forcing her to stand out for the wrong reasons.

'Tobin, you know how dangerous it is to have one of those badges?'

'If I didn't before, I do now . . . apparently Dad's been given some job to arrest everyone wearing them . . .'

'More than arrest,' I mumbled.

'Dad's been arguing with Mum all night, about turning the job down; that he won't arrest his own daughter. Mum's been crying at him that he can't, he'll face Selection. She's insisting we hide Ella . . . Dad's shouting back, that that's impossible . . . which was when Mum started wailing, saying stuff like this was retribution for taking Ella as a baby from another mother . . .'

'She said that?' I swallowed, bit down on my lip, thinking. I shouldn't be gaining hope from this – it was a heinous situation for them to be in. But I had a more pressing life to save. 'Do you think your mum might contemplate saving a baby's life to make up for the one she took?'

Tobin made a perplexed face. I pulled him over to sit down on the bed.

'What are you going on about, Red?'

'I have to tell you something . . . Don't be shocked. Hear me out.'

Tobin plucked absently at the neckline of my nightshirt, as if he wanted to remove it. I pushed his hand back. I needed him to listen.

'You don't really have a clue what it's like, out there. Words like Selection have been dreamt up for people like you – so you don't have to look at the reality. At what your dad's really being asked to do.'

Tobin made another face – showing hurt this time. 'You don't have to go all pious, you're hardly at the rock face of endurance yourself. I *know* what Dad's being asked to do . . . and it's wrong.'

I shook my head; I wasn't doing this right. I couldn't afford a row. I licked my lips as he inched his head away. 'Tobin, I need your help.'

'You need my help?' I almost smiled at the boyish disbelief in his voice.

'I do,' I said.

Tobin shifted back closer to me. 'Okay. As long as it doesn't involve tearing down posters.'

It was an abridged version I gave him, but the facts were still the truth: my only friend; an unapproved baby; her brother a

285

Brown, with the yellow eye like Ella.

'I want us to adopt Sunil – only until we can give him back to Kara. In the meantime I need to bring him here tomorrow – it'll be safer for him; we haven't neighbours close enough to hear his cries.' I took a breath, pressing a hand against Tobin's chest. 'If you can work on Bea, get her blessing to bring him here urgently, I will go to the Leader, ask for his approval for us to be parents.'

I watched him trying to process my words, his eyes squinting at mine as if he were trying to catch me out in a joke. Tobin's life had been so perfectly polished; I couldn't blame him for not being able to see the dirt underneath.

'I get you wanting to help your friend, Red. But, hey . . .' He rubbed a hand over his chin. 'I'm not sure I'm ready to be a stand-in dad, not yet. I mean – we've only just started getting to know one another, properly, these last few weeks.'

'If we don't do something, the baby will die – Kara too. I have to save them.' I stared at Tobin with every inch of emotion that Sunil had reawakened in me.

He held my eyes then, slowly, he replied. 'All right – I mean, if it means that much to you . . .'

'Tobin, thank you,' I said, wrapping my arms about him. I had nearly killed his father – and now I was asking him to risk his own life to help me. My lips found his. From now on, I would let down the defences; I had to be me, whatever was left of me. I owed Tobin that. I kissed him harder, a real, heartfelt kiss, from Christy: Tobin's Pair.

I was drowning. I was surrounded by bitingly cold, translucent blue water, flooding into my mouth, shooting up my nostrils, inflating my lungs. I couldn't breathe, I had no voice to shout for help. A thick hand was clasped round my neck, forcing my head to stay underwater. There was no way out. *I can't die yet*, I was thinking, *I must save him . . . I can't leave them*. Then I heard, above the surface of the water, a familiar voice, urgently calling my name. *Christy, Christy!* My body relaxed. *It's all right, he will fight off my attacker; he will save me . . .*

'Tobin,' I spluttered, my eyes flying open; I hadn't expected it to be him. My mind sleepily readjusted to the sights around me. My warm double bed, my room decorated with silver stars. Curtains open, the glare of natural daylight replacing the artificial glow of the nightlights outside.

'Hey, Red, you were having a bad dream.'

Tobin moved closer, arms drawing me in, enveloping me as I sat up, his breath warm on my neck. Without his tight hold on me I felt like I might sink back into my nightmare. I pulled my face away from his, surveying him like I'd not seen him in a while. 'You're dressed,' I said.

His smile grew, until it reached those round twilight eyes, blinking back at me. 'You're late.'

'I am?' I rubbed at my head and images of yesterday began flooding in, reminding me: Kara and Sunil.

'Yep: let's get on with our mission, Red.'

'Okay, good.' I nodded my head, thinking fast. Time; I had so little time. 'So you'll work on your mum this morning? Play on her emotions, remind her: saving one baby will be a way to make amends for taking another. Use words like that.

'I'll go right away to work on the Leader, try and get him

287

to approve us. Can you meet me at lunchtime? I'll take us to pick up Sunil.'

I pressed my hands onto his chest as he agreed. 'But Tobin . . . If the Leader doesn't approve us then you have to know – hiding Sunil, it could lead to our Selection.'

'Yeah – I know . . . But, we're in this together, right . . . we're a Pair.'

I smiled at him, despite the strain freeze-framing my face. 'We're a Pair,' I repeated back, my mouth playing with the echo of the word. *We* – finally, my Pairing was the answer.

It felt too good to be wrong. It felt too good to have people I cared about in my life again. I included Tobin in that. I walked quickly amongst other Blues and Greys making their way across the Green Mile to the Cross. The day was already warming up, a dry heat that had people peeling off their layers and swigging from white metal water bottles. But I hardly noticed the warmth pricking at my skin. I could only think about this: Tobin and I were going to save Sunil, protect Kara, together. I was no longer alone.

Maybe later, I'd share more. Maybe I'd confide my whole journey . . . Would he forgive me for duping him? For considering murdering his father? Would he understand? If I told him I saw us as a true Pairing now? Tobin – the other half of me.

I climbed the carpeted stairs two at a time.

'He's not in,' the Leader's stiff-faced secretary informed me as I rushed towards his door. 'He's attending an emergency meeting at South Land Council. There were two more bombs there last night,' she added primly.

I tried not to think about more casualties scattered over the street, pieces of people thrown across the concrete. I had to stay focused. I switched my plan round. I'd go and check on Kara now; see the Leader later this morning – there was time before meeting Tobin.

I rushed back to the house. I'd slipped out this morning without seeing Bea or Audley, or facing Ella and her yellow eye – my mind had to stay fixed on Sunil. Luckily they'd all since left. I grabbed the car keys and some more supplies: wine, food, fresh towels, some stuff for Sunil.

I drove out fast from the underground passage, once I'd been waved through the Trooper-guarded gate. But then came to an immediate standstill before the metal rails of West Land Institute. A mixture of State and Youth Troopers blocked my passage as they picked off Greens; pushing them against walls, kicking others down onto the middle of the street. Yellow eye badges were being pressed against chests. They must have been ordered to step up their effort. My breath quickened. I shouldn't be here: I should be meeting One, getting my orders . . . we had to move before the Culling came. Momentarily, my mind fought a brief game of tug – and Sunil won. Of course he did. I had to see him and Kara safe first. I had something to live for again; I wouldn't lose it.

I started manoeuvring the car slowly round the Troopers; Greens using me as a shield to make it across to the Institute gates unseen, unscathed. I pressed down hard on the brakes when a hand banged authoritatively on my bonnet. I straightened up. I couldn't afford to get checked. I'd purposely left my tracer at home this time – I was supposed to be at work. I couldn't risk One or the Leader tracking me to Kara's.

I smiled sweetly out of the front window, a smile that belied every inch of my true state. Somehow it was enough – the Trooper at the end of the stiff arm softened his expression. He gave me a look as if I was one of them, as if I sanctioned their brutality. He cleared a space for me, knocking two Greens down onto the concrete as he did so. I bit my lip; I had to steel myself: Sunil first, Land after.

'Xavier, you've not gone to work?'

'I didn't want to leave them alone,' Xavier replied softly. 'Kara's insides hurt and Sunil stays quiet only as long as he's held all the time.'

At least Kara looked a little better; she was washed and had changed into a clean nightie. 'I brought some more wine,' I told her. 'Xavier says you're in pain still?'

Kara looked up from the bundle in her arms and nodded. 'But Sunil's been so good,' she answered the next question on my lips. 'No one will have heard him . . . he's mostly been sleeping, feeding some. He's looking after us as much as we are him. The one moment when he did start to cry, Xavier went into the bathroom and ran the shower like you said to.'

I smiled and sat down near her; Kara winced as the thin mattress moved. I knelt on the floor instead, leaning down to kiss Sunil's warm cheek, breathing in his milky scent of life. 'I've also got food; more cloths and small towels to make into nappies; glass bottles to store your milk so others can feed him.

'. . . We must make plans, you know . . .' I would need to find the right words not to scare her off again. 'To hide him.'

I watched Kara's arms tighten round her warm package; her eyes darkening with the old distrust that had broken us. 'Kara, we need to keep him safe,' Xavier said quietly from the doorway.

'Listen, first let me make you something to eat. Then we'll talk.' I needed a moment to consider my words carefully. Kara was still using her heart. So that meant – as always – I had to be the one to use my head.

I began frying the meat patties and cutting thick slices of bread from the loaf I'd brought; I'd add some pickled tomatoes to it. I had to keep Kara's strength up. A sudden noise from the stairwell made me jump. The jar I was twisting open slipped from my fingers, smashing on the floor. I'd hardly taken a breath when it happened; the sudden charge of feet coming to a halt at the front door.

Chapter Twenty-nine

I darted back into the hallway just as they slammed their way through the door, knocking it off its hinges.

The Trooper in the lead pushed me hard against the wall as he stalked past, shouting, 'Where's the baby?'

Another, behind him, grabbed me by my dress, twisting it in his fist, bringing my face close to his. 'Nowhere to hide,' he hissed, as two more stormed past. Then he flung me ahead of him, following the others into Kara's room.

I didn't recognise them as Kara's screams at first. Why would I? I had never heard her shriek like that. No one in Land dared use their voice in that way.

Kara was standing up on her mattress, pacing back and forth, holding tightly on to Sunil's blanketed cocoon. His little fists were thrown out in front of him as if he were ready to attack the Trooper pacing territorially with them. White-blond hair showing under his Black helmet, he was jeering at her, enjoying Kara's fear. 'Dirty little mother!' He flicked up the hem of her flimsy nightdress, pretending to jump in to grab Sunil then moving back again, laughing thunderously each time Kara reacted.

'Run, rabbit, run,' the Trooper gripping me joined in, twisting his face close to mine; middle-aged, mottled skin grazing my cheek. 'You're finer, prettier than her, aren't you? Does the fact you're a Blue make you more of a refined whore than your friend?' His breath stank. 'Or are you a fraud, a Brown, dressed up? We get some of them you know.'

I glanced across to Xavier; his back was against the wall, his hands raised, shaking in the air. We had to do something. I had to act, use my training: stay calm, assess the situation; work out a course of action. There were four of them. I had no weapon. Instead I grasped at words for bullets. 'You don't want to mess with me, I'm someone.' The declaration bellowing out of me as if I were shouting to be heard in a dream.

The Trooper held me tighter against his body, and began to laugh. 'Oh, I like you,' he said. I felt his tongue lick my cheek. 'Someone, huh? You gonna spread your legs like her, Miss Someone?' He snaked his face in front of mine, meeting my mouth with his, trying to force my lips apart.

I strained to pull away from his clasp, forcing my elbow sharply back into his chest, winding him. Before he could retaliate I shouted again, at all of them, pushing my wrist out, 'Check it, check my number, you will see . . . I work in government! The Leader will have you sent for Selection if you hurt me or my friends!'

It had stopped them at least. They had all turned, watching me, eyeing one another. It was buying us time. 'Go on,' I shook my wrist at the white-haired Trooper in front of Kara. 'Check my number on the system.

'I have been hand-picked by the Leader!' My voice gained

authority as I went on. I held my poise, glaring round at the Trooper behind me, daring him, *touch me again*.

'Know this – if you are lying I will shoot you on the spot.' The white-haired Trooper tapped the gun holster attached to his thick Black belt. He unclipped the handheld computer beside it.

I kept my wrist out, and stared down at the gun, trying to calculate the time it would take me to reach it. My heart was pounding for me to do it; it was all I could hear above Kara's panicked screams and Sunil's wails – the first time I'd heard him cry loudly. What would be my plan though; shoot them all? Could I even aim that well? I'd only ever practised briefly . . . And if I managed to pull it off, then what? Where would we escape to?

White-hair looked up from his handheld. 'We can't touch *her* – not without top-level approval. Better be careful, lads.' He was moving away from Kara, backing out of the room. 'Let's get out of this shithole.'

I felt my heart jump and slow. It had worked. They were leaving.

'Arrest the mother, take the baby,' he added acidly in his wake.

I heard my own screams meld with Kara's and Sunil's.

One of the other Troopers caught hold of Kara, forcing her and Sunil out with him. The middle-aged one flattened me against the wall, stopping me from moving with them, his face sneering over me.

As he let go, I raced after him – 'I told you who I am!' I kept on his heels, clattering down the communal stairwell. Halfway he turned, pushing at me violently so I tripped, banging my arm, twisting my ankle, but I wouldn't stop. I got straight back up, following them out the door, flying into the street, yelling, 'I will have you all arrested!'

Outside, the bright, hot sunlight shone down on a recently changed scene. I saw the black Selection trucks, two of them, sitting squat across the road, in front of my car.

'Separate them, one in each,' the white-haired Trooper shouted to his colleagues.

More Troopers were in the street; they circled Kara. 'My baby!' she was screaming over and over, turning, twisting – searching desperately for an escape like an animal cornered.

I knocked away the stiff arm of the middle-aged Trooper as he tried to block me, flinging myself, limping, towards Kara and Sunil, but he brought me back against his chest, squeezing my diaphragm; I could hardly breathe.

I panned around, looking for anyone who might help. People were walking on by, their eyes down. Like I used to. No one was going to intervene. *Stay silent. Fix a smile. Keep on walking.* No one was going to help.

Xavier was standing by the doorway to the tenement block, his hands gripping clumps of his hair. Beside him a line of women was forming against the dirty white wall, arms folded, their mouths curling over insults: *Slut! . . . You deserve it . . . Keep your knickers on next time.*

Kara let out a guttural scream, Sunil's competing with hers. They were tearing Sunil out of her arms.

I drew my leg up and kicked hard, jamming my heel square against the leg behind mine until I was free. 'Leave them!' I shrieked, barging through the Black jackets in front of me. My vision seemed to be filling with a red fog. I knew, at last, how they felt – the mothers who had beaten their fists against Troopers' chests, the children who had screamed when their parents were taken. I realised it now. All those years of saying nothing, doing nothing – I should have helped. I should have helped them all.

I wouldn't let them take Kara and Sunil.

I raced in front of Kara, drawing my arms wide to protect them. A punch came against my sore arm; I was thrown sideways, stumbling onto the ground. As I tried to get up, I recognised the click of the gun against the back of my head.

I could hear people in the crowd, laughing behind me; Xavier's weak voice shouting, 'Don't, you'll make it worse.'

I twisted my face, the gun nudged into the corner of my eye. I flew out a fist to knock it away. I had to get to Sunil at least, grab him; run. Two pairs of hands, this time, pushed me down hard onto the ground. A boot pressed onto my back, forcing my ribcage flat against the concrete; dust flew up into my mouth, choking me, robbing me of my voice. 'Kara,' I breathed out hoarsely as I watched her feet retreat. I tried to stare up; Kara was being tugged roughly, screaming, towards a truck. She was thrown inside; I could see the lines of petrified faces she was joining. The doors were slammed shut. Another Trooper batted the black bodywork, right by its slogan, **For the Greater Good**. 'Take it away.' Its engine started up; it began manoeuvring past me.

'And her?' someone shouted.

'Needs approval first,' the Trooper above me replied.

I could see Sunil being passed into the second Selection truck; his sweet face creased and reddened from screaming.

I let out my own that matched his, the sound of the monster Land had made me into.

Chapter Thirty

I kept shouting as the thick white metal door of my cell slammed shut, 'No! No!' over and over, 'No!' All those years of containing my voice . . . now it spread untethered from my lungs, up through my chest till my throat burned raw.

The Troopers who had forced me on foot to West Land Assessment Centre had tied my wrists together. I spun round manically, four windowless white walls engulfed me; a thin mattress rolled out along the rough, concrete floor; a silver bucket next to it. I might be here for days; I wouldn't be able to help them!

What if they were already facing Selection? The idea pierced my insides. I couldn't bear it. I paced the tiny room faster, panting out short, hurried breaths.

I flung myself frantically against the walls. I beat my conjoined fists against them, as if I could bash an escape through the stone, until my knuckles started to bleed, smearing scarlet red across the white paint. Then I launched the side of my body at the cell door, rebounding off it. 'Open this!' I raged, throwing myself into it again. Still no one came. I stopped, pressed an ear against the cold metal. I could hear nothing. Not a sound. The door was trapping in my noise, keeping out theirs. Violently I kicked it then slid down to the ground, repeatedly banging the back of my head against it. I couldn't get rid of it, that last scene: Kara clinging desperately to Sunil; his wails shattering the air as he was ripped away from her.

I hadn't saved them. I thrashed my head back harder into the metal. By giving the Troopers my number all I had done was save myself.

Hours must have passed by the time I heard the door being unlocked. I jumped up, crouched in a position to attack. I would fight my way out of here. Kill whoever I had to with my bare hands, until I got to Kara and Sunil. They wouldn't face Selection!

But it wasn't a Trooper who filled the doorway.

'Christabel.' It was the stiff Black figure of the Leader. My grandfather. One stood uneasily behind him.

I unfurled my fists, forgetting my act of dutiful Land disciple as I rushed towards them. 'You have to save them!'

The Leader lifted his hands up, as if to bar me getting closer. They stepped in; silently my grandfather shut the door.

'Save them?' he asked, coldly calm. 'The girl and her baby who you were trying to protect?' He patted his lips together. They were dry, cracked at the corners. 'Yes. 454111 and I have just been informed . . . Tell me first why I should save even you?'

I swallowed, scanning his expression. What did he want from me? Which part did I have to play for him? I glimpsed at One; he was passing me a silent message with his eyes. I braved a step closer to the Leader and slumped down onto my knees, raising my joined hands up to him. 'I am sorry. I have been stupid . . . I have done a bad thing, a stupid thing; forgive me.' I sucked in a breath. 'I will learn faster. Your blood, your DNA, runs through me still. I will stand by your side. I will fight for you and your vision of Land. Allow me this one weakness.' I bore my eyes into his; nothing but a performance of sincerity strained at my face – I would say anything to save them. 'Please . . . Grandfather.'

The tension loosened a little around his mouth, shifted slightly from the shadows below his eyes. Was it the word? I so rarely uttered it. He still didn't permit me to even think of him like that. 'Grandfather?' I said again, urging it to mean something. I flitted my eyes all over his face, continuing, 'I have your green eyes; the same curve of your chin; even the dip of my hairline is yours. And I am like you on the inside too. Trust me – just grant me this.'

He folded his mouth inwards. I was getting to him. 'Why does this worthless, ignorant little bitch matter to you?'

I lifted my tied wrists higher, pressing my palms against his immaculate Black-clad torso. 'I live for Land. I have no need for anyone. Look how I let Cons – and Stella – go. It's just,' I took another breath, searching for finer words, 'when I was a girl; when I was just an ignorant child . . . she was my playmate. This girl taught me loyalty to Land.' I paused, soaking the lie in saliva so it might come out credible. 'It was she who helped me see how much Land policy mattered when I was young. And so in turn she matters to me.'

'You want her to be saved when every other girl like her is disposed of?'

300

I felt One step towards us. I licked my lips; I had to deliver the right answer. 'It is not right. I know that . . . she should be . . . disposed of. But she is the one person, the only person, I want saved. Give me this. I will never ask for anything again.'

My hands rose further still; resisting the temptation to draw into fists, pummel his rigid, leather-tanned face until he did as I bid him.

'Your *friend* faces Selection or a brothel. Freedom is not an option for a crime like hers.'

'Then brothel . . .' I answered quickly, spotting the lifeline. 'Have her sent to a brothel . . . Just don't let her die.'

The Leader stared down on me; he gave me a look, as if I couldn't have made a worse choice – it made my stomach churn. But at least Kara would be alive, I told myself. I was saving her!

'And the baby?' I pleaded.

'What?' he growled. 'No! All unapproved babies from now on face automatic Selection.'

I pulled myself up, staying close to him. 'But – I want to raise him as my son . . . as the heir to the leadership.'

His hands were on me within seconds, shaking me violently as if I was filled with nothing but air. His fingers darting to my head, squeezing my skull as he hissed in my ear, 'I let them kill Hogan – my own son – and I can do the same to you. Tell me you are no traitor! Convince me you are not weak like your father!'

I could feel an arm between us. One's voice was low, quiet as he beseeched the Leader. 'Leave her be, it's not her fault. She tries her best. She is still young. It took you decades to detach from those you cared for.'

The Leader whipped his glare round at One. 'Get back,' he hissed out, spittle flying with his words. But One didn't – One stayed close; his arm remained bridged between us.

It gave me strength. 'I am not weak. I am no traitor,' I forced out. 'I serve Land . . . *only*. I intend to succeed you.'

The Leader loosened his grip on my head, refocused his eyes on mine; identical irises meeting one another. 'Then you will *act* like it. You will prove to me over and again how you are loyal to the cause. And you will have children when I say so. Children of *your* blood only – *my* genes. You will raise no bastards.'

He stepped back from me, wiping foams of spittle from his mouth with the back of his sleeve.

'Do not kill the son of my friend.' I paced the words out loudly, showing him I had power too. 'I see potential greatness in my friend that has not been unleashed yet – on account of wrongs by her parents. Her son has inherited strong genes. I am not thinking with my heart –' I touched my head with my hands – 'but with this.'

The Leader's eyes narrowed, assessing me as if we were two wild animals, working out whether to attack or retreat.

'She's young,' I heard One say again.

'She has to work on letting her feelings for other humans go. I have become great because I have refused to care.'

I widened my eyes, intensifying their glare – I played my hand. 'You don't care for me?'

The Leader's fierce expression stumbled, then stiffened as he collected himself. Not before I had seen enough. 'I care that my line continues. That is all.'

'Is it?' I said, testing him.

Silence fell between us. A silence that spoke. Evidence for One: I had achieved the goal he'd set me. The Leader straightened up, pulling his lips tight. 'If I do these things for you, you had better step up, *faster*. What we are about to embark on will redefine the fabric of Land; a new refined race. I have to know you are behind me. You need to show me you can take blood on your hands and not wash it off. Prove you have what it takes.'

'I will do anything,' I said simply, 'to assist your – our – shared vision.' I didn't dare speak further for fear he would change his mind.

'454111, you have the arresting report – go do as she asks,' the Leader said coldly, adding as an aside: 'Of course they will probably only live for a few days more. The Culling will get them and then it will be out of my hands.'

I nodded as if I fully understood; as if all this was was an excuse to buy my old friend and her baby a few more days of life before their end. While inside the monster in me stirred, angry and red: I would end his rule before my grandfather's State could touch them again.

'Now you come with me.' He took out a small knife from his pocket and severed the ties around my wrists. 'There is something you need to see. Something I've been meaning to show you for a while. Something that will beat this sentiment, this spineless softness for others, out of you.'

I was being marched down a narrow white stairwell, deep

303

into a basement; through corridors with low ceilings. It smelt damp; the sound of pipes clattered. The Leader was in front, his ever-present Trooper guards following behind us.

We passed a line of doors, white metal. One suddenly opened – screams fell out with the Trooper who rushed from it. He halted to click his heels and salute when he saw the Leader.

Another shout drew from inside the cell before the door slammed shut again.

'What are these rooms used for?' I asked, affecting a blank timbre to my voice.

'Interrogating rebels we've caught . . . but that's for another time. It's not on today's tour.' The Leader slanted his head towards me, a half-curve on his mouth. 'We're here for Selection. It's time you saw the meaning behind the inane word,' he said, as we stopped outside a wide concertina-door to our left. 'The Selection truck drops them at street level, directly into the lift to here.'

I stared up at the ceiling. I'd often seen the trucks reverse right up against metal doors to one side of the Assessment Centre. Like others, I'd blanked my mind to what happened after.

My grandfather was broadening his arms. 'They walk this way.' He paced out strides – as if he were charting some innocuous route – to a door with a square pane of glass, diagonally to our right. There was a gap before another door, thicker, with the same shaped window in it.

'Look, watch.' He indicated for me to step up against the glass.

Beyond: almost a perfect circle of a curved room, painted

white all over – the floor, walls and ceiling. Strip lights flickered overhead, shining down on the faces already inside – about twenty people. They were standing, equidistant apart, pinned back against the wall by wide black leather straps around their legs and arms. Browns mainly, some Greys, a few Greens. Most of them weren't over sixty-six – they were all ages. One small boy could only have been four or five.

Twenty sets of frightened eyes, darting round the room, searching for the means by which they would die, staring panic-stricken at one another. Some had their mouths wide open; their faces straining with making sound; lips moving frantically over words – words the doors blocked us from hearing.

'See the small black hole in the far side of the wall,' the Leader said in my ear, pointing ahead, his cheek near mine, as if he were performing some grandfatherly nature expedition. 'That's where the gas will come through.'

I swallowed, trying hard to keep my breath steady for his benefit. I couldn't let him see it was affecting me.

'I brought Hogan to experience this when he was twelve years old. You might say Hogan's visit here was his downfall. He took against me, the State, soon after. I have higher hopes for you. You have more of me than him in you, I can see that.'

I nodded my head in artificial agreement, as he continued. 'Selection's such a polite term. Shortened, of course, from reference to the fact we are helping nature make its own Selections. *Assisting* natural Selection. Personally, I have always believed we should just cut to the chase and call it what it is: elimination of the weak.

'But many who work with us don't like to face the reality behind their privilege. Few accept their invitation to visit down here; prefer to pretend it doesn't even happen. Not me. I think if you sign the execution papers, you should watch it. See the sheep you eat get slaughtered.'

I nodded my head again. I could no longer find a voice.

'This might be hard to watch, but it is an essential part of your leadership training. If you want to grow life, you harness death. The animal kingdom would never permit a lame creature into their pack.'

The air through the glass was starting to swim and fuzz. The distraught, raging faces beyond the glass seemed to blur.

'Here it comes; remember: don't take your eyes off the sheep, Christy.'

They were starting to gag; the little boy's mouth was stalled mid-crying as if he were choking on a piece of food; he was wrestling with his arm straps to try and raise his hands to his face. Others – their mouths making shapes of screams as they suffocated.

I wanted to shout, *Stop!* Rattle the handle of the door; break the glass – anything to release whatever poison was killing them! Cons, Stella, my dad . . . they had all been here. Loved ones all over Land had ended this way, fighting for air. Their faces now were turning colours – blue, green, purple, white. The Leader's eyes, I could sense, stayed on me. He was looking for it, I knew it, a flicker of weakness; a hint of my father in me. I stiffened my expression. I wouldn't show it. My role was to pretend. I couldn't help these people here. Or those who had gone before. But maybe I could still help the next to come; I could stop it happening to those they left behind, the people they loved – those still to be born.

I could do something. I could.

'Keep watching,' my grandfather hissed.

I did. I watched every last spasm and shudder; I watched eyes almost squeezed out of sockets and tongues stretching inhumanly between lips.

I watched the little boy, his head innocently shaking as if he were saying 'No' while his skin turned mauve. I watched two women, who had twisted themselves to face one another, try and keep their focus on the other as their heads shook violently. I watched an older man bite his tongue, severing it so it fell from his mouth on a sinewy string of muscle. I watched the puddle of yellow wee spreading on the white floor beneath the girl in Green next to him.

I watched them all slowly die.

'So, they'll scoop up all the bodies now,' the Leader continued in my ear, matter of factly, banally, like my tutors might describe a piece of home-study. 'There's a chute, over there – see.' He extended his arm again. 'The bodies are piled into it; they slide down the shaft into a crate that's put back into a Selection truck at night-time, transported to the East Land furnace that was constructed solely to burn bodies. Explains why the pollution in East Land's air has a black and torrid edge to it, doesn't it?'

I turned, facing his continuing test; my head erect, my body taut. Emotion cleared from my eyes; containing, holding still every emotion racing through my veins right now. 'It does indeed,' I said. Whatever distorted feeling my grandfather might now hold for me – I would never match it.

I imitated the faint smile playing on his lips, as I added, 'But it's all for the greater good.'

The Leader and his guards left me there; he wanted me to wait until the last body had been unbound, dragged and crudely loaded down the shaft by the slaves who had entered the room, white gas masks attached monstrously to their faces.

When it was over, I tried to stay upright as I made it down a stream of corridors, ricocheting off walls as I searched for the part of the building I was familiar with. It was unusually empty – proof that Assessments had become defunct.

Eventually I found the exit that led into West Land's shopping precinct, stumbling out back towards Central Land. Outside, torrential rain had broken the cloying heat. I stepped away from the Troopers guarding the door, then froze. I didn't know where to go next. Until I heard a familiar voice in the near distance. 'Christy!'

One and Salinger were standing in front of One's car a block down from me, Blue umbrellas above their heads. It felt like I'd been jolted awake from a nightmare. I blinked, forcing my legs to move towards them, rain showering me, plastering my dress against my body. As I reached the car, I bent round it, retching into its front tyres; severe cramps forcing out only bile and phlegm – I'd not eaten since yesterday. I felt a hand press down on my back as I convulsed again. I clutched at the pain in my belly; they wouldn't disappear – their faces as clear as if I was still watching them in that circular white room.

I straightened up. Salinger's arm lifted away. His brown

eyes worried. I searched out One behind him, Salinger and his umbrella moving with me.

I searched out One behind him, Salinger's umbrella moving with me. 'We need to end this,' I croaked, my voice a bare whisper.

'Get in the car,' One said, his look telling me in an instant: *Be quiet.*

I flexed my hands into fists. I'd had enough of being biddable, silent. I'd had enough of walking on. I wanted all of this to end. 'We *need* to fast forward to the final act.'

One acknowledged me with a cursory nod, then he took my arm, yanking me over and into the car. Unfolding his umbrella, he joined me on the front bench seat. Salinger climbed in behind. I was soaked. I wrung out the skirt of my dress till water pooled in the footwell. I thought of the puddle of wee at that girl's feet; my stomach jerked again.

'It was a stupid stunt for you to pull for that friend of yours,' One muttered as he started up the engine.

I shook my head, violently juggling remorse with rage. 'I don't need reprimanding. I get it now, okay? I get it! Why I'm doing this; what I'm supposed to feel, what I'm not . . . I said, I get it,' I repeated, as One opened his mouth to continue. 'It's not about me, those I care for – it's about Land, its present, its future – nameless strangers facing Selection . . . All right? I'm with you.'

'Good, so you've finally seen the light,' One answered in a mutter. He turned on thick windscreen wipers, squeaking across the glass.

Yeah, I'd seen the light. Those helpless people – '*Assisting* natural Selection' . . . I got it now, why Cons did what she did, why Dad died fighting.

Overcome by a sudden weariness I leant my head against the car window, my finger tracing a fat raindrop down the glass. 'I saw Selection.'

I felt One's eyes briefly on me. He sniffed before he answered, uncommonly softly, 'Those in charge – they are beasts, the lot of them.'

I stared round at him. He looked as if he'd been watching the people die in that room with me; his face was almost drained of colour; his eyes fatigued, smaller; the white scar of a second smile under his chin mocking the downturn of lips above it. 'So let's just finish this.'

'Agreed,' One replied, squinting through the rain to see the road. 'That's just what we are going to do. What *you* are going to do.

'I have spoken with my alliances on both sides . . . we are looking at the day after tomorrow to stage our coup. Once you have played your part.' His voice caught. 'You'll do okay, Christy,' he added and briefly placed a hand on my knee. Only the second time he'd ever touched me. Fleetingly, I remembered how he had stood between the Leader and me just now; the words he had used to Cons all those months ago in our kitchen: that he was *looking out* for me. I wanted suddenly to hug him. But I kept both arms stiff by my side.

'Here – I've brought you home.' One pulled the car over and switched off the engine. 'Go get cleaned up. We'll come in to wait for you and then we'll head over to mine. I'll inform you more about the coup there.'

The late afternoon sky had turned an ominous grey as the three of us climbed out. Rumblings of a storm threatened overhead. The rain was coming down harder, dispelling the hot, clinging air.

My dress still sodden and sticking to my body, I strode ahead of them towards the front door; I wanted to get the end of my story over and done with. Salinger chased me with his umbrella.

As I fumbled with my key, One said, 'You told 433957 about your friend?' His toneless voice was specked with a casual anxiety.

I turned the key in the lock. 'Bea? Tobin was going to . . . How do you know?' I stopped.

One pulled his umbrella in; rain automatically began trickling down his stiff face. He shot a look in answer – it clicked.

'Bea told the authorities about Kara's baby?' Something forced my throat to seize. 'Bea?' Had Tobin betrayed me too? Blood drained to my feet.

'So the arresting notes stated, yes. 433957 reported it direct to Troopers this morning.'

I thought of my tracer that I had purposely left in my room; of Bea and her matriarchal ferocity – she had purposely tracked me!

'But you leave it, okay?' One was trying to catch my gaze again. I could sense Salinger next to me; his dry shirt leaning against my drenched sleeve. 'Don't argue with her. Audley's in trouble – he's resigned as Head of Population Control. We can get them on our side . . .' He whispered under his breath, 'It will achieve nothing to fight against her now. Keep your cool, Christy – or rather, find it again.'

I gave him a look that I hoped was like a slap in the face. 'I never lost it,' I lied, wiping the rainwater from my face.

Bea seemed to spring out from nowhere as I pushed open the front door. 'I thought you might be Ella!' she cried instantly. 'I'm so glad you're here,' she said, ignoring me and tugging One by his arm into the hallway. 'Ella's gone!' She drew a jagged breath. 'Audley's out looking for her – but Troopers have just called for him!'

I stepped inside with Salinger, glaring at her as she continued, her frantic voice appealing to One to help Ella and Audley; my eyes tearing bits off her.

I felt Salinger's light touch on the base of my back again. Now what? Was he trying to keep me quiet? I moved away from it, closer to Bea.

Presently, she paused her emotional diatribe, catching me staring at her. Her hand shot to her open mouth as her eyes swept over me – my torn dress, the cuts, my knuckles inflamed and bloodied. 'What happened to you?'

I made no attempt to press a smile onto my face. 'Oh, I got caught up in some unapproved baby trouble out in West Land this morning – a Trooper arrest.'

'This morning?' Bea gasped, her hostess face instantly tightening. 'But this morning you were at work, weren't you? Tobin said you were at the Cross? That you'd gone –' She halted, swallowed, quietly adding, 'I didn't know you were in West Land.' Her eyes grew as she connected what she had done with my appearance. I didn't care for the intense concern they displayed.

'It doesn't matter,' I said acidly. It didn't. So she hadn't meant

312

for me to get caught too? She'd still sentenced those I loved to death. 'I'm just here to get –' I stopped. One was circling the room; he was asking Bea the same question over and again. Suddenly I realised he'd been speaking for a while, over Bea as she talked to me. I caught the repeated question: 'Tell me where she is. Tell me what has happened to Ella.

'Where has Ella gone?' He said again, more urgently, desperately. As if Ella meant something to him.

Bea's arms were trembling as she reached them out to him imploringly. 'She ran off. Ella's disappeared!' I stared at the agony on her face; suddenly noticing the tramlines of eye make-up cutting a symmetrical path down her cheeks; the raised tufts of hair where her hands must have been gripping it.

'What do you mean, ran off?' I shot out at her, still struggling to keep my eyes on hers without wanting to rip them out.

'Disappeared, how?' One echoed me, his stiff body bearing down on Bea as if he were about to thump her. 'Gone where?' he barked. 'Have you tracked her?'

I glanced over at Salinger; his expression mirrored mine. Was One losing it?

'Her tracer is here! This morning – we had a row, you see – I was only trying to impress on her how she had to behave . . . now that her dad has left his job – that we're being watched! She wouldn't listen! She was screaming back at me about what the Youth Troopers are doing at her Institute – how she can't stand by and let it happen! So I locked her in her room. Better that than she go to the Institute and get herself arrested! When I went to check up on her . . . she'd gone – out the window, down the drainpipe. Audley and Tobin have been out searching for her. But she could be anywhere! And then Troopers came an hour ago. To arrest Audley!'

'How could you let this happen?' One growled at Bea, so fiercely she took a step back.

She began tugging at her hair, as if she were uprooting vegetables. Her legs crumbling beneath her, she slumped onto the marble floor beneath her polished heels. 'She got the yellow eye . . .' she moaned at the floor. 'So Audley had no choice but to resign. It's all falling apart . . .'

One reached down for her, dragging her up as if she were a piece of dirty washing. 'Why didn't you tell me she'd got the yellow eye?' He began shaking her so her tousled hair completely covered her face.

'Because she isn't *yours*! She is *mine*!' Bea said, her voice hoarse. 'You might have wheedled your way into our house through Christy, but you have no right to Ella. She doesn't belong to you!'

'You were supposed to keep her safe, protect her!'

Bea's face crumpled and she started to cry. 'It isn't my fault! Ella doesn't understand . . . what I do, I do because I love her . . . She doesn't see how much I love her. I have turned a blind eye to everything I thought cruel in Land – I have followed every rule – just to keep my family safe!' she said.

She looked directly up at me. 'I have tried to protect you too, Christy. Yours and Tobin's future together! That's why I couldn't hide a baby for him! I don't understand why my children want to put themselves in danger!'

I was looking frantically from one to the other; I couldn't understand what was being said. I glanced back at Salinger;

his expression – it had changed – an anger of his own drawn across it, like he had caught up with this exchange.

'What is it?' I said to him, then to One: 'What is Ella to you?' as Salinger cut through me, his words flying out across the hallway: 'Is it her?'

One seemed to answer him with a flick of his melancholic eyes. He let go of Bea, who crumpled back to the floor. 'Help her,' she was saying. 'If she still means this much to you, find her, bring her back to me! And Audley! Please protect Audley. Don't let them take him!'

Salinger's eyes were fixed on One.

I tried again. 'Ella is . . .?'

'My sister.'

'My daughter.'

They both spoke. At the same time.

'She's my half-sister . . .' Salinger's voice was strangled.

One made a low groan of a sound at the back of his throat. 'Ella's the unapproved daughter of Salinger's mother – and me.' His face turned to beseech Salinger. 'I just wanted to keep her safe . . . I wanted Ella to have a life – it was the only way to ensure she survived – to bring her here.'

'You ordered me not to go looking. You said we must never see her again; you told me we would never know her number.' Salinger swung an arm out, around the room. 'Or which family had adopted her!'

'Because you were a child yourself! Only five years old when Ella was born! By the time you were old enough to be told, it was all too late. Your nature back then; you were fiery, unpredictable – you would have gone to her, I knew that. And

315

I had promised your mother I would fill the role of father for you as best I could.' One was shaking his head; a thick hand drawing down one side of his face. 'I promised her I would protect your life – as well as my own daughter's.'

'You knew where she was all this time! You chose this Pairing for Christy on purpose. So you could see *Ella*!'

'Salinger – it made sense. A chance to check up on her properly . . . I thought maybe Christy and she might get close . . . That it might help them both – after all, they're . . . they're second cousins . . .'

One looked round at the gagging noise in my throat.

'Now you talk of family?'

His eyes seemed to plead in return, for me to understand something distant, behind their stiff stoicism.

'Christy's a relation of yours?' Bea was alert again. 'You chose this Pairing for Christy? No one gets to choose a Pairing…!'

One's jaw shifted. He *had* lost himself, to have spoken so openly. I found myself stepping back. I didn't know who I could trust any more.

'For reasons you can't know, the Leader had a say in Christy's Pairing. It was fortuitous he chose my suggestion of Ella's family,' One said, righting his face with the correct choice of words. He glanced across at Bea, curled up and trembling on her glistening marble floor, then turned back to Salinger. 'For what it's worth, I think Ella's been happy here. Over the years, I watched them as a family, from a distance. In the same way I watched over Christy.'

Salinger was backing away. 'You should have told me the truth!'

'Truth isn't always the route to survival! I did what I had to – to ensure no one did anything stupid!'

A knife was twisting inside me; tearing at the gaping wound from watching all those people die unnecessarily. Ella was One's daughter. Salinger's sister. A second cousin! One had placed me here – for her, not for me, not for what was best for the cause. More family lies, secrets drawn – for survival. I couldn't hear any more.

Bea was mumbling incoherently in the background. I strode to the staircase, taking the steps two at a time. 'I'm going.' I cast my words loudly back over them.

One shouted up at me, 'Christy – what are you talking about?'

'I won't stay here,' I said.

'You can't leave – not now, you live in Central Land,' One said, but I knew his true meaning. Stay in position.

I stopped, looking down at him. 'Don't worry,' I said. 'I'll be back at work tomorrow. I've still got my job to do . . . I know that. I *get* that.'

I paused, looking over at Salinger; his face was set in stone as he stared at One. 'I'm sorry for you,' I said, as fleetingly we locked eyes.

I rushed into my bedroom, grabbed a canvas bag and chucked in a few basic clothes. I marched into the bathroom, lifting up the cistern where I had repacked and hidden the gun. Except it wasn't there. I scouted around; had I stupidly left it out? But I couldn't see it anywhere. Had Bea found that too? If she had, I didn't have the energy to confront her. I would get another gun. I grabbed only essential toiletries and went back to the bedroom, picking up my nightshirt from the chair. I averted my eyes from the bed, from the impressions of mine and Tobin's bodies I imagined under the covers. What I wouldn't do now for the comfort of those arms, his sweet, warm breath and steady rhythm of his sleeping body.

Charging back towards the door, I halted by the wooden table against the wall; my table, *his* table. My fingers trailed over Dad's number first, then *Hogan* . . . I turned away. They could burn it for firewood for all I cared.

Chapter Thirty-one

Vile pictures hijacked my mind in a broken and bruised sleep. Every distorted face I'd watched die in that room. Sunil, alone and unloved in an orphanage crib. Kara – deposited crudely at a state brothel, faceless men taking turns to violate her frail, sore body.

I woke up with a start at the last image, my breath coming in short, shallow bursts; my pillow damp with tears I'd not known I'd cried. I had made the wrong choice for Kara. She had been right. Always, I had been keeping her safe for me, not her.

I fumbled for my tracer on the cabinet beside me – it was six in the morning. I lifted my head, taking in the familiar surroundings: Cons' room. It felt so much a part of my grandmother that half of me expected to find her moving around me; a resonance of her scent in the air. But there was nothing but the swirl and odour of dust, thickly icing all the furniture.

I'd come straight here yesterday. Numb with exhaustion and despair, it was all I could do to jab my points card into the water meter, and force myself in the shower when it turned tepid. I'd tried to make a meal out of the few tins still lodging in the cupboards before I'd gone into her room, sitting down on Cons' sagging mattress. The same linen covered the bed from when I left; from when Cons'd last slept there. A single, coarse, grey hair lay on the pillow, as if she'd just recently raised her head from it. I'd laid it out straight, placed my head down next to it, watching it, as if it might magically grow into a whole head of her grey-laced red hair. So that I might wrap my arms round her and tell her I forgave her. That I understood at last – social conscience had overpowered her feeling for me. But it didn't mean she didn't love me.

I kicked off the thin cover; rose and pulled open the musty curtains. Yesterday's downpour had abated; now the weather was at peace again, it was easy to hear the occasional background hum and crash of gunfire and explosives. The war One had kindled was catching fire, raging closer; soon it would weave its way into Central Land. No wonder we had to act tomorrow – before both sides burned Land to the ground.

I took a breath. I couldn't help them – Kara, Sunil – not any more, not now. I had to blank out their faces and harness myself to those of the people I'd witnessed dying – I had to stop Selection, the Culling, mass elimination. That was who I was now. The girl Cons wanted me to be.

Three brief raps sounded at the front door. My heart squeezed; I recognised it in an instant, from the old days.

'Salinger,' I said, opening the door by a crack. I was still in my nightdress. 'I'll be at work soon, you don't need to check up on me. I'm still *in*.'

The portion of him on view through the slit looked like he

hadn't slept much either; his short curly hair was unbrushed, semi-circles of grey clung to his lower eyelids. His light grey shirt was creased, sweat marks under the arms.

'I'm not here to check up on you. I've come to help you get Kara out. I know where she is.'

'What? No! I'm not doing that – I told you and One. I understand . . . I need to fight – for Land. I've done what I can for Kara, her baby – I shouldn't have done that even. I've only made it worse. I should have left them alone.'

Salinger pressed his face closer to the gap. 'No – you've been the one who was right all along – you've got to fight first for those you care about. If you don't *care* for anyone, then it's all just political.' He sighed. 'The difference between me and you is that for most of my life I've had no one I loved enough to save . . .'

'I don't know what you're talking about. I'll see you at work, Salinger.' I started to push the door shut. It bounded back as he forced his boot in the gap. 'Stop playing around!' I hissed. 'Isn't this what you wanted? Me, focused – the fight?'

'No, that's not fair! I've only ever followed orders! Didn't you see that . . .? I think you should do what you believe in. What do you believe in, Christy?'

I was losing patience. I had to pull on my killer's skin again; get back out there. 'What do *you* believe in, Salinger?'

'I was trained to train you . . . I believe in you – I believe in your strength and your compassion and your irritable, stubborn nature. Like One.' He made a small laugh. 'I want to follow you.'

I pulled a face; he was humouring me.

'What do you believe in, Christy?'

'Why are you even asking me that?'

'Because I've never seen you stop and look – you've never paused to work it all out, what's being asked of you. You've flung yourself from one drama to the next, just doing what they tell you to do – like they know best, not you. Choices might not come easy in Land – but it doesn't mean you can't still make them. So tell me: what makes you *you*?'

My gut answered for me. 'I love my brave friend Kara . . . '

'Then that's what you should believe in . . . So what are you waiting for? Get some clothes on. I have One's car. Let's go get her.'

I don't know why, but I didn't question him again. Who knew what was right? But suddenly, strangely, it felt okay to be doing what I wanted to do – if Salinger was behind me.

I dressed for a fight: a pale Blue blouse tucked into close-fitting trousers, thick ankle boots. I pulled my hair back into a tight ponytail and tucked my final blue pill, a pill for me, in my pocket.

Salinger chucked a white paper bag on my lap as I climbed into the car next to him. 'Here, I thought you might not have eaten much.'

I peered into the bag, hungrily pulling out a bread roll and an apple. 'Why are you being so nice?'

He made a half smile as he started the engine. 'Christy, I've always been *nice*.' He pulled out onto the road. 'You've just always been too untrusting to notice it.'

'This is reckless; you've not thought this through. Don't we need to be at work today, get briefed on tomorrow's coup?'

'We'll go in later.'

'And where will I keep Kara? No one hides in Land.'

'Make Kara a first. With any luck, change will come by tomorrow.'

'If it doesn't?'

Salinger glanced at me as he drove. 'Then we're probably all dead anyway.'

I bit furiously into the apple, suddenly realising how hungry I was. I needed to gain strength. 'So do you know where Sunil is too?'

'One said they were sending him to South Land orphanage. It's opposite the Institute there – you remember where that is from my map?'

I nodded. Suddenly, I missed that map; those training days.

'You won't miss it,' he added wryly. 'It has a slogan above its door: *Sacrifice the Children.*'

'But the brothel's in West Land?' He was driving us straight down the main road, towards West's outskirts; on both sides, the white-painted walls were becoming daubed with freedom messages in black tar; rebel words fighting back against state posters. More windows were smashed; buildings scorched and bullet-marked. Yet still, the morning commute was going on; Browns and Greys and Greens, diligently making their way to work or the Institute, despite the madness unfolding around them.

'Yeah, West Land brothel . . . the same one my mum went to . . .' Salinger's words came out muffled. When I said 'Sorry,' he continued in a leaden voice; 'We save Kara, maybe it'll atone for not getting Mum out.'

'How could you have? You were a little kid.'

Salinger's brows knitted. 'I never forgave myself for not trying . . . For a while I couldn't even forgive *her*, for not letting One help.'

'How is One?'

Salinger fidgeted awkwardly. 'He lied to me.'

'He said he was protecting you.'

'He thought he knew best.' Salinger sighed. 'Don't the adults always know best . . .'

'Ella will be okay,' I said – but he could probably tell that neither of us could believe that.

Salinger gave me a faint smile anyway, then swore out loud, pressing down hard on the brake as a line of Selection trucks careered round us, scattering those walking down the street like pebbles from a jar.

'The Culling,' Salinger said, manoeuvring the car back amongst the reformed patches of pedestrians. 'The Leader gave it the go-ahead late last night, even without Audley to direct it.'

I thought of yesterday's circular white room and slammed my palms on the leather seat. 'One has to make his coup work. He must.'

Salinger flicked a glance at me. 'Are you ready? For what you have to do?'

I looked away. I didn't even want to see for myself what I felt about that . . . My *part*. My grandfather. Instead I said idly, 'So we both share blood with Ella. What does that make us, related?'

'Hardly!' Salinger spluttered out quickly. 'I own her better half, you can have the bad bits.'

Our shared laughter evaporated as quickly as it came. We drove in silence the rest of the way as more Selection trucks thundered past us the further we went through West Land. Some we saw getting loaded, lines of people being passed out of tenement blocks to be packed into trucks as if they were animals.

Now and again, gunfire rippled through the air, shaking and rattling the car. Rebel fighting was increasing. The state offensive was intensifying. Our time for One's 'balance' was overdue.

Finally the road started to run out, the ground under our wheels became pot-holed, bumpy, laden with small rocks; factory dust whirled through the air. We were into the wasteland that bordered every region of Land. The Great White Wall was looming visibly in the distance, sunlight glinting off its expanse of white. I'd never seen it this close up – it reminded me of the giant waves Cons would tell me about that had circled her voyage here, preying on their tiny boat.

'That's it.' Salinger pulled One's car over on the opposite side of a sprawling grey-white block of a building, sat squat underneath a downy umbrella of smoke from the lofty factory chimneys behind. There were no windows on the ground floor; the ones above were narrow and slashed by vertical, thick bars.

We sat and watched. 'What next?' Now we were here I felt even less confident; we were risking One's whole plan if we got caught. An individual over the greater good? It wasn't what I'd decided I was here for. 'This is a bad idea.'

'We're here now. You got your gun?'

'I . . . mislaid it.'

Salinger shot me a look. 'Open the glove compartment. There should be one strapped to its underside.'

I did as I was told, feeling for hard metal. I peeled it off, checking the safety latch like One had taught me. Slotting it into the waistband of my trousers, the main door to the building suddenly flung open. We ducked down. A middle-aged Blue came out. A woman in Brown behind, talking to him. 'Looks like it's still the same brothel madam as when Mum was here,' Salinger murmured. Her dry, yellow hair was back-combed, spun like tarnished thread around her head; her hands fixed proprietarily on comely hips. She was chewing on something in her mouth, masticating as if it were tough and refusing to be broken down.

We watched the man leave. 'Blues and Blacks still seeing to their needs regardless of the war going on. They probably think it won't last long, the State will regain control soon.' Salinger bit down on his lip then glanced at me, 'Okay; I'm going over . . . I'll pretend to be a paying customer. When I'm in, go round the back, to the right of the building – there's a door, it was where One used to take me, to see Mum. Wait for me there.'

Salinger climbed out of the car, adjusting his face to look like the kind of customer they expected. He matched it with a saunter as he crossed the road. I watched Salinger smile his charm at the woman as she came back to the door, then proffer his points card from his back pocket. Her eyes grazed him, her mouth pinched, probably because he was only a Grey, but then he was in.

Quickly I climbed out, eyes down, walking fast. Out of the

car, I caught a distant roll – an explosion like heavy thunder, rebounding off the Great White Wall.

Salinger was already there, opening the door, as I reached the back. Hurriedly, he beckoned me in.

'I'm supposed to be with a girl – we haven't got long before the brothel madam notices I'm not.' Salinger spoke quickly under his breath. 'The numbers of each inmate are painted in red on the door. What's Kara's?'

I recited it for him as, stealthily, we climbed a thin staircase and then began edging through a web of passages. We checked every door, covered in blistered white paint, for its number; many clearly occupied, exuding noises, muffled shrieks, low moans – sometimes, the hard clap of a smack on skin. I tried my best not to listen, not to imagine – just focus on the red painted numbers till I recognised Kara's.

We moved up another wider staircase, its white bannister stained with grubby handprints. On the next passageway, a door opened midway along. We had nowhere to hide, but instinctively Salinger and I pressed our backs against the wall, for all the good it would do. A man with close-cut dark hair and flared nostrils came out. He strode towards us, his gait confident as he shook on a Trooper Black jacket, zipped up his Black trousers. He nodded cursorily at Salinger then stopped short of me. His mouth snaked salaciously. 'How's about this – a Blue who's fallen from grace, eh?' He grabbed my wrist, twisting it round to see my number. 'Your Pair's loss is my gain . . . I'll look for you next time.' Out of the corner of my eye I could see Salinger crouching down, his hand sliding to his ankle; onto the grey metal of his gun strapped there.

'Yeah, come find me,' I replied stiffly, gesturing with my eyes to Salinger not to do anything stupid.

The man narrowed his gaze in conceited assent and carried on with a nod back at Salinger. 'Enjoy her.'

Salinger started, but I pressed my palm against his shoulder. 'Don't.'

'I'm sorry,' he said, as if it were he who had just insulted me; his teeth were clenched, his face flushing with anger.

I drew him on then – 'Here.' I halted, my breath shooting into my mouth as, finally, I caught Kara's six digits drawn in fresh red paint.

'She might not be alone, remember? We act quickly,' Salinger said, stripping his gun from his ankle. In a flash he had opened and closed the door behind us. My eyes tore round the brightly lit cell. Was that Kara? Crushed under that bulky, bare torso? I couldn't see her face to check. Her arms were lifted, wrists tied to a post above her head – yes, her number was tattooed on the brown skin, a new one inflamed beneath it, the red cross of a brothel worker.

The man hadn't noticed us yet; he was thrusting hard against Kara, emitting growls of moans. Before Salinger could move, I strode forward, yanking my gun from my waistband. Twisting it to hold it by the nozzle, I smashed the handle hard, with all the strength in me, against the back of the man's head. He slumped forwards with an elongated groan.

Salinger was by me; together we heaved and dragged the large naked frame off Kara, chest-down onto the floor. Salinger aimed his gun at his head.

'Kara?' I turned back urgently. She looked tiny, her eyes

open but glazed over. Her hair was greased and brushed back from her forehead; her lips painted a garish pink; more pink on her eyelids: someone had pointedly tried to make her look presentable, for *them*. I set to, hurriedly untying the dirty bands pinning her wrists to the bedpost. I could feel heat radiating off her; I pressed the back of my hand to her head. 'Salinger, she's burning up.' The same flimsy white nightie she'd been arrested in was rucked up around her chest – it was drenched in sweat. I pulled it down over her body; there was little fat left around her belly to show she'd only just given birth.

'Kara, are you hurt?' I brought my face close to hers, staring into her blank eyes for signs of life. It was a stupid question. In reply her emaciated frame began to violently shiver as if she were frozen, despite her hot head. Her breath was coming in little bursts of effort. I pulled off my shirt, leaving a Blue vest beneath, and clumsily tugged it over Kara's head, fumbling her flaccid limbs into the sleeves.

'How's she doing? We have to go.' Salinger darted over, helping me pull Kara up from the bed, while keeping his gun aimed at the man. 'We've got to hurry, Christy –'

Kara's eyes seemed to click awake as her bare feet touched the floor. She glanced at me. 'Sunil?'

'Kara.' I was so relieved, just to hear her voice. 'He's okay. Sunil's alive, safe, at the orphanage. We will go to him soon,' I said. 'First we need to get you out of here.'

'I'll carry you,' Salinger said, putting his arms out to lift her up. Kara twisted, as if she were resisting. In a second she had snatched his gun, aiming it point-blank at the back of the dark head facing the floor. The shot rang out, bouncing off the

329

walls. A black hole appeared within seconds in the unconscious man's skull; a thin river of dark red blood seeping out.

'Sunil,' Kara said again, her voice wavering as her legs gave out and she dropped to the floor.

Salinger made a grab at both her and the gun, cradling her up into his arms. He looked at me, alarm in his eyes. 'Others will have heard that – we have to get out of here.'

He was right. The moment we left, the door directly opposite opened, a man emerged, dressed only in underpants and an open Blue shirt. He started shouting into the air when he caught sight of us, weapons in hand, 'Troopers! Rebels, here!'

Salinger swung his gun at the Blue's face until he retreated back behind his door.

Too late. Heavy footfall sounded below us; up the staircase we'd used.

'We're not going to get out!'

'We are; this way.' Salinger rushed on, Kara dangling loosely from his arms like a piece of fabric. 'One sneaked me up a back staircase once.'

He rushed us through a narrow door at the end of the passageway, onto a spiral stone staircase. We clattered down it, shouts and pounding of feet seeming to surround us.

'This must be the ground floor,' Salinger said, about to open the door – till he halted. Voices were right outside.

'They've shot someone,' we heard a man cry out.

'We're trapped, Salinger,' I said. I'd exhausted my nine lives.

'Can you manage her?' Salinger passed Kara to me. I hugged her body close to mine, her arm slung over my shoulder to keep her upright. 'Have you got a plan?'

'A change of plan. I will stall them; you get out.'

I read the idea in his dark eyes before he'd finished the sentence. 'No. You will not sacrifice yourself for us. Either we all make a break for it, or we all die here. We have bullets. I have my pill.'

'Stupid plan. Mine is better. You go – on my own I can pretend to be a paying customer still. I can't protect you if you stay.'

'It's too late, that Blue up there saw you with us!'

'Let me try! I'm irrelevant now. One doesn't need me – but you . . .' His eyes drew hurriedly over mine – 'You are essential.'

He put his hand on the doorknob. 'Once I've diverted them, you go – the exit should be just to your left.'

'Salinger!' I forced out between my teeth before he'd had the chance to open the door. 'Don't you dare.'

He turned, his face bearing down on mine. He looked angry. 'Why did you kiss me? That time after the rebels kidnapped you?'

I shook my head, my breath coming fast. I couldn't speak. I didn't want him to go. I wouldn't lose Salinger.

'That kiss, it meant something to me. In a place where nothing has meaning; that kiss meant something. It woke me up. Let me do this for you. Please.'

The shouts outside the door intensified.

Salinger bent in low, his hand gripping my neck. His lips were on mine just for a second, before he pulled back, grappling the car keys into my palm. 'You make it out of here, you hear me?'

He had gone, the door banging shut behind him.

'No, don't shoot – I'm a client too. I'm tracking the girl

who just killed hers . . . She's gone back upstairs, that way.'
His voice got more distant. The sound of feet followed him;
I couldn't tell if they were chasing him, or they'd bought his
story. I feared the former from the shouts that followed on
the wake of his voice. But I had no time to think. I opened
the door, looking around hurriedly; I pushed at the exit to our
left – back out where we'd started.

I half dragged Kara's limp body around the building. I
couldn't dwell on the warmth of Salinger's mouth, or what
was happening to him now. I just had to make it to the car.

We got there as I heard raised voices coming out from the
front of the brothel. I opened the door, crudely chucking Kara
inside and following after. A group of Blues and Blacks; they
were nearly on us. My fingers trembled as I pushed the key into
the ignition. I started the engine as their bodies slammed into
the side of the car, thrusting my foot hard against the throttle.
Veering forwards, I spun the car around, away from the Great
White Wall, aiming it back at their growing numbers, running
up the middle of the street to stop me; some Troopers with
guns pointed out. They jumped out of the way as I roared
into them; I'd have killed them otherwise. Bullets ricocheted
off the car's body and boot. I glanced in the rear-view mirror,
hoping to see Salinger running, getting away, but only the same
men filled the glass.

Kara was lying in an awkward position, moaning, next to me.
I got off the main road we'd come up as soon as I could. Fewer
people were on the streets now that work and the Institute had
started; it was easier to see the groups of Troopers, marching
those with yellow eyes from their jobs and into Selection trucks.

I pressed a hand down on Kara's head as she released another murmur of 'Sunil . . .'

'Salinger,' I said aloud, reflexively. I blinked rapidly, trying to get that last image of him – his lips coming towards mine – out of my head. I couldn't . . . I had the people of Land to care about; but still, my heart began to shred itself at the thought of him dead.

Chapter Thirty-two

I parked the car on the road behind my tenement block. I had to get Kara in fast – before anyone reported us, before another Selection truck passed.

I was climbing the communal staircase fast, panting under the effort to keep Kara upright against me. I didn't see him until I had propped Kara up, moaning, against the wall, to unlock the flat.

He jumped up from where he had been sitting on the floor, back pressed against my front door.

'Why are you here?' I didn't mean to make it sound like an accusation, but there was no way I could deal with Tobin right now.

His heart-shaped face creased, then crumpled. 'What's going on?' His eyes rushed over Kara, sliding down the wall. 'What's wrong with her? Is this the girl, your friend you wanted to help? Where's the baby?'

I dived forward and slammed a hand against his mouth. My head shook fiercely, my finger jabbing at the doors near ours.

He stared at me, his eyes pained as I pulled my fingers away; but he stayed quiet as I opened the door, helping me get Kara in. We took her into Cons' room, lying her down on the bed. Before I pulled him into the kitchen. 'If you think anything for me, you won't breathe a word about what you've just seen.'

Tobin was staring at me, his head shaking. '*Think* anything for you? Aren't you my Pair? Aren't we supposed to be together in everything? Why are you talking like this? I was waiting for you to bring a baby home to us! You never even *came* home last night!'

I examined his eyes. He didn't know. He hadn't betrayed me. 'Your mother put an end to our parenting dreams.'

'You already know Mum said no to the baby?' His eyes narrowed as his voice rose. 'I was waiting for you – waiting to hear if the Leader had approved us! Why are you treating me like this?'

I turned on him. 'Will you be quiet! You and your privileged life – you've never known what it is to whisper! To be hushed; to move around unnoticed! Stay quiet – or better still, go!'

I ignored his edged silence and filled the kettle, busying myself to play nurse to Kara.

Tobin pulled me round to face him again. 'You're my Pair. I thought that had started to mean something to you?'

I stared at him, licking my lips. I could still taste Salinger there. I dipped my eyes. Why? How could I have deceived Tobin if I'd never been true to him from the start? 'Bloody hell, Tobin, what *does* it even mean?'

He stepped back, dragging both hands down over his boyish features. 'It means – we look out for each other, we go through life together, we survive as one.'

'Well, things have happened. I can't be your Pair any more.'

'What? You're my Pair for life, Christy. We made a promise to one another! It's the way things are; it's the way I want things to be!' His hands reached out, cupping my face.

Something swept round my stomach; I felt my instinct lurch, to hug my body to his, wrap myself up in his arms. This last month, I'd been safe there. But I couldn't. There was no place for me and Tobin in the stories Cons had fed me.

I carried on talking as if I hadn't heard him. 'You will find another Pair . . . when all this craziness out there calms down.'

'I don't want another Pair. I want you,' he said, his face tensing with a mixture of anger and disbelief, his eyes darkening a deeper blue. 'Don't you do this to me. Not now.' He exhaled a sigh of exasperation. 'I need you. Mum's going crazy. Ella's missing! There's a warrant out for Dad's arrest – he's run too, vanished! I have no one . . . except you.

'You're it, Christy. You're my family.'

The temptation in me was so great now, just to reach out with my fingers and touch his cheek, nuzzle against the crook of his arm; place my head against his chest.

Kara's long moan from the other room broke me out of my stupor.

'I need to see to Kara, and I need you to go. I need you to go right now.'

I lay beside Kara all evening, pressing a cold flannel against her head. I had taken her into the shower, seating her there on a kitchen chair so I could sponge her down as gently as possible; washing the cream from her hair, the garish make-up from her face. Her groin area was swollen; dried blood was caked there, that I didn't dare wash away in case it opened wounds. I dressed her in a clean nightshirt of Cons'. Tucked back in bed, I'd fed her – finger pieces of the bits of food Salinger had given me in the car. I kept giving her sips of water to drink. I'd still not heard anything from her, except a repeat of the same breathless word, 'Sunil.'

As the sky turned indigo, I curled up around her. I prayed her fever would break by morning when I would have no choice but to leave her. I had to get to One. I had to play my part – to help end this war.

I couldn't reverse how I'd made Tobin feel. But maybe if I did my job well I could get him his family back. Maybe I could get mine. Even if I didn't live to see it.

Throughout the night, I stirred in and out of consciousness, intermittently daubing Kara's head; making her drink more water.

Every time my mind turned to Salinger I turned it back around. I couldn't let him in; I felt I would crack into a thousand pieces if I let myself dwell on what had happened to him.

I had kept the curtains open, watching the escalating gunfire, the crackle and pop from explosives, litter the street-lit night sky like a meteor shower. But I must have fallen asleep at some point. I stirred as the sun rose, a bright yellow glow emerging, as if it had colluded with Land to take the baton when the streetlights switched off.

My first feeling was one of relief. Kara had warmed me like a coal fire all through the night; now that heat had completely dissipated. I turned to put my hand to her head. I would find her more food before I left.

I shot back from her, dragging my eyes over her face. My blood was pounding in my head, my heart racing as I made a dash for her pulse, on her neck first; then on her limp wrist. No. No! She couldn't be. She wasn't. I dropped her hand; it fell heavily back onto the bed.

Breathing hard, I flattened my palms against her chest; thrusting heavily above her heart, as I'd watched Cons do once to a woman who'd stopped breathing after giving birth. 'Kara, no, come back.' My mouth to her lips – holding her nose and blowing short puffs of air into her mouth. Again, my palms returning, heaving frantically against her chest.

I pulled back; waiting, hoping for something, anything. My throat constricted; this wasn't happening. It couldn't be. I grabbed her shoulders, shaking them, trying to wake her; she was only sleeping.

Her blue eyes stared out glassily. Her tan skin mottled, frozen to the touch.

I slumped onto her; my own chest convulsing in agony. It was my fault. Kara was supposed to die fighting – that was what she had wanted – not like this. I pressed my face against her cold, hollow cheek. The loud wailing sound was so unfamiliar it took me a while to realise it was mine. For the first time since Cons died, tears fled furiously, unchecked, from my eyes.

I lay there, my head and shoulders merging into hers for what seemed an age. A faraway voice in my head was telling me to get up, to go; *focus*. But how could I leave her? My only friend. My Kara. Eventually I pulled back, gazing at her, the still, stiff mask of her once lively, fiercely held face. I stroked the short black hair back from her forehead, remembering when it flowed long like a waterfall, in the days when Kara wore the confidence of a child whose parents weren't facing Selection. I wished we could go back there, back to our childhoods. Back to our dreams and stories.

In the end I had to take note of that inner voice of mine. I had to leave. The sun had formed its circle, spreading daylight into the room. I couldn't give in to thinking, to feeling. To grieving. I couldn't let Kara's death engulf me as Cons' had. I went to the bathroom, splashing my face with cold water to get rid of the last of the tears. I had to do my job – serve another Land. Save life. Fight Kara's fight.

And yet – when I went in to look at her for the final time, I knew what I had to accomplish on the way to that fight. Leaning over the bed, I pressed my lips against Kara's frozen ear, whispering softly, 'I will go for him. I will get him now. I will make sure nothing happens to him. I promise.'

I didn't look at her again; if I did I would falter. I dressed quickly in yesterday's clothes. I pushed the gun into the waistband of my trousers, wrapping and knotting a Blue shawl round my vest top at the waist to conceal its shape. One gun. One blue pill in my pocket. They were all I would need now. I was ready.

I got back into the car, recalling Salinger's map for the route to the orphanage. Taking the back streets to avoid the worst of the trouble; the roads had become more cluttered with debris and rubbish, bringing a strange palette of colour to the usually sparse streets. People were moving uncommonly chaotically, darting in all directions; no one wanted to get caught in gunfire, or worse, by a Trooper and his Selection truck. Order had finally cracked.

I turned right down a street that should lead into South Land at the bottom, and immediately slammed my foot on the brake. A Brown, directly in front of me; he smashed into my windscreen. He was pointing a gun at my face. 'Get out,' he shouted; his young face twisting with hatred. More Browns and Greys drew round the car, male and female, mostly young. A couple of others had guns. Guns One would've supplied them with.

'I'm on your side,' I cried out as they began rattling the door, even if it was a lie. I wasn't on any side. They were breaking my window with a brick; the glass splintered. I had no choice; I unlocked the door, moving back from them as soon as I was out. 'Have the car,' I said, tossing my keys at the Brown with the gun, as the group stalked closer.

'She's a Blue, shoot her,' I heard a Grey girl hiss.

I reached into my waistband and flipped out my gun, swinging it round at all of them. 'I said, I was on your side. I said, have the car. Now let me pass.' Most of them were unarmed; a few of them put their hands in the air. I kept my gun trained from one face to another as I made them form a path for me. I started to walk backwards down the road, my hands shaking; I knew they would shoot my back if I turned. Only as they began squashing into One's car did I run; pushing the gun back into my waistband.

I didn't stop running. As West Land merged into South Land, I saw more buildings smouldering from recent attacks, the occasional fire still blazing and surrounded by fireworkers with charcoaled faces. More Selection trucks rattled past. I pictured that white circular room; I had to hurry. I picked up my pace, crossing the road as the door to a tenement block opened and a group of Browns marked with yellow eyes were herded onto the street by Troopers. I slowed to a fast walk, dipping my eyes but slanting them to watch. My gun seemed to be nuzzling into my stomach, as if it were reminding me to use it. What the hell could I do? I squeezed my eyes shut then glanced back. The group had been lined up alongside a Selection truck. I dragged my eyes back to the concrete in front. One's coup might still save them; the gassings had to be stacking up. So many people arrested and shoved into trucks – they couldn't put them all through Selection, not for days. Rapid gunfire pealed through the air behind me. I twisted round, my heart squeezing like a sponge expelling water. Everyone in the line had fallen, forming awkward shapes on the ground.

It was too late. We were too late. I picked up my run.

There was no time for Sunil. I had to kill the Leader. Take him out. I no longer had a car – I couldn't carry a baby through the streets anyway. I was about to change direction, about to take the road that led directly to South Land shopping precinct – when I saw it. A low-level white building glued between two taller tenement blocks; the slogan drawn in black paint above its wide entrance: *Sacrifice the Children*.

I halted; my mind fighting different courses of action. I thought of Kara's stiff, cold body, lying on Cons' bed. What would she have had me do? I remembered what Salinger said. Do what I believed in.

I dashed across the street as the sound of a bomb exploding tore through a building a few blocks down. It sent tiny pieces

341

of brick and glass flying through the air, scattering like chicken feed on the ground. I kept going to the entrance; a Selection truck was parked ominously outside. I took a breath, pushing back strands of my hair that had become loose and strode up confidently to the large, white-painted front door. I tried not to think of Salinger again, coming here as a young boy, both parents dead – or where he was now; if he was still alive.

There was a square hall beyond, a floor with roughly cut concrete slabs and a long metal desk pushed to one side.

I froze by the entrance – two Troopers were striding in from a far room. The one at the front held two children wriggling to get free, their screams like a siren. Behind him his colleague pushed a state-regulation white perambulator. It was filled with the round heads of at least nine, maybe ten, babies, eyes red and wet with crying, limbs strewn and tangled as if they'd just been piled in on top of one another.

A middle-aged woman with a wide, flushed face and curled brown hair was rushing alongside them, wringing her hands, her voice pleading.

'You can shut up or I will take you with them,' the Trooper in front spat back.

His colleague, pushing the pram, seemed less severe as he explained, 'Lady, we have a quota to make. Those who came to you last, go first.'

They still hadn't noticed me yet; I breathed fast, processing my next move.

'But to take so many of them! They were assessed positively – what have they done wrong now to deserve Selection?'

'I said, shut it.' The Trooper in front twisted and kicked out with his thick Black boot, catching the woman on her calf so she was flung across the room. That made my decision for me before my mind fully registered it. My hand clutched at the metal in my waistband.

'Leave those children alone,' I said, stepping out of the shadows of the entrance.

The Trooper carrying the children eyed me. 'What's this? A rebel Blue?' He made a faint smile. I could see he was working me out – reckoning he could overpower me.

And he was probably right – I'd still not actually fired a gun yet; practising aim in One's garage was nothing compared to the precise target of a human head or heart. What if I shot a child by mistake?

'We've been warned of Blue insiders. But I didn't expect anything as sweet as you. Maybe we can have some fun en route to your Selection.'

He let out a small grunt of a laugh and dropped the two children to the floor as if they were bags of flour; they scuttled towards the middle-aged woman, burying their faces in the folds of her thick Grey skirt as she stumbled back up.

I had to make him take me seriously.

In the second it took him to drop his hand to the gun holster on his belt, I had pulled out mine, pressed the trigger – and fired.

The wall just behind him splintered, shattering white brick onto the floor around them like heavy snowfall. The children's cries escalated.

'That was just a warning.' I kept my voice steady, as stiff as my arms holding up the gun, while my chest quivered from the mis-aim.

Both Troopers lifted their hands; the one who'd been pushing the pram looked scared. He began impeaching me, 'Please, no, don't shoot. I don't want to die.'

I swept their faces with my gun. 'You ask for your life to be saved, but you're prepared to take these children to their deaths?'

The scared one answered, 'I'm just doing what I'm told . . . I'm just doing the job I was ordered to do . . . like we're all ordered to do. I don't want to kill little ones.'

'Many of your colleagues wouldn't care.'

'Many of your rebel colleagues wouldn't either,' the Trooper at the front interjected. 'Blue children have been slaughtered in the bombs too, you know.'

I swung my aim back to his skull, squeezing again on my trigger. I couldn't let the enemy walk free. They might come back; arrest others. But I would need to go point blank to shoot; I'd already proved I wouldn't be able to kill them from here. Could I even do it – murder them in cold blood? That desire to kill; it had faded since Sunil arrived.

The Trooper near the pram was pleading with me again, telling me he was only twenty-three, begging me to trust him; he wouldn't hurt the children. No; I had to block him out. I had to be a machine. A soldier. I had to find the anger I needed. Just another life. Just another number.

'Let them go,' the woman suddenly said, cutting through my thoughts. 'No more violence.'

I glanced at her; she was holding the two small children tight against her legs as they whimpered softly.

'Please . . . I want to live.'

'He wants to live,' the middle-aged woman echoed the younger Trooper. She took a breath. 'I used to accept Land's ways. I understood the reasoning for survival . . . yet this? This is plain evil. But you don't meet evil with evil.'

I could hear children's shouts coming from other rooms, the mewling cries of babies. Sunil? That should have reignited my anger – the thought of him in there somewhere, his mother dead. Instead, the idea of cradling him again – it diluted any speck of killer instinct I had left. It opened the door a crack, let hope sneak back in.

I flicked my gun around them. 'A new regime is going to win. If you want a life then lose the uniform. Take your clothes off; lay your gun on the ground. Pass me the keys to the Selection truck outside.'

I paraded them at gunpoint in just their underpants and vests into the truck. Doing as they had probably done to thousands, I forced them in and locked the black door behind them. To anyone passing I probably looked like a Blue apprehending undesirables.

I rushed back inside, shouting for the woman as she guided the children and the pram away. 'I came here for a newborn – he would have been sent to you just a couple of days ago.'

'Yes. Who are you to him?' she asked.

I swallowed; what was I to him? 'I'm his family.'

The woman bustled towards me. 'Little thing, he's the first we've had in weeks . . . they're not sending them any more. I was feeding him at my desk when those Troopers barged in. I hid him out of sight.'

'Where is he now?'

'Oh, he's still where I put him. Can't you hear him?'

Suddenly I recognised the whimpering and griping that must have been there in the background all this time. I bolted towards it, bending down under the metal desk – on the grey stone floor, a tight white bundle. There – familiar round black eyes staring directly upwards; they were starting to colour, a hint of Kara's blue spreading through his irises. I grabbed him, clutching him to me, breathing in his milky vanilla scent; my arms moulding round his tiny frame. He let out a little scream, then sighed as I scattered kisses over his warm head.

'You're his mother?' the woman asked. I shook my head. 'You knew his mother?'

'Kara,' I said. 'Her name was Kara.'

'Kara,' she repeated softly behind me.

'And this . . . this is Sunil.'

'Of course . . . Sunil,' the woman said simply, nodding over and again. She understood.

Chapter Thirty-three

It took both my hands to release the stiff handbrake; my arms held wide to control the over-sized steering wheel of this beast of death. I pushed my foot down on the accelerator; I could hear my prisoners in the back lurch against the sides of the truck as we juddered away.

I had put on one of the Trooper's Black jackets and helmet, tucking my ponytail up under it. The woman at the orphanage had found me a broad bag, deep enough to conceal Sunil, tucking extra blankets around him. In another large shoulder bag she had quickly packed a few months' stock of milk powder and cloths for nappies. Both bags were now in the well of the front seat.

I drove in a shuddering, swaying charge down the main road towards the shopping precinct. The sky above us was illuminating with bomb blasts, white and orange, like vertical sunsets. Troopers and Browns were openly fighting now, the rebels more visible than before – their war no longer hidden behind broken windows and white lightning-peals of gunfire.

The sound of another bomb erupted nearby; a plume of grey smoke shot out from behind the flat white roofs of a block directly to our right. I swerved to avoid the fallout. There were screams, shouts. More gunfire rolling through the air all around, as dread swirled in my stomach.

I pressed down harder on the accelerator. I had to get us out of here.

I didn't wait for the Trooper guarding the underground road into Central Land to open the gate; I continued on, keeping my left foot wedged against Sunil's makeshift cradle as we crashed through, breaking the wood in half. We dipped under South Land shopping precinct, moving as fast as the speedometer allowed, soon losing the Troopers chasing us.

I took the truck round to a back entrance to the Cross, not bothering to park it properly, simply abandoning it, along with the Trooper jacket and helmet – and the Troopers inside it. I picked up my bags; despite the noise around us, the roar of the engine must have sent Sunil to sleep.

'Where've you been?' One glanced up sharply, agitation etched into every line on his face.

I scanned the room, Salinger wasn't there. Instead, a handful of men and women, six Blues, two Greys, grouped tensely around One's desk. There was a large, hand-drawn map of Land spread out before them like a tablecloth. It reminded my insides to ache for Salinger.

'The Leader's been asking for you since yesterday. He wanted you at last night's war meeting. You know what you have to do. We've been waiting for you.'

Eight pairs of eyes joined his, fixed on me. I could see they knew me already. I could see they questioned me already. The girl who would end their war? Just a girl, dressed prematurely in Blue.

I lifted my head higher. I recognised some from passing in corridors, the occasional meetings. Was their union powerful enough? I doubted them back.

One must have indicated to them to leave, because they started moving away from his desk; their eyes lingering on me as they walked towards the door. I clung on to my makeshift cradle, rocking it gently, willing Sunil not to wake yet as they traipsed past me.

'Reconvene in here in twenty minutes precisely. Use this time to communicate again with your allies – tell them to be ready to act. We must reclaim order on the streets as soon as . . .' One's eyes fell on me again. '. . . As soon as,' he finished.

'You can trust them. They are behind me,' he added as the last had left. I crossed urgently to the corner of the room, settling Sunil down there. 'I'm glad you are here. I thought you'd abandoned us.'

'I lost Salinger,' I said over my shoulder. 'You have to check if he's been arrested, get to him.'

'Already in hand. I tracked him . . . thankfully at least he had his tracer still on him.'

I caught my breath, turning. 'Is he okay?'

'He shouldn't be. Holed up in a cell; waiting his turn at Selection.' One waved a hand at my expression. 'I signed his release. He'll be on his way. I'll save the lecture to you both for later.'

Relief was swimming over me as One stepped closer.

Up-close, I noticed how ashen his skin was; his eyes, less

melancholic – more shot with panic. His tension was palpable. I started refilling with fear. I stared down at Sunil's dainty, sleeping features; were we going to pull this off?

'Are you ready?' One broke my anxious thoughts.

'Just tell me what I have to do.'

He stepped closer still, bending his head low to whisper in my ear. Clearly, we were done with scribbled notes now – we either succeeded and lived, or failed and died. 'The Leader is in a meeting with the heads of state. Go in, get him out, alone in his office. No guards. He'll do that for you – only you.

'It's crucial you kill him with his own gun. It has to look like suicide. That is the message I will be sending out to every citizen in Land on their tracers.'

'And then?'

'Then we take control. With no Head of State Troopers; we will have to rely on the Trooper deputies to follow our orders. Some will be easier than others.'

'And then, no more deaths?'

'Not if we can help it.' His eyes drew down past me. 'What in the name of . . .?'

I gazed around with him at Sunil's little face, crumpled up comfortably. 'Kara's baby. Kara's dead.' I took a deep breath. 'Listen – this is the last thing I'll ask for, I promise . . . If I don't come back, I want you to look after him, find someone to adopt him if you must, someone kind . . . someone from a good family.' I thought of Kara choosing his name. 'A Blue – if colour still exists.'

'Let's just bank on you looking after him yourself,' One said, but his voice lacked his usual gruff confidence. As his eyes caught my expression, he lifted his hands and drew them down his face, pulling at his skin.

'Any news on Ella?' I asked.

One shook his head dejectedly

'This is going to work, isn't it?' I pushed my face towards his. I wanted the old One back; the stiff wooden frame of a man whom no one could penetrate. This version was vulnerable. It scared me.

'Will people follow me?'

'Yes,' I answered flatly. I didn't want him looking to me for direction.

'Why?'

I lifted my shoulders. 'I dunno, because you're you ... Because you're balanced ... Because you are going to put people, not politics, first, right?' I nodded my head till he joined in. 'All we can do is keep going, One. You have a vision – stick to it. Keep moving,' I said, bending down to lightly kiss Sunil's soft, sleeping head. 'I want a new Land for this child, for the others I just left behind. I have killed for that. Cons and Hogan and Stella died for that. Now you make it happen.'

One stared at me obliquely, blinking as if he were confused. He bent down beside me, his fingers rubbing at the white blanket cocooning Sunil. His voice was rendered soft as he said, 'I'm sorry ... I –'

Briefly he seemed to study me. 'I only held Ella as a baby for a moment. You ... I held often.'

I stared openly at him; a lump swelled in my throat.

'I can still recall the way you stared up at me ... Stella and Hogan were so ... they both loved you.' His eyes hung heavy as he watched mine. 'Just in different ways . . . We all dream for the next generation.

'You, Ella, Salinger – you're my next generation.' One made an abrupt twist of his head. 'The Leader . . . if you ask me, I will do this for you – I'll complete the job for you.'

I put my hand on his arm. 'The people need you alive,' I said, wanting to say so much more. 'Besides, this was always my purpose, wasn't it – to get the Leader to trust me . . .? It's the end of my story. It has to be that way.'

The Leader's private office was empty; I rushed through the intersecting door to the state meeting room – there the heads were collected, all standing around the polished walnut table, strained expressions pulling at their hardened features.

'You're late . . . by a day,' the Leader snarled when he caught sight of me.

I rolled my shoulders back. 'I must talk to you in private.' I spoke lucidly. This was my final performance. I had to give it my best.

'Likewise,' the Leader muttered. He circled his arms through the air like wings. 'Keep working – all of you. Tell me how we are going to strangle this rebellion! I want severe solutions!

'Give me five minutes,' he bit curtly at the two Troopers flanking him as he walked towards me.

'Come,' he growled, leading me back into his empty office, closing the door behind him. He was making it all too easy.

'Why have you not been to see me? You are supposed to be proving yourself. One said you were trailing rebel leads with some State Troopers? Don't get all gung-ho on me. You need to stay by my side from now.'

I stared into his fierce green eyes. 'I thought you would want me out there . . . succeeding where your Troopers fail.' I made my voice arrogantly confident as I eyed the bulge of his gun-holster beneath his tailored Black jacket. He was close enough, a few centimetres from my right hand.

'While I commend your vigour, your place is with me, at my right side. An antidote to all these lumbering, whimpering heads in there. You stay by me, unless I tell you to go.'

'Understood,' I said. I stretched my fingers until they were a breath away from the shape of his gun. *Close to his head – it has to look like suicide.*

'I must tell you something. If this war escalates, and I die . . . what I know dies with me.' He watched me to see if I was following. My mind was fogging over. Whatever he was about to confide in me, I couldn't let it sway me from my mission. I had only a few minutes before he resumed his meeting.

I blocked out his voice as it continued. I hardly heard the first words. But I caught the last two. *No sea.*

My hand pulled back. 'What did you say?'

'Are you not listening, child? You must listen! Listen to me! We will not give in. We will fight side by side. This is our Land – but if by some miracle they win, if the rebels overpower government, then you must get out. You must lead those Blues we can trust – the most powerful heads of state, the best scientists – lead them out of here. Get out of Land. Bide your time then come back to attack. Land is yours, not theirs. We cannot allow them to take Land.

'I am trusting you with this.' He strode away from me,

walking over to his desk, starting to unlock a drawer.

'How can I get out of Land? There is no *get out*.' My voice started to rage; I was losing my opportunity by listening to his mad talk. One once said my grandfather lost his mind to the allure of power – now here was definitive evidence.

He returned to me, brandishing a narrow, black metal box. Pulling a small silver key from his jacket pocket, he opened the box. Inside, nestling on Blue velvet, was a thin metal card. He picked this up tenderly and passed it to me, coming in close, as One had only minutes before.

His voice was a hot puff of a whisper against my ear. 'Like I said: there is no sea…'

I slanted my head back, my body motionless.

'Land's best-kept secret . . . our most powerful weapon, that no one in government knows about.'

'There is no sea?' My voice choked; my hand limply accepting the metal card he was pushing towards me.

The Leader's head shook next to mine. I watched him; he had to be delusional, or lying. But why would he lie? 'I don't believe you.'

'My response, too, when the last Leader entrusted me with the secret.' His eyes bore into mine as he whispered curtly, 'We don't have much time. Listen to me. Soon after Land was formed, the then Leader sent a small band of scientists out. They found no sea. Their research proved the sea had receded almost as soon as it had risen. Land isn't built on high ground like everyone thinks; it just happens to be the place survivors found when the waters had pulled back. I have seen it for myself. Beyond the Great White Wall there's land . . . hundreds

354

upon hundreds of miles of land. Any sea is far, far away. Any sea is currently benign.'

'Then why . . .?' I felt my adrenalin of the last few minutes drain away.

'Land grew quickly from a small community to a large society. The Leader back then made a choice. The secret of the sea posed a dual benefit – he needed the best people to stay, not disperse, so he could retain talent, skill, for Land to thrive. And with the need to maintain order, keep down our numbers, the threat of a rising sea became a crucial weapon to incite fear, to build control. It was too good a propaganda not to keep going. Those scientists didn't survive past their uncovering of the truth.

'Now, the Leaders pass the secret on to one another. There is a door in South Land's Great White Wall – the Troopers who guard it believe they merely protect an exit that soon leads to water. No one else knows, besides me . . . and now you. It's in every Leader's benefit to keep the lie going. You will keep the lie going . . . should anything happen to me.

'So if and when I say: get out. You know now what to do.'

'Yes. I do.' I had his gun already in my hand, swinging the barrel round till it registered his skull. I couldn't think. I couldn't feel. His head made a tiny jerk at the sound of the trigger – a curt click of metal at his temple. His neck twisted, the nozzle scraping across his forehead, metal against bone. His eyes bore into mine. Shock, then confusion, then disappointment. That was where they finally settled – intense disappointment. What had I expected? That my grandfather would be proud?

His lips moved thinly. 'I see I have been weak . . . I see I have been swayed by flesh and blood . . . into trusting you.'

I opened my mouth to breathe; it felt as if I were suffocating. I stiffened my arm. 'I have to kill you,' I said. 'I can't let you destroy any more people. Everyone deserves a right to a free life. Everyone.' I pressed the gun harder against his skin.

'I am your *grandfather*.' That word – it meant something to him after all. I could see it in his face; in some perverse way I had become family to him.

'No,' I said, 'I stand alone.' I told myself, *Squeeze the trigger*. My muscles wouldn't oblige my mind. Drips of sweat travelled down my forehead.

'Put the gun down, Christabel.'

The pattern of our breathing seemed to match one another. Within those seconds, I knew I wasn't going to be able to do it . . . Love had come into my life again – through Sunil . . . through Salinger . . . through One and Tobin – it had fought with my hate and won. I knew that, as I felt a hand fold over mine around the gun, a finger take over on the trigger.

The shot cracked with the close impact.

Shards of skull and blood hit my face as the Leader dropped down by my feet.

Numbly I watched Salinger hurriedly press the gun into my grandfather's limp hand as the Trooper guards charged in from the state meeting room.

'He just killed himself,' Salinger shouted out to them. 'I came in to find 823057, and he was shooting himself with his own gun! He said he'd failed! The war was lost! What will we do now? Our Leader has given up!'

I jostled myself to stir, to help, join in – I didn't need to feign hysterics – 'The Leader, he said his time was over. He said this was the only way, then he lifted his gun to his head and fired! The Leader killed himself!' I gulped back a breath. I wouldn't – I couldn't – mourn a cruel man I had never loved.

I felt a tug on my hand. Salinger was pulling me away as the two Troopers bent over the twisted shape of the Leader, checking him for life still, even though part of his head was missing.

We raced back down the carpeted staircase. 'Why did you do that?' I forced out.

'No one should have to kill their own grandfather,' he said, his hand tightening around mine.

We walked fast till we reached One's office. He stood alone, waiting. He looked surprised to see Salinger, then his eyes flicked to me, his head moving as if he understood from the pattern of blood on my face – that it was done. 'Good. Let me go and send the public message immediately, and inform the others. We have to act fast if we are to control the situation.'

'Wait,' I breathed out; I was trembling as if I was frozen. Salinger had turned me to him; he was wiping at my face with a tissue that soon turned red. 'There's no sea.'

'What?' One stalled near the door.

'We've been prisoners here.'

I could hear Sunil, awake now, softly cooing to himself in his corner of the office.

'There never has been any sea, not since the first floods came sixty years ago . . .' I held up the metal card I still had gripped in my hand. 'This is the key that opens an exit to the outside, to land . . . to miles of land . . . no sea.'

I watched their shocked faces as I walked across to Sunil. I lifted him up, breathing in his milky breath. I needed his little body in my arms to bring me back. To remind me of what I was living for.

One had pushed his head forward, holding it as if it had suddenly become too heavy for his neck. Salinger was shaking his. Neither said a word, so I continued. 'The Leader told me. An exit in South Land's wall – the best-kept secret. Our world isn't limited to Land. There is everywhere to go . . . there is anywhere . . .' I pressed Sunil tighter to me.

'Hogan . . . Hogan had hinted at his suspicions of this. I had always thought him delirious.' One's forehead flexed. 'Are you sure?'

'It must be a sick joke,' Salinger interjected. 'A stupid lie.'

I thought of the look in my grandfather's eyes as he told me. 'I don't think so. I think it's the truth.'

One's doleful stare grew wide as he looked between us. 'The door; there's a door where they go to check the sea levels. It must be there.' He put his thumb to his mouth, sucking on it as if it were sore. 'If there's a chance it's real, then – go. The two of you, take the baby. Go. Get out of here.'

I shook my head. 'This is something for all Land's people, not just us. This is freedom.'

'It's a death sentence, is what it is.' One stepped closer to me. 'Don't you see – if the rest of government or the Resistance hear about this, they have it in their power to close the doors to Land to as many as they like. Land's resources and industry . . . I mean, what is out there? Most people wouldn't survive a week without what we have here. People have grown dependent on the State.'

One started pacing his office, his thumb now stretching his lips downwards, tapping against his teeth. 'No, this is something we must use gently, if we claim power . . . then we can gradually open the doors, build other settlements, explore. However, we must protect this secret until that happens. But it doesn't stop you from going. This is a way I can protect you . . . in case we fail . . . we might fail.'

'You need us here,' Salinger said.

'Not any longer. You've done your bit. Don't you see – the two of you will be the first to get executed if we don't get control. I'd rather know you were safe. If I can't take over the State then we all face Selection. If Resistance get in then we will be revealed as traitors. I doubt their leaders would show us any more mercy than this government. Go now; get out if there's a way . . . Leave a trail; I can come and find you if we succeed. If we don't then you can come back and open the doors, liberate the people yourselves.'

'He's right,' I said, placing Sunil back in his bag. 'I need to protect Sunil. I need to go now.'

One was nodding his head. 'You keep driving south, down the main road. Beyond the farms there is one factory at the end, right under the Great White Wall; it says *Water Cooling*. That has to be the door he's talking about . . . there is no other.'

I moved towards him; without thinking, I wrapped my arms around his stiff, broad body.

He patted my back awkwardly. 'There's no time for goodbyes,' he whispered grimly in my ear, but he didn't push me away.

'I hope you get reunited with Ella.'

I felt his body shudder against mine. 'And with you too,' he said. As I moved away from him, his lips gently brushed my cheek. 'With you too, Christy.'

Chapter Thirty-four

Salinger . . . he'd been right. Choices weren't easy in Land.
But you could still make them.

And I had made my choice – I had chosen the people I
cared most about. The two people who rose up from the ashes;
two people beyond all others I wanted to protect, to love, to
be close to . . . more than life itself. They were with me now.

We took the Selection truck I'd arrived in; after we'd emptied
its cargo – two half-naked Troopers. They ran off the moment
I let them out; they wanted to survive.

We went first to One's as he'd instructed us to, packing
the truck full of as many supplies as we could get our hands
on – food, water, clothes, knives, bullets, rope, blankets, soap,
car fuel. I fed Sunil a bottle of milk, while Salinger finished
the last of the packing. Now I soothed him back into his cradle
of a bag, hoping he would fall back to sleep, despite the now
constant whir and crash of warfare all around us.

We pulled back out onto the streets of Central Land. I
was driving. However cumbersome the truck was to operate,
I wanted to. I wanted to leave Land the way I had dreamt I
might, my foot down on the pedal; heading to freedom – those

I loved sitting beside me.

We cut down towards South Land. Some of the houses nearby were starting to light up with fire – suddenly, like the sun's rays were catching alight. The rebels had arrived in Central Land.

I slowed as I began to recognise the line of houses we were passing.

'Tobin might be in there,' I shouted aloud. 'Over there . . . Salinger! Tobin's house is on fire! We have to stop. I must get to him.'

'You want to take Tobin with us?' His tone was hard to translate. 'You want to take him with us,' Salinger repeated, a statement this time, not a question.

I inhaled sharply. 'I have to . . . just see he's okay. He's my –' I stopped myself from saying it – *my Pair*. Why would I say that? Was that what I believed? That I was tied to Tobin for life because Land decreed it?

No. Because I cared. That was it; I cared about Tobin. Maybe even loved him. However farcical it might have been, Tobin had been my only comfort these last months.

I pulled the truck up in front of the house. 'He might be trapped in there – No,' I shot out at Salinger, as he started to climb out with me. 'You stay here with Sunil.'

He ignored me, began running up the path, back bent over. I didn't have the time to argue. Gunshots were firing closer. I worried for Sunil.

The front door was framed with black smoke; bright orange flames licking the house's two storeys, creating a blanket of suffocating heat that shrouded us.

A Selection truck thundered past behind, followed by a force of black cars. 'Round the back,' I breathed out.

'Wait.' Hurriedly, Salinger ripped off his Grey shirt, his skin bare beneath. He tore at the material. 'Hold it over your mouth,' he ordered, giving me the larger of the two shredded pieces.

She flew into us before we reached the back door. Her face was smeared with black soot. Bea and Audley's slave girl. A man in Brown followed after her.

'Are they in there? Are they –' I stopped short, noticing the black gun, held aloft. 'My gun.'

The slave girl waved the metal in her hand. 'So? I found your hiding place. My need was greater than yours.'

I had hardly heard her speak when I lived there. But I would never have attached such a low growl of a voice to her. Hatred was twisting her delicate features. The silent slave; she'd been plotting her own fight all this time.

Her gun floated up, just for a moment pointing at my face, until Salinger barged forwards, knocking it out of her grip. 'We're no different to you,' I heard him cry as his naked torso shouldered hard into the man lurching towards him. 'The Leader is no more, thanks to us.'

The last statement halted them both in their tracks. They stared back at us. 'The Leader's been killed?' The man in Brown said, his fist half raised.

'The Leader's killed himself. Check your tracer, there's a message confirming it to everyone in Land. The war is over. Change is coming. It's coming now. Go spread the word.'

'Are they inside?' I cut through Salinger.

'Inside?' The slave girl laughed. 'Yeah, she's inside, trapped in there like she trapped me . . .'

I pushed past her, Salinger on my heels. Already, I knew she'd started the fire. I didn't want to think yet what part my gun had played. I rocketed through the back kitchen door, stuffing my mouth and nose with Salinger's torn shirt as clouds of smoke hit me. Immediately my eyes began to stream.

The entire kitchen was surrounded by a sentry line of flames, lapping up the walls as if they were trying to swallow the stone whole. Salinger grabbed my shoulder, gave me a look that said, *We need to get out.* But I couldn't stop now.

Fire continued crackling, tearing up furniture and furnishings in the hall, but it hadn't yet made its way upstairs. I bounded up the staircase, my skin prickling with heat, calling his name now that the air was a little clearer. 'Tobin? Tobin!'

I found her on the landing. She was lying stretched out on her side, her back to me. Her head, resting on her arm, pointing in the opposite direction to her legs. She looked as if she were simply sleeping.

'Bea!' I rushed to kneel down by her side, checking her over. Her face was smeared all over with blood. 'Bea?' I scanned her, searching for a wound.

'Christy,' Bea murmured.

Salinger fell beside me. 'Here,' he said, forcing his hand against Bea's chest; a small spray of scarlet spurting out between his fingers.

'You've come back,' Bea murmured, an incongruous smile spreading across her face. 'I'm glad you're here. I wanted to –' She stopped, taking a gulp of air – 'get the chance . . . to make it up with you . . .' Another gulp; her voice, when it returned, was scratchy, hardly audible. 'You do know . . . I only wanted to keep you all safe . . . happy . . .'

'Bea, we will help you. Hold on.'

She sucked in breath then released it. 'I don't know where Audley or Ella are. Tobin left – he couldn't bear to be near me after I told him what I did to your friend. My family, Christy . . . My family have gone.'

'You will find them again,' I answered, my voice a rush. We had to get her out. 'Salinger, can you help lift her?'

'Please, no – find them, stay together, all of you; find them, and look after one another, promise me that you'll . . .' Bea's voice grew fainter.

I bent down lower to hear her as her chest lurched, bubbles of red liquid spouting from her mouth. Her head shook and lolled off her arm and then she became silent.

'She's gone,' Salinger said. He wiped his bloodied hand on his trousers and leant over Bea, closing her eyes. My mind felt lost; for some reason I had the urge to stay with her.

Salinger was tugging hard on my arm. 'We have to get back to Sunil. Now, Christy. She said Tobin's not here. The fire will trap us soon.'

Salinger had my hand, pulling me down the staircase, fumbling to find our way through the hallway's black smoke. My eyes squeezed shut from the stinging pain. We fell back out into the air, gulping it up as if it were water, as we raced to the truck, to Sunil.

'Christy!' She was running towards us as I climbed up into the truck behind Salinger.

'Are they in there? Mum and Dad . . .? Tobin? Are they in

there?' Tears were streaming down her anxious, small face.

'It's Ella,' I breathed out. I jumped back down, grabbing at her, hugging her to me. I didn't want to let her go. I wanted to keep her safe. For Bea. For One and Salinger. For me. I wasn't going to lose anyone ever again.

'I never knew this was going to happen! I've been hiding out with a group of Green rebels . . . but I would have left sooner if I'd known! I only heard they were hitting Central Land an hour ago. I had to come home, to warn them . . . Are you certain they're not in there?' She was really crying now, her body heaving with tears.

I was about to lie again, but instead truth found my tongue. 'You have to be brave, Ella,' I said gently, my eyes tracing her panicked features. 'Your mum, she was shot.' I put out a hand to stall Ella as she started to charge towards the house. 'She's gone, Ella, she's gone.

'Your dad's still in hiding. I don't know where Tobin is; Bea said he left –' I caught her again as she tried to dart away. 'Listen, you have to stay strong, just for now. Save your grief for later . . . because we're going . . . we're getting out of Land. Come with us.'

I tugged at her arm to encourage her to get in the truck. 'There is no sea. We can escape. The sea is one big lie. It's your choice – but we have to leave now or not at all.'

'No sea? . . . Dad! . . . Tobin!'

I thought of the promise Bea had asked me to make. 'We go now, but we can come back for them . . . .when all this is over,' I went on, my face urging Ella to agree. 'We have to get out of here.'

There were large eruptions in the air. I turned round to watch Ella stumble forwards as the ground seemed to shake. 'Come with me, Ella. Let me take care of you.'

She nodded and I pushed her, before she could change her mind, into the cabin next to Salinger. He let out a simple, 'Ella.'

'You know Salinger,' I said to her, as I climbed back behind the steering wheel. The detail of how she knew him would have to wait till later.

I drove fast, avoiding bomb wreckage; swerving people in all colours, running in their masses; past flying debris and wilful bullets as the air rocked around us.

It began to quieten a little as we reached the first of South Land's expansive farming sectors. I'd never been, but the fields and thin dust roads here were just as I'd imagined them: the trees plump with spring leaves, swaying on the furrowed, low hillside; the fish lakes glistening a translucent blue. It was as if nature had no interest in the mess we were making of our lives back amongst brick and stone.

I stopped the car once the Great White Wall was in sight, just a couple of fields away; we sat there while the engine idled.

Ella was resting her head against the window, subdued sobs coming from her. Salinger, next to her, alert for danger, his gun pointing outwards. Sunil, still snugly asleep in his improvised cradle between Salinger's feet.

I gazed up at the Wall through the windscreen. 'I can see it ahead, where One said it would be.' A building, jutting out; wide doors camouflaged white under a *Water Cooling* sign.

Now the moment of our escape was upon us, my mind suddenly raced with second thoughts. One – his dour expression, his melancholic sloping eyes – I hadn't even told him I'd found his daughter. And Tobin? Wasn't I supposed to save Tobin? For trying to save me? My stomach twisted at the thought of anything happening to him.

As if he could read my mind, Salinger pressed his hand down against mine on the steering wheel. 'We have to go, now,' he said calmly.

I looked up into his eyes, mud-brown . . . they no longer seemed so inscrutable. I pressed my foot back down on the accelerator.

I watched as Salinger disarmed the two Troopers guarding the high steel white doors. We weren't going to kill any more.

He kept his gun trained on them as they sneered at him. 'Your truck can't swim; it's suicide.' When they'd followed Salinger's orders and marched away, I got out, swiftly pushing the metal card into a small gap in the wall. It fitted perfectly. Within moments the doors opened. We drove through and they shut behind us. Another set of doors beyond opened with the same card. After this, there was a long, white tunnel.

As I raced us down it, I thought of the supplies we had packed, enough to last us at least a couple of months. We were no different to Cons as a little girl in my favourite of her stories – cramming food and supplies into the family's boat and sailing away from her old, shattered land . . . to find something new.

Maybe we would find what she had, another community. Or hostility. Maybe we would live alone. Maybe we would discover the settings of Cons' childhood.

At the end of the tunnel I jumped out, pushing my card into a slot by another set of doors. I climbed back in, waiting for them to fully open. Sunil began to make small soft cries and Salinger lifted him out, unwrapping him from his blanket. Nestling there, his soft, new skin pressed against Salinger's bare chest, it could have been a father holding his newborn for the first time.

Sunil's eyes – wide open – searched curiously. Salinger's free hand moved across again, his fingers lacing into mine on the wheel, while he glanced at Ella, connecting the four of us.

My new family.

The doors had opened; we were out.

We drove into bright sunlight. Into silence. Around us, there was only land – all around, for miles into the distance. No buildings, no roads, just land, fringed by nature, resplendent and colourful, untouched by human hands, unsullied by civilisation. Ahead, beyond trees, a curve of a hill, a ragged line where the hues of sky met tones of ground.

My rear-view mirror was filled with the Great White Wall; the gates closing, locking shut. My chest tightened then relaxed. In front: a flock of sickle-shaped starlings flew over us. I followed, driving faster over the uneven earth, until the image of Land's pure white grew smaller. As long as we had the ground to drive upon, we could take our journey as far, and for as long, as our fuel let us. Maybe we would just keep going until we found the sea.

Show Sunil the deep blue of his name.

Settle somewhere that had soil to harvest food; water for life. Learn to love one another without fear or oppression or hatred. Before we returned for those we loved.

Salinger bent his head low over Sunil and kissed his nose.

Learn to grow. With hope back on our side. Salinger caught my gaze. He leant into me; briefly, I met his lips, opening my mouth instinctively. Letting him in.

Already, learning to live.

THANK-YOUS

No man is an island – and as much as I often like to make myself into one, I wouldn't be where I am, no chance, without a long list of lovelies who have always fought my corner. So, just to name but a few . . .

Firstly, thank you to my inspirational Laurie for, well, inspiring me to write *LAND*. To Kirsty McLachlan, for believing so heartily in those first forty pages; and to all at Hot Key Books (especially Sarah Odedina, Georgia Murray and Jenny Jacoby) for steering *LAND* so deftly, so warmly.

Huge thanks to Lucie Chichon for reading not only the first, but the last draft, and providing much needed enthusiasm and insight; and to Christina Ioannou (and Harprit and Lisa) for reading other novels past. To my sister, Lucy, for dreaming with me; and to all my family and friends who have encouraged me so unfalteringly along the way. To all those who urged me, 'Don't give up' and 'It will happen' and 'Do try and wash' . . . you were right. I am glad you were right.

But the biggest praise of all must go to Duncan, Laurie and Mae, for anchoring me in this world while my mind travels to many, many others and yet always being there to welcome me back home, with huge hugs, love and laughter. What would I do without you?

Thank you.

Alex Campbell

Alex Campbell announced she was going to be a writer at eight years old. But no one took much notice. After a nomadic education daydreaming in back rows across Luton, Chester, London, Sheffield and Middlesborough – and one English degree later – Alex moved into the world of PR and copywriting. Here she worked on getting other people noticed instead.

Now, living near Bath with one husband, two children and an armful of untold stories, Alex's eight-year-old self's ambition has finally been realised with the publication of her debut novel, LAND.

When she's not gazing dreamily out of windows, Alex can usually be found, notebook at the ready, in dark art-house cinemas, propping up coffee bars, or worse.

Follow Alex on Twitter: @ACampbellWrites